Also by Gyles Brandreth in the Oscar Wilde series

Oscar Wilde and the Candlelight Murders

Praise for *Oscar Wilde and the Ring of Death*

'Hugely enjoyable'
Daily Mail

'A cast of historical characters to die for'
Sunday Times

'A carnival of cliff-hangers and fiendish twists-and-turns . . .
The joy of the book, as with its predecessor, is the rounded and
compelling presentation of the character of Wilde . . . The
imaginary and the factual are woven together with devilish
ingenuity. Brandreth also gives his hero speeches of great beauty
and wisdom and humanity' *Sunday Express*

'Wilde really has to prove himself against Bram Stoker and Arthur
Conan Doyle when a murder ruins their Sunday Supper Club. But
Brandreth's invention – that of Wilde as detective – is more than up
to the challenge. With plenty of wit, too'
Daily Mirror

'Gyles Brandreth's entertainment is an amusing and satisfactorily
unlikely story featuring Bram Stoker, Arthur Conan Doyle, a
locked room and Oscar Wilde in the role of the series detective'
Literary Review

'The plot speeds to an exciting climax . . . Richly atmospheric.
Very entertaining'
Woman & Home

'Sparkling dialogue, mystery piled deliciously on mystery, a plot with pace and panache, and a London backdrop that would grace any Victorian theatre'
Northern Echo

'The acid test for any writer who has enjoyed first-time success is that all-important second novel. Gyles Brandreth, I am happy to report, has sailed through the ordeal with flying colours . . . Irresistible . . . Elegant . . . Rich . . . Enjoyable . . . A classic Agatha Christie-style whodunnit involving some particularly inventive murders with a few well-placed red herrings'
Yorkshire Evening Post

'As much imaginative biography as murder mystery . . . Terrifically well researched, it whizzes along' *Scotland on Sunday*

'*Oscar Wilde and the Ring of Death* is the eagerly-awaited second volume in Gyles Brandreth's series of detective stories and it doesn't disappoint'
The District Messenger, Newsletter of the Sherlock Holmes Society of London

'One of the most enjoyable crime series around . . . I can't wait until the next one'
Scotsman

Praise for *Oscar Wilde and the Candlelight Murders*

'Genius . . . Wilde has sprung back to life in this thrilling and richly atmospheric new novel . . . The perfect topography for crime and mystery . . . magnificent . . . an unforgettable shocker about sex and vice, love and death' *Sunday Express*

'So many real-life figures have been dragooned as detective heroes that readers are likely to be blasé unless a writer can come up with something special. And that's just what Gyles Brandreth has done for this diverting mystery' *Good Book Guide*

'One of the most intelligent, amusing and entertaining books of the year. If Oscar Wilde himself had been asked to write this book he could not have done it any better' Alexander McCall Smith

For details of the first and forthcoming titles in the series, for reviews, interviews and material of particular interest to reading groups, see:

www.oscarwildemurdermysteries.com

OSCAR WILDE

and the

Ring

of Death

Gyles Brandreth

JOHN MURRAY

First published in Great Britain in 2008 by John Murray (Publishers)
An Hachette Livre UK company

First published in paperback 2009

6

A CIP catalogue record for this title is available from the British Library

ISBN 978-0-7195-6960-9

Typeset in Monotype Sabon by Servis Filmsetting Ltd, Stockport, Cheshire

Printed and bound by Clays Ltd, St Ives plc

John Murray policy is to use papers that are natural, renewable and recyclable
products and made from wood grown in sustainable forests. The logging and
manufacturing processes are expected to conform to the environmental regulations
of the country of origin.

John Murray (Publishers)
338 Euston Road
London NW1 3BH

www.johnmurray.co.uk

To Merlin and Emma

Would you like to know the great drama of my life?
It is that I have put my genius into my life . . .
I have put only my talent into my works.

Oscar Wilde (1854–1900)

Preface

My name is Robert Sherard and I was a friend of Oscar Wilde. We met first in Paris in 1883. He was then twenty-eight and already famous – as a writer, wit and raconteur, as the pre-eminent 'personality' of his day. I was twenty-two, a would-be journalist, an aspiring poet, and quite unknown. We met for the last time in 1900, again in Paris, not long before his untimely death. During the seventeen years of our friendship I kept a journal of our times together. We were not lovers, but I knew Oscar well. Few, I believe, knew him better. In 1884, I was the first whom Oscar entertained after his marriage to Constance Lloyd. In 1895, I was the first to visit him in Wandsworth Gaol following his imprisonment. In 1902, I became his first biographer.

When I wrote that first account of Oscar's life I told his story as best I could. I told the truth and nothing but the truth – but the whole truth I did not tell. Not long before his death, I had confessed to Oscar that I planned to write of him after he was gone. He said: 'Don't tell them everything – not yet! When you write of me, don't speak of murder. Leave that a while.' I have left it – until now. I am writing this in September 1939. I am old and the world is on the brink of war once more. My time will soon be up, but before I go I have one last task remaining – to tell everything that I know of Oscar Wilde, poet, playwright, friend, detective . . .

In *De Profundis*, my friend did me great honour. He described me as 'the bravest and most chivalrous of all brilliant beings'. Oscar Wilde was always good to me and I ask you to believe me when I tell you that in the pages that follow I have tried my utmost to be true to him.

RHS
Dieppe, France
September 1939

Regard your good name as the richest jewel that you can possibly be possessed of – for credit is like fire: when once you have kindled it you may easily preserve it, but if you once extinguish it, you will find it an arduous task to rekindle it again. The way to gain a good reputation is to endeavour to be what you desire to appear.

Socrates (c.470–399 BC)

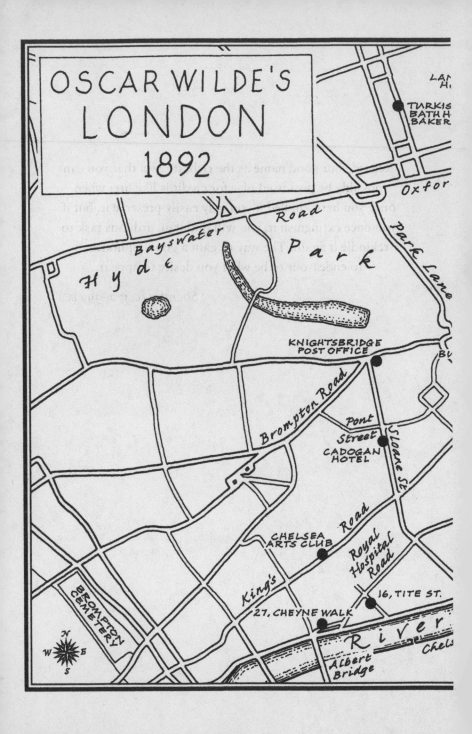

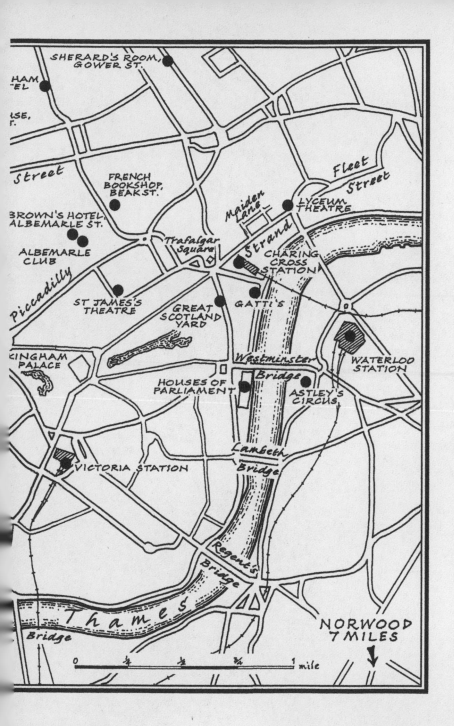

SHERARD'S ROOM, GOWER ST.

HAM -EL

ISE, r.

Street

FRENCH BOOKSHOP, BEAK ST.

BROWN'S HOTEL ALBEMARLE ST.

ALBEMARLE CLUB

Piccadilly

ST JAMES'S THEATRE

Fleet Street

Maiden Lane

LYCEUM THEATRE

Trafalgar Square

Strand

CHARING CROSS STATION

GREAT SCOTLAND YARD

GATTI'S

BUCKINGHAM PALACE

WATERLOO STATION

Westminster Bridge

HOUSES OF PARLIAMENT

ASTLEY'S CIRCUS

Lambeth Bridge

VICTORIA STATION

Regent's Bridge

Thames

Bridge

NORWOOD 7 MILES

0   ¼   ½   ¾   1 mile

1

The Fortune Teller

It was Sunday 1 May 1892, a cold day, though the sun was bright. I recall in particular the way in which a brilliant shaft of afternoon sunlight filtered through the first-floor front window of Number 16 Tite Street, Chelsea – the London home of Oscar and Constance Wilde – and perfectly illuminated two figures sitting close together at a small table, apparently holding hands.

I stood alone, by the window, watching them. One was a woman, a widow, in her early forties, with a pleasing figure, well-held, and a narrow, kindly face – a little lined, but not care-worn – and large, knowing eyes. She was dressed all in black silk and on her head, which she held high, she wore a turban of black velvet featuring a single, startling, silver and turquoise peacock's feather. The colour of the feather matched the colour of her hair.

The other figure seated at the table was quite as striking. He was a large man, aged thirty-seven, tall, over-fleshed, with a fine head of thick deep-chestnut hair, large, slightly drooping eyes, and full lips that opened to reveal a wide mouth crowded with ungainly teeth. His skin was pale and pasty, blotched with freckles. He was dressed in a sand-coloured linen suit of his own design. At his neck, he sported a loose-fitting linen tie of Lincoln green and, in his buttonhole, a fresh amaryllis, the colour of coral.

The woman was Mrs Robinson, clairvoyant to the Prince of Wales among others. The man was Oscar Wilde, poet and playwright, and literary sensation of the age.

Slowly, with gloved fingers, Mrs Robinson caressed Oscar Wilde's right hand. Repeatedly, she brushed the side of her little finger across his palm. With her right thumb and forefinger she took each of his fingers in turn and, gently, pulled it straight. For a long while, she gazed intently at his open hand, saying nothing. Eventually, she lifted his palm to her cheek and held it there. She sighed and closed her eyes and murmured, 'I see a sudden death in this unhappy hand. A cruel death, unexpected and unnatural. Is it murder? Is it suicide?'

'Or is it the palmist trying to earn her guinea by adding a touch of melodrama to her reading?' Oscar withdrew his hand from Mrs Robinson's tender grasp and slapped it on the table, with a barking laugh. 'You go too far, dear lady,' he exclaimed. 'This is a tea party and the Thane of Cawdor is not expected. There are children present. You are here to entertain the guests, Mrs Robinson, not terrify them.'

Mrs Robinson tilted her bird-like head to one side and smiled. 'I see what I see,' she said, without rancour.

Oscar was smiling also. He turned from the table and looked beyond the pool of sunlight to a young man of military bearing who was standing alone, like me, a yard away, observing the scene. 'Come to my rescue, Arthur,' he called. 'Mrs Robinson has seen "a sudden death" in my "unhappy hand". You're a medical man. I need a second opinion.'

Arthur Conan Doyle was then three weeks away from his thirty-third birthday and already something of a national hero. His *Adventures of Sherlock Holmes* in the *Strand* magazine were a sensation throughout the land. Doyle himself, in appearance, was more Watson than Holmes. He was a handsome fellow, sturdy and broad-shouldered, with a hearty handshake, beady eyes and a genial smile that he kept hidden beneath a formidable walrus moustache. He was the best of men, and a true friend to Oscar, in good times and bad.

'I'm no longer practising medicine, Oscar, as you know,' he said, moving towards the window table, 'but if you want my honest opinion, you should steer well clear of this kind of tomfoolery. It can be dangerous. It leads you know not where.' He bowed a little stiffly towards Mrs Robinson. 'No offence intended, Madam,' he said.

'None taken,' she replied, graciously. 'The creator of Sherlock Holmes can do no wrong in my eyes.'

Doyle's cheeks turned scarlet. He blushed readily. 'You are too kind,' he mumbled awkwardly.

'You are too ridiculous, Arthur. Pay no attention to him, Mrs R. He's all over the place. I'm not surprised. He's moved to South Norwood – wherever that may be.'

'It's not far,' Doyle protested.

'It's a world away, Arthur, and you know it. That's why you were late.'

'I was late because I was completing something.'

'Your sculpture. Yes, I know. Sculpture is your new enthusiasm.'

Conan Doyle stood back from the table. 'How do you know that?' he exclaimed. 'I have mentioned it to no one – to no one at all.'

'Oh, come now, Arthur,' said Oscar, getting to his feet, smiling and inclining his head to Mrs Robinson as he left the table. 'I heard you telling my wife about the spacious hut at the end of your new garden and the happy hours you are intending to spend there, "in the cold and the damp". Only a sculptor loves a cold, damp room: it's ideal for keeping his clay moist.'

'You amaze me, Oscar.'

'Mrs Robinson would have uncovered your secret too – by the simple expedient of examining your fingernails. Look at them, Arthur. They give the whole game away!'

'You are extraordinary, Oscar. I marvel at you. You know that I plan to include you in one of my stories – as Sherlock Holmes's older brother?'

'Yes, you have told me – he is to be obese and indolent, as I recall. I'm flattered.'

Conan Doyle laughed and slapped Oscar on the shoulder with disconcerting force. 'I'm glad I came to your party, my friend,' he said, 'despite the company you keep.'

'It is not my party, Arthur. It is Constance's party. The guests are all alarmingly respectable and the cause is undeniably just.'

The party – for about forty guests, men, women and children – was a fund-raiser in aid of one of Constance Wilde's favourite charities, the Rational Dress Society. The organisation, inspired by the example of Amelia Bloomer in the United States, was dedicated to promoting fashions for women that did not 'deform the body or endanger it'. The Society believed that no woman should be forced to endure the discomfort and risk to health of overly tight-laced and restrictive corsetry nor be obliged

4

to wear, in total, more than seven pounds of undergarments. Constance spoke poignantly of the plight of so many women – scores of them each year: young and old, serving girls and ladies of rank – who were either maimed or burnt to death when their voluminous skirts, petticoats and underpinnings accidentally caught on a candle or brushed by a hearth and were set alight.

Oscar and Arthur stood together looking about the room. Conan Doyle leant forward, resting his hands on the back of one of the Wildes' black-and-white bamboo chairs. 'The cause is indeed a good one,' he said. 'Rest assured: I have subscribed.' He smiled at Oscar, adding, 'I remain to be convinced, however, about the complete respectability of the guests. For example, who are those two?' He nodded towards the piano.

'Ah,' said Oscar, 'Miss Bradley and Miss Cooper.'

'They look like chimney-sweeps.'

'Yes,' said Oscar, squinting at the ladies. 'They do appear to have come *en travestie*. I think the costumes are deliberate. They probably wanted to bring us luck. They are not chimney-sweeps by trade. They are poetesses. Or, rather, I should say, "they are a poet". They write together, under a single name. They call themselves "Michael Field".'

'I observed them in the hallway, smoking cigarettes, and kissing one another, upon the lips.'

'Extraordinary,' said Oscar, shaking his head wanly, 'especially when you consider the amount of influenza sweeping through Chelsea this spring.'

'And what about the unhealthy-looking gentleman over there? He has the appearance of a dope-fiend, Oscar.'

5

'George Daubeney?' exclaimed Oscar. 'The Hon. the Reverend George Daubeney? He's a clergyman, Arthur, and the son of an earl.'

'Is he now?' replied Doyle, chuckling. 'Why do I recognise the name?'

'It has been in all the papers, alas. The Reverend George was sued for breach of promise. It was a messy business. He lost the case and his entire fortune with it.'

'He has a weak mouth,' said Conan Doyle.

'And a stern father who declines to bail him out, I'm afraid. I like him, however. He is assistant chaplain at the House of Commons and part-time padre to Astley's Circus on the south side of Westminster Bridge.'

'No wonder you like him, Oscar! You cannot resist the improbable.'

Now it was Oscar's turn to chuckle. He touched Conan Doyle on the elbow and invited his friend to scan the room. 'Look about you, Arthur. You are a man who has seen the world, the best and worst of it. You have journeyed to the Arctic in a whaler. You have lived in Southsea out of season. You are familiar with all types and conditions of men. Consider the assorted individuals gathered in this drawing room this afternoon and tell me which one of them, to you, looks to be the most incontrovertibly "respectable".'

Doyle was entertained by the challenge. He stepped back and stood, arms akimbo, fists on hips. He pursed his lips and narrowed his eyes and, slowly, carefully, surveyed the scene before him. Constance had gathered a motley crowd to her charitable tea party. 'What precisely am I looking for, Oscar?'

'The acme of respectability,' said Oscar. 'The face, the figure, the demeanour, the *look* that says to you: "This chap is sound, no doubt about it."'

'Mm,' growled Doyle, taking in the faces around him, turn by turn. 'They all look a bit doubtful, don't they?' He looked beyond where George Daubeney was standing, to the doorway, where Charles Brooke, the English Rajah of Sarawak and a particular friend of Constance, was holding court. 'Brooke has the look of a leader about him, doesn't he? I know him slightly. He's sound. He's a gentleman.'

Oscar raised his forefinger and waved it admonishingly. 'No, no, Arthur. Don't tell me about people you already know. I want you to make a judgement entirely on appearance. Look about this room and pick out the one person who strikes you as having about him an air of absolute respectability.'

'I have him!' cried Doyle triumphantly. 'There!' He indicated a sandy-haired young man of medium build and medium height who was standing with Constance Wilde at the far end of the room. Constance's older boy Cyril, nearly seven years old, was at her side with his arms clasped around her skirt. Her younger son, Vyvyan, then five and a half, was seated happily on the young man's shoulders tugging at his hair.

'He's your man, Oscar,' said Conan Doyle. 'He's easy with children – and children are easy with him. That's a good sign.'

'He is Vyvyan's godfather,' said Oscar.

'I'm not surprised. You chose well. He has the air of a thoroughly dependable fellow. What's his name?'

'Edward Heron-Allen,' said Oscar.

'A sound name,' said Conan Doyle, with satisfaction.

'Indeed,' said Oscar, smiling.

'A respectable name.'

'Certainly.'

'And his profession, Oscar? He's a professional man – you can tell at a glance.'

'He is a solicitor. And the son of a solicitor.'

'Of course he is. I might have guessed. Look at his open face – it's a face you can trust. It's the face of a good-hearted, clean-living, *respectable* young man. How old is he? Do you know?'

'About thirty, I imagine.'

'And how old is the Hon. the Reverend George Daubeney, may I ask?'

'About the same, I suppose.'

'But Daubeney,' said Doyle, his eyes darting from Oscar to Constance, 'looks ten years the older of the two, does he not? Daubeney's face, I fear, speaks of a life of dissipation. My man's face speaks of The Great Outdoors. He has colour in his cheeks. His jaw is clean-cut, his eyes sparkle, his conscience is clear.'

'My, my, Arthur, you are taken with him.'

Conan Doyle laughed. 'I'm only doing as you asked, Oscar – judging by appearance. Edward Heron-Allen's appearance is wholly reassuring. You cannot deny it. Look at his suit.'

'The tailoring is unexceptional.'

'Precisely. The man is not a dandy. He is a gentleman. His suit is sober: it's exactly the sort of suit you'd expect a solicitor to wear on a Sunday. And his tie, I think, tells us he went to Harrow.'

'He did indeed,' said Oscar, grinning broadly, 'and played cricket for the First XI.'

Conan Doyle caught sight of Oscar's wide and wicked smile and, suddenly, began to beat his own forehead with a clenched fist. 'Oh, Oscar, Oscar,' he growled ruefully, 'have I taken your bait? Have I fallen headlong into an elephant trap? Are you about to reveal to me that my supposed model of respectability is in fact the greatest bounder in the room?'

'No,' said Oscar, lightly. 'Not at all. But we all have our secrets, Arthur, do we not?'

'What's his? Has he embezzled all his clients' money?'

'He is in love with Constance.'

'Your wife?'

'My wife.'

Conan Doyle looked concerned. He was a loyal and conscientious husband. His own young wife, Louisa, known as 'Touie', was a victim of tuberculosis. Doyle went out and about without her, but she was never far from his thoughts. He tugged at his moustache. 'This fellow, Heron-Allen, being in love with your wife, Oscar – does it trouble you?'

'No,' said Oscar, 'not at all.'

'And Mrs Wilde?' asked Doyle. 'How does she feel?'

'It does not trouble Mrs Wilde.' Oscar smiled. 'Mrs Heron-Allen, however, may find it a touch perturbing.'

'Ah,' said Doyle, frowning, 'the fellow's married, is he? He doesn't look like a married man.'

'I agree with you there, Arthur. He looks totally carefree, does he not?'

'He looks quite ordinary to me,' said Conan Doyle. 'That's why I picked him when you started me off on this absurd game. I shouldn't have indulged you, Oscar.'

'Edward Heron-Allen is anything but ordinary, Arthur. He cultivates asparagus. He makes violins. He speaks fluent Persian. And he is a world authority on necrophilia, bestiality, pederasty, and the trafficking of child prostitutes.'

'Good grief!' Arthur Conan Doyle blanched and gazed towards Edward Heron-Allen in horror. The young solicitor was lifting Vyvyan Wilde from his shoulders. He kissed the top of the boy's head as he lowered him safely to the ground. 'Good grief,' repeated Conan Doyle.

'I've seated you next to him at dinner, Arthur. You'll find him fascinating. He's another chiromancer – like Mrs Robinson. Let him read your palm between courses and he'll advise you whether to plump for the lamb or the beef.'

'I'm speechless, Oscar,' said Conan Doyle, still staring fixedly in the direction of Edward Heron-Allen and Constance Wilde. 'I'm quite lost for words.'

'No matter,' said Oscar blithely. 'Heron-Allen can do the talking. He has a great deal to say and you'll find all of it's worth hearing.'

'Are you serious, Oscar?' Doyle protested. 'Is that man really joining us for dinner?'

Oscar chuckled. 'Why not? He looks respectable enough to me. In fact, he's my particular guest tonight. Sherard here is bringing the Hon. the Reverend George Daubeney. Who is your guest to be?'

Conan Doyle was now blowing his nose noisily on a large, red handkerchief. 'Willie . . . Willie Hornung,' he said, hesitating to name the name. 'You don't know him. He's a young journalist, an excellent fellow, one of the sweetest-natured and most delicate-minded men I ever knew.'

'Hornung . . . Willie Hornung.' Oscar rolled the name around his mouth, as though it were an unfamiliar wine.

Doyle returned his handkerchief to his pocket and looked Oscar in the eye. 'Perhaps I should advise Hornung to stay away. Willie's not what you'd call a man of the world.'

'Don't be absurd, Arthur. How old is he?'

'I don't know. Twenty-six? Twenty-seven?'

'Keats was dead at twenty-five, Arthur. It'll do Mr Hornung good to live a little dangerously, take life as he finds it. It's the possibility of the pearl or the poison in the oyster that make the prospect of opening it so enticing. Besides, we have to have him or we'll be thirteen at table.'

'Is Lord Alfred Douglas coming?'

'Bosie? Of course.' Oscar threw his head back and brushed his hands through his hair. 'Bosie is coming, very much so. And he's bringing his older brother, Francis, with him. You'll like Lord Drumlanrig, Arthur. He's about the same age as your young friend, Hornung, and sweet-natured, too. I'm all for feasting with panthers, but it's good to have a few delicate-minded lambs at the trough as well. One can have too much of a bad thing.' He looked around the room. 'Where is Bosie? He should be here by now.'

The Wildes' drawing room was beginning to empty. Katharine Bradley and Edith Cooper, the poetesses dressed as chimney-sweeps, were standing by the doorway blowing kisses towards Oscar. Miss Bradley, the taller of the two, had taken a huge bulrush out of a vase by the fireplace. She called to Oscar: 'I'm stealing this, dearest one. I hope you don't mind. Moses and Rebecca

Salaman are coming to supper. This will make them feel so at home.' Oscar nodded obligingly. Charles Brooke, the Rajah of Sarawak, was handing Constance a cheque and grandiloquently saluting her for her charitable endeavours on behalf of humankind in general and the Rational Dress Society in particular. His wife, Margaret, a plain and patient woman, was pulling at his arm. 'Will he ever stop talking?' she asked.

'Only if we start listening,' answered Constance, with a kindly laugh, kissing her friend on the cheek. 'Thank you both for coming. And thank you, Charles, for your generosity. Every one has been so kind, so good.'

'It's you, Mrs Wilde,' said Edward Heron-Allen, stepping toward his hostess and lifting her hand to his lips. 'You inspire us.'

Conan Doyle spluttered into his red handkerchief and whispered to Oscar, 'The man's intolerable.'

'You inspire our devotion,' Heron-Allen continued, still holding Constance's hand and looking into her eyes. 'We love you. It's as simple as that.'

'We love Oscar, too,' said a voice from the landing. 'But that's more complicated, of course.'

'Ah,' said Oscar, clapping his hands, 'Bosie is upon us.'

Lord Alfred Douglas appeared in the doorway of the Wildes' drawing room and held his pose. Bosie was an arrestingly good-looking boy. I use the word 'boy' advisedly. He was twenty-one at the time, but he looked no more than a child. Indeed, he told me that, later that same summer, a society matron was quite put out when she invited him to her children's tea party and discovered her mistake. Even at thirty-one, people would enquire whether he was still at school. Oscar used to say, 'Bosie contained the very essence of youth. He never lost it. That is why I loved him.'

Oscar did indeed love Lord Alfred Douglas and made no bones about it. Slender as a reed, with a well-proportioned face, gently curling hair the colour of ripe corn and the complexion of a white peach, Bosie was an Adonis – even Conan Doyle and I could not deny that. Oscar loved him for his looks. He loved him for his intellect, also. Bosie had a good mind, a ready wit – he liked to claim credit for originating some of Oscar's choicest quips – and a way with words and language that I envied. He was intelligent, but indolent. When he left Oxford the following year, he left without a degree. (As I had done. As Shelley and Swinburne did, too. Bosie's poetry may not rank alongside theirs, but, nonetheless, the best of it has stood the test of time.)

Oscar Wilde also loved Lord Alfred Douglas because of who he was. Though he made wry remarks to suggest otherwise, Oscar was a snob. He liked a title. He was pleased to be on 'chatting terms' with the Prince of Wales. He was happy that his acquaintance encompassed at least a dozen dukes. And he was charmed to find that Bosie Douglas (with his perfect profile and manners to match) was the third son of an eighth marquess – albeit a marquess with a reputation.

Even in 1892, Bosie's father, John Sholto Douglas, 8th Marquess of Queensberry, was notorious. Ill-favoured, squat, hot-tempered, aggressive, Lord Queensberry was a brute, a bully, a spendthrift and a womaniser. His one strength was that he was fearless. His one unsullied claim to fame was that, with a university friend, John Graham Chambers, he had codified the rules of conduct for the sport of boxing. He was himself a lightweight boxer of tenacity and skill. He was also a daring and determined jockey (he rode his own horses in the Grand National) and a huntsman noted for ruthlessness in the field. He carried his riding whip with him at all times. He was said to use it with equal ease on his horses, his dogs and his women. In 1887, Lady Queensberry, the mother of his five children, divorced him on the grounds of his adultery.

Bosie despised his father and adored his mother. In Bosie's eyes, Sybil Queensberry could do no wrong. 'My father has given me nothing,' he said. 'My mother has given me everything, including my name.' Lady Queensberry had called him 'Boysie' when he was a baby. Oscar called him 'my own dear boy' from the moment they met, early in the summer of 1891. They became firm friends almost at once. By the summer of 1892, they were near inseparable. Where Oscar went, Bosie came too. I liked him. Constance liked him, also. Conan Doyle had his reservations.

As he stood, posed, in the drawing-room doorway, with his head thrown to one side, like a martyred saint upon a cross, Bosie looked straight towards Constance. 'Mrs Wilde,' he cried, '*peccavi*. I have missed your party and I didn't want to miss it for the world. Will you forgive me?' From behind his back he produced a small bunch of primroses tied together with blue ribbon. He stepped forward and presented them to her.

She kissed him, as she might have done a child, and said, 'What a sweet thought, Bosie. Thank you. I'm glad you're here. I'm sure Oscar was getting anxious.'

Bosie, nodding to Edward Heron-Allen, went over to Oscar and Conan Doyle. I moved from my station by the window to join them. 'I apologise, Oscar,' said the young Adonis, furrowing his brow. 'I've had a damnable afternoon. Arguing about money with my father. He's been through £400,000, you know, and won't advance me fifty. The man's a monster. I'd like to murder him.'

Arthur Conan Doyle raised an eyebrow and sucked on his moustache.

'I mean it,' said Bosie seriously. 'I'd like to murder him, in cold blood.'

'Well, you can't, Bosie,' said Oscar, 'leastways, not tonight.'

'Why not?' demanded Bosie petulantly.

'It's Sunday, Bosie,' said Oscar, 'and a gentleman never murders his father on a Sunday. You should know that. Did they teach you nothing at Winchester? Besides, it's the first Sunday in the month and we are going to dinner at the Cadogan. You can't have forgotten, surely?'

2

The Socrates Club

In the summer of 1892 Oscar was at the height of his fame and fortune. *Lady Windermere's Fan*, his first theatrical triumph, had opened at the St James's Theatre in February. He was the toast of the town and collecting royalties at the rate of £300 a week. And yet I sensed he was not content.

We had been friends for nine years. For a brief while, before his marriage and mine, we had shared lodgings in Mayfair. We found each other's society easy: we were good companions. He was seven years my senior and indulged me as he might have done a younger brother. He did not sit in judgement: he accepted me as I was. When my first marriage began to unravel – I had not been as faithful to Marthe as I should have been – Oscar did not reproach me, as my parents did. (As the world at large did, too. Make no mistake, in those far-off days, if your marriage failed, you were reckoned to have failed also.) Oscar simply said, 'Poor Robert!' adding, 'I'm not sure that any marriage should be expected to last more than seven years.' This was that same summer of 1892, when he and Constance had been married for almost eight years.

'But you love Constance still, do you not?' I asked, somewhat shocked. I was the younger brother: the

Wildes were lodestars in my firmament. 'That has not changed?'

'No, that has not changed,' he said – but he said it with a melancholy diffidence. 'She has changed, however. When I married her, Robert, my wife was a beautiful girl, white and slim as a lily, with dancing eyes and gay, rippling laughter like music. In a year or so, after our boys were born, the flower-like grace had vanished. She became heavy, shapeless, deformed.'

'You do not mean it, Oscar,' I protested. Constance, in truth, was none of those things. Constance was always lovely. But, inevitably, she was older than she had been – she was now thirty-four – and Oscar equated age with decay. And, to her husband at least, she was not as amusing as she once had seemed. 'She never speaks and I am always wondering what her thoughts are like,' he said.

Oscar sought to distract himself from this 'domestic *ennui*' (as he termed it) by filling every waking hour with a relentless round of work and play. He posed as an idler, but he was never idle. By day, behind closed doors, seated at his favourite desk (once the property of the great Thomas Carlyle), in a haze of cigarette smoke, he read and wrote, hour upon hour. He had the gift Napoleon most admired: *de fixer les objets longtemps sans être fatigué.** He was one of the most hard-working men I ever knew. He laboured industriously and he played extravagantly. By night, he wined and dined and, then, he drank and ate some more. And between dinner and supper, he took in plays, operas, ballets, concerts and exhibitions. 'What is it to be tonight, Robert? Henry

---

* 'To concentrate on objectives at length, without wearying'.

Irving's Wolsey at the Lyceum or Marie Lloyd's flan-
nelette at the Bedford Music Hall?' He saw *everything*; he
knew *everybody*. And, of course, everybody wanted to
know him. Nobody, I believe, in late-Victorian society,
had a wider circle of acquaintance than Oscar Wilde.
From Monday to Saturday his engagement diary was full
to overflowing. The one day in the week he found testing
was Sunday. 'Nothing happens on a Sunday,' he complained. 'Everything is closed. No one goes out. Nobody
entertains. Even God has to go to church. There's nothing
else to do.' That was why, early in 1892, he formed the
Socrates Club.

The club was named in honour of the great Greek
philosopher. Conan Doyle had suggested Diogenes,
but Oscar said Diogenes was 'a dull dog, a provincial,
without an epigram to his name', whereas Socrates was
'a citizen of the world' with whom Oscar had a fellow-
feeling. 'Socrates was one of the wisest men who ever
lived,' said Oscar, 'but he claimed to know nothing
except the fact of his own ignorance. He's a man to drink
to on a Sunday evening, is he not?'

The club was simply a supper club. It had no premises
and only one purpose: to divert its founder on the first
Sunday of every month. There were just six members:
Oscar, Conan Doyle, Lord Alfred Douglas, myself, Bram
Stoker and Walter Sickert.

Bram Stoker was Conan Doyle's suggestion and Oscar
welcomed it at once. Conan Doyle was not at ease with
all of Oscar's associates, but he felt comfortable with
Abraham Stoker because, as he put it, Stoker was 'sens-
ible' (Stoker was an older man, in his mid-forties), Stoker
was 'sound' (at university, Stoker had been an athlete

and, better still, a scientist). Stoker was also business manager, secretary and friend to Henry Irving, the greatest, most celebrated, actor of the age, and, as a young writer, it was Arthur Conan Doyle's abiding ambition to create a role for Henry Irving. Oscar was pleased to assist in throwing Conan Doyle and Bram Stoker together. Oscar and Bram were fellow Dubliners. 'We go back a long way,' said Oscar. 'We know one another's secrets.' In 1878, Bram had married Oscar's first sweetheart, almond-eyed Florence Balcombe.

Walter Sickert, the artist, was another long-established friend. He was my age (thirty-one), but Oscar had known him since he was a boy. As a young man Oscar had holidayed with the Sickerts in Dieppe and though Wat, as a lad, had been suspicious of Oscar, as the years passed and their intimacy grew, the artist and the writer found that they had much in common. 'We both hunger for laughter, outrage and applause,' said Sickert. He agreed to join the Socrates Club on condition that he was not obliged to change for dinner and that smoking would be permitted even before the Loyal Toast. When Conan Doyle tut-tutted at this, Sickert pointed out that 'Socrates' was an anagram of 'coarsest' and won the point. Conan Doyle and Sickert found they shared a passion for word-play and Henry Irving. Before he became a full-time artist, Sickert had been a part-time actor. Aged eighteen, he had joined Irving's company as a utility player, one of 'the Lyceum young men', as they were known. As well as carrying a spear and swelling the crowd, he was given the occasional line to declaim. 'Irving seemed to like me because I was young and fair-haired,' he told Conan Doyle. 'I worshipped Irving because he was Irving and he noticed me.'

The Socrates Club met in the private dining room on the ground floor of the recently opened Cadogan Hotel, on the corner of Sloane Street and Pont Street, a few minutes' walk from Oscar's house in Tite Street. The hotel had once been the home of Oscar's particular friend (and the Prince of Wales's sometime mistress), Lillie Langtry, and Mrs Langtry (who retained a suite at the hotel) was occasionally to be seen in the hotel foyer, by the porter's desk, wearing one of her famous hats and engaging the notorious hotel parrot, the predictably named Captain Flint, in brittle conversation. The parrot was a vile creature, noisy and noisome. Why Mrs Langtry found him so fascinating none of us could fathom. Why every man who ever met her was taken with 'the Jersey Lillie' was not so difficult to comprehend. She was bewitching, and a survivor. Conan Doyle, who was especially smitten, said she had 'the face of the most beautiful of women, and the mind of the most resolute of men.'

The club 'secretary' was Alphonse Byrd, the resident night manager at the Cadogan, a man in his mid-fifties, who was so thin and pale and bald that he looked like a walking skeleton. His appearance was memorable, but, so far as I could tell, he had no personality to speak of. He rarely uttered a word or looked one in the eye, but Oscar liked him and found his faded appearance strangely comforting. As a young man, Byrd had worked the halls as a conjuror and illusionist, and failed. 'There's mildew is his soul,' said Oscar. 'Failure is so much more interesting than success. I'd much rather read Napoleon's biography than Wellington's, wouldn't you?'

In fairness to Byrd, as club secretary he did a first-class job. He was responsible for the menus, the wines and the table setting and given the relatively modest cost of the meal – half a crown per diner, all in – he did us proud. Oscar insisted on six courses. As well as the customary soup, fish, roast meats and desserts, Byrd laid on a selection of *hors d'oeuvres* – invariably including Russian caviar, Dutch herrings, prawns, lobster, pickled tunny, smoked salmon and smoked ham – and both savoury and sweet, vegetable and fruit *entremets*. Each member of the Club was allowed to invite one guest to each dinner – gentlemen only, or, by permission of the founder, certain actresses. Mrs Langtry came twice, and Wat Sickert sometimes arrived late, bringing one of his theatrical lady friends in tow.

On the evening of 1 May 1892, Oscar's dinner guest was Constance's married admirer, the young solicitor Edward Heron-Allen. Bosie's guest was his eldest brother, Lord Drumlanrig, then very much the 'coming' young man at Westminster, protégé of Lord Rosebery, sometime Foreign Secretary and soon to be Foreign Secretary again.

My guest was also a scion of the aristocracy, though not one with either the promise or the connections of Francis Drumlanrig. The Hon. the Reverend George Daubeney, youngest son of the Earl of Bridgwater, was known, if at all, merely as the man who abandoned his bride-to-be a week before the wedding day and paid the price. I did not know Daubeney intimately, but I felt for him. I married Marthe in haste when we were both too young. Had I left her in the lurch at the altar, it would have saved us both much anguish in the years that followed.

Arthur Conan Doyle's guest that evening was his 'delicate-minded' friend, Willie Hornung. According to

Arthur, the young man was a journalist newly returned from Australia, but Hornung's slight frame, wan look, lank hair and *pince-nez* suggested a nervous country curate rather than a newshound fresh from the Antipodes. 'He's a little shy,' said Arthur. 'I shall speak to him in a little voice,' replied Oscar, in a whisper.

Walter Sickert and Bram Stoker each brought an actor as his guest. Sickert came with Bradford Pearse, a barrel-chested boomer of the old school, a big man with a naval beard and a ruddy face, who seemed much older than his years (he was not yet forty). Sickert and Pearse had first met as juniors in Irving's company and Pearse's claim to fame was that he had understudied Irving in the Scottish play and had even 'gone on' for the great man once at the Lyceum . . . the Lyceum, Sunderland.

Charles Brookfield, Bram Stoker's invitee that evening, had never understudied anyone in his life. He was, I imagine, a leading man from the cradle, enviably blessed with doting parents, admiring older sisters and not a nuance of self-doubt. He was gifted – at Cambridge he was awarded the Winchester Reading Prize – and he was versatile. He played in pantomime and Shakespeare: Ellen Terry rated him, so did Herbert Beerbohm-Tree. He was blessed with energy, ambition, an undeniable presence and what we now call matinée idol looks. Humour and humility, however, were not his long suits. I did not warm to him. I don't believe Oscar much liked him either. I think, bizarrely, Brookfield considered himself, in some way, as Oscar's rival. He was a writer as well as an actor. He arrived at the Cadogan Hotel that evening full of news of his latest enterprise: a play he had written called *The Poet and the Puppets*.

'It opens on 19 May,' he announced, 'my thirty-fifth birthday – it's a present to myself. And it's all about you, Oscar!'

Oscar inclined his head in acknowledgement. 'How clever of you, Charles, to give the public what they want.'

'It's a burlesque, Oscar – a satire on *Lady Windermere's Fan*. It's a little sharp at times, but Bram assures me you won't mind.'

'Praise makes me humble,' answered Oscar, 'but when I am abused I know that I have touched the stars.'

At 7.30 p.m., the hour at which the Socrates Club dinner was customarily served, Oscar enquired of Byrd, 'Are we all gathered? There only seem to be thirteen in the room.'

'My guest is late, Mr Wilde,' answered Byrd, wincing as he spoke. 'It's not like him to be late. My profound apologies. He will be here in the instant.'

Oscar glanced down at the piece of paper on which he had drawn up the seating plan for the dinner. 'Ah, yes,' he said, '"David McMuirtree" . . . I've not met him before, have I?'

'I don't believe so, Mr Wilde,' said Byrd, looking anxiously towards the door.

'He appears to know you, Oscar,' I said.

'You've met him, Robert?'

'Briefly,' I replied, 'just the once.'

'McMuirtree?' said Charles Brookfield, raising an eyebrow. 'I recognise the name. Is he a gentleman?'

'He's what you'd call "half-a-gentleman", sir,' said Byrd, apologetically. 'His mother was a lady, but his father was a footman.'

'A footman!' exclaimed Oscar. 'How delightful. How tall?'

Byrd looked confused. 'I don't follow you, Mr Wilde.'

'How tall was McMuirtree's father? Do you know? The taller the footman, the greater his remuneration.'

'I don't know about the father, Mr Wilde, but McMuirtree must be over six foot.'

'I'm delighted to hear it,' said Oscar, who was more than six foot himself. 'Is your friend a footman like his father? I've no objection to dining with a footman, needless to say, but I'm not sure Mr Brookfield could cope.'

Byrd gave a nervous laugh. 'Oh, no, sir. David McMuirtree's a boxer. He works the fairgrounds. I know him from my time on the halls. He was a champion in his day. I believe he once had the honour of going a round or two with Lord Queensberry. He's never been in service, I assure you. He's a fine figure of a man. You'll like him, Mr Wilde.'

At this point, a tall, broad, handsome man of about forty appeared in the dining-room doorway. His head and face were totally clean-shaven and his dark brown skin had a sheen to it like polished chestnut. His nose was prominent, but unbroken; his eyes were blue-black, but warm. His evening dress was immaculate. He wore a green carnation in his buttonhole.

'I like him very much,' said Oscar.

'I thought you would,' muttered Byrd, evidently relieved. 'Shall I have dinner served, Mr Wilde?'

'If you would, Byrd. Thank you.' Oscar stepped across the dining room and shook McMuirtree cordially by the hand. 'Welcome to our little club, Mr McMuirtree. Socrates taught us that there is only one good and that is knowledge; and only one evil, ignorance. Already, I feel better for knowing you.'

'Thank you, Mr Wilde,' said McMuirtree, bowing his head and speaking in a tone so hushed that he was barely audible.

'There's no need to whisper here,' said Oscar, genially. 'You are among friends.'

'I fear I have no choice but to speak like this,' answered the boxer in the softest of whispers. 'My vocal chords were destroyed some years ago in a bout in Birmingham. I was hammered in the neck by a lunatic.'

'I am sorry to hear it,' said Oscar, lowering his voice to match McMuirtree's.

'Not everyone plays by the Queensberry Rules,' said the boxer with a smile.

'Indeed,' said Oscar. He turned to the room and clapped his hands together loudly.

'Hush!' cried Bosie. 'The chairman speaks!'

'Gentlemen,' said Oscar, 'kindly take your seats. Dinner is about to be served. You will find name cards at your places. The seating plan is my responsibility, but the menu and choice of wines, as ever, have been left to Byrd. He rarely lets us down.'

When we had all found our places, Oscar took up his position at the head of the table and clapped his hands once more. 'Welcome, gentlemen, welcome. I should explain to newcomers, this is a club virtually without rules. To keep Wat happy, you are even allowed to come dressed as you please. We shall say Grace tonight because we are honoured to have a man of the cloth among us –' he nodded towards George Daubeney – 'and, as ever, we shall have a loyal toast because Her Majesty is always present in our hearts. Other than that, we have no formalities – no speeches – and you may say whatever you please –' Oscar looked directly at David McMuirtree – 'you may *whisper* whatever you please, knowing that whatever is uttered or undertaken in this room tonight remains between us.'

A rumble of 'Hear, hear!' ran around the table, interrupted by Bosie who called out, 'We have no rules, Oscar, but we do have one tradition.'

'Do we?' asked Sickert.

'Of course we do,' said Bosie. 'Oscar's game.'

'Oh, yes,' said Oscar. 'After dinner, we play a game.'

'What's it to be tonight, Oscar?' asked Bosie. 'Have you decided?'

'Indeed,' said Oscar, 'I have it in hand . . . or as Mrs Robinson might say, I have it in my "unhappy hand". . . "Murder" is the game we shall be playing tonight. Mr Daubeney – George – will you be so kind as to give us Grace?'

The seating plan
for the Socrates Club dinner at
the Cadogan Hotel on Sunday 1 May 1892

Oscar Wilde

Edward Heron-Allen   Lord Alfred Douglas

Arthur Conan Doyle   Lord Drumlanrig

Willie Hornung   Bram Stoker

Robert Sherard   Bradford Pearse

The Hon. the Rev. George Daubeney   Walter Sickert

Charles Brookfield   David McMuirtree

Alphonse Byrd

3
The Game

Byrd's dinner was exemplary. I noted down the wines in my journal especially: with the fish, an extraordinarily silky white Burgundy; with the beef, an 1888 Margaux so mellow that even Charles Brookfield conceded it had 'merit'. Absurdly, with the brandy, port and liqueurs, Oscar insisted that Byrd also serve a carafe of 'Vin Mariani', a curious concoction, the colour of dung, made from cheap Bordeaux wine treated with coca leaves.

'What's this?' Brookfield asked as Byrd offered him a glass.

'It's not compulsory,' said Oscar from his end of the table. He had the gift of being able to listen to several conversations simultaneously.

'But what is it?' insisted Brookfield. 'It looks disgusting.'

'It's a cordial favoured by His Holiness the Pope,' Oscar explained.

'Well, we're not in Rome now,' said Brookfield, waving Byrd away and reaching for the port decanter.

'Nor in Oporto,' murmured Oscar. 'I asked Byrd to serve the Mariani in honour of Dr Doyle. I believe the beverage contains cocaine. I thought Arthur might care to introduce it to his friend, Sherlock Holmes.'

Conan Doyle laughed obligingly. 'I'd better try a glass then.'

'Her Majesty the Queen is apparently partial to it, also,' said Oscar.

'Never mind the wine, Wilde,' said Brookfield, turning his port glass slowly in his hand. 'What about this game of yours?'

'Oh yes, Oscar,' cried Bosie. 'Let's play the game!'

'Are you sure it's a good idea, Oscar?' asked Conan Doyle, leaning towards Oscar while casting his eyes in the direction of the 'delicate-minded' Willie Hornung.

Oscar addressed the table. 'Arthur has reservations about our game, gentlemen. Last month we played "Mistresses" – and the good doctor felt unable to participate.'

'I did not feel it was seemly,' said Conan Doyle quietly.

'It was most unseemly, as I recall,' said Sickert. 'I think that was the idea.' He turned to his neighbour, McMuirtree, the boxer, to explain. 'Oscar invited us all to select the mistress of our choice. As I recall, he picked Joan of Arc.'

'What has this to do with Socrates?' enquired Brookfield, helping himself to a further libation of port.

'Socrates taught us that the greatest way to live with honour in this world is to be what we pretend to be.'

'I don't follow you,' said Brookfield.

'Oh, but you do, Charles,' said Oscar, 'in everything.'

'Come on,' cried Bosie. 'Let's play the game!'

'Very well,' said Oscar. He looked towards Conan Doyle and whispered, with a kindly smile: 'It's only a game, Arthur.'

'Very well,' said Conan Doyle, nodding to Oscar and patting the back of Willie Hornung's hand by way of offering his young friend reassurance. 'Half a glass of this Mariani wine of yours, Oscar, and I seem to be up for anything.'

'Good man,' said Oscar, getting to his feet. He stood quite steadily at the head of the table and, with an amused eye, surveyed the thirteen of us seated before him. '"Murder" is the name of our game this evening. It was Socrates who first suggested that death may be the greatest of all human blessings, and tonight, gentlemen, we are to visit that blessing upon the victims of our choice. Do I make myself clear?'

There was a general murmur of assent.

'Does everyone here have a pen or pencil about his person?' Oscar asked.

Brookfield muttered to his neighbour, 'We're in the schoolroom now, are we?'

Oscar went on: 'Mr Byrd will pass around the table presently and give each of you a slip of paper and, should you require it, a writing implement. Onto your blank slip of paper – unseen by your neighbours – you are invited to write down the name of the person or persons you would most like to murder.'

'I like this game,' boomed Bradford Pearse. 'What's the name of the theatre critic on the *Era*?'

'When you have written down your victim's name,' Oscar continued, 'Byrd will pass around the table once more, collecting your slips of paper and placing them safely in this collection bag.' He held up a small plum-coloured velvet bag, the size of a hand. 'He will then, on my instruction, draw out the slips of paper, at random, one by one, and read out each name in turn. Our task then, gentlemen, will be to work out who wishes to murder whom.'

'And why,' suggested Charles Brookfield, licking the tip of his pencil.

'Indeed,' said Oscar. 'And why.'

'Will you be playing, too, Mr Chairman?' enquired Lord Drumlanrig. 'Are you allowed to choose a victim, also?'

'Naturally,' said Oscar, sitting down, taking his fountain pen out of his coat pocket and subscribing his victim's name to his slip of paper with the deliberation of a statesman signing an international treaty. 'There is nothing quite like an unexpected death for lifting the spirits.'

While we wrote the names of our proposed victims on the small slips of paper provided to us by Alphonse Byrd, a curious hush fell upon the room. I wrote down the name of my victim-of-choice instantly, without giving the matter much consideration. I then looked about the table and watched the others. Most appeared rapt in concentration, like students taking an exam by candlelight. Bosie was sucking on his pencil, apparently much amused by the thought of who was to be his victim. Bradford Pearse, the actor, was contemplating whatever he had written with what seemed like wary satisfaction. Wat Sickert looked to me to be drawing a sketch of his victim. Like Bosie, Sickert was evidently amused by his choice of prey. Everyone – even the cynical and supercilious Brookfield and mild-mannered Willie Hornung – gave the impression of total absorption in the task in hand. Only Arthur Conan Doyle looked disengaged. He held his pen, unopened, in his left hand and stared vacantly ahead of him, fixing his empty gaze between Lord Drumlanrig and Bram Stoker on the blank wall beyond.

'Suddenly it's quiet as a graveyard in here,' whispered McMuirtree.

'Oh,' said Sickert, smiling slyly, 'I can hear the Angel of Death flapping her wings.'

Oscar looked up. 'Nowhere is there more true feeling, and nowhere worse taste, than in a graveyard,' he said.

Bosie suppressed a giggle. 'That's very good, Oscar. Is it one of yours?'

Oscar was folding his slip of paper in two and placing it in the collection bag. 'It deserves to be,' he said, 'but it isn't, I'm afraid. I first heard it in Oxford years ago. At Balliol, more's the pity.' He held up the velvet bag for Byrd to take it from him. 'Are we all done?' he asked.

'We are,' boomed Bradford Pearse.

'This is rather fun,' said Willie Hornung, polishing his *pince-nez* with a corner of his napkin.

'I'm glad you are having a happy evening, Willie,' said Oscar. 'Help yourself to another glass of Mariani wine.'

When Byrd had been around the table and each of us had placed his folded slip of paper into the collection bag, Oscar took a teaspoon and clinked it against the side of his brandy glass. 'Gentlemen,' he said, 'the moment is upon us. If your glasses are all charged and your cigars are lit, we shall proceed with the game.' He turned to Byrd who was standing at his right shoulder. 'Mr Byrd, if you would be so kind, please draw the first slip from the bag and read out the name thereon inscribed.'

Byrd pulled back his cuff — as a magician might to show his audience nothing was concealed up his sleeve —

and plunged his hand into the bag. He let us see his fingers rummaging about inside the bag and then, with a self-conscious flourish, pulled out a slip of paper and held it close to his eyes.

'This is fun,' repeated Willie Hornung, sitting forward in his place.

Oscar smiled at the young man and then looked up at Alphonse Byrd. 'Mr Byrd,' he said, 'be so kind, would you, as to read out the name of our first murder victim?'

Byrd scrutinised the paper in his hand and looked out across the room. The night manager of the Cadogan Hotel was not an impressive figure – he had the stooped shoulders and watery eyes of a man defeated by life – but he had once been a professional performer and in that brief moment, holding the slip of paper in one hand and his magician's bag in the other, he commanded our attention with an authority that even the great Robert-Houdin might have envied.

Oscar killed the moment. 'Byrd,' he snapped, 'we've heard the pin drop. Read out the name.'

Flinching momentarily, as though Oscar had suddenly struck him across the ear, Byrd did as he was bidden. 'The first victim is to be "Miss Elizabeth Scott-Rivers",' he announced.

The silence in the room that, a moment before, had been so expectant – exhilarating, almost – now became uncomfortable. Every one of us present was familiar with the name of Elizabeth Scott-Rivers. Miss Scott-Rivers was the unhappy bride-to-be abandoned a week before her wedding day by the Hon. the Reverend George Daubeney, my particular guest at the Socrates Club dinner that night. She was the jilted maiden – an heiress

and the only child of elderly parents who had prede-
ceased her – who had gained the sympathy of the public,
and the braying approbation of the press, when, in the
High Court of Chancery, she had sued her former fiancé
for breach of promise, won her case and brought the
wretched man to his knees and the brink of financial
ruin.

'Well, well . . .' said Oscar with a sigh. Conan Doyle
put his fingers to his eyes and shook his head. George
Daubeney was seated on my right. I rested my hand on
his arm. 'Next!' commanded Oscar.

Suddenly, violently, Daubeney pulled his arm away
from me and got to his feet, knocking over a glass of
the absurd Mariani cordial in the process. 'I'm so
sorry, gentlemen,' he blurted out. 'I don't know what I
was thinking of. I despise the woman. I hate her. But I
wish her no harm. I should not have introduced her
name to this game like this. It was inexcusable. May
God forgive me. May you forgive me. I have drunk too
much.'

Oscar raised his right hand and held it aloft, like a
bishop pronouncing the blessing. 'Be seated, George.
Calm yourself. You can't have had more than a glass.'

I put out my hand and took Daubeney's arm once
more. I pulled him back into his chair. 'I'm a fool,' he
muttered. 'A bloody idiot.'

'Come,' said Oscar briskly, 'let us go on. And please
remember, gentlemen, that the aim of the game is for
the rest of us to guess who has chosen whom as a
victim, not for the putative perpetrator of the crime to
offer an immediate confession.' Daubeney sat, in heavy
silence, gazing disconsolately at his empty glass. 'Byrd,'

said Oscar, 'draw out the next victim's name if you please.'

Byrd produced a second slip of paper from his bag and read out the name, this time with rather less ceremony. ' "Lord Abergordon",' he said.

'Who?' asked Heron-Allen.

Byrd repeated the name: 'Lord Abergordon.'

'A curious choice,' said Oscar, taking a sip of brandy.

'Who is he?' asked Sickert.

'We neither know nor care,' boomed Bradford Pearse.

'He's an elderly and obscure member of the government, I believe,' said Bram Stoker.

'He won't be much of a loss then,' said Heron-Allen, with a wry smile.

'Very droll, Edward,' murmured Oscar. 'You're getting the idea. Next, if you will, Mr Byrd – kindly maintain the momentum.'

Byrd produced the third slip of paper, and smiled, and read out the name: ' "Captain Flint".'

'That's more like it,' said Oscar.

'Who's Captain Flint?' asked Willie Hornung.

'The hotel parrot,' said Bosie. 'He's the moth-eaten creature who sits in that cage by the porter's desk. He's impertinent and garrulous and deserves everything that's coming to him. I wanted to murder my father, of course, but Oscar said I couldn't, at least not on a Sunday, so I chose the parrot instead.'

Oscar turned to his handsome young friend and reprimanded him. 'Bosie, you have now spoilt what was a most excellent choice. The object of the game is not for you to reveal who is your intended victim. It is for the rest of us to guess.' He turned back to Byrd. 'On, man, on!'

Byrd produced a fourth slip of paper from the velvet bag and read out the name with a flourish. '"Mr Sherlock Holmes",' he said.

'That's much more like it!' cried Oscar.

'I agree,' said Conan Doyle.

'On, on, Byrd! Don't dawdle, man. Give us the next name.'

The night manager had the fifth slip ready. He looked at it and hesitated.

'Well?' said Oscar.

'"Mr Bradford Pearse",' said Byrd.

'Oh?' said Bradford Pearse, with a shallow laugh. 'Someone here wants me out of the way . . .'

A courteous rumble of dissent went round the table. Conan Doyle spoke up. 'This game is not amusing, Oscar,' he said.

'It's not the game that isn't amusing,' said Oscar smoothly. 'It was Pearse's Fabian that failed to entertain – alas! It's a devil of a part. Several of the critics said poor Pearse deserved to be shot . . .' Oscar smiled benignly at the unfortunate actor. 'It's only a game, Bradford,' he said gently. Pearse nodded and shrugged his shoulders and reached for the decanter of brandy. Oscar turned back to the hotel night manager. 'Onward, Mr Byrd. We're almost halfway. Who is our next victim to be?'

Byrd had the next slip of paper already in his hand. '"Mr David McMuirtree",' he announced.

'Goodness me,' said Willie Hornung.

'This must stop, Oscar,' said Conan Doyle, sharply. 'Enough's enough. Mr Pearse and Mr McMuirtree are our guests. They have come here to be entertained – not threatened with murder, even in jest.'

'I don't take it personally,' whispered McMuirtree from the far end of the table.

'Really?' murmured Charles Brookfield. He was seated directly facing McMuirtree. He looked him in the eye. 'What other way is there to take it?' he asked.

'As our chairman says,' answered McMuirtree, turning away from Brookfield and looking towards Oscar, 'it's only a game.'

'Thank you, Mr McMuirtree,' said Oscar, raising his brandy glass in the boxer's direction. 'We green-carnation men understand one another.'

Conan Doyle growled unhappily and shook his head. Oscar leant towards the good doctor.

'Don't look so serious, Arthur. Humanity takes itself far too seriously as it is. Seriousness is the world's original sin. If the cavemen had known how to laugh, history would have been very different – and so much jollier. Come, Byrd, who's next?'

The night manager stood before us and plunged his hand into the bag once more. He produced another slip of paper.

'Read it out,' said Oscar.

' "Mr David McMuirtree",' said Byrd.

'Again?' asked Heron-Allen, seeming suddenly to wake from a reverie.

'Yes, sir,' said Byrd. 'Again.'

'Pull out another one,' commanded Oscar. 'Let's get on with it.'

'What number is this?' asked Bosie.

'This is the eighth, Lord Alfred,' said Byrd, holding the next piece of paper in front of him.

'Whose name is it this time?' asked Oscar.

'It is the same name, I am afraid,' said Byrd. '"Mr David McMuirtree".'

'Stop this, Oscar,' protested Conan Doyle. 'Stop this now!'

'No,' rasped McMuirtree. 'I'm not put out, I assure you. It really does not matter.'

'Quite right, Mr McMuirtree,' said Oscar, 'Nothing that actually occurs is of the smallest importance.' He delivered the aphorism lightly (it was one of his favourites), but I was watching him as he spoke and I saw the anxiety in his eyes. 'Come, Byrd, continue,' he said crisply. 'We are nearly there. Three of us seem inclined to murder Mr McMuirtree. Let's see if there is to be a fourth. Draw out the next name, if you will.'

Byrd did as he was asked. He held the slip closer to his eyes and paused.

'Well?' asked Bosie.

'"Mr David McMuirtree",' said Byrd once again.

'"Ask not for whom the bell tolls . . ."' murmured Oscar, furrowing his brow and raising his glass once more in the direction of McMuirtree. 'Let's have the next one, Byrd,' he added. 'We're too steeped in blood to turn back now. I'm sure McMuirtree agrees.'

McMuirtree inclined his head towards Oscar and smiled.

'It's decent of you to be so obliging,' said Conan Doyle.

'Who's next?' said Oscar.

Byrd drew another slip of paper from his bag.

McMuirtree, from the far end of the table, looked towards him and enquired quietly, 'Well?'

'The next victim is "Old Father Time",' announced Mr Byrd.

'That's more like it,' said Bram Stoker, gently banging the table with the flat of his hand to indicate his approval.

'Not so exciting though,' said Bosie. 'Perhaps I should have named my father, after all.' He turned to his brother, seated on his left. Lord Drumlanrig was lighting a cigar. 'Why didn't you choose our father as your victim, Francis? You loathe him as much as I do and you stand to gain more from the inheritance.'

'Lord Drumlanrig may well have selected the Marquess of Queensberry as his victim, Bosie,' said Oscar, placing his fingers lightly on the back of his young friend's right hand. 'Byrd still has three names to reveal.' He turned back to the club secretary. 'Who's next?'

Byrd was ready, slip of paper in hand. 'The next victim is "Eros",' he announced.

'Eros?' asked Willie Hornung, putting down his glass of Vin Mariani and looking about the table with a bright-eyed innocence that was endearing. 'Does Eros count? He is a mythical Greek god, isn't he?'

'If you can murder Time,' said Oscar, 'I imagine you can destroy a myth. In fact, I know men who have done both. I think Eros is a permissible victim within the rules of the game, Willie. Continue, Byrd.'

'Yes,' said Brookfield, who now appeared quite bloated with drink. 'Let's have done with it. Who's next for the chop?'

Alphonse Byrd felt inside the bag and pulled out a slip of paper. He held it to his eyes and looked puzzled. He turned it over and examined it more closely. 'It's blank, Mr Wilde,' he said, passing the paper to Oscar.

Oscar held it lightly between his thumb and forefinger. 'So it is, Byrd. Nothing will come of nothing. Next, please!'

'This is the penultimate slip of paper, I believe,' said Byrd.

'Get on with it!' jeered Brookfield.

The club secretary cleared his throat before reading out the name: ' "Mr Oscar Wilde".'

There was laughter around the table. Stoker banged his right hand repeatedly on the cigar box to show his approval. Even Conan Doyle smiled. Oscar acknowledged the mocking ovation with a seated bow. 'I suppose it was inevitable,' he muttered, 'though I'm sorry that my name should have been the thirteenth to be drawn. Come, Mr Byrd, let's name the final victim and be done.'

Byrd, who was now standing at the side of the table, behind Willie Hornung and Conan Doyle, put his hand into his small velvet bag for the final time. He drew out the paper and looked at it. He sniffed and brushed the back of his knuckles against his mouth.

'Come on, man,' cried Brookfield from his corner. 'What does it say?'

'It says, "Mr Oscar Wilde",' said Byrd. He spoke quietly and then shook his head and placed the paper and the bag on the table and looked towards Oscar. 'I'm sorry, Mr Wilde.'

'Goodness,' cried Oscar, grinning. 'I'm almost as unpopular as McMuirtree. I'm not sure whether to be gratified or appalled.'

'Welcome to the club, Mr Wilde,' said McMuirtree, with a husky laugh.

'It's only a game,' grunted Bradford Pearse.

'Indeed,' said Oscar, amiably.

Arthur Conan Doyle was leaning across Edward Heron-Allen, holding the last of the slips of paper Byrd had drawn from the bag. He peered at it intently. 'It's not a game any more,' he said.

'It's only a joke, Arthur,' said Bosie through a cloud of cigar smoke. 'Oscar can take a joke.'

'I think the joke is over,' said Conan Doyle, getting to his feet. He moved to the head of the table and, putting his arm over Oscar's shoulder, held the slip of paper out before him. 'The name of this last "victim" . . . the name that's written here . . . Look at it carefully, Oscar. What does it say?'

Oscar studied the piece of paper that Conan Doyle held before him and read the words: '"Mrs Oscar Wilde".'

4

'We Live and Learn'

Young Willie Hornung filled the silence that had fallen in the private dining room at the Cadogan Hotel. 'Who would want to murder Mrs Wilde?' he asked.

'No one in their right mind,' said Bram Stoker, 'even in jest.' The Irishman stubbed out his cigar on a side-plate and pushed his chair away from the dining-room table. He got to his feet and looked about the room, scratching his beard. 'The game's gone sour,' he said.

'I agree,' said Conan Doyle. He looked sternly around at all of us. 'I don't know about the rest of you, gentlemen, but I'm for my bed.'

Everyone began to move.

'No, gentlemen, no!' Oscar protested. 'We must get to the bottom of this.'

'Not tonight, Oscar,' said Stoker, firmly.

'I insist,' said Oscar. 'I'm the club chairman.'

'But I'm the older animal, Oscar,' Stoker growled, 'and I've had enough excitement for one evening. Mr Irving is embarking on *King Lear* in the morning. First day of rehearsals. Lear can't rely on his daughters, but the Guv'nor likes to think he can rely on me. It's late, Oscar, and, whatever you say, I'm for turning in.'

'We all are,' chimed Wat Sickert, from the far end the table. He, too, was on his feet. 'The iron tongue of midnight hath told twelve,' he said softly. He leant over the dining table, licked the palm of his left hand and cupped it and used it as a snuffer to extinguish the guttering candles that were set in a circle around what once had been Lillie Langtry's favourite epergne. The room was plunged into sepulchral gloom. The only source of light was a pair of gasoliers above the fireplace. ''Tis almost fairy-time,' he said. He turned to Bradford Pearse. 'Come, Brad, you can be my guest a while longer and stay the night at my place. I'll see you don't get murdered in your sleep.'

Pearse laughed. I noticed he was sweating. He had a large white handkerchief in his hand and he used it to wipe the perspiration from his face and neck and brow. 'I'm ready,' he said.

Sickert leant across his friend to shake Bram Stoker by the hand. 'Goodnight, Bram,' he said warmly. 'Give my respects to Irving.'

'I will.'

'If ever he needs a portrait . . .'

'We know where to find you, Wat,' replied Stoker, genially. He peered across the darkened table towards Conan Doyle, who was assisting Oscar to his feet. 'Goodnight, Arthur. Give us a week or three to get *Lear* out of the traps – the Guv'nor has lumbered himself with a plump Cordelia and a troublesome Fool – and then I'll get you in for an hour and you can tell him all about your play. I think he can be persuaded . . .'

'Is Arthur writing plays now?' muttered Oscar in a mock-grumble. 'Perhaps I should consider opening a medical practice?'

'Goodnight, Mr Chairman,' said Stoker. 'The night has been unruly, but memorable. Thank you. And thank you, Byrd, for the feast. We've eaten like princes, as usual. Goodnight all. Come, Brookfield – we'll share a cab.'

Charles Brookfield, his long, handsome face flushed with wine, was already standing by the door. He held himself unnaturally erect: he was deep in drink. 'Goodnight, gentlemen,' he called to the room. 'My play is entitled *The Poet and the Puppets*. It opens on the nineteenth of the month. Your attendance will do me honour.'

As Stoker took Brookfield by the arm and escorted him from the room, Oscar shook his head and murmured, 'Ambition is the last refuge of the failure.'

'Goodnight, Oscar,' said Lord Drumlanrig. 'Thank you for your hospitality.'

'*Bonne nuit, mon cher*,' Bosie called to Oscar, pulling his brother with him towards the door.

'Goodnight, gentlemen,' said Oscar. 'Will I see you tomorrow, Bosie?'

'Murderers permitting,' said Bosie, with a laugh, giving the room a playful farewell wave.

Oscar watched the Douglas brothers depart. 'Bosie is wonderfully amusing, is he not?' he said to nobody in particular.

The remaining members of the party were now exchanging farewells and moving towards the door. McMuirtree was assisting Byrd in clearing the decanters and dead wine bottles from the table onto a large butler's tray on the sideboard. Willie Hornung was telling Conan Doyle that he had had a 'capital evening', 'tip-top', one of the best he'd ever known. Edward Heron-Allen, I realised, had already slipped away, apparently unnoticed. I turned to say goodnight to the Hon. the Reverend George Daubeney and saw that he, alone of the party, was seated still. The poor fellow – my special guest! – was slumped in his place, gazing vacantly into the middle distance.

'Come, George,' I said, 'let's get you a cab.'

Daubeney slowly turned his weary, pock-marked face towards me and, with an effort, pushed his chair away from the table. He started to get to his feet, but, as he did so, lurched forward, stumbled and fell onto his knees, clutching at my legs for support. 'Forgive me, Robert,' he slurred. He put his hands back onto the table's edge as I helped him pull himself up again. 'I have drunk too much,' he mumbled.

'But only from the well of unhappiness,' said Oscar, who was still standing at the head of the table nursing his empty brandy glass.

'Do you want a bed at the hotel?' asked Byrd. 'We can find you a room.'

Daubeney looked up at the night manager and smiled bleakly. 'Thank you,' he said. 'You are kind, but I have business to attend to. I will be on my way.'

'Are you sure, George?' I asked.

'I can walk home,' he said. 'It's not far. The fresh air will do me good.'

He shook me by the hand and bowed towards Oscar and the others and took his leave.

'He is an unfortunate creature,' said Oscar. 'There is something infinitely pathetic about other people's tragedies.'

Oscar handed his empty brandy glass to Alphonse Byrd. 'Thank you, Mr Secretary Byrd,' he said, with a self-conscious half-smile upon his lips. He looked at Byrd's associate, David McMuirtree, and bobbed his head in the bald boxer's direction. 'A pleasure to have made your acquaintance, sir. Four of those seated at this table tonight chose you as their murder victim. I wonder why?'

'I'm a prize-fighter and the son of a footman,' said McMuirtree in his curious croaking voice. 'I had no right to be here. I do not belong.'

'Certainly you are far too well-dressed to pass for an English gentleman,' said Oscar, smiling.

'Am I?' whispered McMuirtree.

'Indeed,' said Oscar. 'Your shoes are very shiny. But it was probably that charming green carnation in your buttonhole that sealed your fate. You have physical strength, personal beauty, an interesting history and exquisite taste, Mr McMuirtree. No wonder people took an instant dislike to you.'

McMuirtree laughed.

'Goodnight, sir,' said Oscar, 'I trust we shall meet again. Perhaps, one day, I shall have the pleasure of seeing you fight.' Oscar shook McMuirtree's hand and continued holding it for a moment. 'At which fairground are you to be found at present?'

'I'm at Astley's Circus for the summer,' answered the boxer genially, looking Oscar steadily in the eye. 'There's a bout on Monday week you might enjoy, Mr Wilde. I'll send you tickets.'

'Thank you,' said Oscar. 'Thank you very much. I should like that.' He called to the club secretary: 'We like your friend, Byrd. Well done. Goodnight.' He turned to the rest of us: 'Arthur, Willie, Robert, come. Let's run the gauntlet of that fearful parrot and find ourselves a cab.'

In fact, the parrot was silent as we crossed the darkened front hall of the Cadogan Hotel. Its cage was shrouded in a huge embroidered shawl. We were fortunate, too, when we reached the street. Two empty cabs were waiting on the rank at the corner of Sloane Street and Knightsbridge.

'Mr Sickert is a fascinating character,' said Willie Hornung eagerly. 'He told me tonight that "Knightsbridge" is the only word in the English language that features six consonants in succession.'

Conan Doyle chuckled. 'Well, I never . . . You live and learn.'

'And then, of course, you die and forget it all,' said Oscar, quietly.

We saw young Hornung into the first cab and waved him on his way towards his digs in Bayswater. As he departed, he looked out of the two-wheeler towards us and called cheerily: 'I'll not forget tonight. Thank you so much!'

'What a delightful young man,' said Oscar, as Willie Hornung's cab disappeared into the darkness. 'The secret of remaining young is never to have an emotion that is unbecoming. I have a feeling that our Willie will be a boy for ever.'

'He's a good lad,' said Conan Doyle.

'He has a good friend,' said Oscar, putting his hand on Arthur's shoulder. 'You'll stay the night in Tite Street, won't you? It's too late to make the pilgrimage to Norwood.'

The three of us climbed aboard the second cab and, as Oscar settled back into his seat, he flicked his gloves lightly across Doyle's knees and said, 'I'm loath to admit it, dear Doctor, but you were right: that game was a mistake. There were strangers in our midst . . .'

'And wine was taken,' added Conan Doyle, 'somewhat too liberally.'

'Indeed,' said Oscar, smiling ruefully. 'But what's said when drunk was thought when sober. Did that last slip of paper really name "*Mrs* Oscar Wilde"?'

'I fear so,' said Doyle. 'It was intended as a joke, of course, but it was a poor one.'

'Could it not have been a slip of the pen?' I suggested.

'It could, I suppose,' said Conan Doyle.

'I don't think we'll mention it to Constance, do you?' said Oscar.

'I think we should all forget all about it,' urged Conan Doyle, emphatically. 'It was only a game, after all.'

When we reached Tite Street, the house was in darkness. The street was in darkness, too. It was one o'clock. The family was asleep and the staff – the three of them: Arthur, Oscar's faithful butler, Mrs Ryan, the cook, and Gertrude Simmonds, the boys' devoted governess – had retired for the night. Arthur had left the hallway gasolier lit low and put out candlesticks to light us to our beds. 'You're in my study, Robert, on the divan,' said Oscar, 'as befits a married man in the throes of a divorce. You're in the guest-room, Arthur, on the second-best bed. I'm leaving it to Constance in my will, of course. Goodnight, gentlemen. Sleep well. Don't brood on the events of the evening. They're done. As Arthur says, it was only a game, after all.'

I slept profoundly. Absurdly, I eased myself towards sleep with playful thoughts of Constance Wilde. My marriage to Marthe was a dead and dreary thing – so dead, so dreary I lacked the energy or interest even to pursue my divorce – and my dalliances with Kaitlyn and

Aniela, once so thrilling, had now run their course. I was thirty-one and in want of love. To think of Constance in terms of romance was utterly ridiculous, of course – she was four years my senior and had no eyes for any man but Oscar – and yet, by way of reverie, nothing more, to picture myself in her arms was something quite delicious.

I did not wake until ten o'clock in the morning. I found Oscar and Arthur, already breakfasted, dressed and shaved, seated in the Wildes' white drawing room reading the morning papers. As I entered the sunlit room Oscar sighed from behind his copy of the *Morning Post*. 'Tell me,' he breathed, wearily, 'why, oh why do I persist in reading this stuff? The newspapers of today chronicle with degrading avidity the sins of the second-rate, and with the conscientiousness of the illiterate give us accurate and prosaic details of the doings of people of absolutely no interest whatever. I must give them up.'

'Good morning, Robert,' said Conan Doyle, amiably, lowering his copy of *The Times*.

Oscar threw down his newspaper. 'I need a hobby,' he declared. 'I must take up sculpture, like Arthur here. Good morning, Robert. Did you sleep well?'

'Good morning, Oscar. Yes, thank you, very well.'

'I hope you dreamt well. Dreaming is your hobby, I know.'

I laughed and looked about the room in the hope that there might be a pot of coffee somewhere to be found. 'Is Constance about?' I asked.

'She and Gertrude Simmonds have taken the boys to Kensington Gardens. They have gone to feed the ducks. Everyone, it seems, has a useful hobby, but I.'

'I'll go in search of some coffee, if I may,' I said.

'Of course,' said Oscar. 'Mrs Ryan will boil you an egg as well. And Constance will be back shortly, I'm sure. But, remember, Robert: when you see her, not a word about last night, if you please. It was only a game, but my darling wife is a sensitive creature and I would not want to distress her for the world.'

'I know,' I said. 'I shan't say a word. But I still can't help wondering which of our motley party would have thought of naming Constance like that, even in jest.'

'Stop wondering,' said Conan Doyle, sharply. 'Forget all about it.'

'I will,' I said. 'I have.'

'Good,' said Oscar, turning his head towards the window. 'It is a golden day, is it not?'

As he spoke, and we followed his eye towards the sun-filled casement, the three of us were abruptly arrested in our thoughts by the sudden crack-crack-crack of what sounded like pistol shots.

'Good God!' cried Conan Doyle, leaping to his feet, 'What's that?'

The triple-crack sounded once more. The noise was louder than before. 'It's someone at the door,' said Oscar, getting to his feet and moving cautiously towards the window. The furious rat-tat-tat continued. 'It's some lunatic gone berserk with the door knocker.'

'Who is it?' demanded Conan Doyle, joining Oscar at the window and peering down into the street.

'I cannot tell,' said Oscar. The knocking had stopped. 'Either he's gone or Arthur has let him in.'

There was a sudden commotion in the hallway downstairs: the sound of two men arguing. There was the noise of a momentary scuffle, followed by the fierce pounding of footsteps on the stairs and then, suddenly, in the drawing-room doorway, there appeared before us, in besmirched and dishevelled evening dress, the shambling figure of the Hon. the Reverend George Daubeney. His hands were covered in blood.

'Miss Elizabeth Scott-Rivers . . .' he cried. 'The woman that last night I said I wanted to murder . . . she is dead! She's been burnt alive.'

5

A Death in Cheyne Walk

'Calm yourself, man,' said Conan Doyle.

'Did you do it?' asked Oscar.

George Daubeney stumbled into the Wildes' picture-perfect drawing room and collapsed upon a low *chaise-longue*. He buried his head in his bloodied hands and began to sob uncontrollably.

'Control yourself, sir!' ordered Conan Doyle. The good Scottish doctor – who was no more than thirty months my senior but always seemed to me to be older than my father – stepped out onto the landing to where Oscar's butler was hovering anxiously. 'A bowl of boiling water, towels and soap, if you please,' he said. 'And perhaps Mrs Ryan could prepare some sweet tea?'

'Shall I fetch the kitchen brandy as well, sir?' called the butler over his shoulder as he hurried downstairs in answer to Doyle's clear command.

'No, thank you, Arthur. I think alcohol has done enough damage for one night. If you can bring up my bag when you come, I'd be obliged. It's by the hat-stand in the hallway.'

In the sun-filled drawing room, Oscar was seated in an armchair immediately facing the wretched Daubeney.

The clergyman's sobbing had given way to a low, pathetic whimper.

'Did you do it?' repeated Oscar. 'Did you murder Miss Scott-Rivers?'

Daubeney lifted his head from his hands. His eyes were bulging, bloodshot, rimmed with tears. The irises were a dirty yellow, the colour of old straw. He looked directly at Oscar, but said nothing.

'He's in a state of shock,' said Conan Doyle, returning to the room.

'He's not alone in that,' said Oscar, quietly.

Conan Doyle got down on his haunches and squatted by George Daubeney. 'We're going to clean you up, man, and you can tell us what's occurred.'

Daubeney shook his head. 'I do not know,' he mumbled.

'What don't you know?' asked Doyle.

'I do not know what happened,' said Daubeney, very slowly. He seemed to be in a kind of trance. He turned away from Arthur and gazed at Oscar, imploringly. 'Help me,' he whispered.

'I can smell fresh smoke,' said Doyle, sniffing at the man's grubby apparel. 'He's been in a fire all right.'

'She's dead,' whispered Daubeney. He was barely audible.

'Did you do it?' Oscar repeated the question for the third time.

'Her face was gone, burnt clean away. Her hair was still alight.'

Oscar got up from his chair and paced towards the window. 'We must get him out of here before Constance returns.' He turned to me. 'Where does he live?'

'I'm not sure,' I said.

'He's your friend, Robert,' Oscar snapped. 'You brought him into our lives.'

'I think he has a room in Wandsworth.' I faltered. 'I barely know him, Oscar.'

'Forgive me,' said Oscar, quickly. It was rare for him to show his temper. As a rule, his demeanour remained serene even at the most testing of times. 'That was uncharitable of me, Robert. Unpardonable. His family have disowned him, I know – you told me. I do not ask you to do the same.'

'I know very little of him,' I protested.

'Help me,' bleated the hapless creature on the *chaise-longue*.

Arthur and Mrs Ryan came into the room. The butler, a towel thrown across his shoulder, was carrying a pail of steaming water and a bar of carbolic soap in one hand and Conan Doyle's bag in the other. The housekeeper brought in a tray crowded with cups and saucers, jugs and pots, a biscuit barrel and a small decanter of cognac. 'There's sweet tea and coffee here,' she said, 'and some brandy – for medicinal purposes.'

'There's no need,' said Conan Doyle.

'The brandy's for Mr Wilde,' said Mrs Ryan crisply. She placed her tray on top of the grand piano. 'Shall I leave you to look after yourselves, gentlemen?'

'Indeed,' said Oscar, beaming at his housekeeper. 'Thank you, Mrs Ryan.' As she left the drawing room, she smiled and dropped a curtsy towards her master. 'There's no need to mention this disturbance to Mrs Wilde when she returns,' Oscar added. 'Best not trouble her or the boys.'

The butler followed the housekeeper out of the room. As he left us, I noticed that Oscar inclined his head towards him and brought his fingertips together as if offering his servant a silent salaam. I helped Oscar pour out the refreshments. He added a generous dash of cognac to my coffee and his own. I took a cup of sweetened tea over to George Daubeney. Conan Doyle had washed the man's hands and face and was now applying tincture of iodine to the torn skin on his palms and wrists and arms. Daubeney winced. I held the tea cup to his lips. He drank from it slowly. I realised, looking into the man's face closely for probably the first time, that Conan Doyle had been correct in his initial assessment: Daubeney had a weak mouth.

'Tell us what has occurred, Daubeney,' said Conan Doyle. 'Take your time, but tell us everything. It may be necessary for us to call the police.'

'The police will already be there,' answered Daubeney, taking the tea cup from me and draining it in a long, slow gulp.

'Where?' asked Oscar.

'At 27 Cheyne Walk – her house.'

'Is that where you've come from?' asked Doyle.

'Yes.'

A silence fell.

'Well?' said Oscar.

'What happened?' barked Conan Doyle. 'For God's sake, man, tell us what happened!'

Conan Doyle's outburst produced the desired result. Daubeney handed his tea cup back to me and looked about the room, as if taking in his surroundings for the first time. 'When I left you last night,' he began, 'I walked down to the embankment and along the water's edge towards Wandsworth Bridge. There was no moon, but it was a fine night and when I reached her house I saw the light in her window.'

'Whose window?' asked Conan Doyle. 'The window of Miss Scott-Rivers?'

'Yes,' said Daubeney, 'Her drawing-room window.'

'Had you gone with the intention of seeing her?' asked Oscar.

'No, not for a moment,' he protested. He had not spoken so loudly before. His sudden vehemence was startling.

'And yet,' said Oscar calmly, 'when you left the Cadogan Hotel, you said you had business to attend to?'

'I was in drink,' replied the man, casting his eyes to the ground.

'You were not drunk,' said Oscar. 'I watched you during dinner, Mr Daubeney. You consumed two glasses of wine all evening, three at most.'

'I did not murder her, Mr Wilde. You must believe me. That is why I have come here now. I need you to believe me.'

'You told us all you wished to see her dead,' said Oscar.

'But I did not kill her.'

'Yet she is dead, you tell us.'

Daubeney shuddered. 'Burnt alive,' he said, closing his eyes.

'What *happened*?' Conan Doyle demanded. 'Pull yourself together, man.'

Daubeney opened his eyes and looked at Conan Doyle directly. 'I reached her house. It's on the embankment, fifty yards or so from the water's edge. I saw the light in her window – in her drawing-room window, on the ground floor. Yes, I admit it. For a while, I did consider going up to the front door and ringing the doorbell, and attempting to gain admittance, but I did not do so. I swear to you, as God is my witness, I did not do so.'

'What did you do?' asked Oscar.

'I sat in front of her house, on a wooden bench on the embankment overlooking the river Thames. I sat and I prayed. I prayed for her soul and for mine.'

'And then?'

'I fell asleep.'

'You fell asleep?' cried Conan Doyle. 'For how long?'

'I do not know. What awoke me was the shriek of the siren from the fire-boat on the river. I heard it. I came to. Then I saw the fire-boat steaming through the darkness towards the embankment. I turned about me and I saw the house . . . There were flames leaping from her window. The drawing room was ablaze. I ran towards the house. I ran up the front steps. I beat on the door. I climbed across the iron railings. That's when I tore my coat. I climbed from the front steps up onto the ground-floor window ledge and beat my arms against the window-pane. The glass smashed. I fell forward and caught myself on the edge of the window frame. And then I saw her, lying by the fireplace, her face all burnt away, the flames dancing around her skull, burning the stubble of her hair as in a forest fire.'

Oscar was on his feet. 'We must go there now.'

Conan Doyle was still crouching at Daubeney's side. 'What happened next? Did you go into the room?'

'The flames beat me back,' said Daubeney, hiding his face behind his fingers as if in shame. 'I climbed back along the window ledge, and jumped over the area steps onto the pavement. I could hear the firemen by the embankment. They were coming ashore. I panicked. I ran away. I took refuge nearby – in All Saints church. I hid in the chapel of St Thomas More. I lay beneath the altar and I prayed for her soul and for mine. And, for a while, I think I slept. And when day came, and the church began to come to life, I crept out and made my way here.' He turned towards Oscar. 'I needed to see you, Mr Wilde. I needed you to know that whatever I said last night when playing that infernal game of yours, I did not murder Elizabeth. By all that's holy, I swear to you I did not.'

Oscar said nothing.

'Mr Daubeney,' said Conan Doyle, getting to his feet. 'Everything you have told us you must now tell to the police.'

Daubeney looked at Oscar imploringly.

'Dr Doyle is right,' said Oscar. 'There is no time to lose. The longer you take to report what you know to the proper authorities, the more suspicious your behaviour will appear to be.'

'I am innocent,' pleaded Daubeney, getting to his feet and turning desperately between Oscar and Conan Doyle.

'I know,' I said, 'but do as my friends advise, George. It will be best.'

'Our cab is here,' said Oscar, looking out of the window. 'Let us go to Scotland Yard by way of Cheyne Walk.'

Conan Doyle looked at Oscar with a puzzled expression. 'A cab is here already?' he asked.

'Yes,' said Oscar. 'A four-wheeler – as I ordered.' He smiled and ushered us towards the door. 'As your man Holmes would say, Arthur: "I have my methods".'

Though the traffic was heavy, the journey from Tite Street to the Embankment took no more than a quarter of an hour. We travelled in silence. George Daubeney and I sat facing Oscar and Conan Doyle, our knees almost touching, but each of us apparently wrapped in his own thoughts. Arthur gazed intently out of the cab window, like a tourist visiting a fascinating foreign city for the first time. I sensed that the good doctor wanted to distance himself from the business in hand. Oscar, by contrast, seemed wholly absorbed by George Daubeney. He looked at him fixedly, studying first his face, then his hands, then his shoes and clothing, then his face once more. Daubeney had his eyes closed and his head bowed. His skin was pale and rough, like gravel. He had no beard to speak of. His nose was thin and pointed. His lips were virtually invisible, but his mouth was noticeable because of the beads of saliva visible at either edge. He was not a pretty sight.

When we reached our destination, our four-wheeler drew up alongside a small hose-cart. Two young firemen, with dirty faces, were leaning against it, smoking cigarettes and drinking tea from tin mugs. 'These are good lads,' said Oscar as we alighted.

We stood by our cab for a moment and surveyed the scene. The house itself, a tall, handsome, red-brick building, built in the first year of Queen Victoria's reign, had evidently survived the fire. The damage done was all concentrated in the ground-floor drawing room, to the right of the front door. The window-panes were shattered: the window frames were burnt away. Even standing in the street, we could see that the walls of the room were blackened from floor to ceiling and the furnishings quite destroyed.

'I have been here before,' said Oscar, looking up at the house. 'Bram Stoker lived here once upon a time.'

'When was this?' asked Conan Doyle.

'Ten years ago, at least,' said Oscar. 'This house is no stranger to unexpected death. Bram told me how he rescued a drowning man from the river and carried him into the house and laid him on the dining-room table. The poor man failed to recover and Bram went in search of the police. He left the house and, moments later, Mrs Stoker, unaware of the drama, entered the dining room carrying a vase of freshly cut flowers destined for the sideboard. You may imagine her dismay at finding the body of a dead stranger lying on her dining-room table.'

Conan Doyle looked at George Daubeney. 'How long had Miss Scott-Rivers been living here?' he asked.

'She bought the house two years ago,' said Daubeney, 'when her parents died.'

'And who stands to inherit?' enquired Oscar, leading our party towards the house.

'During our engagement,' said Daubeney, 'she made a will in my favour, but I imagine, under the circumstances, she will have changed it.'

As we climbed the front steps, there were shards of glass beneath our feet. 'Careful,' said Conan Doyle.

Oscar peered over the iron railings into the area below. 'There is glass everywhere,' he said.

'Aye,' said a booming voice at the window, 'but not for long. We'll have this cleared up in a jiffy. We're almost through.' The voice belonged to a large, red-headed, red-faced Scotsman. He wore a tweed overcoat with the collar turned up. He must have been in his mid-forties, but he looked much younger. Life had not yet got the better of him. He had merry brown eyes, a broad smile on his lips and a pencil behind his right ear. 'What brings you here, Mr Wilde?' he enquired, raising an eyebrow and tilting his head to one side.

'By all that's wonderful,' cried Oscar, 'Inspector Archy Gilmour!' The police inspector and Oscar were old acquaintances. Gilmour was now the senior detective at the Criminal Investigations Department of the Metropolitan Police. His path and Oscar's had crossed on several previous occasions. Gilmour had met me, too, though he did not appear to remember it. Inevitably, he recognised Conan Doyle and, when he opened the front door of 27 Cheyne Walk to us, it was Doyle whose hand he shook first. 'I've just read "The Red-Headed League", Dr Doyle. It's your masterpiece. Where you get your ideas from – it's beyond me.' He looked up at the clear blue sky, narrowed his eyes and sniffed the air. 'It's a bright, crisp morning, ideal for a walk by the river, gentlemen, I agree, but what brings you to this particular doorstep, I wonder? Was it your notion, by any chance, Mr Wilde?'

Oscar smiled. He claimed it as axiomatic that red-headed men over forty were not to be trusted, but he allowed Archy Gilmour as the lone exception to his rule. 'We're here,' said Oscar, 'with this gentleman – the Hon. the Reverend George Daubeney.'

'Ah,' said Gilmour, shaking Daubeney's hand, 'the sometime fiancé of Miss Elizabeth Scott-Rivers. I read about the case.' His manner changed. He paused and took a deep breath. 'I'm afraid that I have bad news—' he began.

'We know,' Oscar interrupted. 'Miss Scott-Rivers is dead. That is why we are here. Mr Daubeney was outside the house when the fire broke out.'

'Ah!' exclaimed Gilmour, 'So this is our runaway witness! The firemen spotted him climbing down from the window ledge as they came ashore.' Gilmour looked at Daubeney. 'I'm glad you've returned, sir. We'll need to take a statement from you.'

'I understand,' said Daubeney, lowering his eyes.

'He's fearful,' said Oscar. 'The circumstances are somewhat delicate.'

'Aye,' said Gilmour, still looking towards Daubeney. 'As I recall, Miss Scott-Rivers successfully sued you for breach of promise and secured substantial damages.'

'Everything I possess,' said Daubeney quietly. 'I had loved her once, so much. I came to hate her. But I would not for the world have wished her life to end like this.' He raised his head and looked towards the burnt-out windows and shuddered.

'Indeed not,' said Gilmour. 'It was a horrible death. A terrible accident.'

'An accident, you think?' enquired Oscar, gently.

'There's little doubt of that, Mr Wilde,' Gilmour answered. 'She was alone in the house. It was a Sunday night and both the servants were away. The front door was locked and securely bolted from the inside. So was the garden door at the rear of the house. So was the basement door at the foot of the area steps. She had locked herself in for the night. And then, tragically, before retiring to bed, in her drawing room, she stood too near the

62

fire . . . her dress caught light and the flames engulfed her. It happens all too often. In London, last year, a dozen women died just like this.'

'I can believe it,' said Oscar. 'May we visit the scene of devastation?' he asked.

'There's nothing to see,' said Gilmour. 'The room's burnt out. Look.' He directed our gaze through the front window to the interior of the room. The walls were blackened with smoke. What once had been furniture was reduced to assorted piles of smouldering black ash. 'It was a miracle the fire brigade arrived when they did or the conflagration might have spread to the rest of the house.'

'Do we know who raised the alarm?' asked Conan Doyle.

'No one,' said Gilmour. 'By blessed chance one of the Met's floating fire-engines was steaming back to Southwark Bridge after a night's patrol and the captain spotted the flames in the window and put ashore.'

'Where was the body found?' asked Oscar, holding on to the railings and standing on his toes in an attempt to get a better view inside the room.

'Immediately in front of the fireplace,' said Gilmour, 'on the hearth.'

'Where is it now?' asked Conan Doyle.

'On its way to the morgue at Millbank.'

'Was the poor woman lying on her front or back?' asked Oscar, still straining to get a fuller view of the room.

'On her back,' said Gilmour. 'Her head and neck were lying across the fender.'

'Were her eyes open or closed?' asked Oscar.

'Open,' said Gilmour.

Oscar stepped back and released his hold on the railings. He turned to George Daubeney. 'Does this accord with your recollection, George?'

'It does,' said Daubeney slowly, 'in every particular. Hell is a place of fire. It was a hell-hole. That is why I ran away.' He lowered his eyes once more. 'I am ashamed of my conduct. I did not behave as a gentleman should.'

'Well,' said Gilmour genially, 'so long as you are ready to make a statement now, that's what matters. We'll do it at Scotland Yard, if you don't mind. Sergeant Rossiter will escort you.' He indicated the uniformed police officer who was just emerging from a police growler drawn up alongside Oscar's cab. 'We won't detain you long.'

'And we won't detain you further, Inspector,' said Oscar, shaking Gilmour by the hand. 'It has been good to see you once again, even under such unhappy circumstances.'

We all shook hands and made our ways down the steps to the waiting carriages. As he broke from our group to join the sergeant by the growler, Daubeney looked at us beseechingly and, with his thumb and forefinger wiping the moisture away from his lips, murmured, 'I apologise, gentlemen, for involving you in this matter in any way. I am so sorry.'

I said, 'We'll see you soon, George. Have a care now.'

Conan Doyle nodded towards him and muttered a brief 'Good day, sir'. Oscar simply raised a hand and waved the unfortunate clergyman farewell.

Daubeney climbed into the police growler with Sergeant Rossiter. Inspector Gilmour crossed the pavement towards our four-wheeler and watched us clamber aboard. As he was stepping into the cab, Oscar paused and turned back towards Gilmour and called out to him. 'Inspector, her eyes were open, you say . . . Are you certain of that?'

'Without a doubt, Mr Wilde,' the inspector called back. 'We have a photograph.'

'Playing with Fire'

As we settled back into our cab and began the return journey to Oscar's house in Tite Street, Conan Doyle tugged at his thick walrus moustache and said, reflectively, 'I don't know what to make of Daubeney, do you?'

'Where did you meet him, Robert?' Oscar asked.

'At the French bookshop,' I replied, 'in Beak Street.'

'Oh?' remarked Conan Doyle abruptly.

Oscar laughed. 'Arthur, you are a Scot with the soul of an Englishman. Anything remotely Frenchified and you're suspicious.'

Conan Doyle smiled. '*Touché!*' he said.

'What was he buying?' Oscar enquired.

'He was browsing,' I said. 'We fell into conversation. I don't why it should have been so, but I was somewhat taken aback to see a man of the cloth in a French bookshop.'

'Did he initiate the conversation?' Oscar asked.

I thought for a moment. 'Yes,' I said, 'I think he did. He struck me as likeable, but lonely.'

'Indeed,' said Oscar. 'He is sad and of a nervous disposition. And, apparently, easily distracted. I noticed last night that his cuff-links did not match.'

'Really?' exclaimed Conan Doyle. 'I'm surprised I didn't notice that when I was tending to his hands this morning.'

'He was not wearing the cuff-links this morning,' said Oscar.

Our cab turned from Cheyne Walk into Royal Hospital Road. As we passed the ancient Apothecaries' Garden on our right, Oscar looked out of the window and remarked: 'Do either of you know this remarkable garden? It contains plants and herbs that can cure every ailment known to man.'

It was Dr Doyle's turn to laugh. 'Every one, Oscar?'

'So an apothecary told me. Or, rather, so an apothecary told Edward Heron-Allen, who told Constance, who told me. Heron-Allen and Constance occasionally take a walk together though the garden in winter.'

'Is that wise?' asked Conan Doyle. 'Is that safe?'

'They wear galoshes,' said Oscar, with a grin.

'You know perfectly well what I mean,' protested Doyle, flushing a little, and moving uncomfortably from one buttock to the other. 'You told me yourself the man is infatuated with your wife and – as he admitted to me over dinner on Sunday night – he has some quite peculiar interests . . .'

'He is a world authority on asparagus,' said Oscar, happily. 'As far as Edward Heron-Allen and I are concerned, it is our mutual admiration for my wife that unites us. As far as Edward and Constance are concerned, it is their shared love of botany that binds them.'

I intervened to change the subject. When Oscar spoke teasingly of Constance, I felt uncomfortable. 'Oscar,' I asked leaning forward and tapping him on the knee, 'Tell me why, just now, you were so interested in the dead woman's eyes?'

'I was troubled by something George Daubeney said,' he answered. 'That's all. This morning, at Tite Street, your *camarade de librairie* – the Honourable the Reverend – when, for the first time, he described to us seeing the body of Elizabeth Scott-Rivers through the window of 27 Cheyne Walk, told us that her face had been "all burnt away" . . .'

'I recall,' I said.

'But, later,' Oscar went on, 'when we were at Cheyne Walk and Inspector Gilmour described the position of Miss Scott-Rivers's body and told us that the poor woman's eyes were most definitely open, Daubeney then said that was his recollection also.'

'I don't think the discrepancy is significant,' said Conan Doyle. 'The man was confused. He'd been through a traumatic experience.'

'Indeed,' said Oscar. 'In any event, Archy Gilmour seems certain that foul play is not involved – and Gilmour's a good man. Reliable.'

'Did Gilmour say that a dozen women a year lose their lives in such-like fires?'

'He did,' said Oscar, producing one of his favourite handkerchiefs from his pocket (a white handkerchief with a strawberry-coloured border) and giving his nose a stentorian blow. 'He did indeed, but I think the figure may be even higher. Two of my sisters died in such a fire, you know.'

Conan Doyle sat up and, with a furrowed brow, looked towards Oscar sympathetically. 'I did not know,' he said.

'I did not know you had two sisters, Oscar,' I said. 'I thought you had just the one.'

'I had three sisters,' my friend replied, smiling gently and gazing out of the cab window for a moment as if to bring the image of them to mind.

Oscar Wilde was a fabulist – and an Irishman. He could tell a tale as only a Dubliner can. When it suited his mood, when he felt inclined for a such a story, he would invent wholly imaginary friends and relations for himself and describe them with such complete conviction – and so much circumstantial detail – that only the most diligent and determined biographer would be able to sort out fact from fancy. I noticed that, often, when indulging himself in this kind of invention, he produced a prop of some kind to assist him in the story-telling. My suspicions were aroused by his strawberry-bordered handkerchief. 'Three sisters, Oscar? Is this true?' I demanded.

'Oh yes,' he said, turning to look at me, 'Quite true. You have heard me speak often of my little sister, Isola. She died when she was ten. I loved her dearly. I keep a lock of her hair about me still. But I had two older sisters, also – Emily and Mary Wilde. My papa was liberal in his favours. As a young man, before he married my mother, he fathered three illegitimate children, a boy and two girls. They were brought up as my uncle's wards, but I knew them as siblings not as cousins. And I loved them.'

'And the two girls were burnt to death?' asked Conan Doyle, anxiously.

'They were,' said Oscar. 'I was seventeen at the time. They were twenty-two and twenty-four and lovely as the day is long. One November night, they went together to a ball in County Monaghan and Emily danced too near the fire. Her dress caught light. Mary rushed to save her sister and the flames engulfed them both. My father never recovered from the tragedy.' Oscar smiled sadly and looked me in the eye. 'I trust you believe me, Robert.'

'I do,' I said.

'They were lovely and pleasant in their lives and in their death they were not divided. And it's because of them that I believe so passionately in the work of the Rational Dress Society and encourage my darling Constance in her endeavours in that regard.'

Our four-wheeler was in Tite Street and drawing up outside Number 16. 'And speaking of angels,' cried Oscar, blowing his nose once more, 'look who's here!'

On the pavement outside the house stood Constance Wilde. She looked as pretty as a picture, in a summer dress of cowslip yellow decorated and fringed with ribbons of eggshell blue. On her head she wore a straw boater with, tucked into the band, a sprig of fresh myrtle. In her way, Constance's dress sense was as arresting as Oscar's – less flamboyant, certainly, but just as original. Her boys were disappearing through the front door with their governess, Gertrude Simmonds. As we clambered from our carriage, Oscar murmured, 'Not a word of this morning's adventure, gentlemen – not a word.'

'Welcome home,' said Constance gaily, looking up at her husband with loving eyes. 'Robert, Arthur – you have timed this well. Luncheon is about to be served.'

Arthur protested that, alas, he could not stay. 'South Norwood – my desk – my wife – my daughter – they all call!' He declared that he must collect his case and be gone immediately. He was sure that, in any event, he had outstayed his welcome already.

Oscar pressed the good doctor to remain, but Arthur was obdurate. Oscar turned to me. 'You will not abandon us, Robert?' he pleaded. I protested that I, too, had a novel that called, but I did so with less conviction and Oscar was very pressing. I felt that my friend wanted me to remain for lunch, not so much because he was hungry for my company, but because he no longer wished to be left alone with his wife.

Arthur departed for South Norwood and I stayed for lunch. It was an excellent lunch – watercress soup, followed by grilled turbot, with cold apple pie and hot custard for pudding – and, throughout it, Oscar was charmingly on song. He spoke of everything and anything – except for the events of the night before and the drama of the morning. As a special treat, young Cyril, a month away from his seventh birthday, was allowed into the dining room to eat with us. Cyril was a delightful child, with bright, inquisitive eyes and impeccable manners. He did not speak much, but he listened intently and, when he did give utterance, his contributions to the general conversation were memorable. At one point, he turned to Oscar and enquired of his father, 'Papa, do you ever dream?'

'Why, of course, my darling,' Oscar replied. 'It is the first duty of a gentleman to dream.'

'And what do you dream of?' asked Cyril.

'What do I dream of?' answered Oscar. 'Oh, I dream of dragons with gold and silver scales, and scarlet flames coming out of their mouths, of eagles with eyes made of diamonds that can see over the whole world at once, of lions with yellow manes and voices like thunder, of ele-phants with little houses on their backs, of tigers and zebras with barred and spotted coats . . .' Eventually, Oscar's stream of imaginings ran dry and he turned to his son and asked: 'But tell me, what do you dream of, Cyril?'

'I dream of *pigs*,' said the boy.

Over lunch that day we laughed a good deal. It was a fine feast and a happy one. When we had eaten, Constance took Cyril off for his afternoon rest, and Oscar and I took a leisurely stroll up Sloane Street, back to the Cadogan Hotel.

'Why are we returning so soon to the scene of the crime?' I asked.

'There has been no "crime" as yet,' said Oscar, em-phatically, 'merely an unfortunate coincidence. We are returning to the Cadogan to meet up with Alphonse Byrd. Next Sunday, at Tite Street, Constance and I are hosting another charity fund-raiser and Byrd has kindly agreed to provide the entertainment – assisted, I believe, by his friend McMuirtree.'

'Ah,' I said, 'that explains why I encountered them both at Tite Street the other afternoon. Constance introduced me, but did not tell me exactly why they were there.'

'When was this?' asked Oscar, stopping mid-stride. 'I don't recall meeting McMuirtree before last night.'

'You were not there, Oscar,' I explained. 'You were at the Savoy, I believe, taking tea with Bosie and his brother. I sometimes think I spend more time at your home, my friend, than you do.'

Oscar rose above my chiding. 'This coming Sunday,' he said, resuming our walk, 'tea in Tite Street will outclass anything dear Cesari at the Savoy has to offer. We shall be furnishing our guests with hock and seltzer, Robert, perfumed teas, iced coffees, cucumber sandwiches, lemon tartlets, Madeira cake and, on the side, a little magic. Mrs Ryan is looking after the comestibles and Mr Byrd is taking care of the magic. You are invited, *mon ami*, but it'll cost you a pound at the door, I'm afraid.'

'I shall come,' I said, wondering at once how I was going to raise the necessary funds. 'The cause is just. I had no idea there was so much danger associated with women's clothing.'

'This is not in aid of the Rational Dress Society, Robert. On Sunday we are soliciting support for the Earl's Court Boys' Club. They want a boxing ring and Bosie has asked me to pay for it! His father is the president of the Boys' Club and Bosie, when not wanting to murder the Marquess, is anxious to ingratiate himself with him. I am doing what I can to help.'

As we approached the Cadogan Hotel, we found a party of young ladies clustered on the front step. 'How wan they look!' exclaimed Oscar in hushed tones. 'I imagine they are Americans starting out on the Grand Tour. American ladies on leaving their native land adopt the appearance of chronic ill-health under the impression that it is a form of European refinement.'

'You are very droll, Oscar,' I whispered as we were about to plunge through the assembly of pale young women.

'And adroit, I like to think,' said Oscar, suddenly taking my right elbow and steering me away from the hotel entrance. 'Down here!' he commanded. Adjacent to the hotel's front steps was a narrow gate set into iron railings. Beyond the gate were steep stone steps leading down to the hotel's kitchens. 'Lay on, Macduff!' hissed

Oscar. 'This way we will avoid the Yankee maidens *and* the yabbering parrot.'

For a man who was undoubtedly overweight and professed an abhorrence of all forms of exercise, Oscar Wilde was surprisingly nimble. I led the way down the steps and he followed, not so much steadying himself with a hand on my shoulder as propelling me on my way. Evidently, Byrd was expecting us and, through the basement window, must have seen our feet descending. When we reached the kitchen door, he was standing at it. He bobbed his head smartly towards Oscar, as an equerry might to a prince, and said, 'Welcome, Mr Wilde. We have everything ready.'

'Good day, Byrd,' said Oscar, responding to Byrd's bow with a curious twitch of his nostrils. 'Do I smell smoke?' he muttered.

'This way, gentlemen,' said Byrd.

I sniffed the air. I detected a trace of something, but I said nothing.

Byrd led us through the hotel's vast, dark and deserted kitchen, along a wide, high-ceilinged corridor to a cavernous pantry beyond. It was a room without windows, dimly lit by oil lamps. There, seated at the end of a long, narrow, deal table that ran the length of the room, was David McMuirtree, the boxer, Byrd's friend and guest from the night before. On the table before him was a coil of rope, a candle in a holder and an assortment of jam jars half filled with variously coloured liquids. In his hand McMuirtree was holding a fiercely burning taper: its blue-green flame shot several inches into the air. As we entered the room, abruptly McMuirtree dropped the taper into one of the jam jars. The flame hissed and sizzled as it died.

'Ah,' said Oscar, glancing at Byrd, 'the source of the smoke . . .'

David McMuirtree stood to greet us. The man's appearance quite took us off our guard. He was completely naked from the waist up and his broad, hairless chest and long, muscular arms glistened with oil. He smiled at us, and bobbed his head just as Byrd had done, and said, 'Good afternoon, gentlemen,' in his strange, rasping, hoarse whisper.

'Good afternoon,' said Oscar, smiling also. 'Byrd told us you were half-a-gentleman. Now I see it is the upper half.'

McMuirtree laughed awkwardly and reached behind him for the towel that was hanging over the back of his chair. 'I don't follow you,' he said, starting to rub himself clean.

'You have the torso of a gentleman,' said Oscar.

'I'll take it as a compliment. What does that mean?' asked McMuirtree.

'No tattoos,' said Oscar. 'You earn your living as a fairground fighter. I would have expected your body to bear witness to your calling, but I see no scars, no blemishes, and no tattoos.'

'You are very observant,' whispered McMuirtree, pulling on a plain white cotton shirt and tucking its tails into his black corduroy trousers. 'I have some scars, but the light is dark in here. I have no tattoos because my body is my stock-in-trade. I live by it – and I do what I can to show it off to best advantage. Hence my shaven head and chest and arms.'

'And hence the oil?' asked Oscar.

'No,' said McMuirtree. 'The oil is for a different purpose.'

Oscar looked steadily at McMuirtree, but said nothing.

'We've been playing with fire, Mr Wilde,' continued the boxer, 'and all in your honour.'

'My honour?' said Oscar, raising a quizzical eyebrow.

'We've been trying out material for your Sunday afternoon benefit, Mr Wilde. The oil is a veneer that protects my skin while I pass a burning flame across it. I may be eating fire in Tite Street on Sunday. We've come up with a varied programme that I trust will meet with your approval. If it does, we shall run through it with Mrs Wilde when we see her tomorrow. It's some years since Alphonse and I have tried our hand at a number of these tricks, but it's amusing to rediscover old friends. Sawing one's assistant in half is amusing. Playing with fire is amusing. You like to be amused, do you not, Mr Wilde?'

'Most of all, I like to be charmed,' said Oscar.

'Indeed,' whispered McMuirtree, smiling. 'That also is one of our specialities.' As he spoke, the coil of rope on the table before him appeared to twitch, and suddenly, inexplicably, apparently unaided, one end of the rope lifted itself slowly into the air and, like a cobra rising from a snake-charmer's basket, rose high above the table. Oscar and I gazed at the spectacle in astonishment. McMuirtree clapped his hands and the rope fell instantly to the table. 'Alphonse – refreshments for our guests, if you please!'

Fortified by brandy and beer, Oscar and I spent two full hours seated in the pantry of the Cadogan Hotel being – as Oscar put it – 'wholly charmed and vastly amused by Messrs Byrd and McMuirtree's box of tricks'. I had understood that Byrd was the magician and McMuirtree the assistant. However, as they took us through the programme of 'drawing-room illusions' that they proposed presenting in Tite Street the following Sunday, it became abundantly clear that, even if Byrd was to be the principal performer, McMuirtree was the driving force within the partnership.

As the afternoon wore on, we became aware of various members of the Cadogan's kitchen staff passing along the corridor outside the pantry, returning to their duties. At what turned out to be a little after half past five, there was a sharp knock on the pantry door and a red-cheeked, freckle-faced young man wearing a chef's bonnet, put his face into the room and said, "Scuse me, Mr Byrd, but we'll be needing the pantry now.'

'We're nearly done, Hawkins,' said Byrd.

'We *are* done!' Oscar declared, reaching out for me to help him to his feet. He turned to our hosts and beamed upon them. 'Thank you for a memorable afternoon, gentlemen. Your programme meets with my approval – in its entirety. You are to have a rendezvous with my wife tomorrow, you say? I am sure she will be equally delighted with all that you have to offer. And, if your delivery matches your description, I believe my sons will be especially enchanted by the "Illusion of the Vanishing Lion", particularly as performed on Mrs Ryan's ginger tom-cat. We're in for a treat come Sunday. The readiness is all.'

It was six o'clock but still light when we reached the street outside the Cadogan Hotel. 'They know their business, those two,' mused Oscar as he peered up and down the roadway in search of a passing cab.

'They're an odd couple,' I said, 'an improbable duo.'

'Yes,' said Oscar, reflectively, 'what is the true hold one has upon the other, I wonder?'

'Shall we walk back to Tite Street?' I suggested. 'The air will do us good.'

'Forgive me,' cried my friend, waving to the two-wheeler that was now coming out of Pont Street and heading towards him. 'I am meeting up with Bosie. We're off to the Lyric, to see *The Mountebanks* – Gilbert without Sullivan. I imagine it'll be the usual story, but at least the tune will be different. You go to Tite Street, Robert. Look after Constance for me, there's a dear. I shall see you at lunchtime tomorrow – at the Chelsea Arts Club, at one. Don't forget.' He clambered aboard the two-wheeler. 'I may even see you later tonight, Robert. I don't plan to be late. Bosie and I will have a bite at Kettner's and then I'll be home. Tell Constance, would you? She'll understand. Have a happy evening. I must go now. Forgive me. *Au revoir, mon ami!* Forgive me!' And, with a wave from the carriage window, and looking suddenly refreshed, my friend was gone.

7

'The Occasional Caprice'

I forgave him. Oscar Wilde was an easy man to forgive. Constance forgave him, too – time and again.

That evening she and I had supper together at Tite Street. There was no need for a chaperone: it was as if Oscar was with us all the while. All evening we talked only of him. Constance spoke of Oscar as a mother might of an adored child. He was perfection: he could do no wrong in her eyes. She simply marvelled at his genius and counted herself 'so blessed' that he was there, the father of her children, the centre of her universe. That he needed time away from home – to write, to think, to see his friends – was wholly understandable. She had no complaints. She was simply grateful that 'a mind so large' and 'a spirit so generous' should be part of her life at all. She told me, solemnly: 'Oscar and I both believe in the concept of a seven-year marriage contract, renewable if, but only if, both parties wish it. Oscar and I agreed to embark on our second seven years together last May. As Mr Browning says, "The best is yet to be." '

At eleven o'clock I told her it was time I returned to my room in Gower Street. As, reluctantly, I rose to take my leave I remarked, 'Oscar will be home soon, I expect.'

'No,' she answered, smiling. 'He'll not be back tonight. He's with Bosie. He'll stay in town, I'm certain. And I'm glad of it. He gets tired. Oscar needs his beauty sleep. He is very beautiful in his way, is he not?'

'It is you who are beautiful, Constance,' I replied. 'Goodnight.' And I kissed her on the lips.

She laughed. 'You are such a romantic, Mr Sherard. No wonder Oscar adores you so!'

In the morning – it was Tuesday morning, 3 May 1892; the sky from my window was blue, the sun shone brightly – I awoke early and spent two hours scratching away at my novel. As soon as I had managed to set down three hundred words, I set off again for Chelsea. I had decided I could not afford a cab and horse-drawn bus journeys in central London in those days were interminable. To while away the hour it took to travel from Oxford Street to the King's Road, I bought the early edition of the *Evening News*. A vivid account of Monday morning's dramatic fire at 27 Cheyne Walk featured over two columns on the front page. There was a photograph of the unfortunate heiress, Elizabeth Scott-Rivers, taken at the time of her eighteenth birthday, and another, taken more recently, of Inspector Archy Gilmour of Scotland Yard. Gilmour was quoted extensively, lamenting 'this tragic accident' and praising the courage of the London Fire Brigade, whose prompt attendance at the scene had prevented the conflagration from spreading and so saved both life and property. There was no reference of any kind to the Hon. the Reverend George Daubeney.

I did not reach the Chelsea Arts Club until nearly one-thirty. The club, still in its infancy, was then located on the ground floor and basement of 181 King's Road, an undistinguished, flat-fronted Georgian house immediately adjacent to the newly built Chelsea Town Hall. I found Oscar with his artist friend, Walter Sickert, in the club mess room, in the studio at the back of the house. They were sitting together, alone, at the far end of the communal dining table. They were drinking Algerian wine, eating Angels on Horseback (oysters wrapped in bacon served with buttered toast) and discussing Degas.

'Day-gas?' expostulated Wat Sickert. 'Day-gas? His name is not Day-gas, Oscar! You know full well – because I have told you so, often – Gas is the name of the French town from which the artist's ancestors come. The name was originally spelled "de Gas". That is how it should be pronounced. Why do you persist with this Day-gas business, Oscar?'

'To annoy you, Wat,' answered Oscar, raising his glass in a mock-toast to the young artist.

'To insult him, more likely,' riposted Sickert. 'He is a great man. He deserves to be treated with respect.'

'His art I respect,' said Oscar coolly, looking up and seeing me, and beckoning me to join them at the table.

'You've not forgiven him his gibe, I know,' said Sickert, wiping his luxuriant moustache with the back of his hand.

'I like to think it was intended as a jest rather than a gibe,' said Oscar. He turned to me as I took the chair next to his and laid my newspaper on the table. 'The great Edgar Degas, to whom I had the honour of being introduced by Wat some years ago, said of me: "*Oscar Wilde?*

Il a l'air de jouer Lor' Byron dans un théâtre de banlieu." *
I thought the line amusing. As you can see, I committed
it to memory.'

'You thought the line insulting,' said Sickert, laughing,
'You've not been able to forget it.'

'How was the comic opera?' I asked Oscar, thinking
it diplomatic to change the subject — and prompted
perhaps by Wat Sickert's wonderful appearance. Wat was
undoubtedly handsome, with sea-green eyes and honey-
coloured hair, but there was something slightly ludicrous about his elaborately groomed moustaches. He
was wearing a guardsman's old scarlet tunic open at
the collar, with a bright green kerchief loosely tied about
his neck. He looked like a character from a music-hall
monologue: a love-lorn Bohemian soldier down on his
luck.

Oscar sniffed and took a sip of wine. 'Gilbert had one
joke which I've forgotten and Cellier had no tune which
I recall all too vividly. It was not a night to reckon
with . . .' He looked at me and smiled. 'Whereas you and
Constance, Robert, as I understand it, had a most charming *soirée*, a cosy *diner à deux* at Tite Street.'

I blushed, foolishly, like a guilty schoolgirl. Wat Sickert
growled with pleasure as he poured me a beaker of the
Algerian wine. 'Ah, so you too are sweet on the delectable
Mrs Wilde.'

'Yes,' said Oscar, an impish grin revealing his horrid
teeth, 'Robert is competing with Edward Heron-Allen for
my wife's affections. I fear it may come to a duel.'

---

* 'Oscar Wilde? He gives the impression that he's playing Lord
Byron in a suburban theatre.'

'Don't be ridiculous, Oscar,' I protested, 'I'm a married man.'

'We're all married men,' cried Sickert, raising his glass in a toast. 'Here's to blessed monogamy – reasonably tempered by the occasional caprice!' He clinked his glass against mine and looked up and saw Lord Alfred Douglas making his way across the room towards us. 'Talk of the devil!'

Bosie, looking like a befuddled cherub, was yawning as he approached. 'Good morning, gentlemen,' he drawled, 'I'm sorry I'm late.'

'Good afternoon, Bosie,' said Oscar. 'We've dined, as you can see.'

'Yes,' replied Bosie, sweeping his blond fringe back over his forehead and sitting himself down next to Sickert. He leant forward and tapped my copy of the *Evening News*. 'And you've read the paper?'

'I have,' I said, opening it out and laying it in the middle of the table.

'I saw it earlier,' said Oscar. 'The report of the fire is graphic if not illuminating.'

'Never mind the fire,' said Bosie. 'Look at the Stop Press.' He took the newspaper and flicked it over and pointed to the Stop Press column on the back page. 'Look,' he said again.

I read out the brief news item.

GOVERNMENT MINISTER DIES
Lord Abergordon found dead yesterday
afternoon in the library of the House of Lords.
Prime Minister issues statement expressing
Government's 'profound shock and regret'.

83

'Who the deuce is Lord Abergordon?' asked Wat Sickert, waving an empty wine bottle above his head in a vain attempt to catch the club steward's eye.

'Under-Secretary of State for War,' said Bosie casually.

'And the second name on our list of murder victims,' added Oscar.

'What?' said Sickert, putting down the empty bottle.

'He was a ridiculous old man,' said Bosie.

'You knew him?' I enquired.

'Quite well, as it happens. He was a friend of the family. My father and he were very hugger-mugger. Had been for years. He was my brother's godfather. Drumlanrig despised him. Doubtless that's why, when we were playing Oscar's game, he picked him as his "victim of choice".'

'Did he?' asked Oscar sharply.

'I think so. I don't know,' said Bosie, taking Oscar's glass from him and draining it. 'At the time I assumed so. Who else would think of murdering an old nincompoop like Abergordon?'

Oscar had drawn the newspaper towards him and was studying the news item intently. 'Where is your brother now?' he asked.

'I am not my brother's keeper, Oscar. I've no idea. The House of Lords, I imagine. Drumlanrig loves his politics. He's quite the coming man, you know: Lord Rosebery's little helper.'

'Do you think your brother could have murdered this man, Abergordon?' asked Sickert, waving the empty bottle about his head once more.

'Don't be absurd, Wat. Francis wouldn't hurt a fly. I imagine Lord Abergordon was killed by an excess of luncheon. One Welsh rarebit too many – that'll be what did for him. He never could resist a savoury. He was a fat old fool – as you'd expect. He was a mainstay of the government. He'll have died in a red leather armchair, sound asleep beneath the open pages of the *Sporting Life*.'

'My condolences to his godson,' said Oscar, easing his chair away from the table, 'and to Lady Abergordon, if there is one.'

'There's no Lady Abergordon,' said Bosie, 'and never has been. The old boy died without issue and without kin. So condolences are not in order either. Brother Francis stands to cop the lot.'

'What?' cried Oscar. 'Your brother stands to inherit Abergordon's estate?'

'Down to the last ten thousand acres!' Bosie looked at Sickert who was still vainly waving his bottle in the air. 'I agree with you, Wat. I could use a drink.'

Oscar got to his feet as, at last, the club steward – an unhappy Creole who had been given his notice the night before – arrived at the table with a suppressed curse and a fresh bottle of wine. 'We shall leave you to your drinking, gentlemen,' murmured Oscar. 'Some of us have responsibilities.'

I got to my feet as well. I liked Wat Sickert (everybody liked Wat Sickert: he was like Oscar in that regard) and, on the whole, I found Bosie's wayward charm diverting, but I'd fallen out of the habit of being my own man. If Oscar wanted my company, he had it – whether I had lunched or not. Somehow, without noticing quite when or how it had happened, I had become Oscar's creature. Unbidden, I did his bidding.

As my friend moved towards the door, I joined him. Discreetly, he pressed a florin into the waiting hand of the unhappy Creole. With a flourish he turned to wave farewell to our companions. Bosie was already refilling his glass. 'See you at seven o'clock at the theatre, Bosie,' he called. 'Bring your brother if he's free – he can buy us supper.' Sickert was lighting a little clay pipe. 'Thank you for luncheon, Wat. It was fun. I think Monsieur Day-gas's *Woman at Her Toilette* is my favourite. Good day! We'll see you on Sunday.'

He chuckled as we made our way through the club billiard room and down the stairs into the street. 'Where are we going?' I asked.

'Back to the Cadogan,' he said. 'Constance is meeting Byrd and McMuirtree at three to review their proposed programme for Sunday's entertainment. I don't want her natural delicacy of feeling to stand in the way of some of their more lurid and melodramatic effects.'

By cab we reached the hotel in a matter of minutes. The scene that greeted us there was not so much lurid and melodramatic as pitiful and grotesque. The hotel reception area – an oak-panelled hallway no more than twenty feet square – was awash with a sea of small green feathers. The feathers were everywhere: on the tiled floor, on the steps to the landing, on the porter's desk, inside the umbrella stand, trapped among the lilies in the vase on the window ledge, floating on the surface of the water of the ornamental fish-tank that stood at the foot of the stairs – everywhere. As we pushed open the front door on our way into the hallway, the sudden gust of breeze we brought with us lifted the feathers from the floor like a sheet being shaken out above a mattress. As the feathers settled to the ground again, we saw that the floor itself was smeared with blood from side to side and end to end.

'What is the meaning of this horror?' I gasped.

'Who would have thought that one small bird could have so many feathers?' said Oscar, shaking his head sadly as he gazed about him.

As we stood on the threshold of the hallway, transfixed, a young kitchen maid – a girl of fourteen or fifteen, with ruddy cheeks and tears in her eyes – emerged from the alcove beneath the staircase facing us. She was carrying a metal bucket and a mop and was followed by a freckled young lad in uniform – one of the hotel pageboys – bearing a dust-sheet and dustpan and brush. The boy and Oscar appeared to know one another.

'Sorry business, Mr Wilde,' said the lad.

'Indeed, Nat,' said Oscar. 'A very sorry business. Poor Captain Flint. Is the manager in?'

'No,' answered the boy. 'He's off sick. Mr Byrd's on duty. He's in the office.'

Gingerly, like boys crossing a stream on stepping-stones, we tiptoed across the scene of carnage and turned off the hallway into a darkened corridor. 'It's here,' said Oscar. He knew his way around the Cadogan. The manager's office had, until lately, been Lillie Langtry's ground-floor sitting room. The door to the room was open. We entered without ceremony. There, standing, grouped together around the manager's desk in the centre of the room, were David McMuirtree, Edward Heron-Allen and Constance Wilde. Seated at the desk facing them, was Alphonse Byrd, ashen-faced and trembling. He looked a broken man. On the desk before him, spread out on the blotting-pad like a specimen awaiting dissection, were the mangled remains of the hotel parrot. The pitiful wings, like stripped branches of a fir tree, were spread wide. The pathetic head hung from the body by a single band of bloody tissue. The bird's eye, like a fish-eye, stared blindly up at us.

No one spoke. Oscar crossed the room and went straight to the desk. He leant forward and, to my astonishment, laid his right hand against the bird's cadaver. Tenderly, he held it there.

'The poor creature's stone-cold,' he said.

'Does that signify?' asked Heron-Allen.

'It does,' said Oscar, quietly. 'It does. Most certainly.'

'This is terrible,' said Constance, stepping towards her husband and linking her arm through his.

Oscar smiled at his wife and asked, 'When did you get here?'

'Two minutes ago,' she said.

'Five at most,' said Heron-Allen. 'Constance and I had lunch together – as you know – and she kindly asked me to accompany her here to see Mr Byrd's projected magic show. We arrived at three.'

'The appointment was for three o'clock,' said McMuirtree, huskily. 'We all arrived together—'

'To find this!' exclaimed Alphonse Byrd, covering his face with his still-trembling hands.

'You came from outside the building?' Oscar asked. The three standing figures all nodded.

'I was upstairs,' whispered Byrd. 'As the hallway clock struck three, I came down and found the horror that you see – exactly as you see it. The blood and feathers in the hallway, the parrot's body on my desk . . .'

'Where was the hall porter?'

'Both porters were on the second floor, collecting the trunks belonging to the American party. We have a group of young ladies from New England departing this afternoon.'

'Did any of them see anything?'

'I don't know,' said Byrd. 'I doubt it. I walked through the hallway at ten to three: it was deserted: all was well. I came down again at three o'clock to find . . .' He turned away from us, his head in his hands.

'Well,' said Oscar, with a shrug, 'We came for family magic and we find macabre melodrama instead. I think we should leave Mr Byrd to his sorrow and postpone our business to another day.' He looked towards Constance and Heron-Allen and smiled at them reassuringly. 'I'll just check that the coast is clear,' he added, excusing himself from the room.

We waited for him in silence. McMuirtree stood, his arms folded across his chest, gazing bleakly at the mutilated bird. Heron-Allen moved closer to Constance and touched her on the arm. Within a minute, Oscar had returned. 'Your admirable staff have cleared away the worst of the carnage, Byrd,' he said, briskly. 'I see you have a hip flask on your desk. I trust it's filled with something fortifying. I suggest you take a nip. You've had a shock. We all have.' He nodded towards David McMuirtree. 'If you'll excuse us, we'll take our leave.' He offered Constance his arm and led her and Heron-Allen and me out of the room. As he reached the door he paused and turned back and looked once more at the dead parrot spread out on the desk. 'Poor Captain Flint,' he said.

As he turned again to depart, David McMuirtree called out, 'Mr Wilde, what would you advise – should this incident be reported to the police?'

Byrd looked up and said at once, 'No! No – it will be bad for business.'

'I agree,' said Oscar. 'There's no need to trouble the police. What can they do?'

When we had regained the street, and moved some yards away from the hotel, walking south along Sloane Street towards Sloane Square, Oscar put his arm around Constance's shoulder and said, 'You have had a most unpleasant experience, my dear. I am sorry.'

'It was horrible, was it not?' said Constance. 'Who would do such a thing? And why?'

'To comprehend cruelty is almost as difficult as to understand love,' he said, stopping in the street and leaning towards her and kissing her tenderly on the forehead. 'What time is it, Robert?' he asked me.

I looked at my watch. 'Half past three,' I said.

Oscar turned to Heron-Allen. 'Edward, would you do me a favour? Would you escort my wife back to Tite Street and sit with her while Mrs Ryan provides you both with a pot of tea and the consoling comfort of crumpets?'

'It's far too warm for crumpets, Oscar,' Constance protested.

'Alliteration is no respecter of seasons, my dear,' he said.

Constance laughed, while Heron-Allen pulled himself up in the manly manner of a well-bred young gentleman, clicked his heels together, and said, 'I should be happy to escort Mrs Wilde home and honoured to take tea with her. We shall not talk of the unpleasantness of the past hour, I promise.'

'Good,' said Oscar. 'Thank you.' He looked at his wife and kissed her on the forehead once more. 'Take care, Constance. You are in safe hands. I'll try not to be too late tonight.'

We watched as Constance and Heron-Allen made their way away from us. We stood in silence looking after them. I thought that they might turn and wave to us, but they did not. I saw Heron-Allen give his arm to Constance and, as she took it, I felt an absurd pang of jealousy. When I was confident they were out of earshot, I said to Oscar, 'Should you not be with your wife this afternoon?'

'Do you think that Heron-Allen is untrustworthy?' asked Oscar, looking puzzled. 'He is a solicitor. I agree, that's worrisome. He's handsome, too.'

'That's not what I mean at all, Oscar,' I said, now flustered and knowing that I had taken on an unattractive, hectoring manner.

'What do you mean then?' he enquired.

'I mean that you have not told Constance of the game that we played on Sunday night.'

'Indeed not.'

'She does not know that she was named as a potential murder victim.'

'Of course not.'

'She may be in danger, Oscar. Your wife is on the list of those chosen as potential victims of murder – and you are going to the theatre yet again with Lord Alfred Douglas!'

'You don't need to remind me of the list, Robert. I have the list,' he said, suddenly producing a sheet of notepaper from his coat pocket and waving it before me. 'I am familiar with the list and I see from the list that Constance's name is the last on it – just after my name! – and those of Eros and Old Father Time! Do not get over-exercised about the list, Robert. Sunday's game was just a game.'

'Was it?' I asked sharply. 'On each of the three days since we played this so-called game each of the first three names on the list of "victims" has died. Is it "just a game"?'

'Who is next on the list?' Oscar asked, unfolding the sheet of notepaper.

'Sherlock Holmes, I believe.'

'Sherlock Holmes it is,' he said, scanning the paper, and, as he said it, the page-boy from the Cadogan Hotel came running along the pavement towards us. Oscar smiled. 'Well, Nat?' he asked. 'What's the answer?'

'It's "Yes", Mr Wilde – in every particular.'

'Excellent,' said Oscar. 'Thank you.' He handed the boy sixpence. 'Spend it all at once, Nat,' he added. 'It's the only way.' The lad laughed and, pocketing the sixpence, ran back to the hotel.

Oscar turned to me with a look of quiet satisfaction. 'Very good,' he said. 'Conan Doyle will meet us in the morning, Robert. He has accepted my invitation to breakfast at the Langham Hotel at nine o'clock. We'll see him then – assuming he survives the night.'

'Oscar's Game'

The 'murder victims' – in the order in which the names were drawn from the bag at the Socrates Club dinner, Sunday 1 May 1892

1. Miss Elizabeth Scott-Rivers

2. Lord Abergordon

3. Captain Flint, the Cadogan Hotel parrot

4. Mr Sherlock Holmes

5. Mr Bradford Pearse

6. David McMuirtree

7. David McMuirtree

8. David McMuirtree

9. David McMuirtree

10. Old Father Time

11. Eros

12. *A blank slip was drawn*

13. Mr Oscar Wilde

14. Mrs Oscar Wilde

8

Breakfast at the Langham

That evening, I dined alone in my room in Gower Street. In those days, I would often dine alone: usually in my room, on bread and cheese or a cold sausage and half a beef tomato; occasionally, across the way, at the Mermaid tavern in Chenies Street, on a mutton chop with onion gravy, the Mermaid's 'speciality'.

Oscar, of course, rarely ate alone. That Tuesday evening, he and Lord Alfred Douglas had abandoned their theatre plans and settled, instead, on a five-shilling bottle of champagne at the Café Royal followed by a two-shilling supper at the Florence Restaurant in Rupert Street.

'There were no nightcaps taken, Robert!' Oscar called out the moment he saw me the following morning. I arrived at the Langham Hotel promptly at nine o'clock and found my friend seated alone at a round table set for three in one of the darker corners of the hotel's absurdly bosky Palm Court. He gestured to me to join him and, without pausing to give or receive a greeting, continued: 'I did as you would have wished, Robert. I was a martyr to self-discipline and uxorial responsibility. I resisted all of Bosie's blandishments. He proposed whisky-and-soda at the Albemarle. He suggested schnapps and ice cream at the Savoy. He even tried to entice me with the promise of a pint of porter at the Empire, Leicester Square. Still, I held firm. "Get thee behind me, Douglas!" I cried, "I am going home." And by half past ten, Robert, I was back in Tite Street.'

'I am glad to hear it.'

'You will be less glad when I tell you what I found there . . .'

'My God!' I exclaimed, suddenly alarmed. 'What? Tell me.'

'I found Edward Heron-Allen there.'

'With Constance?' I shook my head. 'The man knows no shame.'

Oscar nodded solemnly. 'You are right, Robert. He was still speaking of asparagus.' Oscar sat back and burst out laughing. He unfurled his linen napkin with a flourish. 'I have ordered kidneys and poached eggs for us both. The beverages are already present and correct.'

'What did you do with Heron-Allen?' I asked, while my friend solicitously poured me a cup of tea.

'I sent him packing – when I had thanked him for keeping my wife company. Edward Heron-Allen adores Constance.'

'I know,' I grumbled, 'that's why I don't trust him.'

'You should, Robert. I do. We both care for Constance, don't we? She is never safer than when Edward Heron-Allen is there. He loves her. He would lay down his own life to safeguard hers.'

'I had not thought of that,' I said. 'Nevertheless,' I added, lowering my voice, 'I remain mistrustful.' I leant towards Oscar and muttered, *sotto voce*: 'The man's a self-confessed pornographer, is he not?'

Oscar smiled and stirred his tea. 'Given the word's Greek roots,' he answered, lowering his voice to match mine, 'a pornographer, strictly speaking, is concerned with writing of harlots. Heron-Allen's interests are far broader than that. The gross bodily appetites of men and beasts, in all their rich variety, are Heron-Allen's peculiar obsession. The more unusual the practice the more intrigued is our Edward. I am certain he does not speak of these matters to Constance, but the other night he introduced me to a new word whose meaning you may guess at . . . "necrophilia".'

'Good grief!'

Oscar smiled. 'That was Conan Doyle's reaction exactly,' he said out loud, looking up and welcoming the arrival of a rack of toast at our table.

'Where is Conan Doyle?' I asked. 'Are you sure that he's coming?'

'That's what Nat told us.'

'Nat?'

'The page-boy from the Cadogan – you recall? He brought us word from Arthur yesterday afternoon. That's why we're here.'

'Oh,' I said, lamely. I was confused.

Oscar looked at me with a gently supercilious raised eyebrow. 'Yesterday afternoon, Robert, when I realised that poor Captain Flint was the third of our "victims" to be found dead since Sunday night and that Sherlock Holmes was the next name on the list, I thought we should take the precaution of meeting up with Arthur to discuss the situation. Just before we left the Cadogan, I found Nat and asked him to convey my message to Arthur. Just after we left the Cadogan, Nat found us in the street and brought us the good doctor's reply.'

'Was Arthur in the hotel at the time then?' I asked.

'No,' said Oscar. 'Arthur was in South Norwood.'

I fell silent for a moment. 'I can't fathom it, Oscar. If Arthur was in South Norwood and the boy was at the Cadogan Hotel – how on earth did they communicate?'

'By telephone!' said my friend, triumphantly.

I was amazed. 'Does Conan Doyle have a telephone – in South Norwood?'

'Nowhere is a telephone more necessary than in South Norwood, Robert.' Oscar smiled his sly smile. He scraped his butter knife noisily across his toast. 'Arthur has had a telephone installed because he is a medical man. Doctors get priority, apparently. But soon, I'm told, we shall all be linked by telephone – the length and breadth of the land. The telephone is about to revolutionise both the art of conversation and the science of detection. I am thinking of having one installed in Tite Street.'

'Do you know how to use a telephone, Oscar?'

'Not yet, but I have children, Robert. They will teach me.'

I laughed and, as I did so, glanced up to see coming towards our table, simultaneously, side by side, our waiter, bearing our kidneys and poached eggs, and Arthur Conan Doyle, looking distinctly flustered and bedraggled.

'I got caught in a sudden downpour,' he grumbled.

'But worse than that,' said Oscar, 'you have just realised that you left your umbrella in the hackney carriage that brought you here . . .'

Conan Doyle stopped in his tracks and gazed at Oscar in astonishment. 'How on earth did you know that?' he asked.

Oscar smiled. 'I saw you come in at the door just now, looking damp but relatively serene. Suddenly, your face clouded over as, frantically, you looked about you. What had you forgotten? It might have been your hat, but your hair is dry while your shoulders are sodden. It must be an umbrella – most likely your favourite umbrella, the special one with the fine ebony handle . . .'

'It's too early in the day for this, Oscar. Come, man, explain yourself. Have you seen me with the umbrella before?'

'No,' said Oscar, complacently, 'but if you turn around, Arthur, and look behind you – standing at the desk, talking to the *maître d'hôtel*, is a London cabby holding a furled gentleman's umbrella that bears a remarkable resemblance to the one I've just described.'

Instantly, Conan Doyle's troubled face was wreathed in smiles. 'Just tea and toast for me,' he called as he strode off to reclaim his lost umbrella. We watched as he tipped the cabman and shook him warmly by the hand.

'He'll be telling him he's the salt of the earth and the backbone of the Empire,' said Oscar. 'There's no more decent fellow in England than Arthur Conan Doyle.'

When he returned to the table, the doctor was a man transformed. He was bubbling with delight. 'Salt of the earth, that cabby,' he said.

'Where's the umbrella now?' I asked.

'In the cloakroom, I hope, with my hat. The *maître d'hôtel* offered to look after it. We can trust him, can't we?'

'We can,' said Oscar. 'Franco comes from Lake Como.'

'Excellent,' said Doyle, surveying the breakfast table and reaching for the marmalade.

Oscar leant towards me to explain. 'Arthur and his wife enjoyed a particularly happy holiday on the banks of Lake Como two summers ago.'

Doyle bit into his toast and, crumbs flying, exclaimed, 'Oscar, you amaze me! Nothing passes you by.'

'I don't know about that,' said Oscar, tapping his next cigarette against the back of his silver cigarette case, 'but I did at least register the fact that the poor parrot's body was cold – quite cold.'

'Ah, yes,' said Doyle, mopping marmalade from his moustache, 'to business. I was sorry to hear about the parrot. It was found at what time?'

'At three o'clock,' I said.

'But it must have been dead for some while,' said Oscar, 'an hour and more, at least. And the feathers we found in the hallway were not shed by the unfortunate bird in flight. They were stripped from its body and wings and tail after death and deliberately flung about, hither and yon, like confetti.'

'Bizarre,' said Conan Doyle.

'Brutish,' said Oscar. 'The poor creature's blood had been smeared across the floor.'

'In any particular pattern?' asked Doyle.

'No,' said Oscar. 'I looked. It appeared to have been done in haste, at random. Who would do such a thing?'

'Whoever is working their way through our list of murder victims one by one?' I suggested.

'Possibly . . .' said Oscar, drawing deeply on his cigarette and looking up into the leaves of the palm tree above him.

Conan Doyle shook his head and attacked another slice of toast. 'Gilmour of the Yard is adamant that the death of Elizabeth Scott-Rivers was an unfortunate accident, is he not?'

'He is,' said Oscar, returning from his reverie. 'And Lord Abergordon, our second "victim", was an elderly gentleman who did not treat his body as a temple and appears to have died in his sleep to no one's very great surprise.'

'So,' said Conan Doyle, wiping his moustache once more before laying down his napkin with a show of satisfaction and finality, 'We have two chance deaths, easily explained, followed by one inexplicable and brutal murder . . . What next?'

'Next on the list,' said Oscar, producing it from his breast pocket, is a "Mr Sherlock Holmes".'

'Who on earth would want to murder "Sherlock Holmes"?' I asked.

'I do, for one,' said Conan Doyle, sitting back and folding his arms across his chest, 'And the sooner the better.'

Oscar pounced. 'What, Arthur? What are you saying?'

'I plan to do away with Sherlock Holmes myself.'

'So it was you who put Holmes's name into the bag on Sunday night?'

Doyle laughed. 'No, certainly not. I did not wish to be party to your game, Oscar, as you know, but I freely admit it: as far as I'm concerned, Holmes's days are numbered . . .'

'But Holmes has been the making of you, Arthur,' Oscar protested.

'And he could be the undoing of me, too. I have so much else I want to write – romances, adventures, stories that delve into the future and the past. I have poetry to pen, dramas to create. I want to write my play for Henry Irving. One hundred years from now, do I want to be known simply as the man who invented Sherlock Holmes? I think not, Oscar. I plan to kill him in his prime. Indeed, it was on Sunday night that I decided how it might be done.'

Oscar and I were now sitting forward, giving Conan Doyle our rapt attention. I had never known our Scottish friend be quite so passionate. 'On Sunday, before dinner,' he went on, 'inspired no doubt by the prospect of your game, one of our guests asked me for my views on "the perfect murder" – where to commit it and how? It's a question that I have been asked before, so I had my answer ready. "On the White Cliffs of Dover," I said. "Or at Beachy Head. Leastways, on a cliff-top somewhere, where, together, unobserved, the murderer and his intended victim can be taking a stroll. All the murderer has to do to achieve his end is seize the moment. When he is certain the coast is clear, with one sharp lunge, our murderer propels his unsuspecting victim over the cliff's edge to meet his doom. It's simple, it's quick, it's clean and it has several advantages – there are no witnesses, there is no murder weapon and it has all the appearance of an unfortunate accident."'

Conan Doyle was not a vain man, but it was evident that he was enjoying his moment 'holding the floor'. Oscar was an appreciative audience. He picked a fleck of tobacco from his lower lip.

'You spin a fine yarn, Dr Doyle,' he said. 'Pray continue.'

Conan Doyle smiled. 'On Sunday night,' he went on, 'it was the word "accident", I believe, that aroused the interest of your friend Bosie's brother, Lord Drumlanrig. "A body going over the cliffs at Dover or Beachy Head doesn't suggest an 'accident' to me," he said. "Suicide perhaps, but not an accident. If you want to contrive an accident, you need to go to Switzerland."'

'Ah,' said Oscar, 'Drumlanrig told you of his uncle.'

'His namesake, Francis – yes – killed in the Swiss Alps. He was with a party of friends, according to Drumlanrig, seasoned mountaineers mostly. They had successfully scaled a peak, somewhere between Zermatt and the Reichenbach Falls, and they were on their way down when the accident occurred. It was a fine day, clear and cloudless; the snow was settled; the conditions perfect for mountaineering. No one knows quite what happened. One moment, Francis Douglas was alive and well; the next, he was gone. He fell headlong into a deep ravine and was never seen again.'

'His body was not found?' I asked.

'No,' said Arthur. 'His older brother, the Marquess of Queensberry, came out from England to help lead the search. The unfortunate man's gloves, his belt and one of his boots were found – but that was all.'

'When was this?' I asked.

'Twenty-five years ago,' said Oscar, 'perhaps more.'

'The point is,' said Conan Doyle, reaching for the teapot, 'Sherlock Holmes's fate is sealed. When the time is ripe, I shall be taking my hero to Switzerland and tipping him headlong into an Alpine ravine. Holmes will take his final bow and then vanish without trace.'

'What about his gloves and belt and boots?' I asked.

Conan Doyle crunched on his toast. 'I'll have to think about those.'

Oscar was lighting another cigarette and signalling to the waiter for fresh supplies of tea and coffee. 'And Arthur, you still maintain it was not you who named "Sherlock Holmes" as one of our victims on Sunday night?'

'It was not me, I assure you, Oscar.'

'Then who was it?' I asked.

'If you must know,' said Conan Doyle quietly, 'it was my guest – my young friend, Willie Hornung.'

'What?' cried Oscar, with a splutter of disbelief. 'Sweet-natured Willie Hornung? Are you sure, Arthur?'

'He told me so himself. He confessed it, turning crimson as he did so. He apologised profusely. He says that he is wildly envious of my creation.'

'Envy is the ulcer of the soul,' said Oscar, watching the plume of his cigarette smoke rise into the palm leaves above him. 'Socrates teaches us that.'

'Never mind Socrates,' said Arthur, chuckling. 'I told our Willie that, since he aspires to be a writer himself, all he has to do to wreak his vengeance on Sherlock Holmes is create a villainous character of his own to outwit the great detective. Bless the boy – I think he's going to rise to the bait.'

'"Rise to the bait . . ."' Oscar repeated the phrase reflectively. 'Is that why the parrot was murdered, I wonder?'

A tray of fresh coffee and tea appeared. The débris of breakfast was cleared away. Oscar's ashtray was discreetly emptied. Clean cups were set before us. Oscar spread out the list of 'victims' on the table and from inside his silver cigarette case produced a small card-scorer's pencil. 'So,' he said, marking the list as he spoke, 'we know that the Hon. the Reverend George Daubeney named Elizabeth Scott-Rivers as his intended victim – Daubeney confessed it at the time. We also know that it was Bosie who pronounced death upon the unfortunate Captain Flint. Bosie, like Daubeney, spilled the beans there and then. We know too, again from Bosie, that it was his brother, Francis, who named Lord Abergordon as his victim of choice – though we have yet to hear it from Drumlanrig's own lips. And now, Arthur, you tell us that it is Willie Hornung who is responsible for naming "Sherlock Holmes".'

Oscar had marked a small cross by each of the first four names on the list. 'What we really need to discover,' said Conan Doyle, picking up the piece of paper and considering it closely, 'is who named David McMuirtree. Four people in that room chose McMuirtree as the man to murder. *Four*!'

My throat was dry, but I spoke nonetheless. 'I was one of the four,' I confessed. As I said it, I sensed I was turning as crimson as Willie Hornung must have done.

'You?' queried Conan Doyle, putting down his cup abruptly.

'Why, Robert?' asked Oscar, looking at me wide-eyed in astonishment. 'You told me you'd only met the man once before in your life. Why on earth should you choose David McMuirtree as a potential victim for murder?'

'It was only a game, Oscar,' I pleaded. 'You said so yourself.'

'Indeed,' answered Oscar, 'but why McMuirtree – even in sport?'

'I had my reasons,' I said.

'Well?' demanded Oscar, leaning towards me and extinguishing his latest cigarette with undisguised asperity. 'What were they?'

'I don't wish to say, Oscar,' I protested. 'I really don't.'

'Come now, man,' said Conan Doyle, 'spit it out.'

'Please excuse me,' I said.

'We won't excuse you,' said Oscar. He looked me directly in the eye and, suddenly, the anger in his brow evaporated and he smiled at me benignly. 'You're with friends, Robert. You can trust us. Indeed, you must.'

'Very well,' I said. And still I hesitated. 'Very well . . . I chose McMuirtree as my murder victim because . . . because of something he said.'

'"Something he said"?' Oscar expostulated. '"*Something he said*"! When? Where? To whom?'

'He said it to me when I met him briefly at Tite Street. He and Byrd had come to the house to meet Constance, to see the room in which they are to present their magic show. I happened to be there. That's when he said it.'

'What did he say?'

'Something personal – and outrageous. It was unforgivable.'

'He insulted you?' asked Conan Doyle.

'No, it was not about me.'

'Was it about me?' Oscar asked. 'Was my reputation traduced yet again?'

'No, Oscar, it was not about you.' Again, I hesitated. They looked at me expectantly. Eventually, I said: 'It was about Constance – or, rather, it was about her father.'

'Ah,' said Oscar, carefully folding his napkin, 'the late Horace Lloyd QC.'

'I'm afraid you're talking in riddles, Robert,' said Conan Doyle. 'I'm lost. Please, simply explain what happened. Tell us what was said – precisely.'

'Do as the doctor bids you, Robert,' said Oscar, his eyes now focused on his napkin.

'It was as they were preparing to depart. Byrd was downstairs in the hallway with Constance. I was still with McMuirtree in the drawing room. I said something about showing him out and he answered with a pleasantry of some kind. He said how delightful it was to meet Mrs Wilde and I nodded in agreement. Then he asked me how well I knew the Wildes. I said, "Well enough, thank you." He said, "Mr Wilde is a remarkable man." I answered, "Yes," quite curtly, and tried to move him towards the door. I was finding his familiarity irksome. But he wouldn't go. He stood his ground and, looking at me with a horrid smile upon his face, he said, "And Mrs Wilde seems very natural, given the circumstances." I was outraged. I said, "What do you mean, sir?" He said, "Given what we know of her father." I said, "Mrs Wilde's father was a highly respected member of the bar." "So I've heard," said McMuirtree. "He was also notorious for exposing himself to young women in Temple Gardens. Didn't you know?" '

Conan Doyle shook his head in disbelief.

'I wanted to horsewhip the blackguard there and then,' I said. 'Instead, I told him to get out of the house – and when I saw him again on Sunday night and we played that ludicrous game of yours, Oscar, I had no hesitation in choosing him as my murder victim. He's a slanderer.'

'McMuirtree's many things, no doubt,' said Oscar quietly, 'but, in this instance, he's no slanderer. Everything he told you is true.'

'I don't believe you,' I protested.

'Nevertheless . . .' said Oscar, smiling. He picked up his list of 'victims', folded it carefully and returned it to his pocket. 'Poor Horace Lloyd,' he said. 'We all have our secrets.'

9

Another Mystery

Conan Doyle glanced about the dining room of the Cadogan Hotel. 'Does Constance know?' he asked.

'No,' said Oscar, through a cloud of cigarette smoke, 'I don't believe she does. She was just a child at the time. She knows that her parents' marriage was not especially happy, but, to date, she has been spared the details of her father's peculiar peccadillo.' He smiled at us wanly and took a sip of coffee.

'I suppose,' I asked, 'there can be no doubt about the matter?'

'I fear not,' said Oscar, putting down his cup and reaching for the ashtray. 'The scandal was the talk of the Inns of Court for several years. Horace Lloyd QC had chambers at Number One Brick Court – disrespectful young briefs had a lot of fun with that address. What was so remarkable about Lloyd's behaviour was its brazenness. By all accounts, in broad daylight he would parade around Temple Gardens with his breeches unbuttoned and his aroused member on full display.'

'Extraordinary,' muttered Doyle.

'Indeed,' said Oscar, revealing his jagged teeth. 'He was said to be magnificently endowed.'

Arthur was not amused. 'I'm surprised he was not arrested,' he said curtly.

'He would have been,' said Oscar. 'He was about to be when a kindly colleague, a High Court judge, took him in hand – so to speak – and warned him off . . . Poor Horace Lloyd. He died shortly after.'

'Of shame?' asked Conan Doyle, not unkindly.

Oscar smiled. 'Possibly, Arthur. Who knows? The death certificate spoke only of pulmonary problems. He was forty-six years of age – too young to die.'

Conan Doyle sighed and pushed away his tea cup. 'What in heaven's name would make a sane man behave in such a way?' he asked. 'He was a married man. He was a Queen's Counsel. Think of the risks!'

'Apparently, he told his friend the judge that the danger was half the excitement.'

A silence fell among us. It was broken by the arrival at Oscar's side of a tall, lean figure in a frock coat, holding an envelope. 'Ah,' said Oscar, 'my bill. I have no ready money, waiter. Would you put this to my account?'

'Can't do that, sir.'

'Why not?' protested Oscar.

'Let me pay,' volunteered Conan Doyle, reaching for his wallet.

'No, Arthur, no!' cried Oscar. 'You are my guest. My credit is good here, I'm certain. Waiter, why can't you put this to my account?'

'Because, sir, this isn't your bill and I'm not your waiter.'

'What?' snapped Oscar. He looked up sharply. 'Wat!' he exclaimed. For the first time, we all looked at the figure in the frock coat. It was Walter Sickert.

'Nobody notices the waiter,' said Wat, smiling down on us. 'I know: I've been one. It's the fate of the serving classes. No one looks the poor bloody staff in the eye. It's the oldest rule in the book. That's why you'll find it's usually the butler "what done it" – none of the witnesses can recollect what he looked like.'

'What on earth are you doing here, Wat?' asked Oscar, looking about him for a real waiter. The restaurant was now deserted. 'Let's get you a chair. What time is it? I think we might treat ourselves to a mid-morning bracer.'

Sickert pulled up a chair from an adjacent table and sat astride it like a mounted hussar. (His absurd moustachios did give him the look of a comic-opera hero.) 'I'll stay a minute, but I mustn't linger. I'm on my way to Eastbourne.'

'To Eastbourne?' exclaimed Oscar. 'Eastbourne-on-Sea? You'll certainly need a drink.'

A young waiter was now at our table. Oscar inspected the lad. 'What is your name, young man?'

'Dino,' said the waiter.

'Dino,' said Oscar solemnly, 'my friend has just told us that he is on his way to Eastbourne-on-Sea. This calls, I think, for something a little special. A bottle of your 1884 Scharzhofberger, perhaps?'

'Right away, sir,' said the boy. 'And four hock glasses?' Oscar nodded approvingly. The waiter smiled and turned smartly on his heels.

Conan Doyle cleared his throat and tugged at his waistcoat. 'I can't linger, I'm afraid,' he said.

'Stay a moment,' said Oscar. 'Stay at least until we've discovered *why* Wat is on his way to Eastbourne.'

'This is why,' said Sickert, leaning forward over the back of his chair and waving in the air the envelope that a moment ago Oscar had taken for his bill. 'This is why I'm here. This letter reached me this morning – from Eastbourne. I felt I should share it with you. I went to Tite Street and Constance told me that you were here, so here I am.'

'Go on,' said Oscar. 'What is it?'

Walter Sickert opened the small envelope and produced from it a single sheet of notepaper covered, on both sides, in an unruly scrawl. 'It's a note from Bradford Pearse – the actor. You recall: my guest on Sunday night.'

'We recall,' said Conan Doyle, eyeing Sickert carefully.

'His was the fifth name on the list of murder victims,' I added.

'Thank you for reminding us, Robert,' said Oscar, archly.

'I liked him,' said Conan Doyle.

'Everyone does,' said Sickert. 'He's the best of fellows.'

'Well,' said Oscar, 'what does he say?'

'It's a "thank you" letter,' explained Sickert, holding the note out in front of him. 'But there's something about it that perturbs me.'

'Read it to us,' said Conan Doyle. He smiled at Sickert. 'If you don't mind.'

Sickert read the letter. He read it simply, without dramatic emphasis.

Tuesday 3 May. Eastbourne

My dear Wat,

Sunday night was memorable – fine food, fine wines, fine friends. Thank you for your hospitality. Thank you for remembering me. I hope you always will! I shall not forget you or your kindness(es) to me – come what may. To be candid, I don't know what the future holds for me. I'm being pursued and I'm fearful.

I'm in Eastbourne this week. At the Devonshire Park. Come and see the piece – Wednesday night would suit. Bring Wilde. The play is so bad I think it might amuse him. It was an honour to meet him again, of course. He is wise as well as wonderful. Inspiring, in fact. I liked Conan Doyle too – and his shy young friend with the name no one will remember. Hornbeam was it? Chas. Brookfield was as obnoxious as ever. I neither like nor trust him. I never have. Who is to be trusted these days? You are, of course, old friend. Thank you for that.

Come and see me if you can spare the time. I'm frightened to be honest with you. Come and see me.

Ever yours,
Bradford Pearse

Sickert passed the letter, and the envelope, to Conan Doyle.

'What train are you catching?' asked Oscar.

'The three o'clock from Victoria,' said Sickert.

'We'll come with you,' said Oscar.

'I cannot, I'm afraid,' said Conan Doyle, pushing back his chair. 'I have domestic obligations. The doctor is calling to see my wife this afternoon and I need to be on parade.' He got to his feet. 'But I think that you and Robert should definitely go, Oscar – and I think, too, that, with Wat's permission, you should share this letter with Inspector Gilmour at Scotland Yard.' He handed the note to Oscar.

'You think Pearse may be in danger?' I asked.

'Are you feeling melancholy, Oscar?' asked Sickert. 'You don't look it. You don't seem it.'

'We all have our secrets, Walter,' said Oscar, emptying his glass in a single draught and handing the young waiter a second shiny shilling. 'There are no exceptions to the rule . . .' He swivelled in his chair and held his empty glass out in the direction of the doorway to the dining room. 'Look at those two.'

There, hovering at the entrance to the Langham Hotel Palm Court, stood Charles Brookfield and Bram Stoker. They were wearing outdoor coats and anxious faces. Stoker was shaking his head as Brookfield surveyed the room.

'I agree: they do look furtive,' chuckled Wat Sickert.

'There'll be a lady in the case, I warrant,' exclaimed Oscar, waving his napkin in the direction of the door.

The boy waiter was refilling our glasses. 'Dino,' said Oscar, 'ask those two gentlemen to come and join us, would you?'

The waiter brought Brookfield and Stoker to our table.

'Good morning,' said Stoker genially.

'We can't stay,' said Brookfield. 'We have an appointment.'

'With a lady?' Oscar conjectured, with a smile.

'An actress,' said Stoker. 'Brookfield has an emergency on his hands. He's lost his leading lady. I've agreed to help him find another. We're due to meet Miss Tilvert at eleven.'

'She'll be late, I'm afraid,' said Oscar. 'Take off your coats, gentlemen. You've time for a glass, that's certain.'

'Do you know Miss Tilvert then?' asked Brookfield, looking about the room.

'No,' replied Oscar smoothly, 'but I know the type. Have some Scharzhofberger, Charles. It'll settle your nerves.'

'We're not stopping long ourselves,' added Sickert. 'We're off to Eastbourne.'

'Eastbourne,' echoed Stoker, pulling up a chair and smiling as Dino poured him a glass of the German wine. 'I love Eastbourne. Eastbourne has style.' He raised his glass towards Oscar. 'The town's entirely owned by the Duke of Devonshire, you know.'

'It's not His Grace we're visiting,' said Oscar. 'It's Bradford Pearse. He's in a play at the Devonshire Park. We're going to see it.'

Brookfield, who remained standing, waved away the glass of wine that Dino was offering him, and looked down at Oscar. 'You're going to Eastbourne to see a play? It must be frightfully good.'

'On the contrary,' answered Oscar, breathing out a long plume of grey-blue cigarette smoke as he spoke, 'Bradford Pearse tells us that the play is frightfully bad – truly atrocious. It seems it could hardly be worse. That's why I'm determined not to miss it. I do enjoy excess in everything.'

'You're very funny, Oscar,' said Brookfield quietly.

'Give Pearse my best,' said Stoker with enthusiasm, savouring his wine. 'He's a fine fellow and a good actor – and the unlikeliest candidate for murder you could imagine. I don't know why anyone picked him as a victim when we played that game of yours, Oscar. Bradford Pearse hasn't an enemy in the world. I'd stake my life on it.'

'What about his creditors?' asked Charles Brookfield, with a little sniff, folding his arms across his chest.

'I don't know about his creditors,' said Bram Stoker, holding out his glass for a refill, 'but I happen to know his pawnbrokers and they speak very highly of him.'

'I imagine they know him exceptionally well,' said Brookfield, smiling.

'There's no truer friend than an honest pawnbroker,' said Oscar.

'Agreed!' said Stoker. 'I use Ashman in the Strand. Capital fellow. Who do you go to, Oscar?'

'The same. A good man. Ten years ago, when I was in desperate straits, I took him my most prized possession – my Berkeley Gold Medal – and he gave me thirteen guineas for it. *Thirteen guineas!* I said, "Mr Ashman, I don't think it's worth five pounds." He said, "Mr Wilde, I know about this medal. In my day, I was a Greek scholar, too. You won this when you were at Trinity College, Dublin, did you not? It is the college's highest classical award. To you it must be beyond price. I have thirteen guineas in my safe this morning. I am happy to give you thirteen guineas for your medal."'

'What a wonderful story,' said Bram Stoker.

'Ashman is a scholar and a gentleman,' said Oscar.

'And a Jew,' added Charles Brookfield.

'Indeed,' said Oscar, smiling, 'I find that so many of the best people are.'

'Have you seen the paper this morning?' asked Wat Sickert, deftly changing the subject. 'There's a paragraph about the Cadogan Hotel parrot. Apparently, the poor creature was done to death yesterday, in the hotel hallway, in broad daylight. Can you believe it?'

'The parrot is dead?' said Charles Brookfield. 'I'd not heard that.'

'How strange,' said Bram Stoker. 'Brookfield and I took breakfast there yesterday. The parrot was fine, as far as I recall.'

'Who would do such a thing?' asked Sickert. 'It was a messy business, according to the paper – blood and feathers everywhere.'

Charles Brookfield smiled. 'Perhaps it was one of your vampires, Bram?' he suggested. 'Bram's obsessed with vampires, aren't you? I think it comes from working for Irving, the old blood-sucker.'

'It could have been a vampire bat,' suggested Oscar, lightly.

'In Knightsbridge?' exclaimed Brookfield.

'Sloane Street,' Oscar corrected him.

'The notion's ludicrous,' said Brookfield scornfully.

'Unlikely, I agree,' said Oscar benignly, 'but not beyond the realms of possibility. There's a breed of South American bat – the *desmodontidae* – that subsists on blood, and preys on birds and beasts and humans.'

'How do you know this, Oscar?' asked Stoker.

'I went to Oxford as well as Trinity College, Dublin. Poor Captain Flint was a South American parrot. Perhaps he was ravaged by a South American vampire bat?'

'Do you think that's likely?' asked Bram Stoker, draining his glass.

'No,' answered Oscar, shaking his head. 'Frankly, I do not.'

'Then who killed the parrot, Oscar?' asked Charles Brookfield. 'Do tell us.'

'I can't.'

Brookfield looked about the table. 'Oscar sees himself as something of an amateur sleuth – the Sherlock Holmes of Tite Street. Isn't that right, Oscar?'

'I don't know about that,' Oscar answered, widening his eyes and revealing his teeth, 'but I'm certainly an admirer of Holmes's powers of observation and deduction. Thanks to them, for what it's worth, Charles, I can tell that you left home in something of a hurry this morning.'

Brookfield raised an eyebrow. 'And how can you tell that, Oscar?'

'By looking at you, Charles. Your waistcoat's done up with one button adrift, the underside of your chin is not thoroughly shaved and your boots are unevenly shined. You're short of funds: your cuffs are frayed. You have no valet: you clean your own shoes and this morning you spent more time shining your left shoe than your right.'

Charles Brookfield looked steadily at Oscar and clapped his hands together slowly in a show of mock-applause. 'Very good, Oscar. Very good. So who killed the parrot?'

Oscar returned Brookfield's gaze, but said nothing.

'Come on, Oscar,' jeered Brookfield. 'Rise to the challenge, old boy. Who killed the parrot? If, before my first night, you can prove beyond reasonable doubt who it was killed that parrot I'll give you . . .'

'What will you give me, Charles?' asked Oscar.

'I'll give you . . .' Brookfield hesitated and then leant forward and looked Oscar directly in the eye. 'I'll give you . . . thirteen guineas.'

'Very well, Charles,' said Oscar, smiling. 'I accept your challenge.'

10

Murder Most Foul

We caught the three o'clock train to Eastbourne with only seconds to spare. Bustling along the platform, as whistles blew and steam swirled about us, we must have made a curious sight. Oscar, in a crimson cape and white fedora, led the way, striding forward, head held high, like a papal legate hurrying to an international conference. Wat Sickert paced anxiously beside him, the attendant major domo, in his black frock coat and pinstripe trousers, his waxed moustaches as shiny as his stove-pipe hat. I brought up the rear, the humble, bumbling clerk, scurrying breathlessly to catch up with my masters. I was only last, and out of breath, because, as we arrived at Victoria, Oscar had despatched me to buy all the newspapers.

We travelled First Class, thanks to Lady Windermere; we had a compartment to ourselves; and exactly as we reached it and fell back into our seats, the final whistle blew and the train began to judder out of the station. 'We made it!' gasped Sickert, pushing his hat to the back of his head and wiping the perspiration from his forehead with a huge, crumpled, paint-stained handkerchief.

'Did you doubt it?' asked Oscar, carefully removing his own headpiece and caressing the felt fondly as he placed it on the empty seat beside him.

'I most certainly did, Oscar. I thought you and Brookfield were all set to have a duel in Portland Place. What is the matter between you and Brookfield?'

'He does not like me.'

'That's evident – but why?'

'Envy,' I chipped in, sitting forward and recovering my breath. 'Brookfield envies Oscar.'

Sickert laughed. 'We all envy Oscar! I've envied Oscar since I was a little boy. Just because I envy him I don't go about making snide remarks at his expense, do I? I don't put on a play whose sole purpose is to lampoon and belittle him. I don't issue preposterous challenges to him for no apparent reason. There's more to it than common-or-garden envy, that's for sure.'

'Once upon a time,' said Oscar, unclasping his cape and letting it fall from his shoulders, 'I gave Charles Brookfield cause for offence.'

'Ah!' grunted Sickert, stuffing his handkerchief into his trouser pocket, 'I thought so. What did you do?'

'It was in New York, some years ago. I was on my lecture tour. He was appearing in a play. We met at a tea party. He was wearing gloves. It was an *indoor* tea party. A gentleman never wears gloves at tea. I told him so – publicly. He has not forgiven me.'

Oscar was reaching inside his jacket pocket for his cigarette case. We looked at him expectantly. He found a cigarette – one of his Turkish ones – and put it to his lips. He said nothing.

'Is that it?' asked Sickert.

'It is enough, I think,' he replied, lighting a match. 'I wounded Brookfield's pride. I humiliated him – in America, in front of strangers. I spoke without thinking.

It was wrong of me and I regret it.' He turned away from us and looked out of the carriage window as the railway cottages of south London flashed past. 'Watch your thoughts, they become words,' he said. 'Watch your words, they become actions. Watch your actions, they become habits. Watch your habits, they become character. Watch your character, it becomes your destiny.'

'Do you think you'll discover who killed the parrot?' I asked.

Oscar turned round and grinned. 'It'll cost me thirteen guineas if I don't! Hand round the newspapers, Robert. We've work to do.'

I had perhaps a dozen newspapers in my bundle. I divided them up and handed them round. 'What are we looking for?' I asked.

'Anything that's relevant,' said Oscar. 'Further and better particulars of the fire in Cheyne Walk; statements from Inspector Gilmour of the Yard; obituaries of Lord Abergordon; reports of South American vampire bats having escaped from Regent's Park zoo . . .'

'You were not serious about the vampire bats, were you?' asked Sickert, spreading out the *Evening Chronicle* on his knees.

Oscar did not answer the question. His nose was buried deep in the pages of the *Daily Graphic*. 'Look, gentlemen,' he announced, with satisfaction. 'We already have something . . . a photograph of the late Lord Abergordon, Under-Secretary of State for War, on his way to the Epsom Down races with his longstanding friend, the Marquess of Queensberry . . .'

'Is this significant?' asked Sickert.

'Possibly . . . According to the *Graphic*'s graphic correspondent the two noble lords shared "a passionate interest" in all things sporting – "racing, hunting, shooting, boxing, mountaineering . . ." And how about this?' Oscar rustled the newspaper with delight. 'It appears that their lordships first met as young men back in 1865, "at the time of the tragic death of Lord Queensberry's younger brother, Francis . . . Lord Abergordon was a member of the same fateful Alpine expedition as Lord Francis Douglas, but happily survived the mountain-side catastrophe . . ." '

'Is this significant?' repeated Sickert, putting aside the *Evening Chronicle*.

'Probably not,' said Oscar, lowering the newspaper and smiling at Wat Sickert, 'but it's intriguing, you'll allow . . . In 1865, Lord Francis Douglas dies in a mountaineering accident and Lord Abergordon happens to be there. In 1892, the next Francis Douglas – Lord Drumlanrig, Abergordon's godson – says he'd like to see Abergordon dead and within forty-eight hours he is . . .'

'Drumlanrig named Abergordon as his "murder victim", did he?' asked Sickert. 'I didn't know.'

'Yes,' said Oscar, 'according to Bosie. We've yet to talk to Francis himself.'

'But it doesn't mean to say he did it – it doesn't make him a murderer.'

'Of course not.'

'You'll recall,' said Sickert, brushing dust from his trousers with the back of his hand, 'that a year or two ago I was chased through the backstreets of King's Cross by a posse of prostitutes all crying "Jack the Ripper!" after me.'

'I recall,' said Oscar. 'You told me.'

'And I'm not Jack the Ripper,' protested Sickert.

'I know,' said Oscar.

'All I'm saying,' said Sickert, 'is that one shouldn't jump to conclusions on the flimsiest of circumstantial evidence.'

'I agree completely,' cried Oscar. 'I don't; I haven't; I wouldn't; I won't — I assure you.' He waved the news-paper in the air. 'I'm just intrigued by the coincidence, that's all . . .'

Sickert sniffed and twitched his moustaches and looked out of the window. We were passing through Paddock Wood. The platform was deserted.

'You never told me, Wat,' Oscar continued, smiling wickedly, '*why* it was that you were wandering the back-streets of King's Cross in the middle of the night? Was the danger half the excitement?'

Wat turned back from the window to look Oscar in the eye. 'It was not the middle of the night: it was midnight. I am an English painter: I was looking for English sub-jects to paint. I had been sketching at a music hall in Somers Town. I got lost on my way home . . .'

'Were you dressed as you are dressed now?'

'Possibly,' said Sickert. 'This is a favourite coat of mine. It was winter. I wore a cape as well.'

'And the hat? And those moustaches?' Oscar chuckled. 'No wonder the King's Cross chapter of the daughters of joy found your appearance alarming! I'm surprised they didn't mistake you for one of Bram's vampires.' I laughed. Sickert managed a flicker of a smile. Oscar leant forward and put his hand on his friend's knee. 'Nobody believes that you are Jack the Ripper, Wat. And I don't believe that Bosie's brother murdered Lord Abergordon.

123

What's more, Scotland Yard assure us that Miss Scott-Rivers's death was accidental, Mr Sherlock Holmes appears to be safe in the hands of Conan Doyle, and I've no doubt that when we reach Eastbourne we will find Bradford Pearse equally safe and sound – in good health, in good heart and ready to tell us his secret.'

'His secret?' queried Sickert, recovering his composure. 'He didn't say anything about a secret.'

'We all have our secrets, Wat,' said Oscar, smiling. 'I have mine. You have yours. Bradford Pearse has his. He confessed as much in his letter.'

'Did he?' said Sickert, clearly perplexed. 'He told me he was frightened. He made no mention of any secret.'

'Are you sure?' asked Oscar. He reached into his inside pocket and produced Pearse's letter. He opened it and passed it across to Wat. 'Read the final paragraph again.'

Sickert turned to the end of the letter and looked closely at Pearse's scrawl. He read the conclusion slowly and out loud: '"Come and see me if you can spare the time. I'm frightened to be honest with you."' He looked at Oscar. 'It seems pretty clear to me. The man is frightened. He says so.'

Oscar retrieved the letter and examined it once more. 'I wonder . . .' he said, reflectively, '. . . Pearse's lack of precision when it comes to punctuation leaves scope for ambiguity, I fear. I may be mistaken, but I took it that your friend's final sentence was an admission that he is fearful of telling you the truth. He is saying, "Wat, I'm frightened *to be honest with you*" – is he not?'

We reached Eastbourne Station at a little after half past six. The train ran late. There was a points failure at

Polegate. The recently built Devonshire Park Theatre – the jewel in Eastbourne's already well-studded theatrical crown – was situated to the south-west of the town, a tidy walk from the town centre but only a stone's throw from the sea. We arrived at the stage door, at the rear of the theatre, at a minute after seven. We stood in the street, in fading light, addressing the stage doorkeeper through a small square grille cut into the stage door at about head height. From what little we could see and hear of him, he was a lugubrious old codger, who hailed from Lancashire and gave the impression of having spent a lifetime working in the theatre, loathing every minute of it. 'No visitors before the show,' he grunted, without so much as glancing in our direction. He was implacable, moved by neither Wat's pleading nor, more remarkably, by the rattle of Oscar's shiny shillings. 'No visitors,' he repeated.

'Is Mr Pearse definitely in the theatre?' Oscar asked, his face pressed against the grille. The doorman did not answer. We could hear him slurping a beverage of some kind. He belched slowly as Oscar repeated the question. 'Is Mr Pearse definitely in the theatre? We need to know.'

'He'd better be,' grunted the doorman, 'or who else are they going to murder in the fourth act?'

As we abandoned the stage door and made our way around the building towards the box office at front of the theatre, Oscar shook his head and sighed. 'As you will be aware, gentlemen, I have made it my life's work to *entertain* the working classes, *enrage* the middle classes and *fascinate* the aristocracy – but I do believe I've just met my match. Accrington 'Arry here is in a class of his own, beyond my reach.'

We secured three seats for the evening's entertainment without difficulty. *Murder Most Foul*, 'a modern melodrama in the old tradition', had failed to draw the town. Oscar had hoped to be seated in the mid-stalls for the performance, but Mr Standen Triggs, the theatre manager, who chanced to be on duty, proved himself to be one of nature's aristocrats by recognising Oscar the instant we entered the foyer and being evidently, obsessively, utterly *fascinated* by him. Mr Triggs was quite overwhelmed by the honour of having so great a man of letters as Mr Wilde in his theatre and insisted, consequently, that our party be seated in the royal box, as his personal guests, with his humble self in awed attendance all evening. From the moment we arrived at the Devonshire Park to the moment we departed three hours later, I don't believe Triggs took his eyes off Oscar once. He gazed upon him, fixated, as though Oscar were the Queen of Sheba.

Triggs, as bonhomous and voluble as his stage doorkeeper was dour and taciturn, held a certain fascination himself. He was a small man in his mid-fifties, dapper in his dress, dainty in his movements. His diminutive head was quite extraordinary: it was round like a radish and separated from his shoulders by a long, thin, stalk-like neck. As he spoke, it bobbed from side to side like a child's toy. He was virtually bald; his cheeks were pink and smooth, almost velvety; his nose was small but sharply pointed, with a red tip that looked as if it had been applied by means of theatrical make-up; his watery red-rimmed eyes were perfectly round and disconcertingly protuberant. While he spoke repeatedly of the 'great unbridled joy' he felt at our presence, he seemed all evening to be on the brink of emotional collapse. His hands shook; sweat trickled down his face and neck in a constant stream; time and again his bulging eyes filled to overflowing with heavy tears.

Before the performance and during each of three long intervals he entertained us in his office and talked incessantly. His exuberance and enthusiasm were both comical and touching. He served us a warm and peculiarly unpleasant Alsatian wine. 'Excellent, is it not?' he asked, crying and laughing as he spoke. He sang the praises of everybody and everything. His theatre, only eight years old, was 'probably, possibly – no, *certainly*' the finest Italianate theatre outside of Italy. His employers – the Devonshire Park and Baths Company – were, 'without question', the fairest, the most decent you could hope to work for, and, while he had not yet met the new Duke, nor indeed the new Duke's new Duchess, he had heard only good things of them – 'only very good things, *very* good things indeed'. And as for our friend Bradford Pearse . . . 'Ever an Eastbourne favourite . . . Is there a better provincial player of his generation and particular build? I think not. Is there a more popular man of the theatre – present company excepted? I *know* not.'

'Pearse is well-liked by his colleagues?' asked Oscar, whose own eyes now seemed to be watering (possibly on account of the wine).

'He hasn't an enemy in the world,' declared Mr Triggs. 'Indeed,' he added, leaning towards Oscar confidentially, 'so liked and respected – and *trusted* – is your Mr Pearse that we allow him a privilege allowed to no other player on the touring circuit . . .'

Oscar raised his eyebrows enquiringly.

'We permit him to stay on the premises overnight. It's against all the rules.'

'He sleeps here?' asks Sickert.

'Yes,' answered Triggs, still not taking his eyes off Oscar. 'Bradford Pearse is customarily short of funds, but he'll never be short of friends. When he's appearing at the Devonshire Park Theatre we allow him to use his dressing room as his digs.'

'Your stage doorman permits this?' murmured Oscar in amazement.

Mr Standen Triggs nodded solemnly, wiping his eyes the while. 'Such is the standing of Bradford Pearse in his chosen profession,' he said.

It cannot be pretended that the professional standing of Mr Bradford Pearse was much enhanced by his appearance in *Murder Most Foul*.

'This is not bad enough to be good,' Oscar whispered to me as the house lamps were dimmed for the final act. 'The word "tosh" was coined, I believe, in the year 1528. I have long wondered why. Now I know. This play is tedious twaddle. No wonder Mr Triggs is yawning at the back of the box. I do hope friend Pearse is murdered sooner rather than later.'

It was not to be. The last act of *Murder Most Foul* was the longest – or, at least, so it seemed. In the drama, Pearse played the part of a cruel husband and father, a ship's captain, who neglects his wife and family when he is at sea and beats and brutalises them without remorse whenever he returns home. In the final moments of the play, his wife decides she can endure his cruelty no longer and, using a pistol she has stolen from a passing stranger

– a character from the complex subplot: a Peruvian cattle rustler if I remember right! – she shoots her husband in the back as, in a drunken rage, holding a bull-whip, he turns away from her, his hand raised to beat their mis-shapen, cowering, blind, consumptive daughter . . .

It was Oscar who said, famously, 'One must have a heart of stone to read of the death of Little Nell without laughing.' During the final moments of *Murder Most Foul* I noticed my friend leaning over the edge of the royal box at the Devonshire Park Theatre with his teeth clamped around his knuckles.

Sickert, seated immediately behind Oscar, hissed: 'What if the gun is loaded?'

Oscar stifled a snigger. 'If it is, we can shoot the author.'

Sickert persisted: 'Someone threatened Bradford's life. If he's to die, tonight's the night . . .'

Oscar turned to Sickert. 'Hush, man. Let him die in peace.'

As Oscar spoke, on stage the gun exploded. The burst of noise was shocking. From the sparsely filled auditor-ium, there were cries of 'No!'

From the back of the box, a freshly roused Standen Triggs muttered, 'Realistic, eh?'

On stage, the actress playing Pearse's wife dropped the smoking pistol to the ground and covered her eyes in anguish; the young girl playing Pearse's daughter looked, wild-eyed, towards her mother and let forth a piercing scream; and Bradford Pearse himself, centre-stage, swung about to face the audience. His chest and hands were crimson with blood; his eyes were closed, his face con-torted. He staggered, first to the left, next to the right;

suddenly, he stumbled forwards, towards the footlights; for a moment it seemed he might fall into the orchestra pit; instead, with arms suddenly outstretched, he stepped abruptly back and collapsed, like a dead-weight, onto the floor.

The curtain fell.

'Worth waiting for, eh?' exclaimed Mr Standen Triggs, leaping to his feet to lead the standing ovation.

We stood, too, and cheered and gazed down into the near-empty auditorium and saw that others were also standing to offer their applause.

After several moments – the applause was beginning to falter – the stage curtain rose once more. There, behind the footlights, in line, side by side, hand in hand, heads held high, ready to take their call, were all the members of the cast of *Murder Most Foul* – bar one. Bradford Pearse was nowhere to be seen.

11

'I Fear the Worst'

'He's milking it,' chuckled Mr Standen Triggs. 'He'll make his entrance on the second call.'

'I wonder,' murmured Oscar.

The curtain fell and rose again. Still there was no sign of Bradford Pearse. As she took her bow, the leading lady had her eyes cast towards the wings.

'Here he comes,' announced an excited Mr Triggs.

'I think not,' said Oscar, now sounding concerned. 'Let us go backstage.'

As the applause from the auditorium evaporated, the stage curtain fell for the second time. Before it hit the ground – with a disconcerting clanking sound: its hem must have been lined with metal weights – we saw the feet of the actors beneath it breaking rank and moving swiftly off the stage.

'Come!' commanded Oscar.

'Stay!' countered Triggs, stepping to the front of the box and, with a trembling but proud hand, indicating the orchestra pit below. 'We're in the royal box – this is our moment,' he declared. As he pulled himself smartly to attention, the five elderly members of the Devonshire Park Theatre's resident orchestra struck up the National Anthem. They played as though their hands all trembled as much as Triggs's. Oscar stopped in his tracks and stood, stock still, facing the auditorium, chest forward, head erect, face frozen. Though unbearded and thirteen years younger and five inches taller, nonetheless he gave a passable impression of the Prince of Wales.

The moment the anthem was done, Oscar was galvanised. He turned to Sickert. 'We must find Pearse,' he hissed.

'Of course,' said Mr Triggs, taking Oscar by the elbow, 'I hear you, but first . . .' Beaming broadly, nodding happily, his face glistening with sweat, his eyes more bulbous than ever, the theatre manager indicated the orchestra pit once more. The conductor, his baton raised, looked up towards us and, graciously, inclined his head. As Oscar bowed back (a mite less graciously), the quintet of ripe virtuosi embarked on a selection of favourite melodies from the comic operas of Gilbert and Sullivan.

'Ah, *Patience*!' cried Oscar, closing his eyes.

'In your honour, Mr Wilde,' gurgled Mr Triggs, 'and they are raising the house lights for us so that you can appreciate our domed ceiling. The cherubs and caryatids are by Schmidt of Holloway. I know you will admire their finesse.'

'I do!' exclaimed Oscar, despairingly, gazing up towards the plasterwork. 'But I am also anxious about our friend, Bradford Pearse.'

'Indeed,' nodded Triggs, still smiling but now moist-eyed. 'I understand.'

'Forgive me,' said Oscar.

'Follow me,' said Triggs. He waved from the box towards the orchestra pit. The selection from Gilbert and Sullivan ceased abruptly. 'Come, gentlemen. Let us find friend Pearse. Most unlike him to miss his call, I agree.'

Moving lightly, though breathing heavily, like an asthmatic pixie, Mr Triggs led us out of the royal box and along a short curving corridor towards what he called 'the pass door'. 'This takes us directly to the dressing rooms,' he explained. 'We don't have any of your West End comforts here, Mr Wilde, but by provincial standards we don't do too badly.' As we passed through the door, it was as if we had crossed a frontier. Instantly, we left behind the gilt and red-plush of the land of plenty and found ourselves in a dark and barren country: the walls were bare brick, the floors were bare boards, and the light so dim we could barely see the way ahead.

'Pearse's room is the first on the right,' said Triggs. 'Allow me to go ahead.'

'Can you see?' asked Oscar.

Mr Triggs appeared to be feeling his way along the wall. He laughed somewhat nervously. 'It takes my eyes a moment to adjust,' he said. 'That's all.' In the gloom, I could see him peering at a name card fixed to the dressing-room door. 'Here we are,' he said. He knocked. There was no answer. He knocked again.

'Go in,' instructed Oscar.

'I fear the worst,' whispered Sickert.

Standen Triggs felt for the door handle, found it and turned it slowly. 'Visitors, Mr Pearse,' he called as he pushed open the door.

We crowded around the doorway not knowing what to expect.

'Is he there?' asked Oscar.

'Bradford!' shouted Wat Sickert, stepping forward into the room. We followed him in. 'He's not here,' said Sickert, turning to Oscar. 'He's gone.'

The room was small and square, low-ceilinged, windowless and dank, like a prison cell. With four of us standing in it, there was scarcely room to move. It was lit by a solitary gas lamp fixed high up on the wall that faced the door. Below the lamp was a dressing table covered with a half-torn piece of towelling-cloth, littered with assorted sticks of theatrical make-up. On the floor, below the dressing table, was a narrow palliasse that ran the length of the room, with a navy-blue sailor's blanket rolled up at one end to form a bolster. To the right of the table was a small deal wardrobe, its door hanging open. The wardrobe was quite empty. Thrown across the wooden chair that faced the dressing table was Pearse's costume: a pair of breeches, a coat and the blood-soaked shirt he had worn in the final scene of the play. I noticed Oscar dipping his fingers into the blood and bringing them to his lips to taste.

'Look!' cried Wat Sickert with a start. To the left of the dressing table stood a cheval mirror, its amber-coloured glass mottled and pitted. Across the glass, at eye height, scrawled in greasepaint, in large capital letters though barely discernible in the gloom, was the single word: 'FAREWEL'.

Oscar peered at the looking glass and sniffed. 'Bradford Pearse's spelling's as poor as his punctuation.' He turned sharply to the theatre manager. 'We must be on our way, Mr Triggs. Will you kindly escort us to the stage door?'

Perspiring and trembling, Standen Triggs stood gazing at the mirror. 'What is the meaning of this?' he asked.

'It means, I fear, that you should alert Mr Pearse's understudy to the possibility that he may be called before the mast tomorrow night.'

'What do you think has occurred, Oscar?' asked Wat Sickert, his voice hoarse with alarm. 'Do you think it's what we feared?'

'What you feared?' echoed Mr Triggs, now breathing more heavily than ever. 'What did you fear?' He looked at Oscar with his huge eyes full of tears. He seemed at once both desolate and exultant.

'Nothing, Mr Triggs,' said Oscar reassuringly. 'We had hoped to see Mr Pearse tonight and feared he might run off . . . that's all. He worries about his creditors, you know. Come, we must go. We'll find him in one of the nearby public houses for sure.'

Mr Triggs escorted us from Pearse's dressing room down a steep iron stairway to the stage door. It can have been no more than fifteen minutes since the melodrama ended and the curtain fell, but the theatre was already deserted. At the stage door we found the leading lady – Miss Dolly Justerini, 'another Eastbourne favourite' – handing in her dressing-room key to the lugubrious doorman. When Triggs presented us to her, she bobbed a cursory curtsy, but begged to be excused. Her 'walking gentleman' had promised her a large glass of port at The Devonshire Arms, and the price of port and the nature of men being what they were, she was loath to keep either of them waiting.

Having congratulated her on her performance in wildly over-exuberant terms that she accepted entirely as her due, Oscar enquired: 'Are we likely to find Mr Bradford Pearse at The Devonshire Arms?'

'I doubt it,' trilled Miss Justerini, over her shoulder as she disappeared into the street. 'Brad spends most of his time in hiding these days. He ran off before the curtain call tonight. He's probably locked himself into his dressing room, naughty man. Goodnight, sweet princes. Goodnight, Harold.' As we voiced our goodnights, she was already gone. The stage doorkeeper belched softly but said nothing.

'Do you think Pearse might still be somewhere in the theatre?' asked Wat Sickert.

For the first time, the doorman looked up from his newspaper. 'He scarpered twenty minutes ago,' he said. 'Maybe he knew you was coming.'

With a pencil Oscar was writing something on the back of one of his visiting cards. He looked towards Mr Triggs and smiled. 'Does Mr Pearse have his own key to the stage door?' he asked.

'Yes,' said Standen Triggs, who appeared calmer and less heated now. 'But he can only get back into the building until midnight. That's when Harold,' – he nodded towards the doorkeeper without catching his eye – 'turns in for the night. Mr Pearse has a key to the main lock here, but at midnight Harold goes home and secures two further locks before he departs. From midnight until eight in the morning the building is impenetrable.'

'Indeed,' said Oscar.

'Indeed,' said Mr Triggs. He pulled open the stage door and let us out into the street. The moon was pale and high; the air was mild; in the distance, a church clock struck the hour; a seagull screeched in the darkness above us.

'If you see Bradford Pearse before we do, Mr Triggs,' said Sickert, shaking the theatre manager by the hand, 'be sure to tell him that we called. Ask him to make contact as soon as may be.'

'Naturally,' said Triggs, 'I'll tell him you were here. But I'm sure you'll find him yourselves without difficulty. For a moment Mr Wilde alarmed me with his talk of understudies, but if Pearse is not at The Devonshire Arms, he'll be at The Cavalier or The Prince Albert – or the Lamb inn. You'll find him. I know you will.' He shook my hand warmly, though his fingers were cold as ice. He turned to Oscar and looked up at him in awe. 'Mr Wilde,' he said, his eyes glistening anew, 'it has been such a deep honour . . .'

'The honour – and the pleasure – has been all ours,' said Oscar, bowing to our host and handing him a visiting card. 'Make use of that address, Mr Triggs,' he added, as he stepped away from the stage door, 'if you'd be so kind.'

Mr Triggs took Oscar's card and held it to his lips as if it had been a sacramental wafer. 'Goodnight, gentlemen!' he called to us as we moved off down the street. As we went we turned back and saw that the little man had produced a large white handkerchief from his coat pocket and was waving it above his head. He kept on waving until we reached the corner of the street and turned out of his sight into the main road.

'Standen Triggs is a good man, is he not?' said Oscar.

'An odd man,' said Sickert.

'You wrote something on the back of your card, Oscar,' I said. 'What was it?'

'The name of a physician, a specialist, a colleague of my late father's. I believe Mr Triggs suffers from a condition known as Graves' disease. He may not be aware of it, but he has all the symptoms, poor fellow – starting with the protuberant eyeballs. I fear he is not long for this world.'

'I am sorry to hear it,' I said.

Wat Sickert stopped in his tracks. 'You are a phenomenon, Oscar Wilde! You appear to know *everything*.'

'Alas,' said Oscar, stopping also and putting an arm on Sickert's shoulder, 'I do not know the whereabouts of your friend, Bradford Pearse.'

Sickert laughed. 'At least we know that he wasn't murdered in the last act. At least we know that he left the theatre alive.'

'Yes,' said Oscar, absently, 'so the doorman said.'

'Do you doubt it, Oscar? We'll find Pearse in one of the local hostelries, for sure.'

'I think not,' said Oscar, feeling for his cigarette case. 'I doubt very much that we will find Bradford Pearse tonight.'

'But we must search for him, must we not?' insisted Sickert.

Oscar lit a match and Wat's white face and piercing eyes were suddenly illuminated. We stood together in a small circle on the deserted roadway. Up the hill to the left were the lights of the town; down the hill to the right was the road to Beachy Head.

'What time is it?' asked Oscar.

'I heard a clock strike just now,' I said. 'It must be a little after eleven.'

Oscar turned to me and smiled and, narrowing his eyes, held my gaze in his. It was his way when he was about to ask a favour. 'Robert,' he said, 'if Wat and I trawl the taverns of the town, can you stand sentinel here? I'll give you cigarettes to smoke – you'll not be idle. Should Bradford Pearse plan to lodge at the theatre tonight, he will return before midnight. If he turns up,

138

which I doubt, bring him to The Lamb in the High Street. We'll take rooms there.'

'Are we going to The Devonshire Arms first?' asked Sickert.

'Yes,' said Oscar, 'briefly, if the landlord will admit us at this hour. And to The Cavalier and The Prince Consort and whatever other inns we pass along the way. We'll do it, Wat, to ease your conscience – to help you to feel that "something is being done". But we'll not find Bradford Pearse tonight – alive or dead.'

'Do you think he's dead?' asked Wat Sickert, suddenly alarmed.

'I know no more than you do, Wat. If he's alive, as I pray, he's in hiding – for reasons we do not yet know. If he's dead already, killed in the past half-hour, poor wretch, and lying in a ditch or in some dismal Eastbourne alley, it's too late – we're too late – and too dark by far for us to find him now. To please you, Wat, we'll stay on the case till midnight. And tomorrow, when it is light, we can resume the search in earnest.'

Oscar's instinct was sure. Until gone midnight, I loitered on the corner of Compton Street and Hardwick Road, smoking Oscar's cigarettes and watching the stage door of the Devonshire Park Theatre. A solitary dog – a limping cocker spaniel – and two drunkards came shambling past, but I saw no sign of Bradford Pearse. As the church clock began to strike twelve, I saw the stage door open and the stage doorkeeper emerge. He was taller than I had expected him to be – and fitter. To my surprise, he wheeled a bicycle out of the theatre with him and when he had turned back and attended to the locks on the stage door, and looked both ways down the street, he mounted his two-wheeler and rode briskly on his way.

I lingered outside the theatre for fifteen minutes more. No one came, no one went. Sensing my duty done, I made my way up the hill to the High Street. I found Oscar and Wat standing together, smoking, on the front steps of the Lamb inn.

'We've not found him either,' said Oscar. 'He's well-known to the local landlords, and well-liked by one and all it seems, but not a soul has seen hide nor hair of him tonight – they're all sure of that – and no one – no one at all – has the least idea where he might be.'

'I am anxious,' said Wat. 'Pearse is my friend.'

'We'll find him,' said Oscar, casting his cigarette into the gutter and gazing up into the blue-black sky, 'but not tonight.' He put a comforting arm around Wat Sickert's shoulders. 'The stars are weary and so are we. Let's to bed, *mes amis*.' He put his other arm through mine. 'We have rooms here, Robert – and, according to Wat, "they're clean and cheap and welcoming, like the best daughters of joy". And our landlord's wife, Mrs Fletcher, God bless her, is a saint. Leave out your linen and she promises she'll have it laundered and pressed by break of day. This is Eastbourne, gentlemen, where the age of miracles is not past.'

I did not sleep long, but I slept well, and I awoke at 6.30 a.m., surprisingly refreshed, to find our saintly landlady at my bedside with a kindly smile, clean linen, warm towels and a bowl brimming with boiling shaving water. Mrs Fletcher was indeed a paragon: when she had drawn back the curtains and opened the bedroom window, I saw that she was no more than my age and, though a little plump, as pretty as a Watteau milkmaid. I lifted my head from the pillow and said good morning. She simply bobbed a curtsy, said, 'Breakfast will be ready shortly – Mr Wilde has asked for goose eggs,' and went about her business. (Why had I gone to Paris and married a tiresome Polish blue-stocking like Marthe Lipska when I could have come to Eastbourne and found myself a wholesome English girl like Mrs Fletcher?)

I got up and went to the window. Thursday 5 May 1892 offered as bright and fresh an English early summer's morning as you could wish for. The sky was pale blue and cloudless; the breeze was gentle and scented with wall-flowers. I shaved and dressed and tied my tie with special attention, thinking of Mrs Fletcher and smiling at the recollection of one of Oscar's favourite axioms: 'A well-tied tie is the first serious step in life.'

Oscar and Wat had reached the breakfast table before me. They, too, looked remarkably refreshed. Oscar was in especially ebullient form. As I appeared, he rose to his feet, swept to the sideboard and began lifting the lids from the breakfast dishes like a magician producing bouquets of paper flowers or white rabbits from a hat. 'Let me serve you, Robert. You will not be disappointed. Mrs Fletcher has fresh herrings, local ham, devilled kidneys and mutton cutlets to offer you. She also has eggs. An egg is always an adventure, Robert – one is never certain what to expect. But a goose egg . . .'

'I will have one of Mrs Fletcher's goose eggs, if I may,' I said, handing Oscar my plate.

My friend was clearly in a teasing frame of mind. He turned to Wat and whispered, 'Did you hear how Robert said her name? "Mrs Fletcher" . . .' He rolled the words around his mouth as he ladled a fried goose egg onto my plate. He winked at me. 'Robert is in love again!' he declared. 'One day away from Constance and my dear wife is quite forgotten. He's a fickle one, this Robert Sherard . . .'

I added a slice of Sussex ham to my plate and took a crust of bread and sat at the table. 'Don't be absurd, Oscar. My affection for Constance, while profound, is entirely gentlemanly, as well you know.'

'Whereas that of Edward Heron-Allen . . .' said Oscar, grinning wickedly.

'Don't mention that man's name,' I interrupted. 'In my opinion, his interest in Constance is unhealthy.'

Oscar laughed. 'He's harmless, Robert, I assure you. Constance is flattered by his attention and I'm grateful to him. Women give to men the very gold of their lives, but invariably they want it back in small change. Heron-Allen helps me out with the small change.'

Wat Sickert tapped the side of his breakfast plate with his knife. 'Gentlemen, gentlemen,' he cried, 'Isn't it a bit early in the day for this amount of banter? I thought only dull people were supposed to be brilliant at breakfast.'

Oscar smiled. 'There are exceptions to every rule,' he murmured. He sipped his coffee and contemplated the table. 'But you are right, Wat. Let us concentrate on the feast Mrs Fletcher has laid before us.'

'I'm thinking about Pearse,' said Wat.

Oscar put down his coffee cup and paused. 'I am, too,' he said eventually, taking his napkin and slowly wiping his lips. 'I care for you, Walter, I care for you deeply, so I care about Pearse. He is your friend. And I do not forget:

he was my guest. His life was threatened last Sunday – at my dining club, at my table, during the absurd game we played at my instigation. I am conscious of my responsibility.' He put down his napkin and looked at me. 'And have no doubt, Robert, that I care for Constance more than I do for my own life. I will let nothing harm her. Her life was threatened also. She, too, was named as a "victim". I'll not rest until we have unravelled this mystery.' He opened the palm of his left hand and ran his right forefinger over it. 'I see a sudden death in this unhappy hand,' he said. He looked at each of us in turn and smiled. 'Eat up, gentlemen. I have ordered our carriage. It will be here at eight.'

We ate up and we ate well. Sickert was especially delighted that Mrs Fletcher served us Keiller's Dundee marmalade. 'It's the only brand for artists,' he explained, spreading it lovingly onto his toast. 'Degas, when he is in England, will eat nothing else.'

'Degas is a great man,' said Oscar. 'I don't doubt it.'

Our 'carriage', when it arrived, turned out to be a small pony-and-trap. When Oscar had settled our account at The Lamb and we had bidden Mrs Fletcher a fond adieu, we climbed aboard. Oscar and Wat sat side by side within the trap. I perched up front with the young driver. The accommodation was not spacious.

'Where are we going?' asked Sickert as our little party, somewhat unsteadily, set on its way.

'Down the hill,' said Oscar, 'to the edge of town, towards the west – to the headland.'

'To Beachy Head?'

'Yes, Wat. Prepare yourself. I fear the worst.'

12

Beachy Head

We reached the headland within the hour.

I had been there once before, taken as a child by my mother. She was the granddaughter of the poet William Wordsworth (as she never forgot!) and she took me to Beachy Head when I was a small boy because my great-grandfather had taken her there when she was a little girl. She was seven years of age at the time; he was seventy. He told her, so she told me, that with 'its great green sward, its high white cliffs and God's blue sky above, there is no prospect more majestic in all England than that of Beachy Head'.

It would certainly have taken a poet of my great-grandfather's ability to do justice to the stark beauty of the place that Thursday morning when Oscar Wilde, Walter Sickert and I were taken up onto the promontory in search of Bradford Pearse. Our little open carriage climbed the long, steep, deserted approach path haltingly, stopping every fifty yards or so to allow our pony to regain her strength and us to admire the view. Oscar sat upright in the trap, wrapped in his crimson cape, surveying the scene.

'The name "Beachy" comes from the Old French for "beautiful",' he announced, as if he had been a tour guide escorting us through the side-streets of Florence. 'This beautiful headland has been so-called for nigh on a thousand years. Beauty is timeless. As we learn from life and art and nature, all beautiful things – these chalky cliffs, that azure sky, the frescoes of Giotto, the music of Mozart, the profile of the young man who is driving us so expertly this morning – belong to the same age . . .'

Our young driver – he was Mrs Fletcher's nephew as it turned out – looked over his shoulder at Oscar and laughed. He brought the pony-and-trap to a halt. 'Rosie's come as far as she can,' he said. 'If you're going to the peak, you'll have to walk from here.'

'Walk?' exclaimed Oscar, affecting an attack of the vapours. 'If the horse cannot make it with four legs, do you imagine that I shall be able to do so with half as many?'

'It's not far,' said the boy, laughing once more. 'You're nearly there.' His laughter was kindly: it was clear that he found Oscar wonderfully droll. 'Don't worry. I'll wait here to take you down again.'

Wat Sickert was standing up in the trap, shading his eyes with his hands, scanning the horizon. 'There's no one here,' he said. 'There's nothing to be seen. There's no point in going further.'

Oscar, breathing heavily, assisted by the young driver, was now clambering out of the trap. 'There's every point,' he wheezed. 'On a clear day from the summit they say you can see the Isle of Wight. In all probability Her Majesty is on the veranda at Osborne House already waving in our direction. It would be most ill-mannered, not to say unpatriotic, not to return her greeting.'

The boy covered his face and sniggered in happy dis-belief as he accepted Oscar's shilling. 'Don't be absurd, Oscar,' snapped Sickert. 'Must you forever be facetious?' he demanded angrily. 'We're here because Pearse has dis-appeared and you are playing foolish games.'

'You know my rule, Wat,' Oscar replied genially, coming round the back of the trap and offering a hand to Sickert, who was now climbing down from the vehicle. 'One should always be a little improbable – whatever the circumstances.'

'This is not a time for laughter,' answered Sickert.

'I laugh that I may not weep,' said Oscar quietly, turning towards the cliff-top. 'Come, Wat,' he went on, putting a hand on Sickert's shoulder, 'Let's to the peak. That's what we came for. If Bradford Pearse has been here we need to know it.'

In silence, the three of us trudged the final five hundred yards to the highest, furthermost point of Beachy Head. A cool breeze blew into our faces. The grass beneath our feet was soft and wet. Above us seagulls swooped and screeched.

'There!' cried Oscar suddenly, pointing towards the cliff's edge.

'Where?' shouted Wat, alarmed.

'There!' Oscar cried again. 'At the summit, at the very edge. Do you not see it?'

I saw it. For a moment I thought it was the body of a dead dog, half hidden in the grass. Wat Sickert saw it too. Together, as one, we ran towards it, abruptly stopping together, as one, as we came near the cliff's edge. Over that edge, below us – way, way below us – we could see the sea crashing towards the base of the cliff, the spray rising up towards us. At a distance the vast and mighty wall of chalk had indeed looked majestic; at close range, the reality of the sheer drop inspired not awe but terror.

'Take care!' cried Sickert, falling to his knees. 'Get down.'

We must have been five feet at least from the cliff's edge – we were in no real danger – but, suddenly, the brisk breeze that had cooled us as we climbed the hill had become, at the summit, a jabbing wind that threatened to propel us towards our doom. I dropped to the ground. For a moment, the earth seemed to spin about me. I laid my face against the damp grass and breathed slowly. I closed my eyes and recovered my equilibrium. When I opened them, I saw Sickert, on his elbows and knees, inching his way forward towards the object at the cliff's edge. 'Can you reach it?' I called.

'Yes,' he answered, choking as he spoke. For a brief instant, I thought that he was weeping, or whimpering in pain – but he was laughing. 'What a sight I must seem to the seagulls,' he cried. 'Oscar is quite right. One should always be a little improbable.' He was now alarmingly close to the precipice. If he had rolled two feet to his left he would have fallen to a certain death. His right arm was outstretched ahead of him. 'I'm nearly there,' he gasped.

'What is it?' I called.

From behind me, Oscar answered: 'It's Pearse's travelling bag. It's what we came for.' Still lying flat on my face, I turned my head and looked back. Oscar was standing about fifteen feet away, watching us. He raised his hand and waved. 'You're good men,' he called.

'Got it!' cried Wat Sickert. With the fingertips of his right hand he held the very edge of a black leather case – an

147

'He clearly believes so,' replied Conan Doyle. He looked quite grave. 'I liked Mr Pearse – very much.' He glanced at his timepiece. 'I must go – forgive me. Will you keep me informed, Oscar? Thank you for breakfast. Gentlemen.' He bowed to us and went on his way.

Oscar called after him: 'Don't forget your umbrella, Arthur – and don't murder Holmes too soon!'

Conan Doyle turned back and laughed and waved towards us genially. As he departed, he passed Dino, the boy waiter, arriving with our wine. He stopped the lad and spoke to him.

'What did Dr Doyle say to you, Dino?' Oscar asked when the young waiter reached us and was uncorking the bottle.

'He told me to take good care of you, sir.'

Oscar chuckled. 'Did he indeed?'

'Yes, sir,' said the boy, sniffing the cork with the air of a seasoned sommelier. He can't have been much older than the wine: he looked fifteen, sixteen at the most.

'Tell me, Dino,' said Oscar, taking a sip of the Scharzhofberger and rolling it around his mouth a little noisily. 'What *exactly* did Dr Doyle say to you? What were his actual words, Dino?'

'Since you ask, sir,' said the boy, pulling a face as he filled our glasses, 'His actual words was, "Only the one bottle – they've work to do."'

Oscar banged the table with delight. 'I knew it!' he cried. 'You can depend on Arthur! And he is right, of course. We do indeed have work to do and I'm glad of it. As Arthur knows, work is the best antidote to sorrow.'

old Gladstone bag, bulky and battered – and slowly, inch by inch, manoeuvred it about in the grass until he could reach its handle. I watched as he eased himself forward and, finally, grasped the handle tight. 'Yes!' he cried triumphantly and, as he did so, he rolled over onto his back holding the Gladstone bag in the air above him.

'Bravo!' cried Oscar.

'My God!' cried Sickert in sudden terror as he realised that his right shoulder, thigh and leg were poised at the very edge of the cliff-top. Propelled by I know not what power, I stumbled to my feet and lunged towards him, grabbing both his legs and pulling him violently away from the brink. I pulled until I had yanked him several yards inland. Holding the bag fast in one arm and clinging to me with the other, he pushed himself to his feet and, shaking and laughing, together we staggered downhill.

'My heroes!' cried Oscar, opening his arms wide to embrace us. We stood before him, like schoolboys returned from a great adventure.

He took the battered Gladstone bag from Wat Sickert and held it up before us. 'Let us examine the evidence. You risked your life for this.'

Sickert shook his head and wiped his eyes and moustache with his hands. 'Is it Pearse's bag?' he asked, recovering his breath.

'It would appear to be,' said Oscar. 'Here are his initials: B.P. . . .' He ran his hand across the leather. 'It's wet from the dew. It's been here some hours.'

'Wat pulled it through the grass,' I said.

'Yes. But the bird droppings on it are dry – encrusted. The bag was left here last night – or, if this morning,

148

certainly before dawn. What does it contain? Very little, I surmise. It's remarkably light. And unlocked . . .' With thumb and forefinger he unfastened the lock. He bent forward and peered inside the bag. 'As I thought, very little . . . No make-up tin; no hair brushes; no shaving tackle . . . Just papers. Nothing but papers. We can examine them on the train. Come, gentlemen – our charioteer awaits.'

'Where are we going?' asked Wat.

'Back to London. Our business here is done.'

Sickert appeared bewildered. 'But, Bradford—' he protested. 'We must search for his body.'

'We will not find it,' said Oscar, shutting the Gladstone bag and passing it to me to carry. 'If your unfortunate friend jumped off the cliff – or was pushed – the tide will have washed his body away long ago. The tide went out at dawn. We'll report what we know to the police on our way to the station . . . they'll alert the coastguard. Come, let us go.'

'Do you think my friend is dead, Oscar?' asked Wat seriously.

'If he fell from that cliff, he is. It is the highest chalk sea cliff in the land. It has claimed a thousand lives and more. I know of no survivors.'

'Has he been murdered then?'

'That is possible,' said Oscar, looking back towards the cliff's edge. 'There are no signs of a struggle, but that does not signify. There are no boot-marks in the grass, but all that tells us is that whoever was last here departed before the arrival of the morning dew. Yes, it's quite possible the poor man's been murdered.'

'He hadn't an enemy in the world.'

Oscar smiled. 'Most murders are committed not by our enemies but by our friends.'

'Could he have taken his own life?' I asked.

'That is possible also – more suicides are committed from this cliff-top than anywhere else on the planet. Of course,' he added, turning back in the direction of our waiting pony-and-trap, 'to take one's own life at Beachy Head is a little obvious. It smacks of what the French call a *cliché*. But as we saw from last night's melodrama, Bradford Pearse was not averse to the obvious. He was not frightened of a *cliché*.'

Wat Sickert winced and shook his head despairingly.

'Life's a jest,' said Oscar, 'and death is a certainty. If it be not now, yet it will come, Wat – that's for sure. The readiness is all.'

Sickert said nothing. We trudged down the hill towards the pathway.

'Why should he take his own life?' I asked.

'Perhaps his "secret" overwhelmed him,' said Oscar.

'What "secret"?' asked Sickert, sharply. 'I don't believe he had a secret. I've known him for years.'

'We all have secrets, Wat. None of us is entirely as we seem. Beneath that bluff exterior, behind that seafarer's bushy beard, was there another Bradford Pearse – a man you never knew? Remember what he wrote in his note to you? "Come and see me if you can spare the time. I'm frightened to be honest with you." '

We had reached the boy with the pony-and-cart. 'Let us talk of other things,' said Wat as he and the young lad helped Oscar clamber aboard. I sat up front again, on the driver's seat, holding Bradford Pearse's Gladstone bag on my knees. When he joined me our young driver glanced at the bag enquiringly. 'I think Mr Wilde would like you to take us to the railway station,' I said.

'Righto,' said the boy, picking up the reins and twitching them to set the pony on her way.

As we rumbled unsteadily down the hillside, Sickert shaded his eyes with his hands once more and slowly looked about him, surveying the landscape from east to west. 'I want to fix this scene in my mind's eye,' he said. 'I shall paint it one day.'

Oscar chuckled and reached for his cigarette case. 'A landscape without figures, Wat? Only grass and sea and sky? Is that really you? Nature is elbowing her way into the charmed circle of art, I see. I'm not sure I like it.'

'There are plenty of shadows on the hillside, Oscar. You like those.'

'But nothing man-made?'

Wat laughed and took the cigarette Oscar was proffering him. 'To please you, my friend, I'll include the lighthouse.'

'The lighthouse?' exclaimed Oscar. 'Where?'

'There,' said Sickert, pointing to the west, 'on the next headland.'

Oscar leant forward and called up to the boy: 'That lighthouse – how far is it from here?'

'Half a mile, as the crow flies; two miles by road.'

'Take us there, if you'd be so kind,' commanded Oscar. 'And as swiftly as you're able. There's an extra shilling in it for you. The lighthouse keeper may be able to help us. Do you know him? Are you by any happy chance –' he paused – 'consanguineous?'

The boy laughed. He turned round and looked Oscar in the eye and winked. 'I know what you mean, sir. And the answer's "Yes, he is of my blood." He's my uncle. You'll like him.'

It was Oscar's turn to laugh. He slapped Sickert on the knee. 'Tilly-vally! In London, no self-respecting child knows who his father is. In the country, everyone's related.'

The Belle Tout Lighthouse at Seven Sisters point – built, it turned out, by our young driver's great-grandfather in 1832 – was an ugly structure, graceless, square and squat, rough-hewn from stone. It had the forbidding look of a military conning tower. As we approached it, in the building's solitary window, up on what must have been the second floor, below the lighthouse lamp itself, we saw the figure of a large man smoking a pipe. 'Is that your uncle?' asked Oscar.

The boy squinted up at the edifice. 'No,' he said, 'that's not him. That must be one of his men. You can't miss my uncle. He's a character.'

He was indeed. He might, in fact, have been a character from one of the tales of the Brothers Grimm – or even from one of the darker verses of Oscar's poetic hero, Edgar Allan Poe. He was diminutive in stature and in every respect misshapen. His back was twisted; he walked with a limp; he had a club foot; he had a withered hand; his skin was rough and warty; his brown bald head was a patchwork quilt of hollows and carbuncles; he wore a black eye-patch over his left eye. 'He is grotesque,' Oscar murmured as the man shuffled towards us. 'Speak to him, Robert. I cannot.'

Oscar Wilde's obsession with "beauty" bordered on the pathological. Famously, Max Beerbohm said: 'Oscar may not have invented Beauty, but he was first to trot her round.' But the counterpoint to Oscar's passion for what he held to be beautiful was his revulsion towards what he conceived to be ugly. Ugliness to him was a sin, an evil, the devil's work – and he would not look upon it. Oscar was a man of great sweetness and enormous generosity and yet he would cross the road to avoid the sight of an ill-favoured beggar. He pitied the hapless 'Phos girls'– those poor creatures who worked in the Victoria Match Factory and lost their jaws and fingers through tipping matchsticks into poisonous phosphorus hour upon hour, day by day – but when, once, one of them called at Tite Street in answer to the Wildes' advertisement for a scullery maid, Oscar presented her with a ten-pound note on condition she never darkened his door again. He told me the sight of the girl had made 'his soul shrivel and his gorge rise'.

We spent very little time at the Belle Tout Lighthouse. There was no need. Happily, the lighthouse keeper's manner was as benign as his appearance was malevolent. He was a jolly fellow, evidently eager to please, and he answered my questions – and Wat's – with an old-fashioned deferential courtesy that was quite disarming. Alas, he was not familiar with Bradford Pearse – by name, sight or reputation. Yes, he had been on duty through the night and he always kept 'a weather eye' out for 'goings-on' on the peak of Beachy Head – but no, he hadn't noticed anything untoward in the past twenty-four hours and neither had either of his men. He'd observed no strangers on the cliff-top by day and no unexpected traffic, lights or lanterns during the night. Suicides were all too common, he regretted to tell us, and the bodies of the poor unfortunates did not always reappear. When they did it was not necessarily on the next tide, but sometimes days and occasionally weeks later, and, due to the currents, often a mile or more along the coast. He regretted the sad occasion of our visit, was sorry we did not have time to stay for some refreshment and hoped our paths would cross again in happier circumstances.

As we drove away from the lighthouse keeper, and he stood, crooked but contented, waving to us with his withered hand, Wat said, 'What an extraordinary individual — I want to paint his portrait.' I said to our young driver, 'I like your uncle very much.' Oscar said nothing.

On our way to Eastbourne railway station, we stopped briefly at the Devonshire Park Theatre and left a message for Mr Standen Triggs informing him that, sadly, it now seemed certain that the services of Mr Bradford Pearse's understudy would indeed be required. We stopped briefly also at the police station in Grove Road where the sergeant on duty took a cursory note of what we had to tell him, but did so reluctantly and only because Oscar insisted that he should. The sergeant, a God-fearing family man with a ruddy complexion and a black walrus moustache, did not care for Oscar's manner, did not like theatrical folk and had no sympathy for the suicidally inclined. 'Suicide's a criminal offence,' he reminded us. 'If we find the man, we'll charge him. Good day, gents.'

Eventually, at around one o'clock, Oscar, Wat and I, in our compact pony-and-trap, trundled into the forecourt of Eastbourne railway station. As our young driver helped him climb from the carriage, Oscar presented the boy with half a crown. 'You've looked after us well, young man. Thank you. May I ask your name?'

'Brian,' said the boy, touching his cap in recognition of Oscar's munificence. 'Brian Fletcher.'

'Oh,' said Oscar, solemnly. 'I'm sorry to hear that. You'll need to change it when you take to the stage professionally. You can't be called Brian in London, I'm afraid.'

The boy looked puzzled. Wat intervened. 'Pay no attention to Mr Wilde, Brian,' he said reassuringly. 'Brian's a fine name.'

'Fiddlesticks!' said Oscar. 'Name me an artist called Brian! Name me a composer called Brian! Name me the lowliest spear-carrier in Irving's company who boasts the name of Brian! You cannot! Brian is not a name that rides on clouds of glory. If this boy is to be an actor, he has to give up his pony-and-cart and change his name!'

'But why should he want to be an actor?' asked an exasperated Wat Sickert, shaking his head. 'He's happy as he is.'

'Only the dead are happy as they are, Wat,' said Oscar. 'This lad is already an amateur actor of note. Am I not correct, Brian?'

The boy blushed and nodded.

'Indeed, he is a budding Shakespearean. If I'm not mistaken, he has recently scored something of a sensation in the Eastbourne Vagabonds' acclaimed production of *Twelfth Night*.'

'Did you see it, sir?' asked the boy, looking at Oscar, amazed.

'No,' said Oscar, dolefully. 'Would that I had. I saw Mr Irving and Miss Terry in the play at the Lyceum. Not a success.'

Wat Sickert was now standing face to face with Oscar, hands on hips, head thrown back in scornful disbelief. 'How is this possible, Oscar? If you have not met the boy before, how on earth did you know that he has appeared in Shakespeare's *Twelfth Night*?'

Oscar was not looking Sickert in the eye. He was gazing over his shoulder, towards the station cab rank.

'Come, Oscar,' said Sickert. 'Explain yourself.'

Oscar looked at Wat and smiled. 'The boy was familiar with the word "consanguineous" – and proud to be. It's a word that features prominently in Shakespeare's *Twelfth Night*, but not, I imagine, in the daily discourse of the average East Sussex stable lad . . . I jumped to a happy conclusion, that's all – prompted no doubt by my seeing a poster advertising the Eastbourne Vagabonds' production of the play displayed in the foyer of the Devonshire Park Theatre.'

I laughed. 'How did you know that the Eastbourne Vagabonds' production had been "acclaimed", Oscar?' I asked.

'*All* amateur productions are acclaimed, Robert. That is the rule.' He turned back to the boy who was now standing wide-eyed and open-mouthed between us. 'Brian,' he declared, 'I have solved your dilemma. In future, you are to have two names – one for the town, one for the country. In Eastbourne, while you are an amateur actor, you may continue to call yourself Brian. But when you come to London and turn professional, you will need another Christian name – something, if I may say so, with a more romantic ring to it . . .' From inside his coat pocket, he produced his silver cigarette case and began to tap it against his chin thoughtfully. 'What would you say to the name "Sebastian", Brian? Does "Sebastian" appeal to you?'

The boy laughed nervously. 'I don't believe this,' he muttered. 'Sebastian – it's the part I played in the play.'

'Good,' said Oscar. 'I guessed as much. That's settled then.' He put out his right hand and the boy shook it, bowing his head as he did so. 'It's been a pleasure to meet you, Brian,' Oscar went on, now, in his left hand, holding his silver cigarette case out towards the boy. 'Please accept this as a token of my appreciation – and friendship. And as a christening present.'

The lad took the silver cigarette case in both hands and looked on it in wonder. He shook his head. 'I can't, sir. I mustn't . . .'

'You can and you must,' Oscar laughed. 'Indeed, you have no choice. Look inside – you will see that it is already inscribed to you.'

Oscar leant forward and opened the cigarette case for the boy. He indicated inside the lid. 'There,' he said. 'Read what it says.'

The boy narrowed his eyes and read the inscription:

Sebastian from Oscar
with love

Oscar turned to me. 'Do you have Pearse's bag, Robert? We must be on our way or we shall miss our train.' He turned to Sickert. 'Come, Wat. Our business here is done.'

Leaving the boy, standing by his pony-and-trap, turning his silver trophy over and over in his hands, we made our way hastily across the forecourt into the station.

'You're astonishing, Oscar,' exclaimed Wat Sickert. 'I've never witnessed a scene quite like it.'

'I'm a vain old fool,' cried Oscar. 'But I'm *observant*, I'll grant you that. Did you see what I saw – in the station forecourt?'

'No,' said Wat, as we found an empty first-class compartment and began to climb aboard.

'Out of the corner of my eye I saw a familiar figure getting into one of the station cabs. I'd have gone over to him if I hadn't been playing out my little drama for the benefit of the boy. . .'

'Who was it?' I asked, settling back into my seat, still holding Bradford Pearse's Gladstone bag at my side.

'Didn't you notice him either, Robert?'

'No,' I said. 'Who was it?'

'It was Francis Douglas, Lord Drumlanrig – Bosie's brother. What is he doing in Eastbourne, I wonder?'

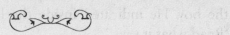

13

'What's in a Name?'

s our train gathered steam, Oscar stood at the carriage window gazing out over the red and grey rooftops of Eastbourne scudding by. 'Drumlanrig turning up like that . . .' he mused. 'It's a curious coincidence, don't you think?'

'Yes,' retorted Sickert, sitting back in the corner seat, contemplating our remarkable friend. 'Not unlike the "curious coincidence" of you chancing to have on hand a silver cigarette case charmingly inscribed to "Sebastian" just when you needed one! How did you pull off that trick, Oscar? Was it a coincidence? Or do you have half a dozen cigarette cases secreted about your person – each inscribed to a different Shakespearean hero?'

Oscar turned back from the window, unhooked his crimson cape, furled it into a bundle and placed it with his white fedora hat on the luggage rack above our seats. He smiled at Sickert and shook his head.

'What would you have done if the boy had been cast to play the part of Fabian, Oscar?' I asked.

'The boy would not have been cast to play the part of Fabian, Robert. The boy is beautiful. He had to have played Sebastian. What else could he have played?' He sat himself in the window seat opposite mine. 'Curio,

I suppose,' he added, 'or Valentine. But they're not leading roles, and I sense young Sebastian Fletcher is destined for leading roles.' He leant across to Sickert. 'May I cadge one of your cigarettes, Wat, my friend? The boy now has all of mine.'

Wat obliged and Oscar lit up. As a smoker, Oscar was a sensualist. With deep satisfaction he filled our compartment with a haze of blue-grey smoke. Through it, waving Wat's cigarette in the air, he announced: 'No one in all literature is a richer source of perfect names than Shakespeare. He is the master of nomenclature. Names, as you know, are everything.'

'Are they?' I asked. 'Are they really?'

'Oh, yes, Robert,' he said earnestly, 'indeed they are. I am as I am because I'm called as I'm called. And so are you. You began with five names, did you not, Robert? So did I. How many names do you have Wat?'

'Just three: Walter Richard Sickert.'

Oscar reflected on them. 'They'll serve,' he said, 'but you should perhaps have started out with one or two more. I began life as Oscar Fingal O'Flahertie Wills Wilde – a name with two Os, two Fs and two Ws . . . It has a fine ring to it, does it not? But a name which is destined to be in everybody's mouth must not be too long. It comes so expensive in the advertisements! When one is unknown, a number of Christian names are useful, of course, perhaps needful – but as one becomes famous one sheds some of them, just as a balloonist, when riding higher, sheds unnecessary ballast . . . All but two of my five names have already been thrown overboard. In time, I shall discard another. The day will come when I'm known by five letters of the alphabet, no more: two vowels and three consonants – like Jesus or Judas, or Pliny or Plato. A century from now, my friends will call me Oscar; my enemies will call me Wilde.'

Wat Sickert smiled and proffered Oscar a second cigarette. 'You still haven't explained the cigarette case inscribed to "Sebastian from Oscar with love" . . .'

'It was a present to myself. Oscar is neither a saint's name nor Shakespearean; Sebastian is both. Sebastian is my *alter ego*. I am Oscar in town and Sebastian in other times and other places. . . . I gave the boy my own cigarette case – on impulse. It was the moment for it, was it not? One should always seize the moment.'

The train jolted to a halt. 'Where are we?' asked Wat, straining forward.

Oscar peered out of the murky window. 'Leap Cross,' he said. 'Names are everything. Shall we seize the moment to examine Pearse's Gladstone bag?'

'Perhaps you should do so,' I said to Sickert, passing the case across to him. 'He was your friend.'

'He *is* my friend,' said Sickert, opening the bag with a heavy sigh and carefully emptying the contents onto the seat beside him. 'I can't believe he's dead. I don't want to. Why should he take his own life? Who would want to kill him?' Oscar said nothing.

The bag disgorged no secrets. 'It's as you said, Oscar – just papers.' Sickert sorted the material into separate piles. 'There's correspondence here with assorted theatre managers . . . postcards from landladies confirming digs . . . bills and statements, plenty of those . . .'

'Is there a bank book?' asked Oscar. 'Or any receipts from pawnbrokers – from the likes of Ashman in the Strand?'

'No, none that I can see. There's the script of *Murder Most Foul*, Tuesday's *Times*, a copy of the Eastbourne *Gazette*, a copy of Bradshaw's railway timetable, more bills, but no bank book and no receipts from pawn-brokers . . .' Wat returned the material to the Gladstone bag. He snapped it shut. 'What do we do with this now?' he asked.

'Keep it safely and, in due course, if need be, pass it on to his next of kin.'

'He had no family, Oscar. His friends were his family.'

'He must have had parents . . .'

'Dead long ago.'

'Brothers? Sisters?'

'None that I know of.' Wat stood up and hoist the bag onto the luggage rack. The train was moving once more. He steadied himself, holding on to one of the leather straps attached to the frame of the compartment door. When he turned around I saw that his eyes were filled with tears. 'Damn you, Oscar,' he hissed. 'Damn you and your confounded game.'

'He may not be dead,' said Oscar quietly.

'But what if he is!' wailed Sickert, sinking down into his seat and covering his face with his hands. From his coat pocket he pulled his crumpled paint-stained hand-kerchief and wiped his eyes. 'Forgive me, Oscar,' he mumbled. 'I should blame myself, not you. It was I who brought him to the Cadogan Hotel on Sunday night. He was my guest, not yours.'

'But it was my game,' said Oscar slowly, 'and on the four consecutive days since we played it, in the exact order in which their names were drawn from the bag, the first four of the game's so-called "victims" have each met their fate.' He had produced the list of 'victims' from his pocket and unfolded it and laid it open on his lap. With his fingertips lightly touching the side of his temples he stared down at the list as if his concentrated gaze might somehow enable him to penetrate its secrets. 'Elizabeth Scott-Rivers died first, burnt to death, but the conflagration could have been caused by accident . . . Lord Abergordon was next to go, but he was sixty and appears to have died in his sleep . . . The wretched hotel parrot was murdered for sure, butchered to death – that much is certain. . . . And now Bradford Pearse has gone . . .'

'Who's next?' asked Wat, blowing his nose.

'Next on the list,' said Oscar, 'is David McMuirtree – the boxer, Byrd's associate, bald yet oddly handsome . . .'

'I recall,' said Sickert. ' "Half-a-gentleman".'

'Who chose McMuirtree as his victim, I wonder?' Oscar pondered.

There was a pause. Oscar and Wat each lit up another cigarette.

'I did,' I said, somewhat awkwardly. 'As Oscar knows.'

Wat Sickert sat back and drew slowly on his cigarette. 'I did, too,' he said quietly.

'What?' cried Oscar. 'Why? Do you know the man?'

'No.' Sickert laughed. 'Not at all. I saw him box once. He's an artist in the ring.'

'But you'd not met him before?'

'No. Never.'

'Then why in all creation?'

'Because of his name, of course.'

' "Because of his name"?' Oscar expostulated. 'What do you mean, man?'

'It was a game, Oscar — you said so yourself. I chose David McMuirtree because of his name.'

'I don't follow you, Wat,' said Oscar, furrowing his brow.

'I was seated on his right, you'll recall, and through dinner, as we talked, as the conversation ebbed and flowed, I idled away the time with my pen — sketching McMuirtree's profile on the back of the menu and playing with the letters in his name . . .'

'Playing with the letters?'

'Rearranging them — making an anagram out of them. I discovered to my amusement that "David McMuirtree", rearranged, makes "A murdered victim" . . . That's why I chose him, Oscar. No other reason.'

Oscar sat back and burst out laughing. It was not his low chuckle: it was his raucous, barking laugh. 'Good God!' he exclaimed, 'Is't possible? Have we condemned a man to death because of his name?'

'It was just a game, Oscar,' said Sickert.

'But a deadly game, my friends, do you not see?' He calmed himself and leant forward once more and put out a supplicating hand to claim the last of Wat's tin of cigarettes. 'I have being trying to work out in my mind what it is — what it could be — that links Elizabeth Scott-Rivers, Lord Abergordon, that wretched parrot and Bradford Pearse. I now realise it may be nothing — *nothing at all*, bar the fact that they were randomly chosen as "victims" when on Sunday I forced us to play that ludicrous game. These four unfortunate creatures — a lady, a lord, a parrot and an actor — not slain for a reason, but *murdered without motive* . . .'

'You mean—' Sickert began.

'Yes, Wat, I mean that just as it amused you to name McMuirtree as your "victim" because you like to play with words, so it may be that, in our midst, there is a cold and calculating killer who finds it "amusing" to take a list of names such as this –' he lifted the list from his lap and brandished it before us – 'and eliminate them one by one, simply for pleasure – playing the game for the game's sake.'

I leant across and took the list from Oscar and studied it. I glanced up and saw that my friend had closed his eyes, as if in prayer. 'I know what you are thinking, Robert,' he said, almost in a whisper. 'I am thinking it, too. The last name on that list belongs to Constance – constant Constance, innocent Constance, the truest and best wife and mother in the world. You love her as I do, Robert. All who know her love her. None who knows her could wish her harm. And yet our murderer does not need to know those whom he seeks to kill. He is playing a game – ticking off mere names on a list.'

He shuddered and opened his eyes. 'Are we approaching London yet?' he asked, getting to his feet. He reached for his cape. 'I'm cold and hungry,' he said. 'It's a while since Mrs Fletcher's breakfast.'

Wat Sickert looked up at Oscar, ashen-faced. 'I fear you may be right, my friend. Bradford Pearse has not taken his own life. He has been murdered – not because of who he was, or what he was, or aught he'd done. He was murdered because his name chanced to be upon that list.'

'But who put his name upon that list,' asked Oscar slowly, 'if, as we all keep saying, he hadn't an enemy in the world?'

The train was slowing down, passing through Croydon. 'What do we do now?' I enquired. 'Go to the police?'

'Yes,' said Oscar, decisively. 'We must do as Conan Doyle advised. We must go to Inspector Gilmour at Scotland Yard. We must show him Bradford's letter and tell him the whole sorry story. There were fourteen of us around the dinner table on Sunday night and at least one of us, I fear, is a murderer.'

'Or an instigator of murder,' suggested Sickert. 'One of our number could have taken the list and hired a killer to do his bidding. Indeed, isn't that more probable?'

'Does the murderer need to have been at the dinner at all?' I asked. 'If it's a random killer, as you suggest, Oscar, couldn't one of our number have simply recounted the events of the night in a bar or a pub – or at his club or somewhere – and been overheard by a stranger?'

Oscar burst out laughing again. 'A stranger bent on murder? A stranger with excellent hearing who happened to be in search of a tidy shopping list of would-be murder victims? Anything is possible, I suppose.'

The train had reached Victoria. 'What time is it?' Oscar asked, while sorting through his small change in anticipation of the coming encounters with station porters and hansom cab drivers.

Sickert put his head out of the carriage window and looked up at the station clock. 'Gone five,' he said.

'I'll take Pearse's bag, if you don't mind,' said Oscar. 'Those bills of his might reveal something – you never know.'

We clambered out of the carriage onto the noisy station platform. 'I'm going home,' said Wat. 'I hope to sell a picture tonight. You'll keep me posted, won't you?'

'Of course,' said Oscar. 'I'll send you a wire when we've seen the police.' He handed me Bradford Pearse's Gladstone bag to carry.

'Are we going to Scotland Yard at once?' I asked. 'It's quite late. Should you not go home, too?'

'If our murderer is following the chronology of the list, Robert, until David McMuirtree is dead Constance should be safe.' He led us across the station towards the cab rank on Victoria Street. 'Scotland Yard can wait until tomorrow. I think first we should find McMuirtree and alert him to the danger he is in.'

'And you must safeguard yourself also, Oscar,' said Wat. 'Your name, too, is on the list.'

Oscar glanced towards Sickert. 'I know.'

Wat suddenly stopped in his tracks. 'Your young friend Bosie keeps a gun, does he not? A pistol of some sort? He boasts about it.'

Oscar laughed. 'Indeed. He tells me he plans to use it to shoot his father!' Oscar stood still and looked about the station concourse and spread his arms wide and laughed again. 'I am surrounded by murderers and madmen . . .'

Wat Sickert smiled and took both of Oscar's hands in his. 'I'm serious, my friend. Perhaps you should borrow the gun from Bosie and keep it at Tite Street until the danger's past.'

'I don't fear for myself, Wat. Death may indeed be the greatest of all human blessings. But I fear for my children – they need their mother and Constance is too young to die.' The poet and the artist embraced one another. They were a curious sight: Oscar, all of six-foot-three, in his crimson cape and white fedora, and Wat Sickert, so much slighter, in his theatrical frock coat with his absurd moustaches. 'You go and sell your picture, Wat,' said Oscar. 'Robert and I are going to the circus.'

14

The Ring of Death

'Why on earth are we going to the circus, Oscar?' I asked as we stood in line in the station forecourt waiting for a hansom cab.

'Because Mr David McMuirtree is a fairground fighter and has a summer engagement at Astley's Circus. I know because he has kindly sent me two tickets for his next appearance – promisingly described as "an historic gala bout". It's scheduled for Monday night. Bosie won't come. He has a horror of boxing. Are you free?'

'Thank you,' I said. I had become accustomed to being Oscar's companion on nights when Bosie was unavailable. 'I love Astley's. When I was a boy, my birthday treat was always an outing to "Lord" George Sanger's circus at Astley's.'

'Yes,' Oscar murmured as we moved up to the head of the queue. 'I recall that you had a troubled childhood.'

I smiled. I sensed that the people behind us were listening in to our conversation. Oscar was not averse to the public's attention. 'What was your birthday treat then, Oscar?' I asked.

'An afternoon in the bluebell wood of Phoenix Park reading Euripides and Theocritus, followed by an evening in the cloisters at Drumcondra with Plato and John Ruskin. I was an uncomplicated child.'

I laughed and we climbed aboard our hansom.

By cab, it took no more than twenty minutes to travel from Victoria Station to Astley's Circus amphitheatre on the south side of Westminster Bridge. This was 1892, the year before the amphitheatre – one of the great glories of Victorian London – was razed to the ground.

Until I was eighteen – until I began to travel and discovered the Paris Opera House, the Fenice in Venice, the Ronda bullring in Andalusia – Astley's was my pleasure-dome. I had never been inside a building so wondrous, so vast, so ornate, so exotic. It was illuminated by a chandelier that burnt five thousand candles. The audience was seated in four steep and curving tiers that rose up to fifty feet above the ground. There was a conventional stage for the musicians, clowns and tumblers to perform on, and, in front of it, in place of the traditional orchestra stalls, a huge circular arena – forty-two feet in diameter – for the performing horses and the dancing dogs.

Philip Astley (whom my grandfather knew) used no wild animals in his shows. He was a horseman – and an acrobat. He invented the circus ring to display his riding skills to best advantage. He realised that by galloping in a tight circle he and his fellow-riders could generate a centrifugal force that would help them maintain their balance while standing on the bare backs of their steeds.

As our hansom trundled slowly down Victoria Street in the Thursday evening rush-hour traffic, I tried to share my enthusiasm with Oscar. He was not interested.

'I seem to recall Sickert telling me that Monsieur Degas also adores the circus,' he said wearily.

'Oh yes,' I replied warmly, ignoring his wan smile and gently raised eyebrow. 'The French all adore the circus. In France they regard Astley as a hero. They call him "*Le roi des cirques*". He died in Paris, you know.'

'Astley's dead?' said Oscar, feigning surprise.

'Long dead. He is buried at Père Lachaise.'

'That tells us nothing,' Oscar replied dismissively. 'They'll take anybody there.'

When we reached Astley's amphitheatre, Oscar instructed our driver to set us down at the stage door. 'No wonder Conan Doyle wants to kill off Holmes,' he grumbled as he clambered down from the cab. 'The lot of the private detective is not an easy one.' He sighed. 'We're now going to have to run the gauntlet of another surly stage door-keeper. Will it be a bearded lady? Or a two-headed dwarf? More probably a hapless acrobat who has succumbed to arthritis.' He handed our driver two shillings. 'I really cannot bear the ugliness of the world,' he said. The cabman touched his cap and nodded in agreement.

But, for once, Oscar was mistaken. The stage door-keeper was no grotesque. He was a handsome young African boy, a shiny-faced youth with huge eyes and brilliant white teeth. 'By all that's wonderful!' cried Oscar. 'I expected to find Cerberus at the gates of Hades. Instead I find an old friend. Robert, this is Antipholus!'

The boy – he must gave been fifteen or sixteen years of age – sprang to his feet and, emerging from the stage doorkeeper's cubbyhole, bowed low to us both. Oscar shook the lad warmly by the hand and at once reached into his waistcoat pocket to find a sovereign to present to him by way of greeting.

The youth beamed at Oscar. 'Thank you, Mr Wilde. You've not changed.'

'Whereas you've grown, my friend,' said Oscar, spinning the boy around and inspecting him. 'Antipholus was a boot boy at the Savoy when first we met,' he added by way of explanation. 'Now he appears to have run away to the circus.' He looked into the boy's face anxiously. 'What are you doing here, Antipholus?'

'I'm going to be a clown, Mr Wilde,' said the boy happily.

'Oh, Mary, Mother of God!' cried Oscar. 'A clown! A clown!' He clapped his hands over his eyes. 'What's wrong with the youth of today, Robert?' he wailed. 'I fear for the future of the empire.'

The boy looked at Oscar and began to giggle. 'You really haven't changed, Mr Wilde,' he laughed. 'It was you who told me that if I was to succeed in life I'd have to learn to walk a tightrope. I'm only doing what you told me.'

Oscar's eyes were pricked with tears, but he was smiling. 'May the gracious Lord forgive me,' he cried. 'It seems it's all my fault!'

Suddenly the laughing boy looked anxious. 'Oh, Mr Wilde,' he said, 'I hope you haven't come to see the circus? The circus has gone to Blackpool for the summer.'

'No, Antipholus.' Oscar raised his fists and punched the air playfully. 'We're here for the boxing. We're in search of a Mr David McMuirtree.'

'"Mighty McMuirtree – David and Goliath"?'

'Is that what he's called?'

'He's inside, sir. With his lordship.'

'With "Lord" George Sanger?' I chipped in, eager to show off my circus knowledge.

'I think not,' said Oscar, looking at me despairingly.

'Oh, no, sir,' said the boy. '"Lord" George is in Blackpool. This is a real lord. I'll take you through. Follow me.'

We followed the boy through a heavy metal door and down some shallow steps. 'Mind your heads!' he called as he ducked down sharply and led us under a stone arch and into a long, dark, low-ceilinged, narrow, curving corridor. The walls were of bare brick; the ground under-foot was sodden.

'It smells of rats,' said Oscar.

'They come back as soon as the dogs are gone,' explained Antipholus. He laughed. 'It's worse than the Savoy kitchens here. Don't stop unless I tell you. Whatever you tread on, keep moving.'

'Are there no gas lamps?' I called. The boy and Oscar were some way ahead of me. I could barely discern their figures in the gloom.

'"Lord" George runs a tight ship.' The boy giggled. 'Don't worry – we're nearly there.'

'The stench is unbearable,' said Oscar.

On the ground a creature scuttled past me. 'This is hideous, Oscar,' I hissed.

'This is the circus, Robert.'

'Stop!' cried the boy. 'We're here!' Through the gloom I could just see the outline of his head. 'Come,' he called, pushing open a door at the end of the tunnel. Immediately beyond the door were heavy black curtains. They were rough to the touch and smelt of rotten apples and sawdust. Antipholus pulled them back and released us from our hole into the vast arena of Astley's amphitheatre.

I had expected the place to be a blaze of light – the shining palace I remembered from my childhood. Instead, it was a deserted cathedral, as dark and cavernous as Fingal's Cave. It took a moment for our eyes to adjust to the half-light. We appeared to have entered the arena from beneath the stage: we were at ground level, facing the auditorium, standing at the outer edge of the circus ring, in the centre of which was what, for a brief instant, I took to be an altar.

It was not an altar, of course. It was a large square dais, raised some four feet off the ground. And standing on the dais, leaning on the ropes of what I now realised was a boxing ring, was the arresting figure of David McMuirtree. He was quite naked. His powerful arms, his broad shoulders, his wide chest – brown and hairless – glistened with sweat. 'Mr Wilde, Mr Sherard,' he rasped, 'Welcome to the Ring of Death!'

I looked back to the curtains beneath the stage. Antipholus had disappeared.

'We've disturbed your rehearsal,' said Oscar, apologetically, removing his hat in some confusion and bowing awkwardly.

McMuirtree murmured: 'I'm a fighter, not an actor, Mr Wilde.' He picked up a plum-coloured dressing gown that was lying in the corner of the ring and, without hurrying, slipped it on. 'I don't rehearse. I train. I practise. I've been sparring with Lord Queensberry. You know one another, I'm sure.'

Out of the gloom on the far side of the ring stepped the squat and anthropoidal figure of John Sholto, 8th Marquess of Queensberry. With small white hands he was tucking his shirt-tails into his grey-check flannel trousers. His cuffs were loose; his feet were bare. He sniffed contemptuously and furrowed his thick black eyebrows. Not acknowledging my presence, he looked directly at Oscar and grunted his name: 'Wilde.'

Oscar stepped forward and bowed once more, this time less awkwardly. 'Your Grace,' he murmured, 'An unexpected pleasure. I've just seen Lord Drumlanrig – in Eastbourne.'

Queensberry sniffed again and wiped his nose with the back of his hand. 'I believe you see more of my sons than I do, Mr Wilde. Doubtless you have the time.'

'Time—' Oscar began . . . But his aphorism was still-born.

'Time waits for no man,' grunted Queensberry, picking up his stockings, boots and jacket from the side of the ring. He ducked nimbly between the ropes and jumped down into the arena. Casting his jacket over his shoulder, without turning back towards us, he strode steadily up one of the gangways and out of the auditorium. He called to McMuirtree as he went: 'Good day, my friend. We're making progress. On Monday we make history.'

When he had gone, McMuirtree stood smiling, gazing after him. 'He's a great man,' he said, in his curious croaking voice, 'but he lacks charm.' He turned and looked down towards Oscar. 'Whereas you, Mr Wilde – you always have something charming to say.'

'When men give up saying what is charming,' Oscar answered, 'they give up thinking what is charming. I hope I'll never do that.'

I was still reflecting on the charmlessness of the departed marquess. 'Is he really such a great man?' I asked.

'If you're a boxing man, he is, Mr Sherard, no question. The Queensberry Rules have transformed the game, turned it from near-lawless brawling into something approximating a sport.' McMuirtree held his arms out wide and looked about him. 'We call this "The Ring of Death" because that's what it used to be. Men fought like dogs and fought to the death – no holds barred. The crowds jeered them on. The referees did nothing. It was brute force and staying-power that won the day. Now, thanks to Queensberry, skill has a chance. Strategy, too. Psychology, even. Prize-fighting was licensed barbarism until his lordship came along. It's taken him more than twenty years to get the rules established, but on Monday we have our show bout here and, if all goes well, after the summer, for the first time, the heavyweight championship of the world will be decided under the Queensberry Rules. Have no doubt: as long as grown men fight, the Marquess of Queensberry will be remembered.'

'He has joined the ranks of the immortals then,' said Oscar, lightly.

McMuirtree had gathered up two pairs of boxing gloves. He stood at the edge of the ring holding them aloft for us. 'Care for a friendly knock-about, gentlemen? No biting, gouging, wrestling allowed – strictly Queensberry Rules.'

'No, thank you,' Oscar protested, waving his hands anxiously in the air. 'I'm not one for the martial arts.'

'But you have a boxer's build, Mr Wilde,' said McMuirtree, bending down and stepping between the ropes. He jumped to the ground in front of us. 'And something of a reputation.'

'I don't know about that,' said Oscar, laughing. I sensed that my friend was unnerved by McMuirtree's physical presence. He was also thrown because he had run out of cigarettes.

'I've heard the stories,' said McMuirtree, fixing Oscar with his eyes.

'The stories?' repeated Oscar.

'How at Trinity College, Dublin, the class bully sneered at your poem and you struck him across the face – and how, when honour had to be satisfied with fists in the open air, within moments you had floored him. How at Magdalen College, Oxford, when philistine students came mob-handed to break up your room, you threw them bodily down stairs – each and every one.'

Oscar stepped back and looked at McMuirtree in amazement. The boxer, still holding the gloves in either hand, turned to me. 'Your friend Mr Wilde plays the aesthete, Mr Sherard, poses as a shrinking violet, but he's nothing of the sort. He can use his fists, I know. He can use a gun, I know. He's a fine shot.'

'Have we met before, Mr McMuirtree?' asked Oscar quietly.

'We have, Mr Wilde. At a shooting party in Connemara. In November '79. With the Hicks-Beach family. The shooting was good.'

Oscar appeared quite flustered. 'I'm afraid I don't recall,' he said. 'Please forgive me.'

'Nothing to forgive,' said McMuirtree genially. 'It was a large party and, in my experience, you're only half noticed when you're only half-a-gentleman.'

Oscar appeared dumbfounded.

'Are you from Connemara?' I asked, feeling that, somehow, my friend needed rescuing. It was so rare for him not to be in command of every conversation.

'No,' said McMuirtree, 'I'm from Dublin, like Mr Wilde. I was brought up in Clare Street, a stone's throw from Merrion Square. I'm three years older than Mr Wilde. I've known of the Wilde family all my life. Mr Wilde and I once had a sweetheart in common.'

Gradually Oscar was recovering himself. 'Oh?' he smiled. 'Who would that be?'

'Florrie Balcombe, of course.' McMuirtree turned to me. 'She was the prettiest girl in Dublin.'

'She was indeed,' said Oscar. 'I had no idea you knew her.'

'I did not know her as well as I would have liked. I only kissed her the once. I did not know her as well as you did, Mr Wilde. Nor as well as Mr Stoker.'

Oscar laughed. 'Bram got the better of us both. He married her.'

A silence fell among us. 'You don't by any chance have a cigarette on you, do you?' asked Oscar.

David McMuirtree, naked but for a dressing gown, let the two pairs of heavy boxing gloves he was holding fall to the ground and, with his fist tightly clenched, reached his right hand out towards Oscar's right ear. Oscar flinched. McMuirtree laughed and pulled his fist away and held it out in front of Oscar and slowly opened it. There, lying in the palm of his hand was a single cigarette. 'Player's Navy Cut, Mr Wilde – not a gentleman's cigarette, but the best I can do.'

Oscar clapped his hands with delight and took the cigarette and lit it at once, drawing on it with deep satisfaction. 'I'm much indebted to you, Mr McMuirtree,' he said. 'You are a phenomenon, sir. I had come to offer you counsel, but it's clear you don't need my help. I'm certain there's nothing I can tell you that you don't already know.'

McMuirtree bent to the ground to retrieve his gloves. 'Is this about your game?' he asked.

'Yes,' said Oscar. 'My foolish game of "Murder".'

'Don't take it seriously, Mr Wilde. I don't.'

'Perhaps you should,' I ventured.

'"Seriousness is the only refuge of the shallow" – is that not so, Mr Wilde?'

Oscar looked at McMuirtree appraisingly. 'You attended my lecture on *The New Philosophy*?'

'I did,' answered the boxer. 'I am interested in modern philosophy.'

'And modern psychology, too, I think,' said Oscar, holding McMuirtree's cigarette out before him and turning it between his fingers. 'You are interested in men's impulses. You like to know what drives them.'

'I am a fighter by trade, Mr Wilde. I look for men's weaknesses – and their strengths. I did not go to the University as you did, but I can read. I read the modern psychologists. I have William James's *The Principles of Psychology* on my bedside table.'

Oscar laughed. 'And I have one of his brother's mighty tomes on my bedside table, too. Who in England now abed needs a sleeping draught while the James brothers are busy scribbling?'

Obligingly, McMuirtree croaked a small laugh of his own. From the side pocket of his dressing gown he produced another cigarette and handed it to Oscar.

'You are a remarkable man, Mr McMuirtree,' said Oscar, nodding his thanks and immediately lighting the second cigarette from the first. Pugilist, psychologist, philosopher – but even you are not invulnerable.'

'You think I am in danger?' rasped McMuirtree, evidently amused.

'I am concerned for your safety, Mr McMuirtree,' said Oscar solemnly.

'Do not be.'

'I feel responsible. Last Sunday you came to our club dinner, as our guest, in good faith . . .'

'And I left in good heart. And I'm safe and sound as you can see.'

'But Mr McMuirtree,' Oscar persisted, 'on each successive day since Sunday last something unfortunate has befallen each successive "victim".'

'Is the bearded actor dead then?' asked the boxer.

'Bradford Pearse has vanished,' said Oscar.

'We fear the worst,' I added.

'I'm sorry to hear that,' said McMuirtree. 'I liked the man.'

'Did you know him?' asked Oscar.

'Our paths had crossed,' answered the boxer. 'I know a lot of people.'

'The point is,' said Oscar, sucking from the first cigarette a final inhalation of delight before drawing at once upon the second, 'if this is murder and there's a chronology to it, you're next, Mr McMuirtree. Tomorrow is your turn . . .'

'Tomorrow,' said McMuirtree, smiling, 'Or Saturday or Sunday or Monday – wouldn't you say? I was named four times, after all.'

'You were,' said Oscar. 'Why do you think that was?'

'I have no idea. None at all.'

'Who might have chosen you as their victim?'

'I cannot tell you, Mr Wilde. I've not the least notion.' He turned and began to walk towards the gangway. He motioned to us to follow. 'Mr Charles Brookfield might have done so, I suppose,' he suggested, without much conviction. 'Brookfield's temper was certainly uneven that night. I don't think he appreciated having the club secretary – not quite a gentleman – seated on his right. I don't think he enjoyed sitting opposite me. I know he was irritated by my green carnation.'

'When we played the game, Mr McMuirtree,' asked Oscar, 'who did you chose as your particular victim?'

'Oh, I played safe. Queensberry Rules. I don't punch below the belt. I chose Eros, god of love.'

'Eros?' queried Oscar. 'Eros is a curious choice for a prize-fighter.'

'Come, Mr Wilde. It's not only the disciples of aestheticism who know that love's a devil.'

We had reached the top of the gangway. McMuirtree held open a glass-fronted polished oak door that led to the amphitheatre's mirrored entrance hall. 'If you'll excuse me, gentlemen, I must go and change.' Evidently our audience was at an end. 'Thank you for coming by. Thank you for the warning.'

'Thank you for the cigarettes,' said Oscar, smiling. 'And thank you for the tickets for Monday night – the gala bout.'

'You're coming?'

'A ringside seat for history? How could I refuse? And, by way of reciprocation, Mr McMuirtree, if you'd be amused to see my play I'm taking a party to the St James's Theatre on Saturday night – I'd be honoured if you'd join us.'

McMuirtree bowed. 'I'd be delighted, Mr Wilde, thank you.' With one hand he was holding open the door for us; with the other he was indicating our way across the vestibule to the exit to the street.

'Excellent,' said Oscar, adjusting his hat, but not yet moving through the doorway. 'I'll leave a ticket in your name at the box office.'

'Excellent,' echoed McMuirtree. 'Forgive me if I go now.'

'Oh,' said Oscar, putting out his hand and touching the boxer's arm, 'One more thing, if you would. The parrot. The Cadogan Hotel parrot. Who do you think killed the parrot?'

'Oh, Mr Wilde, I've really no idea.'

'I'd value your opinion. Please.'

'Well,' said McMuirtree, with a sigh, 'they say, don't they, that those found first at the scene of the crime are the most likely suspects? So it could be you or Mr Sherard, I suppose, or me or Alphonse Byrd, or even Mrs Wilde or Mrs Wilde's friend, Mr Heron-Allen . . . But isn't it most likely to be a disaffected member of the hotel staff or an irate guest infuriated by the creature's constant squawking and yabbering?'

'Do you think Mr Byrd could have killed the parrot?' asked Oscar.

'No, it won't have been Byrd. He truly loved the wretched creature.'

'Then who?'

'I don't know who would want to do such a thing – and in such a brutal fashion.'

'You're interested in psychology, Mr McMuirtree. What would a modern psychologist tell us?'

'All sorts of nonsense. He might tell you that Mr Heron-Allen murdered the parrot because he is in love with your wife. Heron-Allen is a solicitor. He dares not murder you, so instead he kills a defenceless creature whose exotic plumage rivals your own . . .'

'That's an amusing notion,' said Oscar. 'I did not realise that Heron-Allen had made his feelings so self-evident.'

'He might suggest that Mrs Wilde was guilty of the crime because her great-grandfather had a collection of eighty stuffed birds and as a child the oppressive presence of the birds provoked nightmares in the little girl . . .'

Oscar's eyes narrowed. 'How do you know all this?'

'He might even suggest that you are the guilty party, Mr Wilde.'

'Me?' said Oscar, laughing.

'At Magdalen, was not the college organist called Parratt? Was he not a friend of yours? Did he not come to stay with you in Dublin in '74? Did you and he not have a notorious falling-out?'

'Good grief, man! You know everything about me.'

McMuirtree laughed as he held out his hand once more to point us on our way. 'Not everything, Mr Wilde, far from it. Would that I did . . . But I keep my eyes and ears open. It's in the blood. My father was a footman, as you know.'

15

Gilmour of the Yard

'What a remarkable fellow,' said Oscar, chuckling, as we emerged from the deserted foyer of Astley's amphitheatre onto the Westminster Bridge Road. It was a perfect May evening: the low, round, orange sun had turned the stonework on the Thames embankment gold; there was a warming breeze in the air and that special smell of the London of my youth – the comforting smell of hay and horses.

'I don't like him, Oscar,' I said. 'He's arrogant. He's impertinent. He's—'

'He confuses you, Robert. You don't know where you are with him, that's all. If Bosie or Drumlanrig spoke as he does, you'd think nothing of it. They're toffs. They can do as they please. But McMuirtree . . . he's half-a-gentleman. And that ain't easy – for you or him. He's walking a tightrope.'

'I don't like him,' I persisted. 'I don't trust him.'

'Whereas you have no such qualms about my little friend Antipholus?'

'Indeed not.'

'Is it because he's black and knows his place?'

There was no time to protest. We had already crossed the street and were standing face to face with the bright-eyed

African boy whose beaming smile I did indeed trust instinctively.

Antipholus was not alone. He was leaning against the stone parapet overlooking the river with, at his side, an enchanting child – a *petite* black girl of perhaps nine or ten years of age – and, next to her, the Hon. the Reverend George Daubeney. The trio were scrutinising a stout piece of card the size of a quarto volume – and laughing.

The moment he registered our presence, Antipholus sprang to attention.

'Mr Wilde, Mr Wilde's friend, may I have the honour to present to you my sister, Bertha?'

The little girl, who was dressed in the simplest white smock, curtsied low and squeezed her eyes tight shut and bit her lip as Oscar bent down to her and shook her by the hand.

'You are very pretty,' he said to her softly.

'She is very beautiful, Oscar,' declared George Daubeney loudly. 'She is a princess, Robert – a fairy-tale princess.' He leant over to us each in turn and shook us vigorously by the hand.

'You're in fine form, George,' said Oscar, cocking his head to one side as he examined the clergyman. 'You seem dressed *en prince* yourself.' Indeed, since we had seen him last, Daubeney appeared to be a man transformed. His eyes were still puffy and drawn; his skin was rough and grey; there were trickles of moisture at the edge of his mouth; but the man's defeated hang-dog look was entirely gone. He wore his frayed clerical collar as before, but his black serge curate's suit had been replaced by a dandy's frock coat with shiny silk reveres.

'I'm a happy man,' he said, giving one of the girl's little pigtails an affectionate tug. 'I'm a free man. A cloud has lifted.'

'Ah?' said Oscar. 'The inquest.'

'The coroner's court met this morning, at eleven clock sharp, in the front parlour of the Pier Hotel, Cheyne Walk, and the business was done and dusted before the parlour clock had struck the half-hour. The jury followed the coroner's lead and endorsed the verdict of the Metropolitan Police and the London Fire Brigade: "Miss Elizabeth Scott-Rivers – Death by misadventure".'

'Congratulations,' said Oscar.

'You'd have been gratified, my friend. In his summing-up, the coroner – a lovely man, a sort of Mr Pickwick but Irish – made specific reference to the important pioneering work of the Rational Dress Society.'

'Indeed,' said Oscar, pursing his lips and teasing his eyebrows with his index finger. 'When all this is over, I'll report the good news to Constance.'

'Well done, George,' I added warmly. 'Bravo. I think a drink is called for.'

'I've had several already, large ones,' Daubeney cried out happily, 'and I'm proposing to have several more, larger still!'

'Is there news of Miss Scott-Rivers's Last Will and Testament?' Oscar enquired. 'Had she revised it as you feared? Or are useful bags of red and yellow gold shortly to be put at your disposal?'

'You don't miss a trick, do you, Oscar?' Daubeney was now holding both of Bertha's pretty little pigtails and pulling her head from side to side as he spoke. 'It seems that my erstwhile fiancée had advised her solicitor of her intention to change her will, but had not yet done so . . . She had made an appointment to rearrange her affairs, but failed to keep it. It is not entirely certain – there is the possibility that her family will dispute the will as it stands – but, according to your friend Heron-Allen – a capital fellow, by the way, my kind of lawyer – the odds are in my favour. It looks indeed as though the booty will be mine.'

'He has brought us presents, Mr Wilde!' Antipholus announced with glee.

Daubeney released Bertha's pigtails and raised his open palms towards us, adopting a sudden, solemn air. 'I regret my fiancée's passing – of course I do. We were no longer friends, but I wished her no harm. Whatever she has left me I shall use for God's purpose. It shall all be devoted to the education and welfare of the young.' He leant forward and kissed the top of Bertha's head.

'He's brought some shag for me,' said Antipholus, holding out a handful of tobacco, 'and for Bertha these ribbons and this hoop.' The boy held up one of his sister's pigtails to show off the pale blue ribbon tied to the end of it in a dainty bow. The girl, who was holding the wooden hoop in her left hand, tried to hide it behind her brother's back.

'I'm chaplain here, these are my charges,' said Daubeney, offering us a beatific smile.

'You're drunk,' said Oscar. 'I'm not surprised.'

Bertha took hold of the clergyman's hand and kissed him lightly on the knuckles.

'The hoop is in exchange for the photograph,' Daubeney explained.

'Look!' said Antipholus proudly. He held up the piece of card that the trio had been admiring when Oscar and

I had discovered them. It was a photograph – a fine studio photograph – of the little girl in fancy dress. In the picture she was seated on a small three-legged stool, dressed in a patched and ragged skirt with a checked shawl about her shoulders. Her head was tilted to one side, resting against the handle of a kitchen broom. Her hair was untied, full and frizzy. Her shining eyes were looking out straight towards the camera. There were large tears trickling down her cheeks.

'She's playing Cinderella,' explained Antipholus.

'The tears aren't real,' added George Daubeney.

'I trust not,' said Oscar, examining the photograph closely. 'I imagine they are drops of glycerol. He's a clever young man, Master Archer.'

'Who?' I asked.

'The photographer,' said Oscar, pointing to the imprint in the bottom right-hand corner of the picture. It read: *John Archer, Battersea Park Road, London S.* 'I know him. He comes from Barbados, by way of Liverpool and Ponder's End. He's a bright spark, full of intelligence and invention. Every other photographer makes one look like a stockbroker facing a firing squad. Archer's taken my likeness twice – and Bosie's – and, to our mutual amazement, on both occasions we almost liked what we looked like. We appeared quite human. To be natural is such a very difficult pose to keep up. Master Archer knows how to contrive it. The boy will go far.'[*]

Oscar returned the photograph to Bertha, who handed it to George Daubeney, who slipped it into the inside

---

[*] He did. In 1913, aged fifty, he was elected mayor of Battersea and became Britain's second black mayor.

pocket of his elegant knee-length frock coat. 'Did you mention a celebratory drink, Robert?' he asked, circling his index finger in the air, and looking at me while winking at Oscar out of the corner of his eye. 'Shall we get him to take us somewhere rather grand, Oscar? It's not often that one becomes a wealthy widower without having had to experience the miseries of matrimony. I think a glass or two is in order, don't you?'

'I'm spoken for, alas,' said Oscar, bowing his head towards Daubeney. 'Robert will look after you – and Antipholus will take care of me. He'll roll me a cigarette while we talk of old times and then he'll find me a cab – won't you, my friend?'

The black boy stood to attention once more and gave Oscar a brisk salute.

'We'll go Gatti's in the Arches then,' said Daubeney. 'You can pay for the champagne, Robert. The entertainment's free. Come.' The merry cleric shook Oscar by the hand once more, playfully boxed Antipholus on the ear, ceremoniously kissed Bertha on the forehead and put his arm through mine. 'I'm free!' he cried as we turned and set off across Westminster Bridge.

'Take care!' called Oscar as we departed. 'I'll send you a wire later, Robert. The game's afoot. I'll need you tomorrow morning – sober!'

In the event I did not drink heavily that night. In fact, I was back in my upstairs room in Gower Street before ten o'clock, enjoying a solitary glass of bottled beer. Daubeney was not diverting company. As we walked arm in arm along the embankment, from Westminster Bridge towards Charing Cross, he entertained passers-by by singing a selection of his favourites from the Anglican Hymnal. I tried to distract him – and cover my embarrassment – with earnest conversation, but he would have none of it. 'Sing up, Robert!' he cried. 'Praise the Lord! Hallelujah!' From a pocket in his frock coat – a different pocket from the one in which he had secreted the photograph of Bertha – he produced a leather-cased hip flask and, between hymns, he pressed me to join him in taking a libation.

'It's altar wine, customarily kept about me in the event that I am called upon to administer the blessed sacrament in an emergency – but you may take a swig, Robert. Indeed, you must. The Lord wants it. Praise the Lord!'

When we reached the pier below Charing Cross Station, by the corner of Hungerford Lane, quite suddenly, he calmed himself. He slipped the hip flask back into his pocket and, with his long, thin fingers, carefully wiped the saliva from the corners of his mouth and slicked back his hair. 'Do you know the hall beneath the railway arches?' he asked.

'The music hall?' I said. 'Yes. I've been here with Oscar and with Wat Sickert. It's one of Sickert's regular haunts. He's painted it often.'

'Have you been backstage?' asked Daubeney, leading us up the lane and into Villiers Street.

'No.'

'You're in for a treat. For a modest payment, if you're a gentleman, Mr Corazza, the manager, allows you to spend the evening in the chorus girls' dressing room. Armchairs are provided. You can watch the girls as they dress. And undress. You may even play with their titties. With the young ones, you may swallow them whole like peaches.'

Beneath the broadest of the railway arches, at the front entrance of the hall itself, the evening's audience was gathering. The Hungerford Palace Music Hall (better known as Gatti's in the Arches) attracted a universal crowd – butchers, bakers, clerks and costermongers, shop-girls and matrons, noisy swells-about-town and diffident young lovers new to the West End. Other than George Daubeney, however, there appeared to be no one else in holy orders. I followed the frock-coated cleric as he pushed his way through the throng and led us into the shadows, to the arch beyond.

'Here we are,' he said, knocking conspiratorially on an unmarked door.

'I think I'll leave you to it,' I said, 'if you'll forgive me. It's been a long day.'

'As you please, Robert,' he replied, as, slowly, the door opened and a pretty young woman, with close-cropped red hair and a painted face, looked out.

She recognised Daubeney at once and smiled and opened the door further to let him in. 'Is your friend coming, Georgie?' she asked, wrinkling up her nose and glancing at me with amusement. Beneath her chemise I saw the outline of her breasts.

'No, I must be going,' I said quickly. 'Take care, George. Goodnight.'

'We'll look after the padre, mister,' said the girl, laughing and pulling him across the threshold. 'We'll take care of Georgie, never fear.'

At nine o'clock the following morning – Friday 6 May 1892 – as, alone in my room, I breakfasted on a cold pork sausage and a slice of bread and dripping (and thought back to the glories of Mrs Fletcher's goose egg, sliced ham and mutton cutlets of twenty-four hours before), the telegraph boy arrived with Oscar's promised summons:

MEET ME AT GILMOURS OFFICE AT TEN. OSCAR.

I was not in funds. I was writing my novel, but had not yet sold it. I had sold two articles that month, but had not yet been paid for either. My landlord was pressing me for rent that was overdue. My estranged wife's solicitor was pressing me for maintenance payments 'on account'. As Oscar liked to say (and said in different ways on different days): 'Young people imagine that money is everything; when they grow older, they know it.'

I was not in funds, so I took neither the bus nor a cab, but walked in well-worn shoes the three miles across town from Gower Street to Great Scotland Yard. In consequence I did not reach the offices of the Criminal Investigations Department of the Metropolitan Police until gone half past ten.

I found Oscar already ensconced in Archy Gilmour's room and in full flow. The room was gloomy and airless, small and sparsely furnished. My friend was perched uncomfortably on the edge of a hard-backed office chair, dressed in one of his more flamboyant summer outfits – the jacket and trousers were dove grey; the high-fastening waistcoat was canary yellow; over grey ankle boots he wore yellow fabric spats; his buttonhole comprised a golden hibiscus laid against a sprig of lavender; he held a straw boater and yellow kid gloves upon his lap.

When Gilmour's sergeant showed me in, the detective inspector (dressed, much as I was, in a workaday brown worsted suit) was facing Oscar, half standing, leaning against a heavy oak desk, his arms folded across his chest, listening attentively.

'Good morning, Mr Sherard,' he said agreeably (I was gratified that he recalled my name), 'take a pew.' He did not move: he nodded towards the hard-back chair adjacent to Oscar's. 'Mr Wilde tells a tale as few men can. I'm gripped. He should be writing for *Police News and Law Courts Weekly Record*.'

'I have confessed all, Robert. I have broken the Socrates Club solemn oath of secrecy. I have told the inspector all about our dinner at the Cadogan Hotel on Sunday last and about our foolish game of "Murder" – *my* foolish game of "Murder"! He has listened with exquisite courtesy, despite appearing to be familiar already with all the salient details.'

'We had George Daubeney in for questioning, as you'll recall,' explained the inspector. 'He was very forthcoming – co-operative to a fault. He came clean at once – told us all about the dinner and the game and how he'd named his former fiancée as his intended "victim".'

'Do you think, in fact, he might have murdered her?' I asked.

Gilmour shook his head. 'Murdered her? Having first advertised his desire to do so? I think not.'

'He's a drinker,' I said. 'Men do wild and unexpected things in drink.'

The inspector laughed. 'They walk into walls, not through them. At Number 27 Cheyne Walk the doors at front and back and down below were all locked and bolted from within. The Reverend Daubeney was on the outside looking in. He witnessed the fire. He didn't start it. Miss Scott-Rivers was alone when she died.'

'What did you make of Daubeney?' asked Oscar, turning his straw boater around slowly on his lap. 'As a man, I mean? Did you like him?'

'No,' said the inspector emphatically. 'I did not like him. He's an odd fish. He's a drinker, as Mr Sherard says – you can see it in his face. And he's weak. When we'd finished questioning him, he sat there – in that chair where you're seated now, Mr Wilde – and he wept. He wept like a woman. Not a pretty sight.'

'Weeping is always ugly,' said Oscar.

The red-headed policeman sighed. 'Well, gentlemen,' he said, standing upright and rubbing his hands together. 'I'm grateful to you for calling – and, of course, we must keep in touch – but, candidly, I don't think that anything that has occurred this week suggests that there's a new and unknown murderer in our midst.' He began to move towards the door. It was evident our interview was over.

'Look at the list!' pleaded Oscar, waving his yellow kid gloves in the direction of the sheet of folded foolscap that was lying on the inspector's desk.

Gilmour stepped back and picked up Oscar's list of 'victims'. 'I have,' he said. 'I do.' His eyes scanned the paper. 'Elizabeth Scott-Rivers died in a fire caused by accident. That's the coroner's verdict. Lord Abergordon was an elderly gentleman who died in sleep. That's his doctor's opinion – and mine also. The actor, Bradford Pearse, appears to have taken his own life. He was in debt; he was pursued by creditors; his spirit was low. The correspondence you've shown me confirms as much. He has thrown himself off Beachy Head. It's a common enough occurrence, alas.'

'What about the parrot?' asked Oscar. 'What about poor Captain Flint?'

'Killing wild birds is not yet a criminal offence in England,' replied Archy Gilmour.

'Indeed,' said Oscar, getting to his feet. 'Among a certain class, it is a national pastime.'

Gilmour chuckled. 'I do feel for poor Captain Flint,' he said kindly, 'but there's nothing I can do.'

'You're a feeling fellow,' said Oscar shaking the inspector by the hand. 'You are a vegetarian, of course.'

The inspector looked suitably surprised. 'How do you know?'

'By looking at your teeth, Inspector. There's a tiny fleck of lettuce and a crumb of bread and butter on either side of your left canine tooth. Only a truly committed vegetarian would breakfast on a salad sandwich.'

Gilmour burst out laughing and pulled open his office door. 'You're a wonder, Mr Wilde – a prince of party tricks. You're your own detective. You don't need any help from me.'

'Oh, but I do, Inspector.' Oscar stood his ground as Gilmour hovered by the door. 'Look at the next name on that list of potential victims, Inspector . . . Would you be so kind?'

Gilmour glanced at the paper once more. 'Mr David McMuirtree.'

'He's an interesting fellow,' said Oscar. 'A well-connected boxer. A fine figure of a man. He works at Astley's amphitheatre. Four people chose Mr McMuirtree as their "victim". I believe his life might be at risk, Inspector. I have come here to ask you to give him police protection.'

'We already do,' said Archy Gilmour. 'He's one of us, you see.'

An Appointment in Baker Street

'I stand amazed,' said Oscar. 'David McMuirtree is a serving officer with the Metropolitan Police?'

'No longer,' said Gilmour, still holding open his office door and standing by it in evident anticipation of our imminent departure. 'He was.'

Oscar put down his hat and gloves on the inspector's oak desk. 'When was this?' he asked.

'In the 'seventies,' answered Gilmour, running his tongue along his gums to clear the fleck of lettuce from his teeth. 'He joined up soon after leaving Ireland. It's no secret. He was the Metropolitan Police boxing champion for six years in a row. You'll find his name in gold letters on a board downstairs. You'll have passed it in the entrance hall. With your eagle eyes, Mr Wilde, I'm surprised you missed it.'

'But he's not a policeman now?' persisted Oscar, still standing by the detective inspector's desk.

'No. He served ten years and then, rashly in my view, he decided to take his chance as a professional boxer. Joined the circuit – threw his hat into the ring, as it were. He's done well enough, I think. He's survived. But I don't believe he has enjoyed the success he had hoped for. Professional boxing's a dirty game, though it's getting cleaner, slowly, thanks to the likes of Lord Lonsdale and Lord Queensberry.'

'McMuirtree left the Metropolitan Police,' said Oscar reflectively, 'but I take it he did not lose touch?'

'Correct.'

'McMuirtree is a police informant.'

'He moves among all kinds and conditions of men,' replied Gilmour. 'He is intelligent. He is observant. We find him invaluable.'

'And you reward him for his efforts?'

'The labourer is worthy of his hire.'

Oscar retrieved his hat and gloves and turned to Inspector Gilmour and looked him directly in the eye. 'Tell me,' he asked, 'did McMuirtree come to the Cadogan club dinner as a spy?'

'Not at all. He went simply as the guest of your club secretary – Mr Byrd, is it not? I understand McMuirtree and Byrd have been friends for some years. "Fairground friends", you might say. McMuirtree was not at the Cadogan Hotel last Sunday on any business of ours. So far as I know, the Metropolitan Police has no special interest in any members of your club – or in their guests.' Gilmour folded over Oscar's list of 'victims' and handed the paper back to him. 'Our man McMuirtree is not permanently on duty, though I like to think he is always on the *qui vive*. He has nothing to fear from your circle, Mr Wilde, but among the criminal community, certainly, he has enemies – enemies he has made on our behalf. We recognise our responsibility towards him. We keep a watchful eye on David McMuirtree. You can rest easy on that score, Mr Wilde.'

We bade the red-headed detective farewell and took our leave. As we passed through the entrance hallway of Great Scotland Yard we paused to inspect the several honour boards hanging on the side wall adjacent to the stairs. Among the Met's sporting heroes we found McMuirtree's name without difficulty. As we regained the street, Oscar paused and adjusted his boater at a jaunty angle. He chuckled. 'We can rest easy, Robert. Gilmour of the Yard tells us so.' He tucked his arm into mine and glanced up towards the sunshine. 'A celebratory glass of Perrier Jouët is called for, I think, don't you? As we both know, a passion for pleasure is the secret of remaining young.'

Together we stepped across the pavement and into Oscar's carriage. If he liked the look of a cabby – or his horse – my profligate friend thought nothing of keeping a particular brougham waiting on him all day – and all night, too. 'Albemarle Street, driver,' he commanded.

'What now?' I asked, as we settled back into the cab.

'Cheese straws, I think, with the champagne,' he replied, grinning at me wickedly. 'There's a new pastry chef at Brown's Hotel. His savoury sweetmeats are proving controversial among the older *clientèle*. The boy needs our support.'

'What about the case?'

'You heard the inspector, Robert. Rest easy.'

I was surprised to find us going to Brown's. The hotel – founded by James Brown, Lord Byron's former valet – was not one of Oscar's regular haunts. He said he found the oak-panelling gloomy. On our arrival, therefore, I was doubly surprised to hear the hall-porter's effusive greeting of my friend: 'Back again, Mr Wilde? We can't keep you away.'

As he handed the man a shilling, I looked at Oscar enquiringly. 'I was here for breakfast, Robert – and to use the telephone. I have to say it is the most exciting device. It is going to change all our lives – especially if we are playwrights. Think if there'd been a telephone in Shakespeare's day – there'd have been no need for those long-winded and intrusive messengers.'

He led me through the hotel's entrance hall towards a large glass-fronted cabinet the size of a guardsman's sentry box. 'Look inside,' he said. 'There it is – the very apparatus from which Mr Graham Bell made the very first telephonic communication within the United Kingdom. When I'm in the West End, naturally, I come to Brown's to make all my calls. It is like going to the source of the Nile. I have an account.'

'And who were you calling this morning?' I asked, as we moved from the entrance hall into a somewhat dark and humid drawing room. An elderly waiter escorted us to a pair of leather armchairs, half hidden within a forest of potted palms. It was difficult to tell, but we appeared to be alone.

'A bottle of Perrier Jouët,' Oscar said to the waiter, 'preferably the 1880. And a dish, please, of Massimo's cheese straws.' He waited for the servant to leave before answering my question. 'I made two telephone calls this morning, Robert, both long-distance – which may explain why my voice is a little hoarse. The telephone is not yet suited to the whispering of sweet nothings. First, I called the police station at Eastbourne. They were not overly helpful, but they had at least made contact with the coastguard. There is no news of Bradford Pearse, alas – alive or dead. Next, I called South Norwood – the residence of Dr Arthur Conan Doyle.'

'And how was Arthur?'

'I cannot tell you. He would not come to the telephone. According to Mrs Doyle, he was in his shed, working on his sculpture and not to be disturbed. However, she assured me that he is expecting to join us at the theatre tomorrow night *and* he promises to be at the Tite Street fund-raiser on Sunday afternoon.'

'Are you still going ahead with it,' I asked, 'under the circumstances?'

'Of course!' he declared breezily. 'Why not?'

The elderly waiter arrived with our chilled champagne and Cheshire cheese straws. Happily, both fully lived up to their promise and Oscar's high expectation. As he sipped and nibbled, Oscar closed his eyes to savour the moment. When he opened them, he said: 'No civilised man ever regrets a pleasure, and no uncivilised man ever knows what a pleasure is.' He replenished my glass. 'How was George Daubeney?' he asked.

'Last night? I didn't stay long with him,' I said. 'He was drunk, as you saw. I left him at Gatti's, in the hands of a chorus girl.'

'Yes,' said Oscar, slowly draining his glass and smiling. 'The Anglican clergy do have a weakness in that direction.'

I laughed. Oscar broke the last cheese straw in two and offered me the plate.

'Can we really "rest easy"?' I asked.

'McMuirtree, we are assured, is in safe hands.'

'And Constance?' I said. 'Is she in safe hands?'

'At present, I believe so.'

'Is Edward Heron-Allen with her again today?' I enquired. I tried to ask the question coolly.

'He is,' said Oscar, brushing crumbs of pastry from his waistcoat onto the floor.

'Good God,' I exploded. 'Doesn't the man have a home of his own to go to?'

'He does,' said Oscar, 'and that is where his wife lives. He prefers to be at my house because that is where my wife lives. The peach-out-of-reach in the adjacent orchard is always more alluring than the apple on the ground in one's own.'

'Do you trust him, Oscar?'

'I trust Constance, Robert. Completely. But I also heard what McMuirtree said about her and Heron-Allen – and as I listened I read between the lines. Others do not know my wife as well as we do, Robert. I appreciate that I must have a care for her reputation as well as for her safety. You will be pleased to hear that, in consequence, tonight I have cancelled both my dinner with Bram Stoker and my supper with Bosie Douglas. I am going home this evening, to read a bedtime fairy story to my children and then to dine *à deux* with Mrs Wilde. And after dinner, to please her, we shall play a game of *piquet*. There is one thing infinitely more pathetic than to have lost the woman one is in love with, and that is to have won her and found out that her favourite recreation is a game of *piquet*.'

'But you love Constance,' I protested. 'I know you do.'

'I love her, Robert, but I no longer find her quite so *interesting* as once I did.' He looked at me with wide and mournful eyes. 'It happens,' he said. He emptied the remainder of the Perrier Jouët into our glasses. 'And what are your plans for this evening, Mr Sherard?'

'I'm seeing Sickert,' I said. 'We're going to a music hall.'

'Gatti's?' he asked, smiling.

'I don't know. Wherever Wat fancies.'

'Don't let him lead you astray, Robert. Don't stay out too late. I shall be requiring your services tomorrow. As ever, I need you as my witness.'

'We are not abandoning the case then?'

'Far from it. Today we may rest easy. Tomorrow we quiz a would-be murderer – in Baker Street.'

'In Baker Street?' I laughed. 'At 221b?'

'No,' he said. 'At the other end of the thoroughfare, at Number 20. You can't miss it. Our appointment's for twelve noon.'

'I won't be late,' I said.

But I was. Wat Sickert and I had what's known as 'a night on the town'. From dusk to dawn we ricocheted across London with gay abandon. Wat hired a two-wheeler for us for the purpose – and equipped it with crystal glasses and a bucket of champagne. Wat was as wanton with his money as Oscar, although his means were far fewer. We took in the early show at Gatti's in the Arches – where I failed to spot George Daubeney's friend in the chorus – and the late show at Collins's Music Hall on Islington Green – where Wat claimed to be 'hopelessly in love with the girl who plays Godiva'. (Her horse was real, but her hair was not.) We had lamb chops and boiled potatoes in Sydney's Supper House on the Strand and beer and wine and spirits (in which order I cannot remember) in a variety of restaurants and bars and public houses, from the Café Royal in Piccadilly Circus to the Olde Cheshire Cheese on Fleet Street. And everywhere we went Wat found a friend – a bar-maid or a flower-girl, an actress or an artist's model. He was easy with women in a way that I have never been. He was easy with life in a way that I have never dared to be. I noticed that night how he smoked his cigars the wrong way round – lighting that end which most people put in their mouths. He said that, with a Manila cigar, the smaller and more flavoursome leaves were always used at the narrow end. 'It's a shame not to enjoy them.' He claimed, too, that the cigar 'drew better' when puffed from the wider end. 'It's as they smoke them in the Philippines.'

At the end of the evening – when he had run out of cigars and the Cheshire Cheese was closing – Wat took me to a brothel in Maiden Lane.

'Why are we going here?' I asked.

'The address amuses me,' he said.

'But you're a married man, Wat. Is this right?'

'Oh, Robert,' he cried, 'this horrid Christian habit of inventing sins for everyone! I tell you, I don't understand it! I don't know what is meant by it! Let us all be happy. Let us allow a little elasticity in our domestic lives.'

Laughing suddenly, his arm around my shoulder, he marched me across the pavement and into the bordello. 'Robert, I'm bringing you here as much for your sake as for mine. This will do you good. There's no use you pining after Constance, Robert. Mrs Wilde is not to be had – for love nor money. You know it and that makes you sad. But when there's frustration in Tite Street there's consolation to be found in Maiden Lane. Solace and sweetness guaranteed – and five shillings top whack. You'll find no five-pound virgins here. These girls know their business. They won't disappoint. You'll like it, I promise.'

And, of course, at the time, I liked it – after a fashion. I was mad with desire. Wat was right about that. But on the morning after, while he awoke carefree, no doubt, I awoke with a headache and a familiar sense of *ennui*.

That Saturday – 7 May 1892, another 'bright day' according to my journal – I reached 20 Baker Street at one o'clock. I had no difficulty locating the address, but I was startled to find when I got there that it was a Turkish bath house. Its exterior appearance was deceptive. From the outside, the building looked like a Non-Conformist chapel in need of minor repairs; from within, it had the look of a caliph's palace in a Drury Lane pantomime. In the receiving room – a gold-and-green vestibule shaped like the inside of a giant beehive – I was greeted (if that's the word) by a pair of dwarfish attendants, ugly little men with yellow faces. Their heads appeared identical – they might have been twins – but their costumes could not have been more contrasting. One, the slightly taller of the two, wore a rough, brown serge suit and a grubby shirt, collarless and unbuttoned. The other was kitted out in full theatrical fig, dressed not so much as Ali Baba as one of his forty thieves. As I entered, the man in the brown suit glanced at me and then disappeared behind a saffron-coloured curtain at the back of the room. His companion looked at me without apparent interest and said curtly: 'First class or second? Three-and-six or half a crown?'

What tin I had I'd spent in Maiden Lane. 'I believe I'm expected,' I mumbled, not knowing what else to say. 'I'm joining Mr Wilde.'

The attendant grunted. 'Ah, so you's the "guest", is you?' His accent spoke more of the Old Kent Road than Old Baghdad. From a reed basket in the corner of the vestibule, he produced a linen towel and handed it to me. 'They'll be in the hot room by now. Down the stairs, fourth chamber on the left. Take yer time to get there or yer'll faint.' He laughed a little devil's laugh.

'Yer could faint anyway,' said a voice from behind the curtain. 'It's 160 degrees.'

I followed the attendant's advice and took my time. Beyond the vestibule, the building was as dark and dank and silent as a subterranean catacomb. In the first class changing room, where I undressed, there appeared to be no more than half a dozen other piles of discarded clothes. In the first of the steam chambers – it was heated by a brick flue, about three feet high and nine inches wide, that ran along three sides of the room – I found myself seated opposite a silver-bearded and obese old man (Sir John Falstaff, naked) whom I'd have taken for dead had it not been for his snoring; in the second chamber I sat alone, sweating heavily, breathing with difficulty, admiring the exquisite Craven Dunhill tiling all about me, but wondering how and why these curious – and not inexpensive – metropolitan hothouses had become so widespread and so popular so suddenly.

At last, I made my way into the final chamber. The heat in the 'hot room' was overwhelming and the steam so thick and sticky that it took me several moments to see that this is where they were: Oscar and his two companions, seated, close together, naked, on a porcelain slab, like Shadrach, Meshack and Abednego in the fiery furnace.

'Is that you, Robert?' whispered Oscar, faintly. *'Enfin!'*

'I'm so sorry—' I began.

He interrupted me. 'Don't apologise, Robert. We haven't time. I'm wanting his lordship to confess before we all boil to death.'

Either side of Oscar Wilde sat Lord Alfred Douglas and Francis, Viscount Drumlanrig. Oscar lounged between them like a beached porpoise: his skin was grey, with odd patches of livid pink; his arms and shoulders were heavy; his chest and stomach were covered with unsightly fat. He had a towel draped across his knees. Oscar, aged thirty-seven, looked like an old tart *en deshabillé* as drawn by Toulouse-Lautrec. The young men beside him, aged 21 and 24, looked like statues sculpted by Michelangelo. Their skin was white and smooth as alabaster. They were not handsome: they were beautiful.

'Why are we here?' I asked, bemused.

'Lord Drumlanrig is a director of the London and Provincial Turkish Bath Company. We are his guests, Robert. Apparently, this experience will do wonders for our health – cures the gout at a single sitting.'

'I thought we had come to cross-examine a potential murderer,' I said, sounding more irritable than I intended.

'We have. We are. Drumlanrig acknowledges that he chose the late Lord Abergordon as his "victim", but won't tell me why – nor if he did it.'

'Of course, I didn't "do it", Oscar,' replied Drumlanrig, closing his eyes and resting his head against the tiles behind him. 'And it's not just the gout that benefits from a Turkish bath. Dyspepsia, dropsy, scarlatina, impetigo . . . you name it, we cure it.'

'Why?' persisted Oscar, '*why* did you choose Abergordon as your "victim"?'

'Because he was an old booby.'

'That's not reason enough, Francis.'

Drumlanrig turned his head towards Oscar and opened his eyes. They were pale blue. 'If you must know, Oscar . . .'

'I must know.'

'If you must know . . .'

'My wife's life may depend on it,' said Oscar earnestly.

Drumlanrig's brow furrowed. 'I can't see how that can be. I really cannot.'

'Trust me.'

'Trust him,' said Bosie.

'Very well,' said Drumlanrig, sitting upright and covering himself with his towel. 'I did not murder Andrew Abergordon, but I wished him dead and – God forgive me – I am truly glad that he is gone. He made my life a hell.'

'I thought he was your godfather,' said Oscar.

'He was – and as my godfather he saw himself as the guardian of my moral welfare. He convinced himself that I had fallen into evil ways, "descended", as he put it, "into the pit of degradation".'

'What did he mean?' asked Oscar, wide-eyed.

'He accused me of committing unnatural acts with other men. And he accused my friend and patron, Lord Rosebery, of being my corrupter. Lord Abergordon told my father – and God knows who else – that I had committed the act of sodomy with the Earl of Rosebery.'

'With Primrose?' said Oscar.

I laughed. I could not help myself. 'Lord Rosebery is known as "Primrose"?' I spluttered.

'It is his family name,' said Oscar, smiling. 'Names, as you know, Robert, are everything.' Oscar turned back to Francis Drumlanrig. 'And were Lord Abergordon's accusations justified? Is that why you wished to see him dead?'

Drumlanrig got suddenly to his feet and turned towards Oscar. 'In no way were they justified. In no way whatsoever! They were vile calumnies – ruinous to my reputation.' He covered his face with his hands.

'And to that of Lord Rosebery,' said Oscar quietly.

'Indeed,' muttered Drumlanrig, now picking up his towel and wrapping it about his waist. 'Of course. Utterly ruinous – to us both. Abergordon was destroying our lives with his wretched lies – his vile calumnies, filthy falsehoods.'

'Methinks you do protest too much, Frankie,' whispered Bosie, his pretty head tilted to one side.

'I must protest,' cried Drumlanrig. 'It's all very well for you to talk about love among men, Bosie. You can apostrophise the virtues of Greek love for all you like – you want to be a poet! I want to be a politician. Lord Rosebery wants to be prime minister. Different rules apply.' The young viscount turned back towards Oscar. 'Yes, I wanted Abergordon silenced. I prayed that he might die. I wished it. I willed it. But I did not murder him.'

'Why did you go to Eastbourne on Thursday?' asked Oscar, sitting up and mopping his face with his towel.

'To Eastbourne – on Thursday?'

'To Eastbourne on Thursday.'

'If you must know . . .'

'I must know.'

'I went to Eastbourne on Thursday,' said Drumlanrig, 'to see the Duke of Devonshire – to talk politics. He has a house there. He invited me to dine. I am Lord Rosebery's secretary. By the autumn we shall have a Liberal government again. Mr Gladstone will be prime minister once more, no doubt. But even Mr Gladstone cannot go on for ever. When he goes, if the Duke of Devonshire does not succeed him, the Earl of Rosebery might.'

Oscar began to struggle to his feet. Bosie and I assisted him. He wrapped his towel around his waist and found another to throw across his shoulder. He beamed at us benevolently. 'I look like Caesar, do I not?' he asked. We laughed. He put a hand out and touched Francis Drumlanrig on the arm. 'Primrose Rosebery is much older than you, I think?'

'He is forty-five – forty-five today, as it happens. 7 May is his birthday.'

'And you love him? And he loves you?'

'I admire him above all other men. He is a great man. And he . . . he seems to value me. He is recently widowed. He is lonely. We spend much time together. We love one another as two men may.'

'Bring him to the theatre tonight, will you? If he's free, bring him to my play at the St James's. It can be his birthday treat.'

210

17

A Full House

That Saturday night the St James's Theatre was filled to capacity – as it had been on each and every night since 20 February 1892. My friend's play was a triumph from the moment it opened.

I must have been to the theatre a thousand times during the course of my life, but, truly, I cannot recall an evening more memorable – more *sensational* – than the first night of *Lady Windermere's Fan*. Indeed, I doubt that any one who was there on that occasion will have forgotten the experience: the humour and humanity of the play, the *surprise* of it (none of us had known what to expect), the glittering nature of the audience (*le tout monde* was in attendance), and the scandal – the *outrage* – caused by Oscar's curtain speech. When the play ended and there were cries of 'Author!' from the circle and the stalls, Oscar stepped lightly from the wings and walked non-chalantly onto the stage. He stood behind the footlights and slowly surveyed the auditorium. In his buttonhole he wore a green carnation; in his mauve-gloved hand he held a lighted cigarette. The audience fell silent. Oscar held the moment. Languidly, he drew on his cigarette. Eventually, he spoke. 'Ladies and gentlemen, it is perhaps not very proper of me to smoke in front of you, but . . .

perhaps it is not very proper of you to disturb me when I am smoking! I have enjoyed this evening *immensely*. The actors have given us a *charming* rendering of a *delightful* play, and your appreciation has been *most* intelligent. I congratulate you on the *great* success of your performance, which persuades me that you think *almost* as highly of the play as I do myself.'

At that first performance Oscar had supplied several of us with green carnations to wear as buttonholes. He arranged for just one member of the cast to wear one as well. 'What does it mean, Oscar?' I asked. 'What's the significance of the green carnation?'

'It means nothing, Robert, nothing whatsoever. And that's just what nobody will guess . . .'

For the performance on 7 May, Oscar had reserved all fourteen of the theatre's private boxes for his special guests. The evening was intended as a 'thank you' for those friends who had supported Constance's fund-raiser on behalf of the Rational Dress Society and had promised to support Oscar's in aid of the Earl's Court Boys' Club. Our host had arranged for green carnations to be left in each box for the gentlemen to wear. (Not all the gentlemen obliged. 'Not really my style, old fellow,' said Conan Doyle.) At the last minute, I was despatched by Oscar to Covent Garden market to buy small bunches of primroses to present to each of the ladies in honour of Lord Rosebery's birthday. The ladies were charmed and Primrose Rosebery professed himself 'sincerely touched by the gesture – candidly, a little overwhelmed'.

Lord Rosebery and Lord Drumlanrig sat with Oscar and Bosie in the royal box. In the box next door sat Charles and Margaret Brooke, the white Rajah and

Ranee of Sarawak, with Constance and the ever-attentive Edward Heron-Allen. ('Mrs Heron-Allen was invited, I assure you,' said Oscar. 'So was Mrs Conan Doyle. And Mrs Stoker. And Mrs Sickert, too. They are none of them coming. They are all indisposed. Whatever you do to make your fortune, Robert, don't try inventing a cure for the headache. There's no market for it.')

I was seated – with Wat Sickert and Bram Stoker – on the other side of the auditorium, in the box directly facing Constance and her friends. I had never seen Constance looking lovelier. She wore the dress that she wore on each of the many evenings that she went to see *Lady Windermere's Fan*. It was a talisman. She had worn it on that propitious first night and Constance was as superstitious as her husband. It was a dress of blue brocade, with slashed sleeves and a long bodice decorated with pearls and antique silk. The dress was grand, inspired, apparently, by the court dresses of the reign of Charles I, but Constance wore it with great simplicity. Sickert caught sight of me gazing longingly upon her and rounded on me.

'You're a fool to yourself, Sherard,' he said. 'The more you pine, the unhappier you'll become. She has eyes for no one but Oscar. That idiot Heron-Allen fawns on her day and night and she won't so much as let the back of her hand graze his. Look elsewhere, man – while you've still got your sanity.' He handed me his opera glasses and invited me to scan the auditorium. 'Tell me who you fancy,' he said, 'and I'll give you the odds.'

Stung by his reproof, I took Wat's opera glasses and used them to look about the theatre. Certainly, there were some handsome women on parade. There were some oddities, too. In one of the smaller boxes on the upper tier were Oscar's friends, Miss Bradley and Miss Cooper, the Sapphic poetesses who wrote together under the name of 'Michael Field'.

'What on earth have they come as?' I asked Sickert, handing him back the glasses.

The artist peered up at the eccentric ladies. 'Tyrolean goatherds, I'm sorry to say. . . And they appear to be having a detrimental effect on the neighbourhood. It's a full house and the most sought-after ticket in town, but the box next door to theirs is empty.'

The empty box was the box Oscar had reserved for David McMuirtree.

As the house lights dimmed and the orchestra struck up the overture (it was the overture to Mozart's *Il Seraglio*), Sickert murmured to me: 'No news today of Bradford Pearse?'

'None that I've heard.'

'Is it true then?' whispered Stoker from the back of the box. 'The word on the street is that he's topped himself – jumped off Beachy Head. Driven to it by his creditors. When you saw him in Eastbourne, how was he?'

'We saw the play. We didn't see Pearse. He disappeared before we got to him.'

'I can't believe he'd kill himself,' whispered Stoker. 'Not Pearse. Do you think he could have been murdered, poor devil?'

The curtain of the St James's Theatre rose on the sunlit morning room of Lord Windermere's establishment in Carlton House Terrace. The setting was an elegant one (Mr H. P. Hall at his most deft) and provoked a nice round of appreciative applause.

During the interval, Oscar's guests were bidden to join him for refreshments at one end of the crush room at the rear of the circle. The crowd was considerable. I pushed and shoved my way through it to reach my friend. I wanted to alert him to the fact of McMuirtree's absence, but when I reached him, before I could speak, he silenced me.

'I am aware of the situation,' he said, handing me a saucer of champagne. 'Rest easy, Robert. May I present the Earl of Rosebery? It's his lordship's birthday, you know.'

I bowed to the great man who smiled at me with deeply hooded eyes. He was a practised politician: at once he made me feel that we were intimates. 'Isn't the play a joy?' he said. 'Everyone is loving it. And yet young Drumlanrig tells me the critics were divided.'

'Yes,' said Oscar, complacently. 'When the critics divide, the public unites.'

'Indeed, Mr Wilde,' Lord Rosebery continued, chuckling and looking at the multitude around him. 'It's a wonderful turn-out. That's what amazes me. The pit and the galleries are as full as the stalls and the boxes. Who *are* all these people?'

'That's easy,' said Oscar. 'They're servants.'

'What do you mean?' asked Rosebery.

'What I say. Servants listen to conversations in drawing rooms and dining rooms. They hear people discussing my play; their curiosity is aroused; and so they fill the theatre. You can see they are servants by their perfect manners.'

'You are very funny man, Mr Wilde,' said Lord Rosebery. 'The play is to be published, I hope?'

'In due course. My ideal edition is five hundred copies as birthday presents for particular friends, six for the general public and one for the American market.'

The bell rang to signal the commencement of the second act. I bowed once more to his lordship; he gave me once more his politician's smile. As I took my leave, I whispered to Oscar as discreetly as I could: 'You know that McMuirtree's not here?'

Oscar answered, smiling, not lowering his voice at all: 'I have my eye on him nonetheless. Enjoy the play, Robert. Let us meet after the performance at the stage door.'

When I got back to my box I found Sickert and Stoker still shaking their heads over the fate of poor Bradford Pearse, repeating – yet again! – that, of all men, Pearse was the one man without an enemy in the world.

'Where have you been?' asked Sickert. 'Not chasing Mrs Wilde, I hope.' He handed me his opera glasses. 'Take a look in the gallery – at the far end on the left – the young mulatto with the sequins in her hair. Isn't she just your type?'

To indulge him, I took Sickert's glasses and inspected the girl. She was indeed most appealing: Sickert had a practised eye.

'And, see,' added Sickert, 'the Tyrolean goatherds are no longer alone. The neighbouring box has been filled.'

I turned the glasses in the direction of what had been the empty box and saw a tall man in evening dress standing to one side of it looking down into the auditorium. It was not McMuirtree. 'I know him,' I said.

Sickert and Stoker squinted up towards the gods. 'We all know him,' said Bram Stoker, waving towards the distant figure. 'It's Charles Brookfield.'

'He's not here as Oscar's guest.'

'Possibly not,' said Stoker, 'but he's here all the same. He's obsessed with Oscar. He's obsessed with this play. He's putting on his own parody of it, you know. It opens in a fortnight and I imagine we're all invited.'

'Now if someone had murdered Charles Brookfield,' said Wat Sickert, as the house lights faded, 'I shouldn't have been at all surprised.'

When the performance was over, the ovation was extraordinary. Oscar had written a crowd-pleaser, no doubt about it. On this occasion, the author resisted the temptation to take a call from the stage, but, as the audience cheered on, he stood at the front of the royal box and, with a regal wave and head thrown back, silently acknowledged their approbation. And as the audience departed, he stood at the top of the theatre's main staircase, leaning against the brass banister, receiving – as no more than his due – the plaudits of strangers and the thanks of friends.

'Thank you! Thank you, Mr Wilde! I must have a birthday more often,' called Lord Rosebery as he and the Douglas boys slipped past. 'Bravo, Oscar! I'm running for my train,' cried Conan Doyle, speeding on his way. 'I'm sorry Touie missed it. More tomorrow, old man.'

Few lingered, because it was late and, in any event, most of Oscar's friends who were guests that evening were also invited to the following afternoon's fundraiser.

'There's no such thing as a free four-acter,' chortled Charles Brooke, squeezing Oscar's shoulder as he passed.

'This is our Wilde weekend!' chorused Miss Bradley and Miss Cooper blowing kisses towards their host across the crowd.

'They really have come as Tyrolean goatherds,' I whispered to Sickert.

'At least they spared us the *Lederhosen*,' he whispered back.

When the crush had evaporated and I had bidden Sickert and Stoker goodnight, I went to join Oscar on the stairs. As I approached, I noticed Charles Brookfield, on the far side of the stairway. He was standing talking to a diminutive man who was dressed not in evening clothes but in a brown serge suit. Oscar noticed him too.

'Charles! Charles!' he called. Brookfield began to slip quietly down the marble steps, eyes forward. 'Charles!' cried Oscar. 'Don't run away.'

The actor stopped and looked about him, affecting not to know the direction from which he was being summoned.

'Charles!' Oscar called out again. 'Good evening!'

'Ah! Oscar!' Brookfield made his way over to where Oscar and I were now standing. 'I didn't see you there. I was on my way to the cloakroom.'

'I don't think so,' said Oscar. 'It's too warm a night for a coat.'

'Always playing the detective, eh, Oscar?' said Brookfield, cocking an eyebrow. 'Who killed the parrot at the Cadogan Hotel last Tuesday morning? That's what I want to know.'

'How did you enjoy the play at the St James's Theatre this Saturday night?' answered Oscar. 'That's what I want to know.'

'Come to *The Poet and the Puppets*, Oscar, and you'll find out. Come to the opening – on the nineteenth. I'm sending you tickets. You'll have an amusing evening, I think. And no speech from the author at the end of it – that I guarantee.'

'You did not approve of my speech on the opening night of *Lady Windermere*?'

'I was not alone,' said Brookfield, drily.

'Was it the tone or the content that met with your displeasure?' asked Oscar. 'Or my lighted cigarette?'

'All three.'

'You're an old-fashioned thing, Brookfield. You think you're as modern as tomorrow, but in fact you're mired in everything that's yesterday. Yes, the old-fashioned idea was indeed that the dramatist should appear at the end of the play and merely thank his kind friends for their patronage and presence. I'm glad to say that I have altered all that. The artist cannot be degraded into the servant of the public. While I have always recognised the cultural appreciation that actors and audiences have shown for my work, I have equally recognised that humility is for the hypocrite, modesty for the incompetent. Assertion is at once the duty and the privilege of the artist.'

'Thank you for that, Oscar,' said Brookfield, nodding his head. 'Most enlightening.'

'Not at all, Charles.'

'Goodnight, Oscar.' Brookfield turned and descended the now empty staircase, waving a hand in the air as he went. 'But don't forget our challenge . . . Who killed the parrot? That's the question. There's thirteen guineas riding on it, as I recall.'

'Goodnight Charles,' called Oscar. 'I trust you'll find the cloakroom hasn't closed.'

Without looking back, Brookfield marched through the theatre's swing doors and out into St James's. We watched him go.

'Why make an enemy of him, Oscar?' I asked.

'Because I cannot make him my friend, Robert.'

The theatre foyer was now deserted. A pale young man in evening dress – the theatre's assistant manager – was working his way up the staircase, turning down the gas lamps one by one. Suddenly, from behind us, two silent women in shabby coats appeared. For an instant, I took them for Miss Bradley and Miss Cooper unexpectedly returned in a new disguise. In fact, they were cleaning women. One, equipped with a mop and bucket, set to work at once on the Sienna marble floor. The other, with a heavy broom, began briskly to brush each tread of the Indian carpet on the stairs.

'Look at them,' whispered Oscar. 'How plain they are! How ugly! And yet quite young. Industry is the root of all ugliness.'

'Come, Oscar,' I said, taking my friend by the arm. 'We must go.'

'What for?' he cried. 'To drink champagne while they toil and labour here?' He felt inside his trouser pocket and, from it, produced two brand-new five-pound notes. He unfolded them.

'Don't be absurd, Oscar,' I hissed. 'That's three months' wages.'

'What's absurd is that we can afford everything, Robert, and all they can afford is self-denial.' He went over to each of the women and presented her with a five-pound note.

Both looked at him, in silence, utterly bemused. 'With the compliments of Lady Windermere,' he said. 'Goodnight, ladies. Thank you.'

The pavement outside the St James's Theatre was clear. Across the street, Charles Brookfield was standing alone, with his back to us, looking into the window of the wine merchant, Demery & Holland.

'Did you happen to catch sight of his "friend"?' Oscar asked.

'On the stairs just now? The man in the brown suit?'

'Yes – an ugly little man with a sallow complexion and ferret's eyes.'

'I think he's employed at that Turkish bath in Baker Street,' I said.

'Really?' said Oscar. 'You surprise me.' We watched Brookfield walk on alone up St James's towards Piccadilly. 'Whoever he is, he seems a curious companion for a man of Brookfield's refinement.'

A pair of two-wheelers trundled past.

'Has Constance gone home?' I asked.

'She has – with the Brookes and Heron-Allen.' Oscar glanced at me and smiled. 'I shall be going home myself tonight,' he said.

I smiled too. 'I'm glad to hear it, Oscar.'

'It is necessary, I think.'

'Are you very anxious for her safety?'

'No, not yet – at least, not while McMuirtree's living. No, Robert, you'll be amused by this . . . I'm going home tonight because of something one of my boys said.'

I found a match to light his cigarette. 'Out of the mouths of babes . . .'

'Indeed. I was telling them stories last night of little boys who were naughty and made their mother cry, and what dreadful things would happen to them unless they became better – and what do you think one of them answered? Cyril asked me what punishment should be reserved for naughty papas who did not come home till the early morning, and made their mothers cry far more!'

I laughed. 'Wise child. Shall I hail you a cab, Oscar?'

'Not quite yet,' he said, taking my arm and steering me away from St James's into King Street. 'We have an appointment at the stage door.'

'Now?' I asked. 'Won't the actors have gone home?'

'They will. It's not them we've come to see.'

'It's me!' hissed a voice in the darkness.

There was a street lamp nearby and a lighted gas lamp on the wall by the stage door, but I could see no one. 'It's me!' hissed the voice once more. 'Down here.'

I looked and then I saw his eyes shining in the gloom. It was Antipholus, the black boy from Astley's Circus. He was hidden in the doorway, crouching on the ground. As we approached, he sprang to his feet and saluted Oscar.

'How now my little tightrope-walker? What news on the Rialto? Where's Mr McMuirtree been since your last report?'

The boy stood smartly to attention. 'At the Ring of Death all afternoon, sir – training, training hard, working up a sweat. Lord Queensberry came by and stayed for half an hour. Then Mr McMuirtree bathed and dressed and took a cab across town to the Cadogan Hotel.'

'You followed him?'

'I followed him.'

'How?' I asked. 'Not in a cab, surely?'

The lad giggled. 'No, sir! On my bicycle. I held on to the back of Mr McMuirtree's cab and was pulled along, all the way, door to door.'

'And were you seen?'

'Not by Mr McMuirtree, sir. I hope I know my business.'

'What happened at the Cadogan?' asked Oscar.

'He went in with an assortment of coloured boxes.'

'Stage properties, I expect,' said Oscar, 'for tomorrow's entertainment.'

'Then he came out again and took the same cab back to Astley's. The round trip cost him two shillings.'

'And then?' asked Oscar.

'And then, when he should have changed and come here to the theatre as you'd told me to expect, Mr Wilde, he met up with the Reverend George instead.'

'Is that what you call him?' I asked. 'Do you like the Reverend George?'

'Well enough, sir. He's our padre. He's a bit sweet on Bertha, but you know what clergymen are. He tips like a gentleman anyway.'

'And what did Mr McMuirtree and the reverend gentleman do?'

'They went off together – to The Bucket of Blood.'

'The Bucket of Blood?' I queried.

Oscar laughed. 'The Lamb and Flag in Rose Street, Robert. You really have led a very sheltered life.'

'Why is it called The Bucket of Blood?' I asked.

My friend gave me a pitying look. 'Because of the bare-knuckle fighting that goes on there – professional fights, for money, but strictly non-Queensberry Rules.' He turned back to the boy. 'How long were they there?'

'All evening. Till just now. I watched the Reverend George go on his way and then I followed Mr McMuirtree back to his digs behind the circus. I heard the key turn in his lock. I watched the window. I saw the candles put out. He should be safe enough till morning, Mr Wilde – unless, of course, he's murdered in his sleep.'

'Thank you, Antipholus,' said Oscar, handing him a coin. 'Here's your shiny shilling.'

18

'Madame La Guillotine'

Davvid McMuirtree was not murdered in his sleep. Indeed, when next we saw him – on Sunday afternoon in Tite Street for Oscar's fund-raiser – he was brimfull of life. He crackled with energy. Nominally, he was there merely to play his part in the entertainment as Alphonse Byrd's illusionist's assistant, but his bearing and demeanour were hardly those of a humble hired hand. While Byrd, all dressed in black, stood at the far end of the Wildes' crowded first-floor drawing room, silently guarding his magician's table like an undertaker in attendance on a coffin, McMuirtree, also dressed in black, moved easily among the throng, nodding here, smiling there, like the son of the family welcoming distant relations to the wake. McMuirtree was noticeable because of his commanding height and fine physique. He was memorable because of his shaven head, warm blue-black eyes and curious, rasping speaking voice.

'He's very striking,' remarked Willie Hornung, standing by the fireplace, tucking in to a fruit sorbet while surveying the scene.

'He is an odd mixture,' I said. 'I can't fathom him. He has the build of a prize-fighter—'

'And the manners of a Don Juan,' added Conan Doyle, scratching his moustache with the stem of his pipe. 'I'd watch him.'

'We're all going to,' said Walter Sickert, smiling slyly. 'He's the star attraction.'

'Not today,' I ventured. 'Tomorrow, maybe, at Astley's Circus when he has this gala bout to display the merits of the Queensberry Rules. But today, I think, he's somewhat further down the bill. He's the magician's assistant.'

'He's the one we'll watch all the same,' said Sickert, helping himself to a second iced cream from the sideboard. 'I'm a connoisseur of the halls. McMuirtree has what it takes.'

Conan Doyle sniffed and lifted himself up and down on his toes. 'Do you think so? I wonder.'

'I don't,' said Sickert. 'We're talking about the man for a reason – there's something about his presence that compels our attention.'

'Yes,' harrumphed Doyle. 'His cockiness.'

Willie Hornung laughed and pushed his *pince-nez* further up his nose the better to observe McMuirtree's progress.

Sickert waved his dessert spoon in the air. 'I've seen him fight – just the once. And I've met him – just the once, when I sat next to him at dinner last Sunday. I barely know him, but he's made his mark on me. Why? Because, in his way, he's an artist – in the ring and out of it.'

'He's not a very subtle artist, is he?' I said. McMuirtree, as I spoke, was being greeted by our hostess. He raised Constance's hand to his lips as though they were old friends.

'Always remember Whistler's golden rule, Robert – "In art, nothing matters so long as you are bold."'

If David McMuirtree was a star attraction that afternoon, he was not without competition. For a start, he had the Wilde boys to contend with. Oscar and Constance had decked out their sons in fancy dress. They were in orange and green velvet suits, with frilly shirts and buckled shoes. Cyril was costumed as Little Lord Fauntleroy and his younger brother, Vyvyan, because of his naturally curly hair, was dressed to represent the little boy in Sir John Millais's famous painting, *Bubbles*. The boys themselves, as they explained to everyone who stopped to admire and pet them, would much have preferred to come dressed in their matching sailor suits (made of real naval cloth with lanyards with real knives at the end of them), 'but this is what Papa wanted and this is Papa's party'.

In terms of his own apparel, 'Papa' had certainly taken note of Whistler's golden rule. The colour of Oscar's frock coat and trousers was ultramarine blue; his waistcoat was of gold brocade; his tie was crimson; his buttonhole was a columbine flower set against a fan of cymbalaria leaves. The '*tout ensemble*', he explained, was inspired by his cuff-links – 'they came to me from Wat Sickert . . . They are exquisite, are they not? Wat won't tell me where he found them . . . We all have our secrets.'

The cuff-links were enamel, exquisite and extraordinary. They each featured a near-perfect miniature reproduction of Leonardo da Vinci's painting, *The Virgin of the Rocks*. As Oscar explained, his eyes filling with tears as he did so, the colour of his frock coat matched the colour of the Madonna's mantle; his waistcoat was inspired by the Christ child's swaddling clothes; his tie was of the same hew as the angel Uriel's cloak; and his buttonhole included plants depicted in the painting – 'columbine to symbolise the holy spirit and cymbalaria representing constancy'.

Conan Doyle sucked hard on his pipe as Oscar held his cuff up to his friend for closer inspection. 'I'm not sure that I approve, Oscar,' he grumbled.

'And why not?' asked Oscar.

'I'm not sure that I know,' muttered Doyle. 'It doesn't seem quite right, that's all.'

'When's the magic starting, Papa?' Little Lord Fauntleroy was tugging at his father's sleeve.

'Now!' said Oscar. 'This very minute!' And he gathered up his sons and led them to the end of the room where Alphonse Byrd and David McMuirtree were standing waiting to begin their performance. The audience – there were some thirty of us in all – found chairs or stools to sit on, or leant against the piano or the mantelpiece. Constance sat on a sofa near the performers, with her friend, Margaret Brooke, and Mrs Robinson, the clairvoyant, on either side of her, and Charles Brooke and Edward Heron-Allen perched on the sofa's arms. Miss Bradley and Miss Cooper, in immaculate gentlemen's evening dress, sat cross-legged on the floor at the front of the crowd, with Bosie and Lord Drumlanrig and Vyvyan and Cyril at their side. At the last moment, as the clock on the landing struck five, Arthur, the butler, Mrs Ryan, the cook, and Gertrude Simmonds, the boys' governess, crept in at the door to watch the show.

Unbidden, the room settled, and Oscar spoke. His voice was low – we had almost to strain to hear him – and in his eyes there were still the remnants of tears. 'Once upon a time,' he began, 'there was a magnet . . . and in its close neighbourhood were some steel filings.'

'He's going to tell a story!' cried Cyril.

'Hush!' said Constance lifting her finger to her lips.

Oscar raised his voice a little. 'One day two or three little filings felt a sudden desire to go and visit the magnet, and they began to talk of what a pleasant thing it would be to do. Other filings nearby overheard their conversation and they, too, became infected with the same desire. Still others joined them, till at last all the filings began to discuss the matter, and more and more their vague desire grew into an impulse. "Why not go today?" said some of them; but others were of the opinion that it would be better to wait until tomorrow . . . Meanwhile, without their having noticed it, they had been involuntarily moving nearer to the magnet, which lay there quite still, apparently taking no heed of them.'

Oscar reached into his pocket for his silver cigarette case. 'And so they went on,' he continued, his eyes darting about the room as he spoke, 'all the time insensibly drawing nearer to their neighbour . . . And the more they talked, the more they felt the impulse growing stronger, till the more impatient ones declared that they would go *that* day, whatever the rest did. Some were even heard to say that it was their *duty* to visit the magnet, and that they ought to have gone long ago. And while they talked, they moved nearer and nearer, without realising that they had moved. Then, at last, the impatient ones prevailed, and, with one irresistible impulse, the whole body cried out, "There is no use waiting, we will go today. We will go now. We will go *at once*." And then in one unanimous mass they swept along, and in another moment were clinging fast to the magnet on every side. Then the magnet smiled – for the steel filings had no doubt at all but that they were paying that visit of their own free will.'

Oscar paused, and looked about the room, and smiled, and lit his cigarette.

'Bravo, Papa!' called Little Lord Fauntleroy, leading the applause.

Conan Doyle, sucking on his pipe, leant over to Wat Sickert and murmured: 'Who did you say was the "star attraction"?'

Oscar bowed his head briefly, then threw it back, drew slowly on his cigarette and, through a cloud of pale grey smoke which he did nothing to wave away, went on: 'What has drawn you here today, ladies and gentlemen, is your generous impulse. Together, this afternoon, we have raised more than thirty pounds for the benefit of the Earl's Court Boys' Club. Thanks to you, these lads – rough boys, working-class boys, street urchins some of them – will be able to acquire discipline, fitness and skill by learning to box in a proper boxing ring, with real boxing clubs and according to the Queensberry Rules!' This time it was Drumlanrig and Conan Doyle who led the applause.

'Discipline, fitness and skill . . .' repeated Oscar, revealing his teeth in a mischievous grin. 'They're what's wanted in Earl's Court, to be sure. Here in Chelsea, naturally, we incline more to indulgence, indolence and idleness.'

'You're wicked, Oscar!' hissed Miss Cooper.

'That's why we love him,' murmured Lord Alfred Douglas at her side.

Oscar moved towards the mantelpiece. 'Iced champagne and Russian caviar are to be served shortly,' he announced. 'But, first . . .' He held out his arm towards the arena he had just vacated: 'The entertainment!'

'Yes! Yes!' cried Cyril and Vyvyan simultaneously.

'Ladies and gentlemen, would you please welcome this afternoon's master of magic and prince of illusion, late of the Victoria Music Hall, Solihull, sometime toast of the West Midlands circuit, now darling of the Cadogan Hotel pantry, *Mr Alphonse Byrd*, together with his able assistant, the David and Goliath of Astley's Circus, *Mr David McMuirtree!*'

Oscar raised both hands above his head and clapped them together loudly as Byrd, alone, stepped from the corner of the room and took a bow. He was thin and pale and, for an entertainer, disconcertingly solemn. When he bowed, he bowed low, letting his arms hang forward so that his fingers almost touched the ground. The crown of his head was bald and mottled, and what little hair he had was white and wispy. He stayed bent forward, sustaining his bow for longer than was comfortable, and then, suddenly, as the applause subsided, he stood up abruptly, stretching his arms out wide – and, as he did so, two huge bouquets of brightly coloured paper flowers appeared in either hand! As we gasped and laughed and cheered, Byrd stepped towards Constance and carefully laid both bouquets on her lap like a mourner placing floral tributes on a grave.

His entertainment lasted half an hour. His skill was considerable. Effortlessly, without emotion, with barely any commentary, and with minimal assistance from McMuirtree, he made playing cards vanish and top hats disappear. From an empty cardboard box – which he pierced repeatedly with a rapier – he produced a violin. He transformed oranges into lemons, lemons into billiard balls and a furled umbrella into a union flag. Oscar especially liked it when he turned a jug of water into a carafe of wine. 'Always a favourite,' he murmured.

The climax of the entertainment involved neither snake-charming nor fire-eating, as I had hoped. Constance had vetoed both. Instead it was a celebration of what Oscar described gleefully as 'the worst excesses of the French revolution'.

'Finally,' said Alphonse Byrd, 'or should I say "*finalement*"?' – it was the only hint of humour in his entire presentation – 'may I introduce "Madame La Guillotine"? It is her birthday. Let us wish her well.'

As Byrd spoke, McMuirtree stepped forward carrying a tall and weighty object, draped in a black silk sheet. It was about five foot high and two feet wide, a little smaller than a cheval mirror. With a flourish, he pulled away the sheet and revealed what appeared to be an exact replica of a guillotine. The Wilde boys squealed with pleasure. Miss Bradley and Miss Cooper giggled. The other ladies in the room all gasped.

'This instrument of execution,' said Byrd, unflinching, 'was first used in the streets of Paris – in the Place de Grève, to be precise – one hundred years ago this week. Our model is smaller than the French original, but it's quite solid – the beams are made of Welsh pine, the blade is made of Sheffield steel, the block is English oak – and it works well enough . . . See!'

From a basket beneath the magician's table McMuirtree produced a large white cabbage and held it high in the air, on the points of his fingers, for all to see. He passed the cabbage to Byrd, who took it, and felt its weight, and laid it on the execution block, lowering a narrow wooden beam shaped like an ox's halter onto the vegetable to secure it in position. Then, with some ceremony, the magician untied the thin rope that held the blade in place at the top of the guillotine. He held the rope taut so that the blade did not move. 'Watch,' he whispered softly, closing his own eyes and turning his head away from the scene. He paused. He took a long, deep breath and held it. 'Now!' he cried, with a sudden, terrifying vehemence, releasing the rope and letting the blade fall. It came down at once – sharply, swiftly, silently – and landed with a small thud on the oak block. The cabbage fell to the floor, cleanly cut in two.

The room was silent. Alphonse Byrd opened his eyes and looked on what he saw with satisfaction. McMuirtree bent down and recovered the two halves of the cabbage. He held them aloft in either hand and bowed.

For the first time that afternoon, Alphonse Byrd smiled. 'Thank you,' he said. 'Your present attention is even more welcome than your former applause.' He looked at the apparatus at his side. 'Our guillotine appears to be in working order,' he continued. 'It is time now to put it properly to the test. One hundred years ago, in Paris in the late spring of 1792, a gentleman by the name of Nicolas Jacques Pelletier was the first man to lose his head to the blade of Madame La Guillotine. One hundred years on, in London in the late spring of 1892, do we have a volunteer brave enough to follow in his footsteps?'

'Yes!' called Little Lord Fauntleroy, jumping to his feet and waving his hand in the air.

'No – please!' gasped Constance Wilde, reaching forward towards her boy. Together Miss Bradley and Miss Cooper pulled Cyril back onto the floor.

'Why not?' the little fellow demanded furiously. 'Why not?'

'Mrs Wilde is right,' said Byrd. 'This is not a game for little boys.'

'I shall be seven on the fifth of June!' cried Cyril.

'Nevertheless,' said Byrd solemnly, 'I think we require the services of a slightly older gentleman for this assignment.' He looked about the room with darting eyes. 'Who would like to place his head upon the block?'

From the fireplace, Willie Hornung stirred. He raised an arm and said amiably: 'I'll give it a go.' With a quick hand on the shoulder, Conan Doyle held his young friend back. No one else moved.

Byrd turned slowly towards McMuirtree. 'Well,' he said, 'in that case I must ask my assistant to assist.' McMuirtree smiled and began to remove his jacket. Byrd turned back to the guillotine and raised the blade and secured it afresh at its departure point. He produced a silk handkerchief from his pocket and brushed the shards of cabbage from the cutting edge. He lifted the wooden halter that had held the cabbage in place and invited McMuirtree, who had now removed his tie and collar and shirt stud, to lay his neck upon the block.

The boxer, still smiling, knelt down behind the guillotine. With his large brown hands he gripped the sides of the block, leant forward and put his head in place. He turned his face upward and stared out towards the audience. Byrd brought the wooden halter down around his neck to pinion him.

'Is this suitable for a children's party?' demanded Conan Doyle from his position by the fireplace.

'Yes!' cried Cyril Wilde, clapping his hands with glee. Vyvyan had crawled across Miss Cooper and was now lying across his mother's lap.

'We're nearly done,' said Byrd. 'In a moment, our revels will be ended. The decapitation itself takes no more than one thirtieth of a second.'

'How does he know?' Bosie giggled.

Alphonse Byrd looked down at David McMuirtree. 'Are you ready, sir?' he asked. 'Are you prepared for what's to come?'

'I am,' rasped McMuirtree.

'Do you wish for a blindfold?'

'No, I do not.'

'Very well,' said Byrd quietly. 'The moment of execution is upon us.' He turned to the guillotine and solemnly untied the rope. With one hand he held it taut. With the other he reached out to the blade and lightly ran his forefinger along its edge. He winced and sharply drew in his breath. He held his finger out towards the room. A pinprick of purple blood bubbled into a drop. He put the finger into his mouth and for a moment held it there. Then, as he had done before, he closed his eyes and turned his head away. 'Watch,' he whispered softly. 'Watch closely.'

McMuirtree lowered his head. We could no longer see his eyes, but at the very apex of his cranium, within a shallow indentation, clearly visible, a pulse beat steadily. Byrd stood motionless. We waited. There was no sound but of Oscar drawing on his cigarette.

'Now!' cried Byrd, with a vehemence even fiercer than before. He let go the rope and the blade fell. It fell, crashing down to the oak block in an instant.

There were cries of alarm and disbelief from every corner of the room.

'What's happened, Oscar?' hissed Sickert.

'Is he dead?' asked Cyril Wilde expectantly.

'It's only a game!' called Oscar.

'Indeed!' cried Alphonse Byrd, smiling for a second time.

The blade had apparently passed through McMuirtree's body – you could see it clearly on either side of his neck – but he was not dead. Far from it. Slowly, he raised his head and opened his eyes wide. He smiled and, in his rasping voice, declared: 'It seems I have survived.'

As McMuirtree spoke, Byrd set to work, swiftly raising the blade, lifting the wooden halter and releasing his assistant from the guillotine. The boxer rose to his feet at once and, stepping round the deadly apparatus, took his place immediately at Byrd's side. Together they bowed. Suddenly the drawing room at 16 Tite Street was filled with laughter and applause.

'How did you do it?' demanded Cyril, running towards the two men open-mouthed with admiration.

'Congratulations gentlemen,' said Miss Bradley and Miss Cooper getting to their feet.

Constance called over to the butler. 'Arthur, we are ready for our champagne now.'

'I think we need it,' said Edward Heron-Allen.

'I think we *deserve* it!' said Margaret Brooke. 'My nerves are all a-jangle.'

Her husband wiped his large red face with his handkerchief and chuckled: 'I'm not sure whether my charitable donation should be larger or smaller because of this.'

Mrs Ryan and Gertrude Simmonds were already passing through the room carrying dishes piled high with inch-long wafers shaped like tiny rowing-boats, each wafer filled with a spoonful of black caviar.

Oscar went forward and shook both of the entertainers warmly by the hand. 'Mr Byrd, Mr McMuirtree,' he said. 'Thank you. I doubt that Mr Irving himself could have commanded the room more brilliantly.'

'How did they do it, Papa?' asked Cyril, tugging at his father's ultramarine frock coat.

'We must not let daylight in on magic,' replied his father.

'Why not, Papa?'

'Because a secret that was beautiful becomes banal when it's revealed.'

The boy, unconvinced, set about examining the guillotine as Byrd and McMuirtree began to dismantle it. 'Look, Papa,' he cried, excitedly, 'the magician's finger is still bleeding.'

'Only a little,' said Byrd, tying a handkerchief around it.

'Mr Byrd takes risks for his art,' explained Oscar. 'All artists must.' Oscar smiled at McMuirtree who was wrapping the guillotine blade in a baize cloth. 'I'm relieved you survived your ordeal, Mr McMuirtree.'

The boxer laughed and looked Oscar steadily in the eye. 'And if I survive until midnight tomorrow, Mr Wilde, I think we can consider the case closed.'

'Can I keep the cabbage?' asked Cyril, lifting up one half of it and holding it close to his chest.

'You may,' said McMuirtree, 'if your father will allow it.'

Oscar sighed. 'I try to set an example. I wear a columbine in my buttonhole inspired by Leonardo's *Virgin of the Rocks*, and my son craves half a cabbage salvaged from the guillotine . . . What is to be done?'

'Is that a "yes", Papa?' enquired the little boy and, assuming that it was, without waiting for an answer, he ran off to find his mother to show her his trophy.

The butler stood at Oscar's side with a tray of champagne.

'A drink, gentlemen? You've earned it.'

McMuirtree was about to take a glass, but Byrd stopped him. 'I think not, Mr Wilde. It's not really our place, is it? We'll just gather up our bits and pieces and be on our way.'

'As you please,' said Oscar. He dismissed the butler with a nod and a smile, bringing his fingertips together in a silent salaam. Oscar turned back to Byrd and McMuirtree. 'I'm in your debt, gentlemen. I'll call at the Cadogan tomorrow and we can sort out the crinkle.'

The entertainers continued packing up their paraphernalia as Oscar set about working the room. He found me nearby, at the piano, scoffing caviar, and having my hand 'read' by Mrs Robinson.

'Do you see murder also in Robert's palm, Mrs R?' he asked teasingly.

The lady, who was seated on the piano stool, tilted her head to one side and looked up at him. 'No, Mr Wilde,' she said firmly. 'We are each unique. Every hand is different. In Mr Sherard's hand I see no sudden death, no murder – but much matrimony!'

'I am hoping to be divorced, Mrs Robinson,' I said softly.

'That's as may be,' replied the lady soothingly, 'but you'll be married again – twice more.'

'I don't believe it!' I cried.

'You may not want to believe it,' she said, 'but it's clearly written. Look . . .' She held open my palm. 'Your life-line flows long and strong – from here to here – and cutting across it, as you can see, are tiny sets of parallel lines, like bridges. Each bridge represents a marriage. Along your life-line there are three . . .' She looked up and smiled at me. She turned to Oscar and took his right hand and turned it over and laid his palm next to mine. 'Now, when we consider Mr Wilde's life-line, what do we see? It's deeper than yours, wider – the river flows faster, the currents are deeper and more powerful . . .'

'And how many little bridges cut across my life?' Oscar enquired, leaning forward the better to see his hand.

'Just the one,' she answered. 'Here.' I saw the tiny parallel lines she spoke of.

'And where is this "sudden death" you say you saw in my unhappy hand?'

'There,' said Mrs Robinson letting her pointed finger-nail rest on a concentrated confusion of tiny lines that were undoubtedly evident in Oscar's palm – and as certainly absent from mine.

'Your hand is the map of your life, Mr Wilde,' explained the fortune teller, running her fingers lightly across my friend's palm. 'I look down onto your hand and I see a landscape laid out before me – with hills and valleys, dense forests and open fields, and flowing through them the principal river – your life-line – with, running into it, tributaries, so many of them – smaller rivers, streams, rivulets, brooks and gullies, each one representing a different current in your life. Where this brook abuts this field, Mr Wilde, I see a whirlpool . . . and it worries me.'

'"Where this brook abuts this field . . ."' repeated Oscar. 'Do you choose your words with care, Madam?'

'I hope so,' replied the lady, 'but I work more with pictures than with words. The lines of your hand form shapes. I see the landscape of your life, but I see also pictures of many of God's creatures hidden there. And each picture tells its story. Look at the base of Mr Sherard's ring finger and what do you see?'

I peered closely at my own hand. 'A triangle?' I suggested.

'Yes,' she said.

'And another triangle set across it?' I ventured.

'I see a starfish, Mr Sherard,' she said.

'And what does a starfish signify?'

'An island, usually.'

'Well,' I said, 'I was brought up on the island of Guernsey . . .'

'Yes,' jeered Oscar, 'and I was brought up on the island of Ireland, but I see no starfish at the base of my ring finger.'

'No,' said Mrs Robinson, lifting Oscar's palm close to her eyes, 'but there's a creature drawn there nonetheless – a bird.' She held Oscar's hand towards me. 'It's as clear as day, is it not?'

'A bird?' exclaimed Oscar. 'A bird, you say? Is it a parrot?'

Mrs Robinson laughed and pushed Oscar's hand back towards him. 'Don't be absurd, Mr Wilde. It looks nothing like a parrot. Look at the long legs, look at the elongated bill . . . a heron, perhaps?'

Alphonse Byrd and David McMuirtree brushed past, carrying their stage properties. Edward Heron-Allen followed them, with Cyril on his shoulders. Little Lord Fauntleroy was still clutching his half-cabbage to his chest. 'We're on our way, Mr Wilde,' said Byrd. 'Apparently you ordered a four-wheeler for us – much obliged.'

'Excuse me, dear lady,' said Oscar, extricating his hand from Mrs Robinson's. 'I must just see these gentlemen to their carriage.'

We followed them to the landing where Constance was standing talking with Conan Doyle and young Willie Hornung. 'Thank you for a quite wonderful entertainment, gentlemen,' she said.

Alphonse Byrd simply nodded his skull-like head and said, 'Good day, Mrs Wilde,' but David McMuirtree put down his cases and prepared to take his hostess's hand. As he did so, as he was bending forward towards Constance, quite suddenly, he clutched desperately at his own chest, turned away from her and fell headlong down the stairs.

We stood transfixed. Cyril, on Heron-Allen's shoulders, cried out in alarm and let go of the cabbage, which tumbled down the stairs in McMuirtree's wake. As it reached the foot of the stairs and rolled towards the boxer's body, Oscar, peering over the banister, laughed and began to clap his hands. He looked back towards his son. 'Don't worry, my boy,' he said. 'It's only a game.'

19

The Virgin of Guadalupe

'But how on earth did you know that he was playing a game, Mr Wilde?'

'Are we to be friends, Mr Hornung? We have only been acquainted for a week and a day, I know, but already we are lunching together on a Monday. And, Mr Hornung, just as a lady never wear diamonds in the country and a gentlemen never wears brown shoes in town, so it is that two gentlemen never take luncheon together on a Monday unless they see true friendship in prospect.' Oscar raised his glass of Le Montrachet 1865 in Willie Hornung's direction. 'If we are to be friends, Willie, and I think that we are, my name to you is Oscar . . .'

Oscar was at his most mellow. It was the next day – Monday 9 May 1892 – and my friend and I were lunching with Willie Hornung and Arthur Conan Doyle in the oak-panelled dining room of the Cadogan Hotel. Hornung, Conan Doyle's shrinking violet, gently watered by Oscar, was developing into an altogether more robust bloom. The young man raised his glass to our host, pushed his *pince-nez* up his nose and repeated his question: 'How did you know that it was a game, Oscar?'

Oscar smiled and contemplated his plate. He had ordered what he called 'a light lunch – a Monday lunch':

cold lobster and fresh mayonnaise, with cucumber salad, tomato jelly and new potatoes.

Hornung persisted: 'We all thought that he was dead. And then, when you laughed and he got up and took a bow, we didn't know what to think . . . Had he told you that's what he was planning to do?'

'No,' said Oscar, skewering a piece of lobster on his fork and dipping it into the mayonnaise. 'But I sensed at once that what we were witnessing was play-acting – comedy not tragedy.'

'It looked real enough to me,' said Conan Doyle, tucking into the new potatoes.

'Yes,' said Oscar. 'He clutched the left side of his chest as a man might when suffering a heart attack, but there was something I thought you might have noticed, Arthur, as a medical man . . . When confronted with sudden pain, the genuine patient tenses up, does he not? But McMuirtree, I observed, as he turned away from Constance at the top of the stairs, far from stiffening his sinews, appeared deliberately to relax his entire body. He was readying himself for the fall. He tumbled down that staircase head first, loose-limbed, not like a man in agony, but like an old trouper on his day off from Astley's Circus.'

'But why did he do it, Mr Wilde – Oscar?'

'I imagine, Willie, that he did it on the spur of the moment, because the opportunity arose.' Oscar balanced a small dollop of tomato jelly on a slice of cucumber. 'I imagine, Willie, that he did it for any number of reasons . . . to show off . . . to amuse himself . . . to upstage Alphonse Byrd – Byrd had scored rather well during the entertainment, after all . . . I imagine, too, that he did it for the benefit of those of us who were there yesterday afternoon and had been here at the Cadogan Hotel last Sunday night. Perhaps he wanted to show his contempt for whomever it was had chosen him as a "victim" last Sunday night. He was defying them and their idle death threat. He was cocking a snook, as the saying goes.'

'He was certainly running a risk,' I said. 'It's his big fight tonight. He might easily have broken a limb taking that fall yesterday.'

Oscar chuckled. 'A short flight of stairs in Tite Street holds no terrors for "David and Goliath" McMuirtree, Robert. Besides, risk to a man like that is what a second bottle of this charming white Burgundy will be to us – part and parcel of a well-filled day.' Oscar waved a hopeful hand in the direction of the sommelier.

'No more wine for me, thank you, Oscar,' decreed Conan Doyle firmly. 'I'm on my way to the *Strand* magazine. I have an afternoon of heavy negotiations ahead of me.'

'Are you still planning to murder Sherlock Holmes?' I asked.

'In my head, in my heart, he's dead already,' answered Doyle, mopping his walrus moustache with his napkin. 'But in my bank book, he quivers and twitches still.' He sniffed and shook his shoulders as if he had suddenly been caught in a draught.

Hornung leant into the table and whispered conspiratorially: 'The *Strand* is offering Arthur a thousand pounds for a dozen stories.'

'Money isn't everything,' muttered Conan Doyle, embarrassed by his young companion's revelation.

'Oh, but it is,' murmured Oscar, almost to himself. I said nothing. (For my short novel, *Agatha's Quest*, I had recently received from Trischler & Co. the grand sum of fifteen pounds and fifteen shillings.)

'Money, of course, is important,' Hornung added eagerly, 'but it is genius, surely, that we should aspire to?'

'No, no, no,' wailed Oscar, at the same time signalling to the sommelier that a second bottle of Le Montrachet was definitely overdue. 'Do not aspire to genius, Willie. The British public is wonderfully tolerant, but it has its limits. It forgives everything – except genius.'

We all laughed. Conan Doyle put down his napkin. 'You and the British seem to rub along well enough, Oscar. They love your play. They tolerate your eccentricities.'

'They despise my buttonholes,' said Oscar, with a heavy sigh. 'As I walk down the street I see the passers-by glancing at my left lapel and I know what they are thinking . . .'

'All they are thinking, Oscar, is that their taste is not quite as your taste is,' said Conan Doyle, sitting back and grinning broadly at his friend. 'I mean to say, old man, look at you now. It's a beautiful May morning out there and you're sporting an overblown black tulip on your jacket. It looks like a dead crow.'

'It is in honour of Gustave Flaubert,' said Oscar, looking mournfully at the tulip. 'He died twelve years ago yesterday. He was a master. I revere him. And on the eighth of May every year I buy tulips in his honour. I remember him as he would wish to be remembered. Flaubert said, "*Il est doux de songer que je servirai un jour à faire croître des tulipes.*"*

---

* 'It is sweet to think that one day I will serve to grow tulips.'

'Yes,' chuckled Conan Doyle. 'He always was one for *le mot juste*.' The sommelier arrived with our second bottle of Le Montrachet. Doyle glanced at his pocket watch. 'Monsieur Flaubert, of course, did not have to contend with the editor of the *Strand* magazine. I must be on my way in a moment, Oscar. Might I be allowed a quick cup of coffee first – while you finish your wine and order your dessert? I must hear about your morning's endeavours before I take my leave. You've been questioning the staff here at the hotel, have you not?'

Oscar was tasting the new wine approvingly. He put down his glass and looked steadily at Conan Doyle. 'We have,' he said.

'And is there any vital point to which you would wish to draw my attention?'

'Merely, Arthur, to the curious incident of the parrot in the morning – in the hours immediately preceding its unfortunate demise.'

'From what I understand, the parrot did nothing in the morning.'

Oscar smiled his sly smile. 'That is the curious incident.'

Conan Doyle shook his head. 'I'm not sure I follow you.'

'Robert and I have been here since ten o'clock this morning,' explained Oscar. 'We have questioned every member of staff who was on duty at the hotel last Tuesday. The parrot was last seen alive and well, perched in his cage, shortly after breakfast. Nat, the page-boy and Nellie, one of the maids, will both testify to that. Thereafter, no one appears to have given poor Captain Flint any thought of any kind until his devastated body was discovered at three o'clock.'

'Is that so surprising?' asked Conan Doyle, dropping two sugar cubes lightly into his coffee.

'Captain Flint was a talkative creature,' said Oscar. '"Impertinent and garrulous", according to Bosie – that's why the dear boy wanted to murder him. Customarily, the Cadogan Hotel parrot made his presence felt. That morning, it seems, he did not do so. Curious, don't you think?'

'Not necessarily,' said Conan Doyle. 'An occasional visitor to the hotel, like Lord Alfred Douglas, would notice the parrot no doubt, but the staff, passing through the hotel hallway all the time, might very well take his presence for granted. Was the hotel busy that morning?'

'Exceptionally busy – and short-staffed. Both the day manager and the assistant manager were indisposed, which is why Byrd was still on duty. According to the hotel register there were seven new arrivals during the course of the morning and, in the early afternoon, a party of four-teen American females was set to depart. All day, by all accounts, there was much coming and going through the hallway. The page-boy and the hall porter recognised a number of the regulars – Bram Stoker and Charles Brookfield were here for breakfast; Mrs Langtry was at her usual table, over there, for lunch; as you know, Constance and Edward Heron-Allen arrived a little before three.'

'Was the hallway deserted at any stage – even for a moment?'

'Oh, yes,' said Oscar, who now had a Kentish straw-berry skewered on to the end of his dessert fork and was dipping it happily into his glass of wine. 'The hall porter acknowledged that he had frequently to leave his post to help bring down luggage for the American ladies. And, at regular intervals, Nat, the page boy, was similarly engaged. The hallway was often empty. The front door was always open. The truth is: *anyone* with access to the hotel that morning could have had access to the parrot's cage. Anyone might have murdered Captain Flint.'

'Anyone might have done it . . .' reflected Conan Doyle, turning his coffee spoon round in his fingers. 'Yes . . . anyone might have had the means and the opportunity . . . but who had the motive?' The doctor added another sugar cube to his cup. 'Who owned the parrot? Did he belong to the hotel?'

'No, he belonged to Alphonse Byrd. He came to the hotel with Byrd when the hotel opened. According to the hall porter, Byrd and the parrot were inseparable.'

'I can believe it,' said Willie Hornung eagerly. 'I kept a parrot when I was in Australia – "Captain Cook" I called him. Parrots are extraordinary creatures – they are like people in many ways. They can converse, you know, and count. Captain Cook could count to ten. And they form strong attachments. They can be fiercely jealous.' Hornung stopped. Evidently he felt he had spoken out of turn. He gulped at his wine and muttered: 'Well, anyway, that was my experience in Australia.'

Oscar smiled at the nervous young man and laid his hand on his. 'When I look at the map,' he said, 'and see what an ugly country Australia is, I feel that I want to go there and see if it cannot be changed into a more beautiful form. Perhaps you will take me there one day, Willie? Would I feel at home in Sydney?'

'Gentlemen,' growled Conan Doyle, clearing his throat. 'Can we stick to the matter in hand? Byrd was fond of his parrot—'

'He adored the creature,' said Oscar emphatically, removing his hand from Willie Hornung's and looking Conan Doyle directly in the eye.

'Did Byrd have enemies?'

'Byrd has few friends, it seems, other than McMuirtree, but he has no known enemies. Those who work with him at the hotel appear to accept him for what he is – a cold fish. They don't warm to him, but they don't dislike him. They don't despise him, certainly. There is nothing to suggest that the unfortunate Captain Flint was slain by someone with a grudge against Mr Alphonse Byrd.'

'So the parrot's death remains a mystery,' said Conan Doyle with a short sigh. He took his pocket watch from his waistcoat. 'I must go,' he announced, pushing back his chair and getting briskly to his feet.

'I'll come with you,' said Willie Hornung, taking a final gulp of wine and pulling his napkin from his shirt. 'We can share a cab into town.'

Oscar and I got to our feet and shook hands with the good-hearted doctor and his young charge. My friend's vast circle of acquaintance included all types and conditions of men. Almost all of them were fascinating in their way, but with a number I felt distinctly uncomfortable. With Arthur Conan Doyle and Willie Hornung I always felt at ease.

'Will we be seeing you tonight?' Oscar called after them as they made their way towards the door. 'McMuirtree's bout begins at eight o'clock.'

Conan Doyle waved as he went. 'We have our tickets. We'll be there – without fail.'

When they had gone, and Oscar and I were seated once more, lingering over the last of Le Montrachet '65, I said to my friend: 'If McMuirtree survives tonight, if tomorrow morning he's still alive and well, will it all be over do you think? Will you feel the curse has been lifted?'

'I'll feel I can sleep more safely in my bed,' he answered slowly. 'And I'll feel that my dear wife can sleep more safely in hers. But I'll still ponder on the fate of Bradford Pearse. Did he fall or was he pushed? And I'll still need to solve the riddle of Captain Flint – or else be obliged to give the wretched Brookfield thirteen guineas.' The yellow wine in his glass was now peppered with strawberry. Oscar gazed into it reflectively. 'Who killed the parrot, Robert? That is the question. *Qui a tué le perroquet?*' He reached for the bottle. It was empty. 'Flaubert kept a stuffed parrot on his desk to give him inspiration, did he not? I believe he used the parrot in *Un Cœur simple*. I have not read the story. Have you? I must.' Suddenly he was galvanised. 'I shall! This very afternoon. Do you have a copy, Robert? I don't. We shall go to the French Bookshop in search of it. I shall get the bill and we shall go to Beak Street at once. Who knows, we might also find your friend the Hon. the Reverend George Daubeney there, might we not? It's where you first met. The French Bookshop is one of his haunts, didn't you say?' He waved his napkin cheerily towards the head waiter. 'I look forward to telling our cabby that we are going to Beak Street in search of a simple heart. It will amuse him. Drink up, Robert. The game's afoot.'

The drive from Sloane Street to Beak Street took half an hour. It would have taken less long if, along the way, Oscar had not insisted on stopping at every tobacconist's shop until he found one that could supply him with a tin of Player's Navy Cut cigarettes. 'McMuirtree did me a great service introducing me to these, Robert. As he noted, they are not a gentleman's cigarette – but it's their very roughness that lends them their charm. It's what a man needs after lobster, strawberries and white Burgundy.'

Our cabman, who Oscar claimed was 'an old friend', gave not the least impression of knowing who Oscar was nor of understanding any of the array of quips, observations and reflections on Flaubert that Oscar lightly tossed his way. Whenever Oscar spoke, the man merely sniffed and sucked on his own cigarette. When we reached our destination and, with much ceremony, Oscar asked him to kindly wait for us and presented him with a silver sovereign by way of 'interim payment', the man gave a perfunctory nod and pocketed the sovereign as if it had been a sixpence.

The *Librairie Française* in Beak Street was a magnet for civilised souls in the London of the 1890s. From the outside it had the reassuring air of a milliner's shop in a novel by Jane Austen, but behind the Regency shopfront with its enticing window of many panes, was a dimly lit smoke-filled emporium that smacked more of Paris or Marseilles (or even Athens or Algiers) than of Bath or Cheltenham Spa. As well as books and journals of every description (including quite a number a respectable writer might be loath to describe!), Monsieur Hirsch, the Frenchman who had opened the shop in 1889, stocked a rich assortment of Gallic luxuries that could not normally be obtained in London – French toiletries, French cigarettes, French cheeses, continental-style prophylactics, bottles of absinthe. 'Smell the corruption,' said

Oscar as we pushed open the door and a little bell tinkled to signal our arrival.

Within the shop the air was close, heavy with incense. We closed the front door behind us and the bell rang again. We appeared to be only customers, but we were not alone.

'Good God!' cried Oscar in alarm as a mass of green and yellow feathers flew violently towards us. 'Is that a parrot?'

A small bird ricocheted about the crowded room, frantically hurling itself against walls and lamps and pictures. We cowered helplessly by the door. Eventually, the creature came to rest on top of a high bookshelf.

'It's a canary,' I said. 'One of a pair.'

Oscar peered up at it suspiciously. 'Known as "Edmond" and "Jules" no doubt.'

'Yes, as it happens. How on earth did you know?'

'I didn't. I guessed. We are in a French bookshop. That the owner should name his twin canaries in honour of the Brothers Goncourt is to be expected.'

I smiled. 'Monsieur Hirsch keeps a monkey as well.'

Oscar sighed. 'Does he dress it as a matelot? How depressing.'

'*Bonjour, messieurs!*' A familiar voice greeted us through the haze. It was the Hon. the Reverend George Daubeney. He emerged, smiling, from behind a narrow beaded curtain at the far end of the shop. He was unshaven, his eyes were bloodshot, his mouth was thick with saliva, but he appeared in the best of humour. He was carrying an artist's portfolio tied together with blue ribbon. He laid it on the cluttered counter and took each of our hands warmly in his. 'This is an unexpected pleasure,' he said, wiping the edge of his lips with his thumb and forefinger, 'but a considerable one.' He was wearing white cotton evening gloves.

'What news of your inheritance, George?' asked Oscar, offering the clergyman one of his new cigarettes.

'Still encouraging, though not yet entirely settled.'

'We thought we might find you here,' I added, holding a match to light both his cigarette and Oscar's.

'What can I do for you? I'm minding the shop for Charles – for Monsieur Hirsch. He's out walking the monkey. It's Monday afternoon. It's very quiet. You're my first customers.'

Oscar's eye was fixed on the artist's portfolio. George Daubeney grinned.

'I've been exploring some of Charles's hidden treasures.' Gingerly, he undid the ribbon and pulled open the portfolio. 'Prints of masterpieces by Peter Paul Rubens. I know you appreciate an ample bosom, Oscar.'

We gazed down on a fine reproduction of Rubens' celebrated painting of Cimone and Efigenia. 'Delicious, aren't they?' gloated the clergyman, running his fingers across the ladies' sumptuous breasts.

'Does he?' I asked, surprised. 'Do you, Oscar? Do you "appreciate an ample bosom"?' Much amused, I looked enquiringly at my friend. His face betrayed nothing as he gazed in silence at the painting and drew slowly on his cigarette.

'Indeed he does,' continued Daubeney, gleefully. 'I recall the advertisements well – posters promoting "Madame Fontaine's Bosom Beautifier", endorsed by the "doctor of aesthetics" himself. "Just as sure as the sun will rise tomorrow, just so sure will it enlarge and beautify the bosom."'

'The words were not mine,' said Oscar, coolly.

'But your portrait was on the poster, Oscar, alongside a spray of lilies, a profusion of sunflowers and, as I remember, the prettiest full-breasted maiden you ever saw.'

'Is this true, Oscar?' I marvelled. 'Did you give your blessing to "Madame Fontaine's Bosom Beautifier"?'

'It was some years ago,' he said. 'I think you were living in Paris at the time.'

'Oh, yes, Robert,' continued Daubeney, with lubricious relish, 'Our Oscar is a noted connoisseur of the female form.'

'My taste has become somewhat more refined with the passing years,' said my friend lightly, feeling in his pocket for another Player's Navy Cut.

Daubeney turned over the first print to reveal another. 'So, Oscar, you prefer something less obvious nowadays, do you? More subtle, less obtrusive, more *gamine*. Is this more to your liking?' The naked girl in the painting was standing on a sheath of red silk, wrapped in fur, gazing out to the artist. Her round breasts rested on her folded arms. 'We are told her name is Helen Fourment. More than that we do not know.'

'She was someone's daughter,' said Oscar, quietly, 'someone's sister . . .'

Daubeney laughed. 'But not yet someone's wife. Look at her innocent face. Look at her mouth. She is a virgin – you may be sure of that.' He turned to the next print. 'This is my favourite. I notice the cuff-links you are wearing, Oscar. I think this may prove to be a favourite with you, too.'

Oscar was wearing the enamel cuff-links that he had worn the day before, the ones that featured a miniature reproduction of Leonardo da Vinci's painting, *The Virgin of the Rocks.* The Rubens print that George Daubeney now displayed was entitled *The Origin of the Milky Way*. It was a painting of the Virgin Mary offering her left breast to the Christ child. With his gloved hands, Daubeney held up the picture for Oscar to inspect more closely. 'Feast your eyes upon the teat, my friend. It quite revives your faith, doesn't it?'

Oscar drew deeply on his cigarette. 'Is this enthusiasm of yours, George, entirely seemly in a man of the cloth?'

'God gave us seed that we might spill it, Oscar,' replied the clergyman, almost in a whisper. He closed the portfolio and began to tie up the blue ribbon. 'If you have had satisfaction from *The Virgin of the Rocks*, I have other, similar cuff-links in stock. Just in from the Americas, I have *The Virgin of Guadalupe* . . .'

'And the price?' Oscar raised his eyebrows and tilted his head. 'Five pounds, as ever?'

'Indeed,' said Daubeney, 'and, as ever, the quality is guaranteed.'

Oscar paused and contemplated Daubeney. 'I now know why you removed your cuff-links when you took refuge in the church on the morning after the fire in Cheyne Walk. It wasn't because the cuff-links didn't match. It was because you realised that you would shortly be interviewed by the police . . .'

Daubeney smiled at Oscar and with the tip of his tongue collected the flecks of moisture from either side of his mouth. 'You noticed?' he said. 'Yes, I removed the cuff-links because I feared that they might send out the wrong signal. In my limited experience, the officers and men of the Metropolitan Police do not appreciate the subtleties of fine art in the way that we do.'

Oscar snapped shut his cigarette case and turned away from the shop counter to look about the room. 'As it happens, George, what we're in search of this afternoon is simply a book. *Un Cœur simple*, a short story, *de Gustave Flaubert*.'

Daubeney wiped his mouth with the back of his hand and moved quickly across the room. He stopped to scan a particular shelf. He ran his fingers alone the spines of assorted volumes. 'Alas, Charles does not appear to have it.' He turned to Oscar and shrugged. 'I can offer you *Madame Bovary*. She had fine breasts.'

'Is that a feature of the novel?' asked Oscar, laughing.

'It is when I read it,' Daubeney replied.

'We must go,' Oscar announced, moving me briskly towards the door. 'Doubtless we shall see you tonight, George – for McMuirtree's bout.'

'Of course. I am the padre. It requires my blessing.'

'*À tout à l'heure*, then, *mon ami*. Give our regards to Monsieur Hirsch.'

Our sullen cabman was waiting where we had left him, at end of Beak Street, outside the Crown tavern. As we climbed aboard the two-wheeler, Oscar remarked: 'At least we've learnt something this afternoon, Robert.'

'And what is that?' I asked.

'That Miss Elizabeth Scott-Rivers was spared a great deal when the Hon. the Reverend George Daubeney broke off their engagement.'

Oscar called up to the driver: 'We failed to find a simple heart in Beak Street, cabby. We're now on our way to the Ring of Death, by way of Gower Street and Tite Street, if you'd be so kind.'

20

The Queensberry Rules

To our surprise, when we reached Astley's Circus amphitheatre that evening, at a few minutes before eight o'clock, we discovered that the steel filings of London town had not been drawn irresistibly towards the magnet of the Ring of Death. The upper tiers of the amphitheatre were all closed and, on the ground floor of the auditorium, the seats around the boxing ring were, at best, a quarter filled.

In vain, we looked about for a familiar face. In due course, searching for the consolation of a drink, we found a handful of our friends clustered together at one end of the rear-stalls bar. Oscar, in a midnight-blue evening suit, with a simple red rose for a buttonhole, stood in the centre of the near-deserted room, his arms outstretched. 'Where is everybody?' he enquired.

'At your play, Oscar,' answered Charles Brookfield, amiably, 'or possibly queuing along Shaftesbury Avenue in the hope of booking tickets for mine. We at least offer *drama*, after our fashion. What's on offer here tonight is but a charade – a "demonstration bout". It counts for nothing.'

'Why are we here then?' asked Oscar, gratefully accepting one of the beakers of cheap champagne being held out to us by Bram Stoker.

'In Queensberry's honour,' said Brookfield. 'The Marquess is a good man. We're supporting him. Simple as that.' He accepted one of Oscar's cigarettes. 'In a few weeks' time, "Gentleman Jim Corbett" will take on "Boston Strong Boy John L. Sullivan" in the heavyweight boxing championship of the world – the first-ever title match prize-fight to be fought with padded gloves according to the Queensberry Rules. History will be made. This is the curtain-raiser – a chance for those who don't know the Queensberry Rules, or still have their doubts about them, to see the rules in action.' He glanced at his pocket watch. 'This evening – somewhat later than advertised, by the look of it – your friend McMuirtree is going head-to-head with another old codger in a "friendly" to demonstrate "fair fighting, Queensberry-style". McMuirtree claims he'll pull no punches – but no blood will be spilt either, that I guarantee.' Brookfield looked about the empty bar. With the corner of his left eye he winked at Oscar. 'No blood: no crowds.'

'Has anyone seen McMuirtree?' I asked.

'We all have,' said Edward Heron-Allen. 'He's in his dressing room, holding court. Your friend, the Reverend Daubeney is in attendance, sprinkling him with holy water.'

'Sickert's there, too,' added Bram Stoker, evidently much amused by the notion, 'sketching the great man as he prepares himself for the ring.' He topped up our champagne.

'And Lord Queensberry?' asked Oscar.

'He's there, as well,' said Brookfield, smiling to himself while studying the plume of smoke rising from his cigarette. 'Very much so.'

Stoker chuckled. 'His lordship is a man obsessed. He keeps whispering his mantra into McMuirtree's ear: "No wrestling, no hugging, nothing below the belt."'

We laughed. 'As you know, Oscar,' said Brookfield, looking up, 'The Queensberry Rules are very clear about hugging and anything below the belt.'

Oscar smiled and took a sip of champagne. 'Were you a boxer at school, Charles?' he asked.

'Not really. Cricket was more my game. I rather fancied myself in "whites".'

'I always think that the postures adopted by those who play cricket are somewhat indecent,' said Oscar lightly, dropping the butt of his cigarette into the dregs of his champagne. He touched my arm. 'Let us go and wish McMuirtree well, Robert.' He looked to Edward Heron-Allen. 'Where did you find the great man's court?'

'Just behind us here,' said Heron-Allen, indicating a painted brown door marked 'Private' to one side of the bar. 'The dressing rooms are along the corridor to the left. McMuirtree's is the first.'

We found it without difficulty. And in it, standing in the centre of the room, we found McMuirtree in high spirits, surrounded by a numerous and oddly assorted entourage. Inspector Gilmour of Scotland Yard was of the party; so were Arthur Conan Doyle and his young friend, Willie Hornung. The Hon. the Reverend George Daubeney was there, changed and shaved since we last we saw him, not sprinkling holy water, as reported, but apparently assisting the boy, Antipholus, who was standing immediately behind McMuirtree, on a three-legged wooden stool, applying oil of some kind to the boxer's bare back and shoulders. On his hands McMuirtree wore large, ungainly, padded leather boxing gloves, bound tightly about his wrists with leather laces. The lacing was being tied for him, not quite by two handmaidens, but, on the left hand, by a young police officer, one of Gilmour's men, dressed in the official uniform of the Metropolitan Police, and on the right, by Walter Sickert, dressed in what appeared to be his own version of the uniform of the Transylvanian national guard. 'Tighter, gentlemen, please – tighter!' commanded McMuirtree, laughing as he gave the order.

Crouched at the boxer's feet was the ape-like figure of John Sholto Douglas, 8th Marquess of Queensberry. He was in full evening dress, but his appearance was anything but *soigné*. His face was red and covered in perspiration. His hands were black. He was squatting, seated uncomfortably on his haunches, holding McMuirtree's right foot in his lap, examining the boxer's boot much as a farrier inspects a horse's shoe. 'No boots with springs allowed,' he muttered. 'No kicking, gouging, butting, biting. No hugging. No blows below the belt.'

As we entered the dressing room and surveyed the scene, McMuirtree called to us: 'Gentlemen, welcome. I'm still alive, you see.'

Conan Doyle, Hornung, Gilmour, Sickert, all spoke a word of greeting. Lord Queensberry looked up at Oscar. 'Are my sons with you?'

'Not Lord Alfred, my lord,' replied Oscar, pleasantly. 'I understand he is dining with his mother. But Lord Drumlanrig hopes to be here, I know. He is a firm believer in the benefits of boxing – and of the Queensberry Rules.' He bowed towards the semi-recumbent marquess. 'Drumlanrig has been raising useful sums for the Earl's Court Boys' Club, I understand.'

'Is Primrose with him?'

'I do believe Lord Rosebery hopes to be here also, yes, sir.'

'Good,' grunted the Marquess, shifting his attention to McMuirtree's other boot. 'They can see how real men fight.'

Behind us, at the dressing-room door, a short man in a tall hat appeared. He carried a large hand-bell which he rang three times. 'The fight's to begin in ten minutes, gentlemen. Kindly clear the room. Only side-men and seconds to remain. The fight's to begin in ten minutes. Kindly clear the room.'

Without debate, we did as we were told, wishing McMuirtree good fortune as we went.

'Is Byrd not one of your supporters?' Oscar asked as we took our leave.

'No,' answered the boxer, now running on the spot and jabbing the air with alternate fists. 'Byrd's on duty at the hotel tonight, but no matter – he's seen me fight often enough. Lord Queensberry and Inspector Gilmour are kindly looking after my interests – I'm in safe hands.'

The entourage was gone. Oscar and I were the last of the visitors to leave. McMuirtree stopped running and stood, alone, between the police inspector and the marquess, towering above them, head erect, arms held out, glistening like a Roman gladiator. Oscar stood in the doorway facing him. 'Good luck, my friend. I've no doubt tonight the better man will win.'

'Thank you,' rasped the boxer. 'And by breakfast, Oscar, all your worries will be over. I will have survived and you'll know for certain that it was only a game.'

We caught up at once with the rest of the party and made our way back, through the rear-stalls bar, to the auditorium. Francis Drumlanrig and Lord Rosebery had now arrived and were seated together, alone, in the centre of one of the rows McMuirtree had reserved for his guests. Oscar went at once to join them, taking Conan Doyle and Willie Hornung with him. I sat in the row immediately behind them, with George Daubeney, Walter Sickert and Edward Heron-Allen.

I did not like Edward Heron-Allen. He was too charming, too intelligent, too well- and widely-read. Whatever the topic of conversation, Heron-Allen had an opinion to voice, an experience to share. When, in the row in front of us, Lord Rosebery, chatting to Conan Doyle, made a passing reference to Sherlock Holmes's beloved Stradivarius, Heron-Allen leant forward to offer his own thoughts on the history of Italian violin-making, reminding us that he had himself been apprentice to George Charnot, 'the greatest violin maker of our time', and that his (Heron-Allen's) treatise, *Violin Making As It Was and Is*, was now in its fifth printing. When Wat Sickert remarked casually that we were having to wait so long for the boxing to begin that he regretted not having brought his library book with him, Heron-Allen immediately embarked on an account of the hours that he had been spending in the Bodleian Library in Oxford preparing his literal translation of *The Rubaiyat of Omar Khayyam*. Medieval Persian, marine biology, meteorology, prostitution, prize-fighting – Edward Heron-Allen had something to say on them all. What was infuriating to me was the way in which his trick of turning every topic back to himself seemed so to amuse everyone else. Others found Heron-Allen immensely engaging – it cannot be denied. And that some of what he had to say held a certain fascination cannot be denied either.

In the moments before the boxing began, the conversation turned to cock-fighting. Heron-Allen, inevitably, was an authority. In North Africa, apparently, he had lived with tribesmen who bred fighting birds – gamecocks, birds of prey and parrots. Heron-Allen had been taught how to cut the comb and wattle off a cock, how to hood the creature to keep it calm before a fight, and how to sharpen the natural spurs on each of its legs. In some cultures, in India and parts of Africa, he explained, birds were set to fight with 'naked heels', using only their natural spurs as weapons. In others, in Europe and America, the birds had man-made 'gaffs' or 'cockspurs' – curved, sharp spikes, sometimes two and a half inches long – tied to their legs with leather bracelets. At his home in Chelsea, Heron-Allen told us, he had a prized collection of silver cockspurs from various lands.

'None from England, I hope,' said Conan Doyle.

'One from Scotland,' answered Heron-Allen, proudly. 'Cock-fighting is still quite legal north of the border.'

'I'm sorry to hear it,' responded the good doctor. 'When Lord Rosebery and his party are returned to government, I trust they'll put a stop to such barbarity.'

Rosebery smiled at Conan Doyle. 'Yours to command, doctor.'

Eventually – perhaps thirty minutes after we had taken our seats – the human bout began. The delay, we later learnt, had been caused by nothing more sinister than the late arrival of McMuirtree's challenger. Alfred Diego (conceived in Lisbon, born on Merseyside) had travelled from Liverpool for the fight. On his home turf, Diego had a reputation: in London he was virtually unknown. Lord Queensberry – who knew British boxing as well as any man alive – had chosen Diego as a suitable opponent for McMuirtree on grounds of 'fairness'. The two men were of comparable age and weight and build. Both were known as 'clean fighters', both had experience of fighting with gloves and both were said (and claimed) never to have been the loser in a prize-fight. The bout in the Ring of Death was not, technically, a prize-fight, of course, but there was a purse attached to it nonetheless. Queensberry was paying each man a fee of £10 for his efforts, with a bonus of a further £10 to be awarded to the victor – on condition that, during the course of the fight, none of the Queensberry Rules was transgressed.

When the opponents appeared together in the ring for the first time, a low roar rumbled around the auditorium of Astley's amphitheatre. When the bell sounded and the first round began, instinctively every man in the hall got to his feet.

'It quickens the blood, does it not?' said Lord Rosebery.

'They're an ill-assorted pair,' remarked Oscar. 'It's Beauty and the Beast.'

Oscar had reason. The two fighters were well-matched in terms of height and size, but their physiognomies could not have been more different. McMuirtree's features were well-proportioned; his eyes were clear and open; his skin was as smooth and unblemished as a girl's. Diego, by contrast, had skin that appeared rough and grimy, like a warthog's, and an ugly, bruised and battered face that looked as if it had been beaten about with a spade. For all that, as the sparring began, Diego looked to be the fitter and faster of the two.

For the first five rounds, McMuirtree barely moved as Diego danced about him nimbly. McMuirtree stood his ground well enough, but he kept his gloves close to his face, defensively, and on the few occasions when he threw a punch, always with his right hand, it landed wide of the mark.

Between each of the three-minute rounds, the fighters retreated to their corners for sixty seconds. While Gilmour wiped a sponge across McMuirtree's face and Queensberry whispered instructions in his ear, Edward Heron-Allen gave us the benefit of his wisdom. 'It's going to be a long haul. I reckon our man's pacing himself deliberately. We could be in for twenty rounds.'

'In real life,' said Wat Sickert, 'there's only one round. Most spontaneous fights last no more than ten seconds. The blow is struck, the blade goes in, a shot is fired – and it's over.'

'This is sport,' said Conan Doyle.

'No,' said Sickert, 'this is pantomime – Punch and Judy for grown-ups.'

The second five rounds were as lacklustre as the first. Diego stayed on the offensive and did not appear to tire. He circled his opponent relentlessly, jabbing away at him, throwing punches high then low then high again in quick succession, forcing McMuirtree to retreat but still not managing to lay a glove on him.

'I see how Beauty retains her loveliness,' said Oscar. 'She keeps out of the sun. She lurks in the shadows, out of harm's way.'

'The crowd won't like it,' murmured Heron-Allen.

'Have patience,' said George Daubeney. 'Patience will be rewarded. Patience always is.'

In the fifteenth round Heron-Allen's prediction came true. The rumble of discontent began at the back of the hall with a single, angry cry: 'For God's sake, McMuirtree, start fighting!' The lone voice was joined at once by others close by, and then the cries spread, like rolling thunder, across the auditorium. Within moments, two hundred men were shouting in unison: 'Fight, fight, fight!'

Curiously, it was Diego – who, for almost an hour, had made all the running – who seemed spurred on by the jeers of the crowd. He moved in close on McMuirtree and instead of pounding his opponent from the front began to throw first a right, then a left hook towards his enemy's head. McMuirtree was now forced to duck and weave to avoid the blows. He kept his guard up at all times, but began to move about the ring more energetically, darting to left and right, forward and back, taunting an increasingly frenzied Diego to chase after him.

It was in the nineteenth round that the nature of the encounter changed decisively. As the referee called 'Round Nineteen' and the starting bell sounded, David McMuirtree, like a man suddenly possessed, sprang upon his opponent. He leapt towards him, jabbing at him with a powerful right fist. Taken off guard, Diego stumbled backwards and fell awkwardly against the ropes, tearing his ear as he fell. Incredibly, instead of going after him, McMuirtree now appeared to retreat, jumping backwards and pounding the empty air with shadow blows while seemingly waiting for his opponent to recover his strength and return to the fray. Diego rose to the bait and lurched towards his assailant with his fists insufficiently raised. As he got within striking distance, for a fraction of a second the scene froze and the hall fell silent as McMuirtree pulled his right arm back and then, with astounding force, landed a single punch in the very centre of Diego's misshapen face. The man's head jerked back, his blood sprayed the ring, his knees buckled. He fell slowly to the ground, like a collapsing tower.

He was down. 'One, two, three . . .' called the referee. 'Four, five, six . . .' roared the crowd.

'Wait!' cried George Daubeney.

'Good God, he's getting up,' gasped Lord Rosebery.

'A little touch of Lazarus in the night,' murmured Oscar.

Alfred Diego was down, but he was not out. Far from it. As the referee called, 'Seven, eight, nine . . .' the man, bloodied but resilient, pushed himself onto his knees and, throwing his head back, rose up quite steadily, seemingly laughing, as if defying McMuirtree to do his worst. In the event, McMuirtree did very little more that round. For the next sixty seconds, until the bell went, the two boxers circled one another warily, throwing and parrying punches without conviction, as if merely sparring to pass the time.

'Twenty rounds,' said Heron-Allen when the break came. 'What did I tell you?'

'Do you think this one will decide it?' I asked.

'Don't you?'

I looked at Lord Queensberry and Inspector Gilmour going about their business in McMuirtree's corner. The policeman was wiping the boxer's torso with a towel and squeezing a wet sponge around his mouth. The Marquess was on his haunches, whispering urgently into his champion's ear.

'My father will be impossible tonight,' muttered Lord Drumlanrig. 'When he's triumphed, he's unbearable.'

'Seconds out! Round Twenty!' called the referee.

The round did not last long. This time, Diego anticipated McMuirtree's pounce and avoided it neatly, feinting to the left before jumping to the right, bringing McMuirtree on after him. Diego, however, held the advantage for only a moment. It was clear that he had given his all; he had nothing more to give: his legs could carry him no longer. The crowd sensed that the climax was upon us. 'Kill! Kill! Kill!' they thundered, stamping their feet and waving their fists, as McMuirtree moved lightly forward and, with alternate fists, began, almost methodically, to pound his opponent about the head.

'He's beating him senseless,' cried Oscar. 'This must be stopped.'

'It will be,' called Heron-Allen. 'Look at the blood.'

In the ring, suddenly, blood was everywhere. Both boxers were awash with blood. Blood was pouring from them onto the canvas. Still the crowd bayed for more: 'Kill! Kill! Kill!'. As the referee ran towards the combatants shouting 'Break! Break!', David McMuirtree delivered his final blows: a left jab, a straight right, a formidable left hook. Alfred Diego crumpled to the ground.

'It's over!' cried Oscar.

'Thank God,' muttered Conan Doyle.

George Daubeney broke away from us and ran down the gangway towards the ring.

In his corner at the ringside, I saw the Marquess of

Queensberry, with his hands raised about his ears, dancing a victory jig.

Inside the ring, David McMuirtree stumbled away from Diego's body and turned triumphantly to face the crowd. His face was white, but his eyes blazed. He held up his arms in salute and as he did so we saw the horror of it. There was blood flowing freely from each of his wrists. It was streaming down his naked arms. As George Daubeney and the referee reached him, his eyes closed and he fell dead into their arms.

21

A Charm Bracelet

'**I** am certain that neither death, nor life, nor angels, nor powers, nor principalities, nor things present, nor things to come, nor height, nor depth, nor anything else in all creation will be able to separate us from the love of God in Jesus Christ our Lord. Amen.'

The Hon. the Reverend George Daubeney, kneeling over the body of David McMuirtree, crossed himself with trembling, bloodied fingers and turned to look up at us. There were tears in his eyes. Daubeney and the referee had dragged McMuirtree's body from the auditorium to the dressing room. They had laid him on an overcoat on the floor.

'Is he dead?' asked Oscar.

'There was no time for the last rites,' said Daubeney.

'Is he dead?' repeated Oscar.

Arthur Conan Doyle was crouching by McMuirtree's head, feeling for the pulse in his neck. 'He's dead, I'm afraid, old man. There's no doubt about that.'

'I thought so,' said Oscar, quietly. 'One can always tell. When a man dies, his spirit vanishes. It never lingers. It is gone at once.'

'What in God's name has happened?' The Marquess of Queensberry, like a rampaging bull, burst into the dressing room. He had a whip in his hand. He cracked it again and again against the three-legged wooden stool that Antipholus had used when oiling the boxer two hours before and roared: 'In God's name, will someone tell me what has happened?'

'Something outwith the Queensberry Rules,' murmured Oscar. 'Your champion is dead, my lord.'

'He can't be!' cried Queensberry, swinging round in a circle like a dervish, holding out his whip as if to keep us all at bay.

'It seems he is, Lord Queensberry,' said Inspector Gilmour. He drew himself to attention as he spoke. 'I'm very sorry.'

'Sorry?' roared Queensberry. 'Sorry? I've never heard of such incompetence.'

'A man lies dead before us, my lord,' said Oscar quietly, 'and you talk of "incompetence"?'

'What else is it?' raged the Marquess. 'Gilmour said he had the building crawling with police officers in plain clothes. How has this happened?'

'I do not know,' said Inspector Gilmour, gravely. 'I do not know, but I intend to find out. McMuirtree was one of ours.'

'Yes,' growled Queensberry. 'So you told me.' He pointed his whip towards McMuirtree's body laid out upon the floor. 'We can all see how you take care of your own.' He looked about the room angrily. 'Where's the referee gone?'

'He's gone to see Diego and his supporters,' explained Daubeney, getting to his feet and backing away from the body on the floor. 'He felt he should.'

'Two of my men are with Diego,' said Inspector Gilmour. 'I will interview him as soon as he's recovered.'

Oscar shook his head. 'Alfred Diego has nothing to do with this sorry business.'

Conan Doyle had moved to the side of McMuirtree's body and was now kneeling on the edge of the overcoat inspecting the dead man's wrists and arms. 'This is the devil's work,' he muttered.

'I don't doubt it,' said Oscar, forcing himself to step closer.

'This is utterly grotesque,' continued Doyle, slowly unravelling the blood-soaked laces that had bound the boxing gloves to McMuirtree's wrists.

'Fiendishly ingenious by the look of it,' said Oscar grimly. He bent over the cadaver and through half-closed eyes peered closely at McMuirtree's lifeless arms. 'Like a martyr's wounds . . . May God forgive whoever has done this terrible thing.'

'It is truly terrible,' said Conan Doyle, shaking his head. 'In all my experience, I've seen nothing like it.'

Queensberry had calmed himself and was standing, whip in hand, arms akimbo, gazing down at the blood-drenched body on the floor. 'I admired this man. He was almost like a son to me. He was better than the sons I've got. He was blessed with a natural nobility. He was proper fighting man, fit and strong. And he had intelligence and guile. He could pace himself – that's rare. He was a decent man, too – clean-living. That's rarer still.'

Archy Gilmour crouched down beside Arthur Doyle. The policeman was by several years the older of the two, but he did not seem it. With his light red hair and fair, freckled, anxious face, he looked like a young actor playing the part of a detective inspector for the very first time. He tried to speak with authority, but sounded merely bewildered. 'Well, Doctor?' he enquired.

'It is as horrific as it appears to be, Inspector,' Doyle replied, carefully turning back the leather wrist-band of one of McMuirtree's boxing gloves to reveal a two-inch-long jagged blade. He tugged at the wrist band with his fingers and tore apart the sodden leather, exposing a second blade – smaller than the first – and then a third, and then a fourth. 'Do you see?'

'I don't see,' growled Queensberry. 'What is the meaning of this?'

'It's very simple,' said Oscar. 'Someone has sewn a series of tiny blades – jagged, sharp and lethal – into the leather lining of the wrist-bands of McMuirtree's gloves. During the fight, over time, as McMuirtree began to sweat and the laces loosened, with the movement of his wrists the blades cut through the lining . . . The more he punched, the harder he punched, eventually the blades cut through the veins in his wrists as well.'

'Not just the veins,' said Conan Doyle. 'He might have survived that. The arteries were cut, too – sliced through.' With his forefinger the doctor indicated each side of McMuirtree's bloodied wrist. 'On both hands, both the radial and the ulnar arteries have been severed.'

'Is that why there is so much blood?' asked the red-haired policeman, contemplating McMuirtree's arms and chest and legs all covered in gore.

'Yes,' said Conan Doyle. 'It's the quantity of blood that he lost – and the speed at which he lost it – that killed him.'

'The wretched man was streaming blood,' said Oscar. 'Look at Daubeney. He's covered in it now.'

We all turned to look at the Reverend George. He had carried McMuirtree from the ring and brought him to the dressing room. He stood before us now, like Banquo's murderer, his hands and shirt-front glistening with the dead man's blood.

Edward Heron-Allen was standing just behind Daubeney, by the gas lamp in the corner of the room. 'Forgive me for speaking,' he said, a little too loudly, 'but my uncle was a surgeon and I always understood that a single cut across a healthy artery is not dangerous because an artery – unlike a vein – has an in-built muscle that contracts to staunch the blood.'

'Indeed,' said Conan Doyle, studying Heron-Allen with interest. 'That is correct. On its own a single, clean cut across the wrist might not prove fatal – as many a half-hearted suicide has learnt.'

'And whoever did this knew that much also,' said Oscar, lowering himself with difficulty onto his knees and squinting at the wrist-bands of McMuirtree's boxing gloves. 'Hence the multiplicity of blades – and the variety of angles.'

'Yes,' said Conan Doyle in a business-like way, sitting back and scratching his moustache. 'The blood vessels in this case have been sliced *repeatedly*, and – more to the point – sliced *vertically* as well as diagonally.'

'Would he not have felt the pain?' I asked.

'No,' answered the doctor, shaking his head, 'not in the heat of battle.'

'A man can lose a leg in the heat of battle and not notice it,' said Lord Queensberry, curtly.

'With your permission, Inspector . . .' Oscar, still on his knees, leant forward over McMuirtree's body and, with his right thumb and forefinger, picked out one of the tiny blades and held it up. It was no more than three-quarters of an inch long and an eighth of an inch wide. As he lifted it off the fringe of the glove, we saw that it was attached to a second blade by a slender piece of thread. The second blade was tied to a third, the third to a fourth, and so on. Oscar held the chain of little blades aloft. There were seven of them in all.

'It looks like a charm bracelet,' said Heron-Allen.

Oscar looked at his wife's friend without his customary, indulgent smile. 'Of a sort, Edward,' he said coldly.

'He's been ... murdered?' asked the Marquess of Queensberry falteringly, as though the truth were only just dawning upon him.

'Or he's taken his own life,' suggested Oscar.

The police inspector looked up at Oscar, incredulous. He held his hand out over the boxer's bloody corpse. 'Like this?' he demanded.

'You were in the room, Inspector, when he put on the gloves. One of your men helped lace them up for him, as I recall – assisted by Wat Sickert. I distinctly recollect McMuirtree asking you to pull the laces tighter. He made a point of it. Perhaps Mr Heron-Allen is right: perhaps to David McMuirtree these were charm bracelets of a kind. Perhaps he sought a public death . . .'

'As a form of absolution?' asked the Reverend George.

'Exactly,' answered Oscar. 'A public suicide – on a stage, in an arena, within "the Ring of Death" . . .'

'This is absurd, Oscar,' said Conan Doyle.

'McMuirtree was not a man for suicide,' barked Lord Queensberry.

'In certain circumstances, is not suicide allowable, my lord? Laudable, even . . . Nay, in certain circumstances, heroic?' He paused and looked about the room. 'There is something heroic in this bloody scene, is there not?'

'No,' answered Conan Doyle abruptly. 'Sometimes, Oscar, you go too far.'

Oscar began to struggle to his feet. He seemed almost to be laughing to himself. As I helped him up, he squeezed my arm.

'I agree with Dr Doyle,' said Inspector Gilmour. 'Suicide is out of the question. We were all with McMuirtree before the fight. He was evidently in the best of spirits. He did not appear in the least to be a man who was about to take his own life.'

'The same could be said of Bradford Pearse,' said Oscar.

'*Why* should McMuirtree take his own life, Mr Wilde?'

'Why should Bradford Pearse, Inspector?'

'Who is Bradford Pearse?' demanded Lord Queensberry. 'What's he to do with it? What's his involvement?'

'None, my lord,' said the police inspector quickly. 'He is a friend of Mr Wilde's. He has nothing to do with this matter.'

'Are you certain?' asked Oscar, raising an eyebrow.

'I am certain, Mr Wilde. I am certain that David McMuirtree has been murdered – and that his tragic and untimely death has nothing to do with you or any of your friends, nothing to do with your dinner or your foolish game.'

'What's this all about?' grumbled Lord Queensberry impatiently, beating the side of his own thigh with his whip.

'Nothing, your lordship,' said the police inspector. 'I simply want Mr Wilde to understand that David McMuirtree has been murdered because he was one of us — because he was on the side of law and order. David McMuirtree was a police informer. Such men are necessary. Such men are brave. They put their lives at risk and sometimes they pay the price. McMuirtree had enemies — hardened criminals, evil men who sought to kill him for what he was, for what he knew.'

'These hardened criminals of yours are blessed with wonderfully theatrical imaginations, Inspector,' said Oscar mockingly. 'You might expect a police informer to be beaten to death with a cudgel, or knifed in a dark alley, or even shot as he was alighting from a carriage — but to be killed, as McMuirtree has been killed, by a pair of deadly bracelets sewn inside his boxing gloves suggests a band of desperadoes that is — to say the least of it — a little out of the ordinary.'

'If you will forgive me, Mr Wilde,' said the police inspector, 'we have work to do.' He looked around the room, widening his eyes and clearing his throat. He held his hands out, palms open, as if to sweep us from the room. 'I'd be grateful if Dr Doyle could remain until the police surgeon arrives, but, otherwise, gentlemen, you are free to depart. Thank you for your assistance.'

'Do you need me further?' grunted Lord Queensberry, rubbing the back of his neck with his whip and taking a final look at McMuirtree's body lying on the floor.

'No, thank you, your lordship — you're free to go.'

'But, Inspector,' said Oscar, 'surely you want to ask Lord Queensberry about the gloves?'

'What about the gloves?' asked Gilmour irritably.

'Who gave McMuirtree the boxing gloves that he was wearing?'

'I did,' said Lord Queensberry. 'A week ago. They were brand new – as required by the Queensberry Rules.'

'Did you inspect them before you gave them to McMuirtree?'

'I did,' said the Marquess. 'They were in perfect condition. Made by Messrs Sims and Pittam, the best boxing gloves that money can buy.'

'And you brought them here yourself, last Monday?' The police inspector listened impatiently as Oscar pursued his line of questioning.

'I did,' said Lord Queensberry. 'In that box.' With his whip the Marquess pointed to an empty cardboard box that lay open on the floor in the corner of the room.

'Did McMuirtree inspect the gloves?'

'He did. He tried them on. He expressed himself well satisfied with them.'

'Did he then wear them during his training?'

'No. That would have been contrary to the rules. As far as I know, he left them here in that box until today.'

Gilmour was about to intervene, but Conan Doyle put his hand on the policeman's arm to stop him. 'And between last Monday and this evening,' Oscar continued, 'who in your view, Lord Queensberry, could have had access to this room and to that box?'

'Anyone, so far as I know. At least, anyone who had access of any kind to the building. There are no locks on the dressing-room doors.'

Oscar smiled. 'You noticed that?'

'I notice a good deal, Mr Wilde. You'll find that there's more to me than some suppose.'

'I don't doubt it, my lord,' said Oscar graciously. He stepped towards the dressing-room door and stood within the threshold. He turned and glanced from left to right along the corridor. He turned back and surveyed the room. 'There are no locks on the dressing-room doors and the entrances to Astley's Circus amphitheatre are many and varied.'

'We've been watching them,' said Inspector Gilmour sharply.

'I'm sure you have, Inspector. McMuirtree was one of yours, after all. May I ask: at any one time, how many men did you have watching the building?'

Gilmour hesitated.

'Well?' said Oscar.

'Two.'

'There are six public entrances to this building, Inspector. Five of them are shut, except on performance days. One of them is open every day when the box office is open. There are, additionally, three tradesmen's entrances. And there is a stage door leading to an interesting passageway that runs directly from the Thames embankment to the circus arena itself. Let us assume that the boy, Antipholus, who guards the stage door is not part of the conspiracy and that your two officers were not corrupt, that still leaves a multitude of entrances and opportunities for anyone who wished to do so to slip into the building and tamper with the gloves – assuming that it was not McMuirtree himself who did it . . . I agree, Inspector. You have work to do. We must not detain you. We will be on our way.'

We nodded our goodbyes and left the circus at once. Outside, in the darkened street, as we stood on the kerb, we noticed, underneath a lamp-post, immediately facing us, on the other side of the road, leaning against the embankment parapet, a small, familiar figure in a shabby suit. The light shone brightly on his yellow face. As we waited to cross the road, a police growler trundled past and the little man scuttled into the darkness.

'Is he watching us?' I asked.

'Watching,' said Oscar grimly, 'or waiting . . . Waiting for his moment to pounce.'

Oscar's Grid

O n the following morning – the morning of Tuesday, 10 May 1892, when, according to my journal, the streets of London were 'damp and dismal' and the sky was 'overcast and threatening' – I joined my friend Oscar Wilde in the oak-panelled dining room of the Cadogan Hotel at a little after half past ten. I had gone in answer to his urgent summons – a telegram that reached me in my room in Gower Street at nine o'clock:

> COME TO THE CADOGAN AT ONCE. BRING GALOSHES AND INSPIRATION. OSCAR.

I found my friend seated at a corner table, alone, the débris of breakfast all around him. In his right hand he held both a pencil and a lighted cigarette; in his left he nursed a glass of Portuguese Arinto wine. Before him lay a sheet of foolscap writing paper, densely covered with lines and dates and names and emendations.

As I approached, he looked up at me. His hair was well-brushed and he was freshly shaven, but there were ochre circles beneath his red-rimmed eyes. 'Has it stopped raining?' he asked, smiling at me gently and drawing slowly on his cigarette.

'For the moment,' I said. I sat down beside him and looked around the table for a coffee cup. 'How are you this morning?' I asked.

He closed his eyes and through his nostrils exhaled a long, slow, mistral of cigarette smoke. 'I am *exhausted*, Robert, utterly.' Still holding the cigarette and pencil, he picked up the coffee pot and poured me a cup. 'I thought that breakfast might revive me. I ordered kippers. The folly of it, Robert! Kippers for breakfast are like cobblestones in a cathedral close – charming in prospect, deuced hard work when you get to them. I have spent an hour picking away at the tiny bones.'

'What's this?' I asked, indicating his sheet of foolscap.

'This is the reason for my summons, Robert. This is my grid.'

'Your "grid"?' I repeated, puzzled.

'A new word to the language, Robert – a back-formation derived from the word "gridiron". Since the fourteenth century the gridiron has served as a simple grate for broiling food upon. In the nineteenth century, the "grid" has become an essential tool of scholarship.' He waved to the waiter to bring me a glass of wine. 'You will recall, Robert, that in 1871 I was called to Trinity College, Dublin, where I won the Berkeley Gold Medal for Greek and was elected to a Queen's Scholarship. You will further recall that in 1874 I went up to Oxford, taking a scholarship at Magdalen College and, in 1876, I achieved First Class honours in Classical Moderations. Two years later I took a further First in Literae Humaniores and, in 1878, my university career came to a fitting climax when I read my Newdigate Prize Poem in the hallowed hall that is the Sheldonian Theatre.' He paused as the waiter poured me

'Oscar's Grid'

The 'gridiron' created by Oscar Wilde over breakfast at the Cadogan Hotel on Tuesday 10 May 1892

Name of 'victim'	Who chosen by	Date & occurrence
Miss Elizabeth Scott-Rivers	The Hon. the Rev. George Daubeney	Sunday 1 May – death by fire
Lord Abergordon	Lord Drumlanrig	Monday 2 May – death by natural causes
Captain Flint	Lord Alfred Douglas	Tuesday 3 May – psittacicide
Sherlock Holmes	Willie Hornung	Wednesday 4 May
Bradford Pearse	?	Thursday 5 May – murder or suicide?
David McMuirtree	Robert Sherard	Friday 6 May
David McMuirtree	Walter Sickert	Saturday 7 May
David McMuirtree	?	Sunday 8 May
David McMuirtree	?	Monday 9 May – murder or suicide?
Old Father Time	?	Tuesday 10 May
Eros	David McMuirtree	Wednesday 11 May
A blank slip	OW *and* Arthur Conan Doyle?	Thursday 12 May
Mr Oscar Wilde	?	Friday 13 May
Mrs Oscar Wilde	?	Saturday 14 May

a glass of Arinto and topped up his. Oscar sipped at the wine and then continued: 'These scholastic accomplishments were something, Robert, to be sure – at least my mother felt so – but they were not enough, not nearly enough . . . I can dream dreams in Virgilian hexameters; I can translate Homer on sight; I can unravel Thucydides in the twinkling of an eye; but to get to grips with the case in hand, Robert – to *begin* to get to grips with it – I need a grid!'

I obliged him with a chuckle. 'So what exactly is this "grid"?' I enquired.

'It's an ingenious network of uniformly spaced perpendicular and horizontal lines. It's the sort of thing that Michelangelo or Galileo should have conceived centuries ago, but apparently failed to do so. In essence, it's a device for ordering one's thoughts. In this case to date, mine have been a jumble.'

'And now?'

'Now, at least,' he said, passing me his sheet of foolscap, 'I see the nature of the jumble. I have laid out what information we have within the grid.'

I studied his piece of paper. It was easy to read. Oscar's manner was flamboyant; his speech was florid; but his handwriting was surprisingly neat. 'And what does all this tell us?'

'It tells us what we do not know, which is much – and it tells us, also, that some of what we know makes no sense.'

I looked at him, confused.

'We know who was at the fateful meeting of the Socrates Club on the night of 1 May, but we do not yet know, in every instance, which diner chose which victim.

We need to find out. This morning, before breakfast, I telephoned Arthur Conan Doyle.'

'And how was he?' I interjected.

'In fine fettle. Never better. Convinced that Inspector Gilmour is right and that McMuirtree's bizarre and bloody death has nothing to do with us. "Just an unlucky coincidence," according to Arthur. It was not yet nine o'clock when I put through my telephone call. The good doctor had already completed his morning course of callisthenics and breakfasted – sensibly, on porridge not on kippers. He told me that he was planning to spend the morning in his hut, moulding his damp clay while contemplating ways and means of doing away with Sherlock Holmes. He was as brim-full of good cheer as a choirboy at Christmas – until I asked him a question about the night of 1 May . . .'

'Ah,' I murmured, leaning forward.

Oscar smiled at me. 'You are a good audience, Robert. You will never lack friends.'

'Well?' I said. 'What did you ask him?'

'I asked Dr Doyle if he had chosen *me* as his particular "victim" on the night when we played that foolish game of "Murder". He seemed taken aback by the question – quite shocked by the suggestion, in fact. "Why should I name you, Oscar?" he asked. "Why not?" I replied. "Willie Hornung named Sherlock Holmes as his victim," I reminded him, "and Willie is your friend." "Willie's just a foolish boy," said Arthur. "Was it you who named me, Arthur?" I repeated. "Certainly not," he said. He said it quite indignantly. "Then who did you name?" I asked.' Oscar paused and took another sip of wine. He swallowed it slowly and closed his eyes.

'Well?' I prompted him, impatiently.

Oscar opened his eyes and looked at me steadily. ' "No one," said Arthur. "I named no one." '

'What on earth did he mean?'

' "What do you mean, Arthur?" I asked him. "You named no one?" "I named no one," repeated Arthur. "I did not wish to participate in the game, so I named no one. Mine was the blank piece of paper drawn from the bag." '

'Ah . . .' I said.

'You may well say "Ah!", Robert,' Oscar smiled. 'I said to Arthur on the telephone: "Yours cannot have been the blank piece of paper drawn from the bag, my friend." "And why not, pray?" he asked. "Because, Arthur," I explained, "the blank piece of paper drawn from the bag – it was mine." '

'But, Oscar,' I said cautiously, 'I was at the dinner. I was watching you as we played the game. I'm sure I saw you writing a name on your slip of paper . . . I'm sure of it.'

'The eye can deceive, Robert. You certainly saw me applying the nib of my pen to a slip of paper, but the nib was dry. I moved the pen across the paper, but I left no mark.'

'Gracious me,' I murmured, putting down my glass. 'This means—'

'Yes,' mused Oscar, lighting another cigarette, 'just one blank slip of paper drawn from the bag, but two people claiming credit for it – and two people one likes to think one could trust. The glass darkens, Robert. The plot thickens. The mystery deepens. Despite my grid, I'm at a loss. Perhaps, like poor, doomed Holmes, I should resort to drugs or the violin as aids to inspiration. Do you keep cocaine in your rooms, Robert? Do you have a Stradivarius I might borrow?'

'No,' I answered, laughing. 'The only musical instrument I own is a triangle. You're welcome to that.'

'A triangle? How wise, Robert – so much easier to pack.'

I smiled and looked down at his 'grid'. 'What is "psittacicide"?' I asked.

' "The killing of parrots",' he answered. 'I grieve for your classical education, Robert. You are the great-grandson of William Wordsworth!'

I decided to rise above his banter. 'The deaths in this case are certainly unusual,' I remarked.

'Are they not?' he said, leaning forward. 'Elizabeth Scott-Rivers is consumed by fire; Bradford Pearse is thrown to the waves; for David McMuirtree it is death by a thousand cuts . . . This is manslaughter on an apocalyptic scale.'

'Lord Abergordon died in his sleep,' I said, returning his sheet of foolscap to him.

'So we are told.' He drained his glass and extinguished his cigarette briskly. He waved towards the waiter for our bill. 'How do you think the murderer plans to despatch me?' he asked, smiling.

'Do you truly believe your life is threatened, Oscar?'

'You've seen the ugly little man with the sallow skin and the ferret's eyes. He's trailing me for a purpose, Robert – and it's not a benign one. My life is threatened, without doubt . . . And Constance's life, also. I have loved her. I owe her much. I married her. I must protect her now.'

'Perhaps you should ask Gilmour to put a police guard on Tite Street,' I suggested.

'Not yet. Constance knows nothing of this still. I do not want to alarm her before I must. According to the logic of the grid, we should both be safe enough till Friday. These deaths occur sequentially and on the day appointed.' He glanced down at his 'grid'. 'I am not surprised that Friday the thirteenth is destined as my doomsday.' Smiling, he folded the sheet of paper and placed it carefully in his jacket pocket. 'We have three days in which to solve the mystery, Robert. Three days in which to find our murderer.' He pocketed his pencil and his cigarette case, wiped his lips with his napkin and tossed it lightly onto the table.

'Can it be done?' I asked, puzzled at how sanguine he seemed under the circumstances.

He got to his feet and straightened his waistcoat in a business-like fashion. 'When you think what our Lord managed in three days at the end of Holy Week, I am full of hope, Robert. With your assistance, my friend, and with the aid of our grid, anything is possible. Come.'

I got to my feet. 'Where are we going?' I asked.

'To meet the suspects, one by one. In turn, to interview each of those who attended the Socrates Club dinner – to learn his secret. We shall start here. I trust you have brought your notebook with you?'

In the entrance hallway of the Cadogan Hotel, we found young Nat, Oscar's friend, the freckled page-boy.

'We're looking for Mr Byrd, Nat,' said Oscar, slipping the lad a sixpenny piece. 'Is he about?'

The boy glanced at the grandfather clock at the foot of the stairs. 'He'll still be in his bedroom, Mr Wilde, but he should be awake. Shall I take you?'

The boy led us through a series of baize-covered doors, along a labyrinth of dark corridors to a narrow stone staircase at the very back of the building. 'It's seventy steps, Mr Wilde,' said the boy solicitously. 'Can you manage?'

'I have no idea!' exclaimed Oscar. 'I have never attempted anything so hazardous before.'

In the event, Oscar climbed the stairs quite nimbly. At every landing, he paused and asked the boy a different question. What did Nat think of Mr Byrd? He liked him: Byrd was a magician and Nat liked that. Did Mr Byrd have many friends? Beyond Mr McMuirtree, none that Nat knew of. Mr Byrd kept himself very much to himself. How had the hotel night manager felt about Captain Flint? According to Nat, Mr Byrd thought the world of the parrot. 'He loved that parrot, Mr Wilde – doted on it.' Had the boy seen Mr Byrd on the previous evening? Yes, Mr Byrd was in and around the hotel all evening, as usual. 'He was mostly in his office or in the lobby. I was on duty till ten, Mr Wilde, like normal. I'm sure Mr Byrd never left the building all night.'

When we reached the attic floor, Nat led us along a narrow uncarpeted corridor, where the ceiling was so low Oscar had to duck his head. There were unpainted, unvarnished pinewood doors on either side of the corridor and the only light came from a round window at the far end. 'All the male live-in staff sleep up here,' explained the boy. 'I share with Billy, the other page-boy, and with Dan and Jonty, the two kitchen lads. We're opposite Mr Byrd. He's here.' We had reached the last door in the corridor.

'Thank you, Nat,' said Oscar, producing another coin for the boy. 'You have brought us to the summit. We'll do our best to find our own way down.'

The boy took the coin in his left hand and, with his right, gave us a smart salute. With a grin, he then opened his left hand to reveal that the coin had disappeared. Next, he passed his right hand lightly over his head and held out his right palm to reveal Oscar's coin lying on it.

'Bravo!' I said.

'How old are you now, lad?' asked Oscar.

'Fifteen, sir,' said the boy, 'sixteen nearly.'

'Romeo's age – a perfect age. Stick with it, Nat. The secret of remaining young is never to have an emotion that is unbecoming. You understand that, don't you?'

'I don't understand a word you say, Mr Wilde, but I know it's good stuff.'

The boy scampered off down the corridor and Oscar, smiling, knocked on Byrd's bedroom door.

'Come!' called a voice from within.

We entered the room. It was dark and uncomfortably hot. There was an unsavoury stench in the air, the odour of sweat and sour milk. 'You do not lock your door, Mr Byrd?' asked Oscar.

'I have nothing to fear, I hope,' said Byrd. He was sitting on the edge of his bed, clothed but unshaven. He did not stir as we came into the room. He sat as he was, his narrow shoulders slumped forward, his cadaverous head bowed low. An oil lamp glowed dismally on the bedside table.

'You have heard the news?' Oscar enquired.

Byrd nodded. His hands were clasped together on his lap. Between them he appeared to be kneading a small piece of coloured cloth, pressing it and turning it between his clenched right fist and his cupped left palm. 'Yes,' he said, barely above a whisper, 'I have heard the news. Mr Sickert and Mr Brookfield came to the hotel late last night. Not to see me, of course. They came by for a night-cap, that's all. But when they were leaving they passed me in the hallway. They told me what had happened.'

'I am sorry,' said Oscar.

'McMuirtree was my friend,' said Byrd, looking up at us for the first time. In the dim light I saw the anguish in his eyes.

Had you known him long?' asked Oscar.

'Twenty years,' said Byrd. 'Half a lifetime. We met at the crossroads.' Slowly he turned his head and looked about the room, as if he were seeing it for the first time. I followed his gaze. The room was crowded with boxes, trunks and cases, the stage properties and paraphernalia from his magic show. A silence fell.

'The crossroads?' repeated Oscar, eventually.

'The crossroads,' answered Byrd sharply, 'where McMuirtree, half-a-gentleman, took the high road to fame and fortune, and I took the low road that led to where you find me now.'

'Ah,' said Oscar. 'You were a gentleman . . . I did not realise.'

'Did you not?' said Byrd, looking directly at Oscar. 'My father was a gentleman, a merchant, from Liverpool. My mother was a lady. She died soon after I was born. My father died on my eighteenth birthday. He shot himself. He owned a ship and he lost it in the China seas. When his ship went down, his fortune sank with it. A merchant without means ceases to be a gentleman. I was at the university at the time, Mr Wilde – your university, where you won all those prizes.'

'I did not know,' said Oscar. 'What college were you at? I was at Magdalen.'

'I know,' said Byrd, looking down at his hands once more. 'I was at New.'

'Ah,' said Oscar amiably. He turned to me. 'What was your college, Robert?'

'I was at New College, too,' I said.

'I thought so.'

'And I did not complete my degree either,' I added.

'I did not complete my first term,' said Byrd. 'I left Oxford within a fortnight of my father's death. I took to the road. I followed in the footsteps of my childhood heroes – Maskelyne and Cooke, the great illusionists. My father had taken me to see them perform at the Egyptian Hall in Piccadilly. I marvelled at all that they did. I wanted to be like them. I went to work for them. I was apprenticed to them for two years. They taught me my craft.'

'You learnt it well,' I said.

'I learnt the craft of it. I mastered the tricks. My technique was impressive, but according to John Maskelyne, I lacked "the immortal spark". I did not "engage" the audience.'

'You did not look them in the eye,' suggested Oscar.

'Precisely,' replied Byrd, staring steadily at Oscar. 'Exactly so. I lacked the courage. According to John Maskelyne, to be a great illusionist requires daring and what he called "panache". I had neither.'

'But David McMuirtree had both . . . enough for two?'

Byrd gave a hollow laugh. 'You appear to know my story, Mr Wilde.'

'I guess at it, that's all,' said Oscar kindly.

'McMuirtree came to work for Maskelyne and Cooke as well. We were of an age, but he was everything that I was not. He was strong; he was handsome; he could engage the crowd. I was the better magician, but he was the bigger man. We completed our apprenticeship with Maskelyne and Cooke and took to the road ourselves.'

'As "McMuirtree and Byrd"?'

'Exactly so.'

'And did you prosper?' Oscar enquired.

'We might have done. Thanks to Mr Maskelyne, we had contacts. We got bookings. We were at the bottom of the bill, of course, because we were young and unknown, but we had prospects. We might have prospered, given time. But McMuirtree was impatient – and easily distracted. He took up boxing. He saw it as a more certain path to glory. And then, of a sudden, almost on a whim, he joined the Metropolitan Police. They gave him opportunities to box and a steady income.'

'He abandoned you?'

'He went his own way, but we kept in touch. We never lost touch.'

'But you abandoned the stage?' asked Oscar.

'Without McMuirtree, I had little choice. John Maskelyne was right, Mr Wilde. I lacked courage and panache. And I was not tall enough to join the Metropolitan Police.' He looked up at us both and grimaced and opened his fingers to let a handful of green feathers flutter to the ground.

'Poor Captain Flint,' said Oscar.

Byrd leant forward and carefully picked up each of the tiny feathers. There were thirteen of them in all.

'Where is your parrot now?' asked Oscar.

'I have laid him to rest,' said Byrd.

I looked about the room, wondering in which box or trunk or magician's cabinet the unhappy hotel manager had placed the mortal remains of his feathered friend.

'Not here,' he said, with a dry laugh. 'At my allotment – by Brompton Cemetery.'

Oscar looked surprised. 'You have an allotment, Mr Byrd?'

'A small one. Gardening is my only pleasure now. I work nights here at the hotel so that by day I can dig my patch of earth. I lead a simple life, Mr Wilde. "Having the fewest wants, I am nearest to the gods."'

Oscar smiled. 'I recognise the line.' He looked down at Alphonse Byrd and shifted the weight between his feet. 'And speaking of Socrates, Mr Byrd, let me come to the point and then Mr Sherard and I can leave you in peace. At our club dinner the other Sunday, during my foolish game, you will recall that it was Lord Alfred Douglas who named Captain Flint as his intended victim?' Byrd nodded, but said nothing. Oscar continued: 'I am certain that Lord Alfred meant the bird no serious harm. It was just one of his less happy jokes – and for it, and on his behalf, I apologise. So the question remains: who do you think killed the parrot, Mr Byrd?'

Byrd gazed down at the feathers in his hand. 'Who would do such a thing?' he murmured. 'I have no idea. None whatsoever. A monster, that's for certain.'

Oscar pressed him. 'You have no idea, Mr Byrd?'

'None at all. None.'

'And who do you think might have killed David McMuirtree?' asked Oscar.

'Oh,' answered Byrd, without hesitation, 'I'm certain the police will be able to tell you that.'

'Really?' countered Oscar.

'David McMuirtree worked for the police. He was a police informer. He will have been killed by a member of the criminal fraternity bent on revenge. Of that I'm certain. His life always hung by a thread. He knew it.'

'Is that why, at the Socrates Club dinner, when we played the game of "Murder", you named your friend as your victim of choice?'

Byrd looked up at Oscar and laughed. It was an easy laugh. 'How did you know that, Mr Wilde?'

'I did not know it, Mr Byrd.'

'It was a joke, that's all. It was a joke that he appreciated. I told him about it afterwards. He often joked about the possibility of being murdered. It did not seem to trouble him.'

'He had courage and panache,' said Oscar.

'"Nothing can harm a good man, either in life or after death",' said Byrd, taking a deep breath and closing his hands around his parrot's feathers.

'Ah,' said Oscar, 'Socrates once again.' He turned to me and nodded, indicating that it was time for us to leave.

'I was a classicist once, Mr Wilde,' said Alphonse Byrd, not stirring from his bed.

'Indeed,' said Oscar, bowing towards him. 'And a gentleman.'

23

Ever Thus

'What now?' I asked as we came down the steps of the Cadogan Hotel onto Sloane Street.

There was colour in Oscar's cheeks and a sparkle in his eyes. He stood for a moment considering his next move and then announced: 'We turn left, I think.'

He took my arm and steered me in the direction of Knightsbridge. At the very moment that he did so, there was a sudden, sharp, crashing sound behind us. We turned abruptly and saw, smashed into pieces on the pavement immediately behind us, the remains of a large black slate that had fallen from the roof of the hotel. In silence, we looked up at the building. On every floor the windows were all shut. No curtains twitched. A pair of pigeons hovered about the rooftop and landed on the chimney stack.

'Let us go to the police,' I said urgently.

Oscar laughed. 'Because of a loose tile on a hotel roof? That was an accident, Robert . . .'

'You might have been killed.'

'But I wasn't,' he said calmly. 'And nor were you.'

'Let us go to the police,' I repeated.

'All in good time,' he said. 'I need to visit the post office first. I have telegrams to send – to Oxford, to Eastbourne, to Bosie and to Constance.'

'To Constance?' I queried, as he took my arm once more and steered me in the direction of his choosing. 'I thought we were lunching with Constance in Tite Street?'

'We are,' said Oscar, happily. 'My telegram will arrive after luncheon. It will show her that we anticipated how grateful we would be.' His arm was linked through mine. His large head was erect and held back (he liked his chestnut hair to catch the breeze), but his sloping eyes glanced down towards me and he smiled. 'When Constance and I first met, Robert, we telegraphed each other twice a day – at least! – and at a moment's notice I rushed back from the uttermost parts of the earth to see her for an hour and do all the foolish things that wise lovers do. Romance lives by repetition. Do you think that if I behave once more as once I did, I will feel once more for her as once I felt?'

I did not answer him. What could I say?

As we reached the corner of Knightsbridge and Brompton Road and paused at the kerbside, Oscar took his arm from mine and reached for his cigarette case. 'What did you make of friend Byrd?' he asked, offering me a cigarette.

'He struck me as being a somewhat pathetic creature,' I answered.

'Indeed.' He struck a match and cupped his hands around the flame. He lit my cigarette. 'But I was intrigued to find that the great John Maskelyne had been among his mentors.'

'Is Maskelyne one of your heroes, Oscar?' I asked, drawing on my cigarette without much satisfaction. It was a Player's Navy Cut and more to Oscar's taste than mine.

'As a master of theatrical illusion,' said Oscar, 'Maskelyne has no equal.' There was a gap in the traffic and he stepped out into the road. I followed him. 'Of course,' he added, laughing, as he steered us between an omnibus and a milk float, 'if he was to be run over in the street tomorrow, who knows how he might be remembered?'

'I don't follow you, Oscar,' I said.

'Maskelyne is world famous now for his bag of tricks, for his conjuring and his feats of levitation – but what will posterity make of him?' We had reached the safety of the pavement opposite. 'I reckon John Maskelyne's lasting claim to fame will rest on his one non-theatrical invention: the lock for the public convenience which requires a penny coin to operate.'

'Good grief,' I exclaimed, dropping my cigarette into the gutter. 'Did Maskelyne invent that?'

'He did,' said Oscar, 'and the euphemism "spend a penny" that goes with it. I am a poet and a playwright who has spent a lifetime spinning words, Robert, and yet, were I to live for a thousand years, I doubt very much that I could come up with a phrase destined to be half so famous! Alas, we cannot choose the nature of our own immortality.'

I chuckled. 'I wonder how you will be remembered, Oscar?'

We had reached the crowded doorway of the Knightsbridge post office. Oscar paused. Customers brushed past us as they went about their business. 'For my downfall,' he said, smiling gently. 'In my end will be the beginning of my notoriety. I am certain of that. I always have been.' He held his open palm up in front of me. 'Mrs Robinson has seen it in this unhappy hand.' Oscar spoke often of the prospect of his premature demise and usually did so with melodramatic relish. 'If I should be murdered at the end of this week, Robert, I will be known for all time as the playwright who died on Friday the thirteenth. I will be the Kit Marlowe of the nineteenth century, remembered as much for the manner of my death as the matter of my life.'

'You're not going to be murdered on Friday,' I insisted.

As I spoke – as I uttered the very words 'You're not going to be murdered on Friday' – a man's arm pushed between me and my friend and I saw the silver barrel of a gun suddenly pointed at Oscar's chest. My heart stopped. My head reeled. 'For God's sake,' I cried without thinking, grabbing the hand that held the pistol and wrenching it up into the air.

'Hold on, old boy!' cried Bosie Douglas, shrieking with laughter and pulling himself free of me. 'It's not loaded.'

I stepped back and looked in appalled amazement at the beautiful young man who stood before us. He was wearing white cricket flannels, a pea-green blazer, a yellow boater and a broad and ridiculous grin. He embraced Oscar, kissing him on the cheek, while holding out his open palm towards me. Within his palm nestled the most remarkable firearm I had ever seen. It was no larger than a cigarette case: the chamber for the cartridges was circular, silver, and embossed like a snail's shell; the single barrel of the gun was no longer or wider than a finger. 'Beautiful, isn't she?' purred Bosie. 'She's French. Made by a Monsieur Turbiaux in Paris. Apparently her muzzle velocity is pitiful, but what do

I care? I shall only be using her once – at very close range. My dear papa won't feel a thing . . . But, then, has he ever?'

'Put it away, Bosie,' cautioned Oscar, turning away from the young aristocrat and shading his eyes with the backs of his hands. 'You are making an exhibition of yourself.'

Lord Alfred Douglas laughed, kissed the barrel of the little palm pistol and slipped it into his blazer pocket. 'I've just wasted a shilling sending you a wire, Oscar,' he said, stepping away from the doorway of the post office and looking disdainfully at the members of the public who were staring at him open-mouthed in astonishment. 'I have to go to Oxford tomorrow. My tutor is demanding my presence. He says that if I fail to appear in his rooms by twelve noon, essay in hand, I shall be sent down.'

'And what has this to do with me?' asked Oscar warily, raising an eyebrow.

'I want you to come with me to Oxford tomorrow, Oscar. You can write my essay for me on the train.'

'Don't be absurd, Bosie.'

'Don't be unkind, Oscar. *Please*. It doesn't need to be a very long essay. Or very good. Just a page or two on "The Evolution of the Moral Idea". I've not the first notion of where to begin. You'll do it so beautifully, Oscar, so charmingly. Please, Oscar, *cher ami*. My whole academic future depends on it.'

Oscar looked at the young man and sighed. He pushed the boy's boater to the back of his head so that a heavy flop of fair hair fell across his right eye. 'Lord Alfred Douglas, you are utterly ridiculous. You will not be sent down from the university for failing to produce an essay on time. You might be for parading in the streets of London in possession of a firearm with intent to kill. However . . .' He smiled and shook his head wearily. 'For your own protection, therefore,' he continued, 'and for no other reason, I will accompany you to Oxford tomorrow.'

Alfred Douglas clapped his hands together and cheered. 'Thank you, old fellow. Thank you! And the essay?'

'We shall work at it on the train *together*.'

The young man punched his older friend affectionately on the shoulder. 'You're the business, Oscar. You're the best.'

'And now, Bosie,' said Oscar, firmly, 'when I have despatched my telegrams, I trust you will join us for luncheon in Tite Street.'

'No,' said the boy at once, 'I can't. I'm sorry. I'm lunching with Mama. I promised. We're celebrating Father's latest humiliation.' He glanced at his timepiece and grimaced. 'I must go. I'm late.' Suddenly he looked at us both and grinned excitedly. 'Of course, last night – you were there! At the Ring of Death – in at the kill. Apparently, there was blood all over the shop. The papers are full of it. Poor McMuirtree – murdered even though he played by the Queensberry Rules!' He brought his boater forward onto his head. 'You must tell me all about it tomorrow, Oscar. Write the essay tonight, old man, then we can *talk* on the train. That'll be so much more fun. "The Evolution of the Moral Idea" – a thousand words will do it. Nine o'clock at Paddington. The usual Oxford platform. Will you get the tickets? Bless you, Oscar. Goodbye, Robert.'

He shook my hand. He embraced Oscar. And he was gone. With Lord Alfred Douglas it was ever thus.

Oscar went into the post office to send his telegrams. I found a news vendor and bought a selection of the early editions of the evening papers. All featured the mysterious murder at Astley's Circus on the front page – and most did so in lurid detail. The *Standard* described McMuirtree as 'a well-known figure in boxing circles who, it now transpires, led a double life as a police informant'. The *Evening News* reported that Inspector Gilmour of Scotland Yard already had a number of potential suspects in his sights, 'notorious villains bent upon destroying Mr McMuirtree because of what he knew'. On an inside page, the *Star* carried photographs of some of the distinguished audience who had witnessed the tragic events of the night before, including the Marquess of Queensberry, the Earl of Rosebery, Dr Arthur Conan Doyle and Mr Oscar Wilde.

In the cab to Tite Street, as we scanned the press, and Oscar clucked and tutted at what he read, I suggested that, perhaps, we should try to keep the papers away from Constance.

'The prose style is appalling, Robert, I agree,' Oscar answered, shaking his head despairingly. 'We must protect my lamb as best we can. She is quite sensitive.'

'Be serious, Oscar.'

He looked at me and smiled. 'We can hardly keep last night's massacre a secret, Robert. McMuirtree was a guest in our house two days ago. His sudden death – the horrific manner of his murder – the servants will be speaking of little else . . . But I agree – there is still no need to tell Constance about the Socrates Club dinner and my foolish game and its deadly consequences . . .'

'Should we not warn her, if her life is in danger?'

'To what purpose? In my experience, a worry shared is a worry doubled. In any event, I believe she is safe enough till Friday.'

At Tite Street, Arthur the butler greeted us at the front door. 'I was sorry to hear about Mr McMuirtree, sir. Nasty business.'

'Indeed, Arthur. Very nasty. Is Mrs Wilde about?'

'She is upstairs, sir. Luncheon will be served in fifteen minutes.'

We made our way upstairs. Oscar went on to the second floor, 'to spend a penny', he said archly, and to find his wife. I let myself into the first-floor drawing room. It was my favourite room at Tite Street. It was, by the standards of the time, extraordinarily uncluttered. The white wallpapered walls were hung with etchings by James Whistler and Mortimer Menpes. The unique ceiling was Whistler's work as well: it featured an awning of peacock feathers! I made my way over to the painted grand piano that stood in the corner of the room and looked out onto the Wildes' small and somewhat barren back garden. As I stood by the window I was overcome by a curious sensation . . . I felt I was being observed by an unseen power; I became conscious of an invisible 'presence' nearby.

I turned and looked about the room. There was no one there. I turned back and gazed out of the window once more. Again I felt a hidden 'presence'. I looked down towards the floor. My eyes followed the painted white skirting board to the fringed edge of the white velour curtains that framed the window. Beneath the curtain's fringe I saw a pair of feet in leather ankle boots.

Appalled, unthinking, I pulled back the curtain and grabbed the figure lurking there. I took him by the throat and threw him to his knees. Then I saw who it was. I barked at him: 'What the devil are you doing here?'

Slowly, Edward Heron-Allen got to his feet, dusting down his trousers and adjusting his collar. 'Steady on, old boy,' he said. 'This ain't your house, you know.'

I looked at the man and felt my gorge rise with loathing. He was so at ease with himself, so self-assured, so complacent.

'What the deuce were you doing behind that curtain?' I demanded.

'Waiting for Constance,' he said lightly.

He made me burn with rage. 'Waiting for Constance?' I repeated angrily.

'We were playing a game of hide-and-seek. We play games together. It's quite natural. It's what brothers and sisters do.'

'You are not Mrs Wilde's brother,' I hissed at him.

'Would that I were,' he said. 'I love her as a man should love his sister – easily, without complication.'

'I don't understand you,' I said.

'I see that,' said Heron-Allen. 'You love Constance, too – but your love is tinged with guilt. You don't love her as a brother. You love her as a man loves a woman – you love her with desire in your heart, with lust in your eyes. And that's not easy for you because you love Oscar also and Constance is Oscar's ever-faithful wife.'

'I don't know what you're saying.'

'It matters not,' said Heron-Allen. 'Lust and love are particular interests of mine, that's all.'

'Along with violin-making, cock-fighting and the forbidden literature of Persia,' I added, making no attempt to conceal my contempt.

'In the matter of the no-man's-land between lust and love, we can learn much from the Persians,' he said, moving past me towards the mirror that hung above the fireplace. He peered into the looking glass. With delicate hands he adjusted his hair. With his tongue he moistened his forefinger and carefully pushed back each of his eyebrows. 'In matters of carnality, other cultures have much to teach us. I have studied bestiality, you know – congress between man and beast. And necrophilia. Where lust ends and love begins . . . it's all very intriguing.'

'And is this the sort of stuff with which you edify Mrs Wilde,' I asked, 'when you two are playing your "games" together?'

'No,' he laughed. 'Of course not. Mrs Wilde and I are friends – true friends. That's all. My wife has been away for a month, visiting her sister and her sister's new-born baby. Oscar is always otherwise engaged. Constance and I have made time for each other because we take delight in each other's company. We play together and are happier because of it. In England only children are allowed to play. That is a pity.'

Suddenly, the drawing-room door was opened. It was Constance, looking as lovely as I had ever seen her. 'Is this where you two have been hiding?' she chided. 'Luncheon is served. Come now. Oscar is growing impatient.'

Over lunch – pea soup, griddled lamb chops, and blackcurrant-and-apple pie – I said very little. Edward

Heron-Allen said a great deal. Oscar, drinking white Burgundy, and Constance, drinking lemonade, looked on him with unaffected admiration as though he were a favourite child, an infant prodigy. The range of his interests was certainly extraordinary and the depth of his erudition undoubtedly impressive. In fairness, I could not fault him either on grounds of decorum or discretion. We talked of McMuirtree's murder, inevitably, but Heron-Allen glossed over the most horrific details of the boxer's death and went out of his way to steer the conversation towards sunnier topics: the beauty and intelligence of the Wilde children, the origins of the English eating apple, the subtlety of Mozart's late violin sonatas, the absurdity of the new paintings at the Royal Academy, the prospects for Mr Irving's *King Lear*, Oscar's continuing triumph at the St James's.

After lunch, Constance invited Heron-Allen to join her and her boys for a walk in Hyde Park. To my astonishment, Oscar (who regarded a stroll down Piccadilly as a two-mile hike and a two-mile hike as an utter impossibility) proposed that he and I should join them.

'Oscar,' exclaimed his wife, as amazed as I was, 'what on earth has come over you?'

'Don't I say in my play that health is the primary duty of life?' Oscar answered, getting to his feet and breathing deeply while placing his fingers lightly across his diaphragm. 'I think a post-prandial perambulation will be most invigorating.' He exhaled slowly and then, apparently exhausted, began to feel in his jacket pocket for his cigarette case. 'But you may be right, my dear – going as far as the park might be overdoing it. Perhaps we could just amble up the road to Brompton Cemetery?'

'Take the boys to a graveyard, Oscar?' said Constance, furrowing her brow. 'Something *has* come over you!'

'Not the graveyard,' said Oscar quickly. 'The allotments to the south of the graveyard.'

'Do you have allotments nearby?' asked Heron-Allen with enthusiasm. 'I should love to see your allotments.'

Together, Oscar and I burst out laughing.

'What is so funny, gentlemen?' Constance enquired reprovingly.

Oscar spluttered: 'Edward saying he'd love to see our allotments . . . I believe he means it.'

'I do,' said Edward Heron-Allen, seriously. 'The development of urban horticulture is a particular interest of mine.'

It took us no more than half an hour to reach the small plot of allotments to the south side of Brompton Cemetery. Oscar and Heron-Allen led the way, with Oscar proudly pushing his older son, Cyril, along the street in a child's chariot while Heron-Allen carried his godson, Vyvyan, on his shoulders. Constance and I followed behind them, arm in arm. It was a delightful walk. Heron-Allen was right: when Constance held my arm tight as we crossed the road my feelings towards her were indeed tinged with guilt.

The allotments, when we found them, were an unimpressive sight: ten small plots of ground, each no more than fifteen feet square, all overgrown, all unkempt. 'These do not look much loved,' said Heron-Allen sadly, lifting his godson to the ground. The two Wilde boys scampered around the allotments happily, jumping across the beds, sniffing at what flowers there were, pulling at the greenery. Almost at once, at the edge of the allotments, by the railings that bordered the cemetery, the boys discovered a small mound of newly turned earth and began to poke at it with small sticks of wood. 'Is this a sand-castle, Papa?' asked Cyril.

'No,' said Oscar, 'I think it is a parrot's grave.'

Constance did not hear him. She was talking with Heron-Allen. 'It's all a bit sad, is it not?' she said.

'There's nothing sadder than an unloved garden,' said Heron-Allen.

Vyvyan ran up to his mother holding a handful of weeds and grasses. 'I've picked a posy for you, Mama,' he announced, bowing low and presenting his mother with his little bunch of greenery.

'Thank you, my darling,' said Constance, moved by her child's offering and bending down to kiss the little boy. 'Perhaps Uncle Edward can tell us what you've picked for me.'

Constance handed the green posy to Heron-Allen, who examined it carefully.

'There are herbs here, as well as weeds,' he said approvingly. 'Well done, godson.' He knelt down beside the boy and, like a good teacher, took him through each leaf in turn. 'This, I think, is wild carrot. This, believe it or not, is the leaf of a parsnip. You can eat the parsnip, but you can't eat the leaf. This leaf you can eat, however. It's delicious.' He bit into the curly sprig of vegetation. 'It's called parsley.'

'Correctly known as "*petroselinum*",' added Oscar, bringing Cyril over to join in the lesson. 'We Wildes are all classicists, Edward. My boys have been Latin scholars *ab ovo*.'

Heron-Allen laughed obligingly. 'Well,' he went on, 'this then, I think, is *conium maculatum*. It's a pretty flower, but you mustn't eat it.' He pulled out the smooth green stem and threw it onto the bank. 'But this one – which isn't quite so pretty – is really delicious.' He held the delicate leaf beneath Vyvyan's nose and scratched it. 'Can you smell it? It's very good for you. It's *foeniculum vulgare*.'

'Common fennel?' I guessed.

'Indeed,' said Heron-Allen, getting to his feet. 'Beloved of the Persians also. They call it *"raaziyaan"*.'

On the return journey to Tite Street, Constance walked ahead pushing Cyril in the chariot, with Heron-Allen, with Vyvyan back on his shoulders, at her side. Each time they crossed a road I felt an absurd pang of jealousy as the young solicitor put out his hand to touch and steady Constance's slender arm.

As we walked, Oscar and I smoked our cigarettes, but said very little. As we turned into Tite Street itself, Oscar paused. 'There's much to be done between now and Friday, Robert. We know who killed the parrot, don't we?'

'Do we?' I asked.

He smiled. 'I think we do . . . But who killed David McMuirtree? That's the question. And why? And the blades that slashed the poor man's wrists . . . were they cockspurs?'

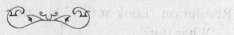

24

Questions

At the end of the afternoon Edward Heron-Allen went on his way. The family gathered at the front door of 16 Tite Street to wave him off. Oscar embraced his young friend warmly; the two boys threw their arms around his legs to try to prevent him from taking his leave; I watched Constance tenderly stroke his ear and cheek as she kissed him goodbye.

'I must go, too,' I said, when Constance had taken the children upstairs for their bathtime and fairy stories.

'A glass of champagne before you go?' suggested Oscar. He went to the end of the corridor and called down towards the kitchen: 'Arthur!' He took me into his red-and-yellow study on the ground floor. The floor was cluttered with untidy heaps of papers and tottering piles of books. Like an overweight frog hopping between lily-pads, Oscar negotiated his way across the room towards his celebrated writing desk – the desk at which Thomas Carlyle had written his History of the French Revolution. 'Look at this,' he said.

'What is it?'

Between his thumb and forefinger he held up a tiny curved object that looked like the clipping of a fingernail encased in silver. 'It is a Mexican cockspur – according to

Heron-Allen. It's the pride of his collection, apparently. He brought it over this morning. He thought I'd be intrigued to see it.' He handed me the miniature blade. 'Take care,' he said. 'It's razor-sharp.'

I examined the shiny cockspur carefully – it was highly polished: it gleamed – and returned it to Oscar who placed it back upon the desk. 'So many questions, Robert,' he murmured. 'So many questions and so little time.'

'If this is a race against time, Oscar,' I said, lowering my voice, 'if you truly believe that your life could be threatened on Friday, is your visit to Oxford tomorrow essential?'

'It is,' he said, not looking at me but picking up a book from the top of one of the piles and leafing through it. 'And not just for Bosie's sake.'

'Who killed the parrot, Oscar?' I asked. He said nothing, but carried on reading. '*Who killed the parrot?*' I hissed.

He looked up at me. 'You're beginning to sound like Charles Brookfield, Robert.'

'But if you know, Oscar, you must tell me.'

He laughed. 'Now you're beginning to sound like Bosie. You must write your own essay, Robert: test the evidence yourself, Robert; make your own deductions; come to your own conclusion.'

'Ah . . .' I said, smiling, leaning back and folding my arms across my chest. 'You don't know for certain, do you?'

He snapped shut his book. 'You are right, Robert. I think I know, but I am not certain. I am not at all certain. As Socrates reminds us, true knowledge exists in knowing that we know nothing. The jigsaw is still a jumble. There are secrets still waiting to be found out.'

Arthur the butler arrived with the Perrier Jouët. He placed the champagne tray on the side-table by the study door and bowed towards his master. Oscar bowed back.

'Pour the wine, Robert. We need to empty the bottle and clear our heads. Do you have your pencil and note-book handy?'

As we drank the sparkling wine – it was wonderfully crisp and cool: 'as pure and yellow as a May moonbeam,' said Oscar – I took a note of my friend's instructions. While he was to be in Oxford, I was to remain in London. I was to return to Byrd at the Cadogan Hotel and reserve the private room there for a dinner on Friday night. Oscar told me to instruct Byrd to invite all those who had been present at the Socrates Club gathering on Sunday 1 May to return to the Cadogan for a special dinner – 'a com-memorative dinner' – on the evening of the thirteenth. 'Tell Byrd there will be fourteen for dinner, as before. Tell him I want the same menu as before – and the same wines.'

'And the same seating plan?' I asked.

'Not exactly,' he said. 'You can tell Byrd that I shall look after the *placement*. And, Robert, you can contact Inspector Gilmour at Scotland Yard and ask him if he might be free to join us. Ask him to bring a fellow officer as his guest.'

'You want the police at the dinner?'

'Yes,' he said, looking into his champagne some-what dreamily. 'Without David McMuirtree and poor Bradford Pearse, we'll be two short at table.'

He stepped carefully between the lily-pads of books and papers and stood gazing out of the window onto Tite

Street. 'And while you're with Gilmour, try to find out what progress he is making in rounding up the "notorious villains" he suspects of McMuirtree's murder. And see if he's had any news from Eastbourne – from either the police there or the coastguards.'

I emptied my glass and returned it to the tray. 'I shall be busy,' I said, pocketing my pencil and notebook.

'I hope so,' he replied, turning to me and smiling. 'And, if you've time, perhaps you could call on more of our witnesses. We've not interviewed young Willie Hornung. We've not heard all that Wat Sickert has to say.'

'Will they have "secrets", Oscar?'

'They will have secrets, Robert – that is certain. Whether their secrets are relevant to the case in hand – that is the only issue.' He looked back out of the window. 'And here is your two-wheeler,' he announced, 'on cue.'

'I didn't order a two-wheeler,' I said, surprised.

'I know,' he answered, beaming at me. 'I did. It's my treat.'

'When did you order it, Oscar?' I asked suspiciously.

'Just now,' he said.

'Just now?' I repeated, bemused.

'Yes,' he said. 'Just now.'

I looked at him. The wine had given colour to his cheeks. He appeared suddenly exultant.

'When Arthur brought in our champagne,' he explained, 'I gave him the signal. It's an arrangement we have. I bring my hands together by way of a salaam. If I bring together the four fingers of each hand it means that I require him to go out into the street and find me a four-wheeler. If a two-wheeler is required, in my salaam I just press together the tips of two fingers from each hand.' He bowed towards me and brought his hands together by way of demonstration. 'I knew that you needed to get home after we had had our drink. I thought you might appreciate a cab. That's all.'

'You are extraordinary, Oscar.'

'I like to think so,' he said happily. 'And you are a good friend, Robert – although you do need to learn to be a little more observant.' From his jacket pocket he produced his green snakeskin wallet (it was his favourite) and extracted three pound notes. He held them out towards me. 'Your expenses for tomorrow, my friend. Don't protest. You have very little money and I have plenty. If I don't give it away now, it will merely be stolen from me in the fullness of time.'

'Thank you,' I said. 'I'll keep a note of what I spend.'

'Don't! For God's sake, don't!' He sounded quite alarmed at the prospect. He put his arm about me as he walked with me towards the door. 'You're not a bank clerk, Robert. You're not a bookkeeper. You're a published poet, the great-grandson of a laureate. You of all people should know that ordinary riches count for nothing. Ordinary riches can be stolen from a man. Real riches cannot. In the treasury-house of your soul there are infinitely precious things that may not be taken from you.'

I looked at his flushed face and smiled. 'Have I heard that somewhere before, Oscar?'

'Did we drink the champagne too quickly?' he asked, kissing me on the forehead. 'Goodbye, Robert.' He waved me on my way. 'If I get back in time tomorrow night, we'll take a nightcap at the Albemarle. Shall we say ten o'clock – eleven at the latest? Meanwhile, *bonne chance, mon brave*!' As I stepped into the waiting two-wheeler, he called out: 'I don't think Heron-Allen's our man, do you?'

I did not know what to think. I did not know where to begin my thinking. Oscar made a fine detective because, though he was a poet, he was also a classicist. His way with words was elaborate and ornate, flowery and full of fanciful flourishes, but his way of thinking was precise. He was not just a spinner of fine phrases: his understanding of grammar and syntax was profound. He had a poet's imagination, a painter's eye, an actor's ear and a scholar's nose for detail and capacity for close analysis. On the following morning – the morning of Wednesday 11 May 1892 – I was grateful that, at least, I had a written note of his instructions.

I did exactly as he had bid me. I began the day by taking a cab to the Cadogan Hotel in Sloane Street. I saw Byrd and asked him to make the necessary arrangements for the Socrates Club dinner on Friday night. He assured me he would be happy to oblige. From the hotel, I telephoned Arthur Conan Doyle and, from him, got the details of where I might expect to find his young friend, Willie Hornung. From Sloane Street I took another cab to Fleet Street and found Hornung, in his shirtsleeves and *pince-nez*, sitting in the darkest corner of the ill-lit basement offices of a 'popular publication' of which I had never heard.

Hornung, it transpired, was the recently appointed assistant editor of the *Gentlewoman: An Illustrated Weekly Journal for Gentlewomen*. The poor fellow, perched on a high stool, inky pen in hand, managed to look distraught and despairing at the same time. 'I can't stop to talk,' he said, putting down his pen and running his hands anxiously through his thick fair hair. 'I have to finish an article about chewing-gum by lunchtime. Chewing-gum! I ask you! They say it's all the rage in America and that over here by Christmas every forward-thinking gentle-woman will be chewing Mr Wrigley's extraordinary sweetmeat. I just don't believe it – but the editor insists. He's an ogre. I wish I'd taken the job on *Forget-Me-Not*. That's another women's weekly, but it's mostly pictorial. I would only have had to write captions for photographs. Arthur said I should go for this job – so I did. But I'm not enjoying it, I can tell you. I'm not enjoying it a bit.'

I stood for a few minutes with the unhappy youth in his desultory corner, consoling him with the thought that Oscar had served his time as editor of a women's maga-zine, while plying the poor boy with questions about the night of 1 May and pressing him to reveal to me his 'secrets'. He said he remembered very little about the Socrates Club dinner. He had been 'rather overwhelmed' by the occasion. He did recall that Bradford Pearse, who sat opposite him during dinner, appeared to have drunk a great deal and he recollected what he described as 'an unhappy exchange' between Charles Brookfield and Arthur Conan Doyle.

'Can you remember what was said?' I asked.

'Arthur was saying that he thought that Oscar had missed his vocation, that Oscar – had he so chosen – could have become a private consulting detective quite as brilliant and perceptive as Sherlock Holmes. Brookfield scoffed and said, "Oscar Wilde as a detective is a prepos-terous notion. Indeed, Oscar Wilde as a person is a preposterous notion. Oscar Wilde is a charlatan."'

'He said this at dinner?'

'After dinner, as we were preparing to leave. I imagine he was drunk.'

'Did Conan Doyle rebuke him?'

'Arthur was very calm, very dignified. He said. "Mr Brookfield, history will show you that the so-called charlatan is always the pioneer. From the astrologer came the astronomer, from the alchemist the chemist, from the mesmerist the experimental psychologist. The quack of yesterday is the professor of tomorrow. Mr Wilde is by no means preposterous. He is merely ahead of his time."'

'And what did Brookfield say to that?'

'"That's a very pretty speech, I'm sure, sir, but it don't change my opinion of Mr Oscar Wilde."'

As he spoke, Hornung kept looking over his shoulder as if fearing the imminent arrival of the monstrous editor he was employed to assist. 'Forgive me, Robert,' he said. 'I must get back to my chewing-gum.'

'And what about your "secret"?' I asked. 'Oscar says everybody has a "secret". What's yours?'

Hornung laughed nervously and pushed his *pince-nez* up his nose. 'Oscar already knows mine. It's my name . . .'

'Your name?'

'I call myself William – everyone knows me as Willie – but that's not my first name.'

'And that's your secret?'

'Yes,' he said, running his hands through his hair again.

'And what is your first name?' I asked.

'Ernest,' he said. 'My name is Ernest. Oscar seemed to think that was very funny indeed.'

I left Hornung and walked in the spring sunshine from Fleet Street to the Strand, down Savoy Hill to the Embankment, past Gatti's in the Arches (George Daubeney and Wat Sickert's favourite music hall), past Charing Cross railway station, to Scotland Yard. Inspector Gilmour was not in his office and not expected back before dusk. He was out on a case – 'in the East End', on the trail of some 'notorious villains' – and his deputy and his deputy's deputy were both with him. According to the desk sergeant, an amiable officer of riper years, I could expect 'progress in the matter of the McMuirtree murder any minute now – certainly within the week'. I left Gilmour a note, signed on Oscar's behalf, inviting him to come to dinner at the Cadogan Hotel on Friday night, at half past seven, bringing one of his deputies with him.

From Scotland Yard I walked on towards Westminster Bridge where I picked up another cab and travelled on to the King's Road, to the Chelsea Arts Club. I found Walter Sickert in the club mess room, the large studio at the back of the building, sitting alone with a plate of ham and pickled onions and a bottle of Algerian wine. He was reading a letter when I arrived. He looked up at me with tears in his sea-green eyes.

'Get yourself a glass,' he said, pushing his bottle of wine towards me. 'I am reading a letter from a friend of mine in Paris. He knew Van Gogh – the Dutch artist who killed himself.'

I poured myself a glass of wine.

'Van Gogh's paintings are so full of life, so full of sunshine and colour, and yet the poor man was so wretched in this world that he killed himself.' He waved the letter he was holding in my direction. 'Do you know what Van Gogh's dying words were? "*La tristesse durera toujours.*"'

'"The sadness will last forever,"' I translated.

'No,' said Sickert, raising his glass to his lips. '"The sadness will never go away." There's a difference . . .' He skewered a pickled onion with his fork. 'Do you think Bradford Pearse felt like that?'

'Have you had any news of Pearse?' I asked.

'None,' he said. 'Has Oscar?'

'I don't believe so.'

Sickert blew his nose on a huge blue handkerchief and nodded towards the small, torn buff-coloured envelope that lay beneath his letter on the table. 'Oscar sent me a wire. He said you might drop by. Oscar's a good man – a touch absurd, of course, but fundamentally good.'

I smiled. It was amusing to hear Wat Sickert, with his outsized bow-tie, his yellow spats and waxed moustache, describe Oscar as 'a touch absurd'.

Sickert went on: 'I have known Oscar since I was a boy. He used to come on holiday with us, you know. He was wonderful to my mother when my father died. Mother was inconsolable – until Oscar came to call. He talked to her of my father with such sweetness, such gentle humour. He taught her how to laugh once more.' He wiped more tears from his eyes and waved the empty wine bottle in the air in the hope of attracting a waiter's attention. 'Of course, some people can't abide Oscar – think he's the most dreadful bore. Wasn't it you who told me that Victor Hugo actually fell asleep during one of dear Oscar's wittiest set-pieces?'

I laughed. 'It was.' The waiter arrived with a fresh bottle. 'Of course,' I added, 'Monsieur Hugo was very old at the time.'

Sickert recharged our glasses. 'Let us drink to Oscar,' he said. 'He's a great man. And a darling. And a good friend, too. He's going to unravel the secret of these mysterious deaths, you mark my words. Who killed the parrot? Who pushed poor Bradford Pearse to his doom? Who slashed the boxer's wrists? I've no idea – none at all! – but Oscar will uncover the truth, I know it. He has a genius for this kind of thing.'

I took one of the pickled onions from Sickert's plate. 'Gilmour of the Yard is also on the case,' I said.

Sickert put down his glass dramatically, splashing wine onto the table. 'Forget Gilmour of the Yard,' he expostulated. 'Oscar will do it – alone, unaided. Two artists sit side by side painting the same subject. Only one of the paintings works. Whistler taught me that. Whistler used to say that "the bogey of success only sits on one palette". Oscar will do it single-handed.' He laughed and poured more wine into his glass. 'Which is fortunate as, sadly, I have no help to offer. No useful recollections, no helpful *aperçus*. I must drink up and return to my studio. What are you doing this afternoon, Robert? I am discovering the delights of a new model this afternoon. I am spending the rest of the day with skin that's quite unblemished, with tiny ankles, lissom thighs, a slim waist and breasts so firm and small that they might be a boy's . . . Have you ever painted a virgin, Robert?'

'No,' I said, 'I'm not an artist.'

'Or slept with one?' he added, waving his glass in the air. 'It amounts to the same thing.'

25

Questions, Questions

At eleven o'clock that evening, my head aching from a surfeit of Algerian wine, I made my way into the smoking room of the Albemarle Club, 36 Albemarle Street, Piccadilly. To my surprise, Oscar was already there. He was standing by the fireplace, his right elbow resting gently on the oak mantelpiece, his right hand nursing a large glass of brandy. He was not alone. Seated in the low leather armchairs on either side of the fireplace were the Douglas brothers. Bosie, who appeared to be wearing tennis clothes, was lying back languidly, his arms flopping on to the floor, his head cast to one side, his eyes closed. Francis, Lord Drumlanrig, by contrast, was in evening dress, sitting forward on the edge of his chair, his face flushed and his eyes alert. He was gazing resolutely towards Oscar.

'You've not forgotten us,' cried my friend, as I arrived. 'We thought perhaps you had.' Oscar, I sensed at once, was in a teasing frame of mind.

'How was Oxford?' I asked, going to the sideboard and helping myself to a weak brandy and soda. 'Have you made progress?'

'Oxford,' said Oscar, who looked extraordinarily fresh given the lateness of the hour and the length of his day, 'was all that we dared hoped for. Our essay, I'm proud to tell you, Robert, was considered Alpha material. Socrates, Spinoza, Saint-Simon, Sappho – we brought them all into play and Bosie's tutor was suitably impressed. The dear old gentleman did not appear to notice that our references were chosen entirely for their alliterative allure. He chewed happily on his handkerchief throughout our reading and offered us each a glass of sherry at the end of it.'

'You read Bosie's essay out loud for him?'

'I wrote it; I read it; Bosie takes the credit. It is extraordinary what you can get away with if you try. I'm sure Sickert will have shared Whistler's maxim with you: "In art, nothing matters so long as you are bold." In my experience, that's true in life as well.'

Lord Drumlanrig was still gazing fixedly at Oscar. He was twenty-five years old. He was not as beautiful as his younger brother. Francis Drumlanrig had what Oscar called 'utilitarian good looks: they serve, they don't inspire'. The young aristocrat shifted further forward on his chair. 'If that's all, Oscar,' he said, somewhat awkwardly, 'I'll be on my way. I must look in on Lord Rosebery before midnight. I'm expected. Thanks for the drink.'

He got to his feet and offered Oscar his hand. Oscar took it and held it and turned to me. 'Francis kindly joined us after dinner,' he explained. 'I had some questions for him and he has answered them all – most helpfully. I have to say he submitted to my cross-examination with an extraordinarily good grace.' Oscar let go of the young man's hand. 'He blushes. He is embarrassed. There is no need. I asked Lord Drumlanrig if he had met the late

David McMuirtree on any occasion prior to the 1 May gathering of the Socrates Club. He acknowledged that he had – just the once. It was a secret meeting, a brief encounter, an assignation on Westminster Bridge – arranged by McMuirtree at McMuirtree's request.'

The young peer stood to attention, with his arms at his side, his cheeks burning, his eyes now firmly fixed on the empty fire grate.

Oscar went on: 'McMuirtree told Lord Drumlanrig that rumours were circulating – rumours of a most unsavoury nature, rumours suggesting that the older man was exerting an unnatural influence over the younger. As you know, Lord Drumlanrig is Lord Rosebery's political secretary. McMuirtree warned him that certain people – the Marquess of Queensberry among them – were saying that Lord Drumlanrig and Lord Rosebery were lovers.'

'I denied any wrongdoing,' said Drumlanrig hoarsely, still staring into the grate. 'I denied it absolutely.'

'He denied it absolutely,' repeated Oscar gently. 'He told McMuirtree not to meddle in matters that did not concern him. He told McMuirtree to mind his own business. He told him so in no uncertain terms.'

'Did he threaten him?' I asked.

'Yes,' said Francis Drumlanrig, turning and looking at me with dark, bewildered eyes, 'I threatened him – in a manner of speaking. I threatened him, but I did not murder him.' He bent over and picked up a newspaper from the floor. 'I must go now, Oscar. Forgive me. Goodnight, Oscar. Goodnight, Sherard.'

'Well . . .' I said, with a sigh, after Drumlanrig had gone. 'Well, well . . .'

'Indeed,' said Oscar. 'There is much to ponder. And I imagine, Robert, there is also much to report. We've had busy days the both of us.' He drained his glass and put it on the mantelpiece. 'Let's to bed now. I'm sleeping at the club tonight. I'll pick you up in Gower Street at noon.' He put his arm around me and led me towards the door. 'Come, let's tiptoe out. We'll leave Bosie sleeping here. His triumph in Oxford has exhausted him.'

I was exhausted, too. And foolish. I reached my room in Gower Street as midnight struck and yet I did not put out my lamp until gone three in the morning. First, I allowed myself to be distracted by re-reading and attempting to draft a reply to yet another importunate letter from my estranged wife's solicitor; next, I decided to write up my journal while the events of the day were still relatively fresh in my mind; finally (and fatally!) I began to read a licentious volume George Daubeney had encouraged me to buy on one of our visits to the *Librairie Française*. When, eventually, sated with the absurd antics of the libidinous nuns and novices of the *Couvent de la Concupiscence*, I put the book aside and closed my eyes, I fell asleep almost at once. I was dead to the world for nigh on nine hours. It was Oscar who woke me, rat-tatting on the front door with his sword-stick.

I looked out of my window and waved down to him. He was dressed immaculately, wearing a dove-grey frock coat and lemon-yellow gloves. (He kept clothes in an assortment of London clubs and hotels.) He raised his black silk top hat to me and indicated the four-wheeler at the kerbside that awaited us. I threw on my clothes – the clothes I had worn the day before! – and ran down the stairs to join him.

'I've not had time to shave,' I apologised as I climbed into our carriage.

'No matter,' he said. 'We are going to a public house. Your appearance is exactly *comme il faut*.'

'I must look like a scarecrow,' I said, realising that I had not even brushed my hair, 'whereas you, Oscar, you look so . . . *civilised*.'

He chuckled. 'With a high hat and a well-cut frock coat anybody, even an accountant, can look civilised.' He fingered the rosebud in the lapel of his coat. 'I am rather pleased, however, with my button-hole. This rose is named in honour of Euthymius the Enlightener. Tomorrow is his feast day. Today, this rosebud is white. Tomorrow, the flower will open and you will see petals as red as fire will be revealed.'

'Tomorrow is the thirteenth,' I said. 'Friday the thirteenth.'

'Quite,' said Oscar. 'Unlucky for some.'

I turned and looked him – this extraordinary, supremely intelligent, highly educated, profoundly civilised man. 'You really are deeply superstitious, aren't you?'

'I take some of it with a pinch of salt,' he said.

I laughed.

He looked at me earnestly. 'The truth is: I love superstitions, Robert. They are the colour element of thought and imagination. They are the opponents of common sense. Common sense is the enemy of romance. Leave us some unreality. Do not make us offensively sane.'

Our four-wheeler turned southwards into the Charing Cross Road. 'Where are we going now?' I asked.

'Nowhere very romantic, alas. To a public house in Wellington Street to have beer and sandwiches with Bram Stoker and Charles Brookfield. They are the last of our "witnesses".'

'What about George Daubeney?' I asked. 'Have you cross-examined the Honourable Reverend?'

'Not yet. He and I are having a *tête-a-tête* this afternoon – at his suggestion. He has something to show me. Something he tells me will please me greatly.'

'Am I invited, too?'

'No, Robert. Whatever he has to offer is, apparently, for my eyes only.'

'He's a curious sort of clergyman, isn't he?'

'Not at all,' cried Oscar. 'In my experience they're all obsessed with carnality and corruption. I think they regard it as their stock-in-trade. The bishops are often the worst.'

I was beginning to feel more awake. Oscar's banter was reviving me – and his quirkiness, his lightness of touch and his easy acceptance of the foibles of others were serving to remind me of why I found him to be the best company in the world.

As our four-wheeler trundled down Charing Cross Road towards the Strand, at his behest I gave Oscar a brief account of my encounters of the day before. When I'd done I said: 'I'm afraid I didn't make much progress, Oscar. I'm not in your league, alas. Nor that of Sherlock Holmes.'

'Forget Holmes,' said Oscar genially. 'You covered the ground, and covered it well. I'm grateful.' He slapped me on the knee by way of congratulation.

'And you?' I asked.

'I made some progress, I believe,' he said lightly, looking out of the carriage window. Our four-wheeler had stopped momentarily: our horse appeared to have been distracted by a road-side water-trough. Oscar turned back to me. 'What did you make of young Drumlanrig?' he asked.

I hesitated.

'Go on,' he said.

'Can I follow Whistler's advice?' I asked. 'Can I be bold?'

He laughed. 'Are you going to tell me that Lord Drumlanrig is our murderer?'

'It's possible, is it not?' I said. 'They are a strange family the Douglases . . . moody, headstrong, touched with madness . . .'

'Indeed. "Douglas" in Gaelic means "dark water", you know. And *"Nomen est omen"* is my philosophy. But of all the members of the family I've encountered thus far, Francis Drumlanrig seems to me to be the least touched with madness, the most down-to-earth.'

'But Francis Drumlanrig chose his godfather, Lord Abergordon, as his victim – and Lord Abergordon is dead. By his own admission, Francis Drumlanrig threatened David McMuirtree – and David McMuirtree is dead . . .'

Our carriage began to move once more. Oscar lit a cigarette and nodded to me as if to say, 'Go on.'

I went on, uncertain as to whether or not I should. 'Francis Drumlanrig,' I said slowly, 'is heir to the Marquess of Queensberry . . . is he not?'

'He is.'

'But Francis is estranged from his father because his father does not much care for the kind of company the young man keeps. Lord Queensberry does not much care for the likes of Lord Rosebery and . . .' I hesitated.

'. . . the likes of Oscar Wilde?'

'Yes,' I said. 'The Marquess of Queensberry does not approve of either of his sons' intimate association with Oscar Wilde. If Francis Drumlanrig were to rid the world of all the Wildes, would that not endear the young viscount to his monster of a father?'

'Ingenious, Robert, as well as bold,' said Oscar, smiling at me benevolently.

Encouraged, I went on: 'Aside from the parrot, there were six people on the list of victims. Who else had a motive to murder at least four out of the six?'

Our four-wheeler was drawing to a halt. Oscar threw his cigarette to the floor and extinguished it under foot. 'Oh, Robert,' he cried, pushing open the carriage door. 'Beware of dangerous assumptions!'

'What do you mean?'

'I mean: do not assume that anyone had a motive to murder more than one of the victims . . .'

I helped my friend out of the four-wheeler. 'I do not follow you,' I said.

'Could our murderer not simply have had just one victim in mind – and be busy murdering all the rest simply to cover his traces, to cause confusion in his wake, to throw sand in our eyes?'

I stood with Oscar on the corner of Wellington Street and the Strand and looked up at the cloudless sky. I was perplexed.

Oscar paid off our cab and led the way into the saloon bar of the Duke of Wellington public house. 'Beer and sandwiches,' he murmured unhappily as we entered the crowded, smoke-filled room. We saw Bram Stoker at once. He was standing at the bar, looking towards the door, waiting for us. There was no sign of Charles Brookfield.

'He sends his apologies,' said Stoker, handing us each a pint pot of warm, dark ale.

'Does he?' asked Oscar, looking down at the beer with wide eyes and undisguised mistrust.

Stoker laughed. He was a big bear of a man. He was as tall as Oscar – six feet two inches at least – and quite as broad, but while Oscar seemed overweight and flabby, Stoker appeared well-built and strong. He was deep-chested and broad-shouldered. When he laughed, his whole frame shook. 'No, Oscar, you're right,' he growled through his laugh and, with the back of his nails, he scratched at his untidy red beard. 'Brookfield does not send his apologies. He's simply decided not to join us.'

Stoker picked up his pint pot and led us towards a boxed stall in a dark corner at the back of the room. Set out on a table within the stall were knives and forks, plates, wine glasses, napkins, one dish overflowing with cuts of cold meat, another piled high with portions of dressed crab and two open bottles of Alsatian wine. 'Take a pew, gentlemen,' said Stoker amiably. 'I've never thought of Oscar as much of a sandwich man.'

'By all that's wonderful,' purred Oscar gratefully, lowering his bulk onto one of the benches within the stall. 'My spirits soar. Thank you, Bram.'

Stoker struck a match and lit two candles in the centre of the table. He had bright blue eyes and ruddy farmer's cheeks. He smiled at me. 'Oscar and I go back a long way.

His parents were very good to me in Dublin when I was a boy. Sir William Wilde was something of a hero of mine.'

'My father was an author and antiquarian as well as a medical man,' Oscar added by way of explanation.

'He was a great man, a good man, a *strong* man,' said Stoker, filling our wine glasses, 'until the case broke him.'

' "The case"?' I queried. 'Was Sir William by way of being something of an amateur sleuth also?'

'No,' answered Oscar, smiling. 'Sir William was by way of being something of a professional ladies' man. "The case" was an unfortunate libel action. My father stood accused of having chloroformed and raped a female patient. It wasn't true, of course, but that he and the lady in the case had enjoyed an illicit, if consenting, relationship could not be denied. The case ruined him. Bram is correct. It "broke" him.'

'There's a lesson there for us all, gentlemen,' said Stoker, beaming across the table at us. 'Keep out of court at all costs. Cheers!'

We raised and clinked our glasses. 'Now,' said Oscar, helping himself to a portion of dressed crab, 'explain to me why Brookfield is not here.'

'He has an aversion to you, Oscar — it's as simple as that. He is obsessed with you, but can't stand the sight of you at the same time! I imagine at the Socrates Club dinner, when we played that infernal game of yours, *you* were his intended victim. He is insanely jealous of you. We all are.' Stoker looked at me and winked. 'I have been ever since I was a young man.'

'This is balderdash, Bram,' said Oscar happily, helping himself to a further portion of dressed crab. 'Poppycock.' He looked at me. 'I'm the one who was insanely jealous.

Stoker here stole my sweetheart – saw her, stole her, swept her off her feet.'

'I had the advantage of years, Oscar,' said Stoker.

'Yes,' replied Oscar, sniffing the wine with satisfaction, 'I have that consolation.' He took a sip of the Alsace and placed his glass back on the table. He leant towards me confidentially. 'Florrie Balcombe – Mrs Stoker – is very beautiful.'

'I know,' I said. 'I have been to first nights at the Lyceum. I have seen the gentlemen in the stalls and in the balconies standing on their seats to get a better view of her.'

'Constance Lloyd – Mrs Wilde – is very beautiful, too' said Bram Stoker, without affectation.

'Indeed,' I said, my cheeks suddenly reddening.

'Robert is a little in love with my wife,' murmured Oscar, gently patting the back of my hand.

'I'm not surprised,' said Bram Stoker. 'I imagine most men are.'

'And yet,' said Oscar, leaning back in the stall and lighting his first cigarette since we had taken our seats, 'one man wants to murder her.'

'It can't be so,' said Stoker. 'I won't believe it.'

'Yes, it is so,' said Oscar quietly. He leant forward towards our host: 'Who did you choose as your "victim", Bram, when we played my wretched game?'

'"Old Father Time",' answered Stoker, smiling. He tugged on his beard ruefully. 'I shall be forty-five this November.'

'And what is your "secret", my friend?'

'My secret? My secret is laughable. My secret is that in my heart I am still only twenty-five.'

'Oh,' said Oscar, draining his glass. 'In my heart I'm not yet nineteen.'

We finished the two bottles of Alsatian wine and ordered a third. We talked of youth and beauty, of fine wine and good food. Bram cautioned Oscar against a third helping of dressed crab. Dressed crab, he claimed, had led him to dream of vampires; we talked of Charles Brookfield's satire on *Lady Windermere's Fan* and of Walter Sickert's paintings of actresses *en deshabillée*; we talked of George Daubeney and house fires and women's undergarments – Bram's grandfather had been a manu-facturer of ladies' stays. We talked of parrots and monkeys and murder – Bram had been given a pet monkey by W. S. Gilbert and spoke of an acquaintance of his* who admitted to murdering a stranger once, 'casu-ally and without cause'. It was a wonderfully congenial lunch, and we touched on many topics peripheral to our 'case', but I was not sure how much solid progress we had made.

At three o'clock, however, standing once more on the corner of Wellington Street and the Strand, Oscar expressed himself well satisfied. Bram Stoker had returned to the Lyceum (to the rehearsals for Mr Irving's *King Lear*), having insisted on paying for our entertain-ment ('I got the girl, Oscar – you may have the dressed crab') and having agreed to be in attendance at the Cadogan Hotel the following evening for what he called 'the extraordinary extra gathering of the Socrates Club'.

'I hope you know what you're doing, Oscar,' Bram called out merrily, as he strode away from us up the street

---

* Sir Richard Burton (1821–1890), translator of the *Arabian Nights*.

towards the theatre. 'And have no fear . . . I'll deliver Brookfield to the dinner for you – that much I promise.'

'What now, Oscar?' I asked.

'Be free, my Ariel! At least for this afternoon . . . Go back to Gower Street. Get to grips with your wife's solicitor. I'm looking in briefly on Inspector Gilmour. I need to be certain he'll be with us tomorrow night. Then I have my assignation with the Hon. the Reverend George Daubeney – in Beak Street, behind the arras. He assures me I'll not be disappointed . . . And then, Robert, believe it or not, I am going home. I am returning to the bosom of my family. I shall be dining with my wife tonight.'

'I'm glad to hear it,' I said, suddenly shaking my friend warmly by the hand. 'That's as it should be, Oscar. And tomorrow?'

'Tomorrow is the thirteenth,' he said. 'Tomorrow is another day.'

'Shall we take breakfast?' I asked.

'No, not tomorrow,' he said, waving his swordstick towards a passing cab. 'Tomorrow, Robert, I shall be spending the day in Eastbourne. I shall be taking the early train. And you, Robert, if you would be so kind, if you can spare the time, will be spending the day in Tite Street. Mr Heron-Allen will not trouble you. Mrs Heron-Allen is back in town, so Mr Heron-Allen, also, is returning to the bosom of his family. . . Tomorrow, Robert, I need you to be Constance's guardian angel. Go to Tite Street tomorrow morning at ten o'clock, Robert. And, until I send you word, do not let my wife out of your sight.'

The seating plan
for the Socrates Club dinner at
the Cadogan Hotel on Friday 13 May 1892

Oscar Wilde

The Hon. the Rev.	Willie Hornung
George Daubeney	
Edward Heron-Allen	Lord Alfred Douglas
Arthur Conan Doyle	Lord Drumlanrig
Robert Sherard	Walter Sickert
Inspector Roger Ferris	Bram Stoker
Charles Brookfield	Inspector Archy Gilmour

Alphonse Byrd

26

Friday the Thirteenth

In south-west London, Friday 13 May 1892 was as Sunday 1 May had been: a crisp, cold day, though the sun shone clear and bright. I did as Oscar had asked. I arrived at 16 Tite Street, Chelsea, at a minute before ten o'clock. Arthur the butler seemed to have been expecting me, but Constance did not. When Arthur showed me into the first-floor drawing room I found Mrs Wilde seated at the table by the window, reading a book.

She looked up and, as she saw me, she cried out: 'Robert! What a lovely surprise! You've just missed Oscar. He's gone to Eastbourne. You will stay and visit with me instead? I am so happy to see you. Edward's wife has come home. He's returned to his nest. I've no one to play with. I'm all alone.'

She closed her book. She got to her feet and ran towards me and kissed me lightly on the mouth. She thought nothing of it, I am certain: it was just her way. I held her in my arms. I felt the warmth of her body against mine. I revelled in the softness of her touch. Oscar had told me, not long before – one night, at the Albemarle Club, when we had drunk two bottles of champagne – that he could no longer love his wife as a husband should. 'I don't blame her, poor creature – I blame nature,' he said. 'Nature is disgusting. It takes beauty and it defiles it. It defaces the ivory-white body we have adored with the vile cicatrices of maternity. It is loathsome. It befouls the altar of the soul.'

I had known Constance for eight years, since the time of her engagement to Oscar, and, to me, her allure had increased, not diminished, across the years. She was now thirty-four and her figure was a touch fuller than it had been in the days of her virginity, but time and motherhood had given her a bloom — a radiance — that she had lacked as a girl. When I first met her, her natural loveliness was masked by her natural reticence. She was pretty, but she was so shy she was almost gauche. Now she was beautiful and, though still sometimes awkward among strangers, as a rule she had a composure — an unassuming self-confidence — that I found utterly compelling. Oscar was my dearest friend: being with him was always exhilarating, but, to be candid, it was not always comfortable. In Oscar's company I was often on edge: in Constance's company I was always at ease.

When I released her from my arms, she did not move away from me. She looked up into my eyes and smiled. I wanted to kiss her again. Instead, I glanced towards the table by the window and said, 'What are you reading?'

She blushed. 'My own book, I am ashamed to say!' She broke from me and, laughing, covered her face with her hands. 'I have been reading my own stories, Robert!'

'Is this your new book?' I asked, moving with her to the table. 'I loved your first book, as you know.'

'They were children's fairy stories, Robert,' she teased. 'You can't have "loved" them!'

'I did,' I insisted. 'What is the new book called?'

336

She picked up the slender volume, bound in blue leather, and passed it to me. '*A Long Time Ago*,' she said. 'More fairy stories. Oscar has been most complimentary about them.'

'I shall be, too!' I declared. 'Read me one, will you, Constance?' I pressed the book into her hands. 'Read them all to me!'

'You are ridiculous, Robert,' she said, but she did as I asked.

We sat together all morning, side by side, at the table in the front window of Tite Street. The stories were delightful, as charming and fantastical as Oscar's own fairy tales, but not quite so melancholy, nor so baroque in their phrasing. Each time Constance finished one of the tales, I pressed her to start another. Each time she protested; each time she acquiesced. And while she read, turning the pages of the book with her right hand, I held her left hand in mine. Now and then, as she read, she lifted her eyes from the page and smiled at me. Once, when I had laid the back of her hand flat against the table and was slowly caressing her palm with the tips of my fingers, she asked: 'What are you doing, Robert?'

'I am studying the lines on your hand,' I said. 'I want to know what the future holds for you.'

She closed her fingers over mine. 'Do not look too close,' she said. 'Even Mrs Robinson will not tell me all that she sees hidden in my hand.'

At a little after twelve noon, Gertrude Simmonds, the boys' governess, knocked on the drawing-room door. She was holding little Vyvyan Wilde by the hand. She had come to ask if Mrs Wilde wanted to join her sons for luncheon and to enquire whether or not I would also be of the party.

'Oh, yes,' cried Constance getting to her feet and going to the door, 'Mr Sherard certainly wants to see the boys.'

As Constance was talking to the governess, and kissing her young son, I stood looking out of the window onto Tite Street. On the pavement opposite, standing beneath a lamp-post, looking up at the house, I recognised two familiar figures: Antipholus, the black boy from Astley's Circus, and his sister, Bertha. He was holding his sister's hand and she was holding the wooden hoop that George Daubeney had given her. When they saw me staring down at them, Antipholus raised his arm and gave me a friendly wave. I raised my arm and waved back.

'Who are you waving to?' asked Constance.

'Nobody,' I lied, turning towards her. 'Somebody I thought I recognised,' I added, 'but I was mistaken.' When I turned back to the window, Antipholus and Bertha were gone.

We lunched with the boys in the nursery. They were delightful children, well-mannered and wise beyond their years. When Cyril said, 'Papa is teaching us Latin, but it's all Greek to me,' and I laughed, Cyril added proudly: 'That's my own joke, you know – it isn't one of Papa's.' When we had eaten, we left the boys to take their after-noon rest and returned to the drawing room.

Over coffee, Constance told me how much she loved Oscar and what a perfect husband and father she found him to be.

When I said, 'I fear he neglects you sometimes,' she protested.

'Never! We are always in his thoughts – always. I expect a telegram to arrive from Eastbourne any minute now. He sends me loving messages wherever he goes.'

'What's he doing in Eastbourne?' I asked. 'Do you know?'

'It will be some literary matter, I expect,' she said sweetly, 'or Bosie suddenly needing a breath of sea air. Oscar needs more stimulus than we can supply here. I understand that.' She smiled at me. 'I don't resent it. I am married to Oscar Wilde, the cleverest man in Europe. And one of the kindest. I count my blessings, Robert.'

A silence fell between us. I glanced towards the window.

'Before lunch,' she said, 'when you waved to someone in the street, was it a young black boy and a little girl?'

I looked down into my coffee cup and murmured that it was.

'They are often there,' said Constance. 'I believe Oscar sends them to watch over me.'

That afternoon in Tite Street gave me something that none of my three marriages has afforded me – a taste of domestic contentment. Constance and I played *piquet*; we took afternoon tea (with Mrs Ryan's best scones and home-made plum jam and thick, buttercup-yellow Cornish cream); together we helped Gertrude Simmonds bath the boys and I read them one of Constance's fairy tales as their bedtime treat. At six o'clock, Arthur lit a small fire in the drawing-room grate and Constance and I stood in front of it and raised a glass of sherry wine to one another. It was all so uncomplicated and easy, so comfortable and comforting. It was what, I realised, I most wanted for my life.

As the clock on the mantelpiece struck seven, we heard the sound of hooves and rattling wheels in the street. Constance ran towards the window.

'That'll be Oscar,' she cried.

We looked down as a hansom cab drew up outside the front door. We expected somebody to step out, but nobody did. Instead, a boy suddenly jumped down from the driver's seat. It was Nat, the freckle-faced page-boy from the Cadogan Hotel. He was holding an envelope.

A moment later, Arthur entered the drawing room bearing the envelope on a small silver salver. 'It's for Mr Sherard, Ma'am.'

'It's from Oscar,' I said. I tore open the envelope and read the note:

All is well – and we are ready. Come to the
Cadogan now. Come as you are and come at once.
Do not delay. Constance will be quite safe.
Antipholus is on guard and the police are apprised.
Tell my wife nothing – except that her husband
loves her and will be home by just after midnight.

I folded the note and slipped it into my jacket pocket. 'I must go,' I said.

'Oscar calls?' she asked. 'Oscar summons?'

'Yes.'

She asked nothing more – not where he was or with whom or why.

'He says he'll be home just after midnight,' I added.

'Oh good,' she said, walking with me to the door, linking her arm with mine. 'I'm glad of that. Give him my love. I am so grateful to him for sending you to me today.' She held her shining face up to mine. 'It has been lovely, has it not?'

'It has been perfect,' I said and I kissed her on the lips.

Twenty minutes later, when I arrived at the private dining room of the Cadogan Hotel, to my amazement, I found the room *en fête*. Laughter, loud conversation and the sound of clinking glasses filled the warm and smoky air. 'Everyone seems very jolly,' I remarked to Walter Sickert, whom I found standing alone by the door nursing a large whisky and soda.

'Very jolly,' he repeated. 'You've heard of the condemned man who ate a hearty meal? I think the principle's the same. They're all here – and they all seem to be in *riotously* good form. Have a cigar!' He offered me one of his favourite Manilas. I took it, remembering to put it in my mouth the wrong way round.

'Are we celebrating something?'

'We are,' he said, striking a match and holding it for me. 'That picture I hoped to sell – I sold it! No more one-man exhibitions and gallery shows for me. I no longer believe in vomiting your whole past, present and future in a lump into a dealer's room for three weeks – the virginity of the pictures gone . . . No, like a cunning mother, I now marry my daughters one by one, quietly, some well, some badly. This one – well! Have another cigar – for later.' He pushed a second Manila into my breast pocket.

Wat was clearly already drunk. It was barely half past seven and yet I sensed that he was not alone. The mood in the room appeared to border on the hysterical. To the right of us I caught side of the Hon. the Reverend George Daubeney, his face flushed with wine, his right hand resting on Willie Hornung's head, apparently offering the lad some kind of absolution. Just in front of us stood Conan Doyle and Bram Stoker, booming at one another.

'News of the giant rat of Sumatra,' cried Arthur. 'That is a tale for which the world is not yet prepared!'

'Tell it, man,' thundered Bram, beating the doctor on the shoulder with a clenched fist. 'Tell it – and *terrify* your public. That's what they want. That's what I plan to do with my vampires.'

'You will, Stoker, you will,' chipped in Charles Brookfield from the sidelines.

'I'd better go and show my face to Oscar,' I murmured to Wat Sickert.

'No need,' said Wat, draining his glass. 'He'll have seen you. He doesn't miss a thing.'

Oscar was standing with Lord Alfred Douglas and Francis, Lord Drumlanrig, at the far end of the room, by the head of the dining-room table. Sickert was right. Oscar had already noticed me. As I pushed my way towards him through the throng, he struck the side of his champagne glass with a fish knife and called for silence.

'Mr Sherard has arrived. Dinner can be served. *À table*, gentlemen, *à table*.'

The company gathered and shifted around the dining table, peering at the name cards to check their places.

'The menu and the wines are as they were when last we met,' Oscar called out, 'but the *placement* has been altered in certain instances.' With his forefinger he beckoned George Daubeney and Willie Hornung towards him. 'I'm having the padre and the *Gentlewoman*'s friend on either side of me.'

'I see that I'm below the salt as usual,' remarked Charles Brookfield, 'between the police and the club secretary.' He called down the table: 'Am I your chief suspect, Oscar?'

'You're seated with men of rank, Charles,' Oscar answered genially. 'I thought that you would appreciate that.'

When everyone had found his place, Oscar tapped his champagne glass once more. 'Silence, gentlemen, please.' We took up our positions behind our chairs and looked towards our host. He lowered his glass and returned the fish knife to the table. As the room fell quiet, he held the moment. Lit from below as he was by the table's flickering candlelight he looked like a figure in one of Wat Sickert's theatrical paintings: the leading actor standing before the footlights about to deliver the prologue to the play. In truth, of course, that's what he was.

Slowly his eyes scanned ours. 'Gentlemen,' he said, eventually, 'thank you for your kind attendance tonight. I am grateful to you all for making yourselves available at such short notice. When we have eaten, I shall explain exactly why I have brought you here – and why I have asked Inspector Gilmour and Inspector Ferris of Scotland Yard to be of the party. We welcome them wholeheartedly to this unusual gathering of the Socrates Club.' He nodded in the direction of the police officers as a low murmur of approval rumbled around the dining table. 'They've not come unaccompanied,' he added, casting his eyes towards the dining-room door. 'I understand there are eight policemen in and around the hotel tonight – one of whom you'll recognise, Robert.' He lowered his voice and leant across the table towards me. 'The ugly little man from the Turkish bath turns out not to be an assassin, but a police spy. And it's not us he's been watching, Robert. It's Lord Rosebery. Apparently, the former Foreign Secretary and his associates are kept under permanent police surveillance . . .'

Lord Alfred Douglas clicked his tongue impatiently. 'I thought you said dinner was about to be served, Oscar.'

'Quite right, Bosie.' Oscar beamed at his young friend and nodded apologetically to the table. 'Let us say Grace and, as we do so, let us pause for a moment and remember those we have lost since we last met in this room a dozen nights ago.'

Oscar lowered his head and closed his eyes and with his long, elegant fingers gripped the back of his chair. We stood in silence for at least a minute – it may have been longer – and then, without prompting, George Daubeney spoke the Grace.

'*In nomine Patris, et Filii, et Spiritus Sancti. Benedic, Domine, nos et haec tua dona, quae de tua largitate sumus sumpturi, per Christum Dominum nostrum.*'

In unison, briskly and quite loudly, we chorused: 'Amen.'

As we sat down to eat, the heightened festive spirit that I had sensed as I arrived in the room returned immediately. As the hotel waiter – our only server – laid the *hors d'oeuvres* before us, Alphonse Byrd, the only one of us in evening dress, moved about the table serving the first of several fine wines. It was an extraordinary *crémant d'Alsace* that bubbled and sparkled and complemented the caviar, lobster and pickled tunny quite perfectly. I was seated opposite Wat Sickert. He raised his glass towards me and whispered: 'The condemned men enjoyed a hearty meal.'

As I sipped my wine, I looked about the table. I looked at each of the faces in turn. I could not see a murderer in our midst. Not one of my fellow diners appeared to me to have the mark of Cain upon him. Even Edward Heron-Allen – talking loudly across the table to Lord Alfred Douglas of fornication among male monkeys in the rain-forests of Peru – gave the impression of a man with a wholly easy conscience. At every corner of the table, I saw guilt-free fellows engaged in comfortable conversation. At the foot of the table, Charles Brookfield was chatting amiably with the two police inspectors. At the head of it, Oscar, smiling, was holding both George Daubeney and Willie Hornung by the sleeve. He leant across them and called to Conan Doyle: 'How goes the sculpture, Arthur? It's nearly finished, I imagine.'

'It is, as it happens. Did Touie tell you?'

'No – but you have been so deeply engaged upon it I assumed that you were working to a deadline. It is a gift I take it – for a birthday?'

'Right again, Oscar. But whose birthday? Are your powers of deduction up to that?'

'It's bound to be a lady,' said Oscar. 'No man cares about giving a birthday present to another man.'

'Except when you give me cigarette cases for mine!' cried Bosie. 'Beautiful cigarette cases, charmingly inscribed.' He produced one from his pocket and waved it in the air.

Oscar ignored his young friend. He continued to look beadily at Conan Doyle: 'It won't be for your wife, Arthur – her birthday is in August, I remember. It won't be for your mistress – I know you, my friend: you're a gentleman: you'll never have one. So, it must be for some female relation . . . your mother, your aunt – or your sister?' He let go of Daubeney's sleeve and with his right hand banged the table triumphantly. 'Do you have a sister, Arthur? I think you do!'

'He does,' cried Willie Hornung, 'and she is very beautiful. Very, *very* beautiful.'

Oscar swivelled round in his chair and looked upon Conan Doyle's young friend. I saw tears glistening in both their eyes. 'You are in earnest, Willie, I can tell. You are in love with Arthur's sister. I'm certain of it. Propose to her, my boy – on her birthday!'

Willie Hornung turned crimson and Arthur Conan Doyle laughed and beat his fingers on the table by way of applause. Oscar called down the table to Alphonse Byrd who had just taken his seat between Charles Brookfield and Inspector Gilmour. 'Byrd!' he cried. 'Byrd! What does Socrates say about matrimony? You're a classicist, you're a New College man, you must know . . .'

Suddenly the table fell silent and all eyes turned on Alphonse Byrd. The club secretary hesitated for a moment, then rose slowly to his feet and looked towards Willie Hornung.

'"My advice to you is to get married. If you find a good wife, you will be happy. If not, you will become a philosopher."'

'Yes!' cried Oscar rapturously, leading the table in a chorus of laughter and applause.

As we ate our meal the mood in the room remained mellow, but as one course followed another – and Byrd and the waiter filled and refilled our glasses with fine wine – the banter subsided. The conversation around the table continued easily, but the edge of hysteria began to dissipate. At ten o'clock – I was seated next to Conan Doyle and he checked his Hunter regularly – when the roast meats had been cleared away, but before the desserts or savouries had been served, I watched as Oscar summoned the waiter and, shaking his head, whispered some instructions in his ear. He then said out loud, to no one in particular, 'We are all much calmer now. I think we can begin.'

27
Answers

Oscar pushed back his chair and laid his napkin carefully on the table. Alphonse Byrd was at his side with a fresh glass and a small decanter of yellow wine. 'Just half a glass, thank you, Byrd. I've work to do.'

He tapped the tips of his fingers lightly on the table's edge and rose to his feet. The room fell silent. The candles flickered obligingly.

Walter Sickert leant towards me and whispered: 'The show begins . . .'

From his place among the policemen, Charles Brookfield, cupping his hands around his mouth, called down the table: 'Who killed the parrot, Oscar? That's what we want to know!'

Oscar smiled as he lowered his head towards a candle to light his cigarette. 'All in good time, Charles,' he said. He said it gently, almost playfully. 'One has to learn to pace these things,' he added, still smiling. 'We'll get to the parrot in due course, but with your permission, Charles, we'll begin at the beginning.' He stood back and, for a moment, placed his hands lightly on the shoulders of George Daubeney and Willie Hornung who were seated either side of him. He looked around the table and drew slowly on his cigarette. When he was certain that all eyes were upon him, he began.

'Thank you, gentlemen,' he said. 'Thank you again for your kind attendance tonight.' His voice was mellow, easy on the ear. Sickert likened it once to the sound of 'a 'cello playing in a nearby room'. 'I'm obliged to each of you. As you'll recall, when last we gathered here, at my instigation we played a game – a game called "Murder" – a game of unintended and quite dreadful consequences . . . How much I regret that game I cannot tell you. My poor excuse is that by it I meant no harm.'

Inspector Gilmour stirred uncomfortably.

'True enough,' said Oscar, looking at the police inspector. 'All but one of those who have lost their lives during these past thirteen days might have been murdered come what may. But that my foolish game acted as the trigger for a deadly chain of events, as it did, when it did, cannot be denied – and because the game was my idea, and mine alone, I believe that it is my responsibility to unravel the mystery of its aftermath. I have asked you here tonight, gentlemen, to do my duty by you: to tell you which of you murdered whom – and why.'

'Are you saying there's a murderer in our midst, Oscar?' asked Willie Hornung, his face aglow with excitement.

'I am.'

Inspector Ferris half raised his hand, like a tentative schoolboy at the back of the class. 'If he's about to be exposed, Mr Wilde, why has this murderer of yours turned up?'

'Good question,' muttered Inspector Gilmour.

349

'Out of curiosity,' murmured Charles Brookfield. 'Oscar's irresistible. We all want to see Oscar Wilde on song.'

'And Byrd does lay on a frightfully good spread,' purred Lord Alfred Douglas, leaning back in his chair and winking at our host.

'To have declined my invitation for this evening – to have stayed hidden – to have run away – would have been tantamount to an admission of guilt,' said Oscar looking directly at Inspector Ferris. 'Our murderer is here tonight by way of asserting his innocence. That's his style. It has been from the outset.'

The room settled once more. Oscar turned towards his right and looked down on the Hon. the Reverend George Daubeney who smiled up at him with watery eyes. 'Your wine glass is empty, George,' he said. 'Have mine.' Oscar handed the clergyman his glass of yellow wine. 'Let us begin at the beginning,' he went on, 'here, with the Reverend George . . .' George Daubeney raised the glass to Oscar and smiled. Oscar turned back to address the table as a whole. 'You will recall, gentlemen, that when we played our game of "Murder" a week ago last Sunday, the first slip of paper to be drawn from Mr Byrd's velvet bag was that of Mr Daubeney . . . Mr Daubeney named his sometime fiancée, Miss Elizabeth Scott-Rivers, as his intended "victim". We know it because he told us so. Indeed, as you'll recollect, he made quite a palaver of telling us . . . Methought at the time that he did protest too much – as he did again later that same evening when he kept repeating that he had drunk too much when, with my own eyes, I had seen him drink two glasses of wine at most.'

Daubeney looked steadily at Oscar. He wiped the moisture from his lips. 'Do not forget that we are friends, Oscar. We know each other quite well, don't we?'

Oscar looked at him. 'I believe I know you better, George, than you know me.'

Daubeney laughed and glanced about the table. 'Elizabeth's death was an accident,' he said emphatically. 'Ask the coroner. Ask the police.'

'It was no accident,' said Oscar, putting out his cigarette. 'It was murder, George – murder most ingenious – murder inspired by a conversation you had on the afternoon of Sunday 1 May at 16 Tite Street – with my wife.'

Daubeney shook his head incredulously. 'I don't know what you're talking about, Oscar.'

'Oh, but you do, George,' said Oscar calmly. 'That afternoon, at our little charitable fund-raiser, Mrs Wilde told you all about the work of the Rational Dress Society. She told you how each year, in London alone, scores of women lose their lives in domestic fires – burnt to death in their own homes, on their own hearth-rugs, their clothes set alight accidentally by spluttering candles or falling coals or stray sparks from the grate. What my wife told you *inspired* you – to murder your former fiancée by burning her to death . . . You wanted to rid the world of the woman who had ruined you once and might ruin you again. That afternoon, quite innocently, my well-meaning wife suggested to you the perfect means. Constance gave you the idea, George. With my unhappy game, I gave you the opportunity.'

A silence fell as Oscar lit a second cigarette.

'Mr Wilde,' said Inspector Gilmour, 'you appear to forget that when we found Miss Scott-Rivers's body her house was securely locked from the inside. I know. I checked all the locks myself.'

'When you arrived on the scene, Inspector, the house was indeed secured from within. But when Mr Daubeney arrived at 27 Cheyne Walk, it was not.'

Inspector Ferris pushed his chair away from the table. 'Don't worry, Inspector,' said Daubeney turning towards him and raising his glass in his direction. 'I'm not planning to run away. I've nothing to hide.'

Oscar's eyes narrowed as he looked down at the clergyman. 'You have so much to hide, George – so much. And your genius, if such it be, is to be so apparently open that no one would believe you capable of so much evil . . .'

'May God forgive you, Oscar – I thought that we were friends.' Daubeney shook his head and drank his wine. He was so calm that it was indeed difficult to believe that he might be guilty. He looked along the dining table and smiled at his fellow guests. 'The house was locked from within, gentlemen. The fire was burning furiously when I tried to break my way in through the ground-floor window. I was beaten back by the heat and the flames. If I could have rescued Elizabeth, I would have done so. That's the truth of it.'

'No, George, that's not the truth of it.' Oscar turned towards the Reverend Daubeney and gazed at him unflinchingly. Until he had finished his narrative he did not lift his eyes from him once. 'This is the truth of it, George. At around midnight on Sunday 1 May last, you left the Cadogan Hotel and walked from here, down Sloane Street, across the King's Road, to the Thames embankment. Steadily, purposefully, you made your way to 27 Cheyne Walk, the home of Miss Elizabeth Scott-

Rivers. You saw a light in your former fiancée's drawing-room window. You knocked at the front door. The lady of the house admitted you herself. Her servants were not at home. She was alone. She told you so – and the moment that she told you so you seized your opportunity. You killed her there and then – in an instant, ruthlessly, remorselessly, in cold blood.'

Daubeney wiped his mouth with a shaking hand. 'How?' he asked. 'How did I kill her?'

'I cannot be certain,' said Oscar. 'I imagine that you strangled her. Her eyes were wide open when her body was found.'

'This is grotesque,' muttered Conan Doyle.

Oscar's gaze remained fixed on George Daubeney. 'It gets worse, Arthur, believe me.' He leant further towards Daubeney. 'You killed Miss Scott-Rivers and you dragged her body across her drawing room towards her own hearth. You laid the body by the grate. You then returned to the front door and locked and bolted it securely from within. You went downstairs to the basement and ensured that the door to the front area and the door to the garden were locked and bolted as well.' Oscar drew on his cigarette. 'The scene was laid . . . all you now had to do was go back to the drawing room and light the match – or, with the fire-tongs, lift a piece of burning coal from the grate and use it to set fire to your victim's dress . . . You set the poor woman's body alight and waited for the flames to blaze before making your escape. It was easily done. You watched her burn, and then you broke your way out of the drawing-room window. And the firemen on the embankment who saw you standing on the window ledge simply assumed that you were trying to get into the house, not out of it, because, in the moment that they saw you, that's how it appeared to them—'

'That's how it was,' said Daubeney urgently.

'No, George. There was so much broken glass in the area below the window – the window had to have been broken from the inside out, not from the outside in.'

'It was an accident,' Daubeney protested. 'Her dress caught fire!'

'If her dress had caught fire by accident, George, her body would not have been found by the fireplace. When a woman sees that her dress is alight, she does not remain right by the source of the fire. She runs from it – she tries to escape. Elizabeth Scott-Rivers's body was found by the hearth because that is where you placed it.'

Archy Gilmour got to his feet and nodded across the table to his fellow officer. 'Charge him with murder!' he commanded.

Oscar laughed. 'And so much more besides!' He held up his right hand. 'We're not done yet.'

George Daubeney made no attempt to move. He closed his eyes. 'I do not feel very well,' he whispered.

'Take him away!' barked Gilmour.

Oscar turned towards the policeman. 'There's more to be told, Inspector – if you're inclined to hear it.'

'Haven't we heard enough?' asked Conan Doyle.

'We've heard enough to hang a man, for sure,' said Oscar. 'We've heard the "what", Arthur; we've heard the "how". We've not yet heard the "wherefore"; we've not yet heard the "why".'

I looked up at Oscar. 'Surely he murdered the poor woman to retrieve his fortune – to inherit hers . . .' I said.

'No, Robert. At the time that Daubeney killed Elizabeth Scott-Rivers, he assumed that she had changed her will. He did not kill her for her money – that came as an incidental bonus. He killed her to exact his revenge – and to silence her. She knew his secret.'

'We all have secrets, don't we, Oscar?' giggled Lord Alfred Douglas, reaching across his brother to Wat Sickert and stealing a cigar from Wat's coat pocket.

'We do,' said Oscar quietly. 'Elizabeth Scott-Rivers discovered her fiancé's secret a week before the day intended for their wedding. At once, privately, she broke off their engagement. Shortly afterwards, publicly, she sued him for breach of promise and, in the process, ruined him. He said nothing in his own defence. Why? Why did George Daubeney – a supposed gentleman, an apparently eligible bachelor, the son of an earl, a man of the cloth, an assistant chaplain at the House of Commons – *why* did he accept the humiliation and ruin that this breach of promise action brought upon him? Because he had no choice – because he had a secret.'

'There'll be a lady in the case,' murmured Bram Stoker. 'There always is.'

'Or perhaps a young man,' suggested Charles Brookfield. 'Oscar has some funny friends.'

'What is this secret, Oscar?' demanded Conan Doyle impatiently. 'Come on, man. Don't play with us. Spit it out.'

Oscar held his head back. Two thin blue-grey plumes of smoke rose from his nostrils. 'George Daubeney is a trafficker in child prostitutes,' he said. 'He has a speciality: young girls. He sells virgins – at five pounds a piece.'

Daubeney said nothing. He sat in his place, his head now in his hands. Inspector Ferris stood immediately behind him.

'How do you know all this?' asked Arthur Conan Doyle.

'Because of the cuff-links,' said Oscar, simply.

'The cuff-links?' repeated Willie Hornung.

'The cuff-links,' said Wat Sickert, quietly.

'Yes, Wat,' said Oscar, looking at the artist. 'The cuff-links.' Oscar's eyes ranged around the table. All but George Daubeney had their gaze fixed on him. 'At the Socrates Club dinner I happened to notice that the Honourable the Reverend George Daubeney was wearing unusual cuff-links – cuff-links that did not match. One was a simple silver cuff-link, undecorated, unremarkable, but the other was exquisite. It was a cuff-link with an enamel facing that featured a reproduction of a favourite painting of mine: a Madonna by Bellini. When I next saw Daubeney – a few hours later, when he found his way to my house in Tite Street in the aftermath of the fire – the cuff-links were missing. He had removed them. I wondered why.'

Oscar paused and held the moment. He looked at Wat Sickert expectantly. Wat ran his fingers along his moustache and said nothing. Oscar went on: 'On the night of the Socrates Club dinner I had been especially struck by George Daubeney's Bellini cuff-link because I knew someone else who had a pair of cuff-links not unlike it . . . a friend, my friend – our friend – the artist, Walter Sickert.'

Oscar stretched out his left arm in Wat's direction. Sickert leant urgently across the table.

'I bought the cuff-links from Daubeney, Oscar – I told you that when I gave them to you.' He looked around at the rest of us. There was a sudden desperation in his eyes. For a moment, he seemed quite frantic. 'The cuff-links featured Leonardo's painting, *The Virgin of the Rocks*. Oscar admired them, so I gave them to him. No, that's not true. I *sold* them to him.'

'For five pounds,' said Oscar.

'Yes,' answered Sickert, 'for five pounds. That's what I had paid Daubeney. That's what I told you.'

'You told me that the cuff-links had cost you five pounds . . .'

'They did,' cried Sickert. 'They had!'

'But you did not tell me, Wat, that when you bought the cuff-links from Daubeney for five pounds Daubeney promised that the cuff-links would be delivered to you personally by a special messenger – a child of thirteen, a young girl, guaranteed a virgin . . .'

Sickert pushed his chair back from the table. 'I did not touch her, Oscar. I swear to it. I wanted her as a model – nothing more. I wanted to paint a girl on the brink of womanhood. I wanted to paint a virgin – a true virgin. That is all.'

'You undressed her?'

'She undressed herself. I did not touch her. Believe me, Oscar.'

Oscar smiled and lit yet another cigarette. 'I believe you, Wat. You are my friend and I know you to be a gentleman. And, strange as it may seem, in this matter I'm indebted to you. You sold me those cuff-links because I took a fancy to them and I'm glad that you did because, by chance, I wore them on the day that Robert Sherard and I visited the French Bookshop in Beak Street. George Daubeney was there. He saw me wearing the cuff-links. And he assumed that I, too, was a man in want of a five-pound virgin . . .'

'Well, well . . .' murmured Charles Brookfield.

'Last night, Daubeney invited me to Beak Street and took me to an upstairs room and introduced me to a little Spanish-speaking girl called Rosa. She was the prettiest child. She had round black eyes and long eyelashes like a baby giraffe's. She can have been no more than eleven or twelve years of age. Daubeney said she was newly arrived from Mexico. He called her "*Nuestra Señora de Guadalupe*". He said that he had "examined" her and that her young breasts were "newly formed and quite, quite perfect". She was "hairless", he assured me, and "blemish-free". He had a certificate from a reliable midwife guaranteeing her virginity. He told me that the child's maidenhood was mine for five pounds – and that I would receive the most charming cuff-links as a souvenir of our encounter.'

'My throat!' cried George Daubeney, lifting his head from his hands, 'My throat is burning. My neck is swollen.'

'Your neck will be broken soon enough, sir,' said Inspector Gilmour of Scotland Yard. 'Get him to his feet, Ferris. Take him to the growler. Get the men to keep him in the wagon till we're done here. Tell them he's to be charged with murder. Don't mention this other business. We need him to survive the night.'

28

Answers, Answers

Alphonse Byrd returned to Oscar's side with a fresh glass and the small decanter of yellow wine. 'You've not touched your wine, Mr Wilde,' he said.

Oscar smiled and rested his hand on the club secretary's arm. 'Forgive me, Byrd. I gave it to Daubeney. I felt his need was greater – under the circumstances.'

'Will you take some now, sir?'

'Thank you – just half a glass.' He turned to the waiter who was standing by the sideboard. 'Make sure everyone has all that they require – if you would be so kind. And then join us at the table.'

'The waiter is to join us at table?' asked Heron-Allen, with an amused look on his pale face. 'I admire your democratic impulse, Oscar.'

'It's all happening tonight!' cried Bosie Douglas, raising his glass towards our host.

Charles Brookfield leant across to me and murmured, 'Am I right – Oscar's always had a liking for the lackey class?'

'It's not a matter of democracy,' said Oscar benignly, resuming his seat and holding his glass of wine up to the candlelight. 'It's a question of superstition.' He looked at George Daubeney's empty chair.

'Dinner's not over and we can't possibly be thirteen at table.'

'It's getting late, Oscar,' said Conan Doyle. 'Are we not done yet?'

Oscar put down his glass and offered the doctor his ungainly, boyish grin. 'You'll be on your way to South Norwood soon enough, Arthur – I promise. We've just a few loose ends to tidy up.'

Conan Doyle put away his timepiece. 'I take my hat off to you, old friend. You've nailed your man most effectively.'

Oscar inclined his head towards the doctor. 'However, I might have got there sooner had I listened to you in the first place, Arthur. The moment you clapped eyes on Daubeney you mistrusted him. You told me that he had a weak mouth.'

'Did I say that?'

'You did – but, romantic that I am, I was distracted by knowing of his association with the circus! I saw clowns when I should have smelt corruption. He was a chaplain at the House of Commons and a circus padre. The sheer improbability of it so delighted me I was disarmed.'

At the far end of the table, Archy Gilmour was taking notes. 'When did you begin to suspect him, Mr Wilde?'

'At dinner, I was puzzled by his show of drunkenness – when I knew him to be sober. I was puzzled, too, by the cuff-links. I guessed that they might be a sort of sign, a symbol, like a club tie – but I presumed that his interest was in women not in children. My suspicions were not properly aroused until I saw him with a child – a little girl, the sister of a boy who works at the circus. I was perturbed by the way that he touched her. I was concerned when I saw how he cherished a photograph that he had of her – dressed as Cinderella, apparently shedding tears.'

Inspector Ferris, crackling with energy, returned to the dining room. His face was flushed and shiny, though he brought with him a gust of cold night air. The candles on the table dipped and flickered. As the young inspector resumed his seat, between me and Charles Brookfield, Oscar waved to the waiter who was standing in the shadows to join us. The waiter – a large man, clean-shaven and unassuming – slipped quietly into Daubeney's old seat at Oscar's right hand. Inspector Ferris, when, noisily, he had pulled in his chair, rubbed his hands together and nodded towards Archy Gilmour with a show of satisfaction. 'He's in the growler now – hand-cuffed. I've put three men with him. He's quite secure – and totally docile. He's complaining that he's sick.'

'He's sick all right,' said Charles Brookfield.

'Desire at the end is a malady, or a madness, or both,' said Oscar.

'They whip child molesters, don't they?' asked Brookfield.

'What constitutes a "child" nowadays?' enquired Bram Stoker.

'Fifteen and under,' said Lord Drumlanrig. 'The age of consent was raised from thirteen as part of the 1885 Criminal Law Amendment Act.'

'You're very well informed, my lord,' said Brookfield, raising an eyebrow. 'The 1885 Act? That's the one that puts the buggers to hard labour, isn't it?'

'The Act was designed to protect the young and vulnerable,' said Drumlanrig seriously. 'Lord Rosebery can claim some of the credit.'

'Well done, Primrose!' said Brookfield, raising his glass towards Drumlanrig.

'I think you'll find George Daubeney is hanged before he's whipped, Mr Brookfield – if he's found guilty of murder, as I suspect he will be. Mr Wilde has made a convincing case.' Gilmour looked down the table towards Oscar. 'We'll need a full statement from you in the morning, Mr Wilde.'

Oscar nodded. 'Of course, Inspector. Mr Sherard has kept notes. I trust you'll find them helpful.'

'The question is,' said Willie Hornung eagerly, leaning forward and lighting his cigarette from Oscar's, 'Did George Daubeney commit the second murder on the list? Did Daubeney murder Lord Abergordon? If Daubeney was a chaplain at the House of Commons he must have had access to the House of Lords.'

Oscar chuckled and rested his hand on Hornung's. 'No, Willie. For once, I believe the medical men may have got it right. Lord Abergordon was an elderly gentleman who died in his sleep – of natural causes. He was not murdered.'

'But McMuirtree was murdered,' said Heron-Allen emphatically, tapping the table with a clenched fist. 'There's no doubt of that. We were there. Daubeney was there. Did George Daubeney murder David McMuirtree?'

'No!' cried Inspector Gilmour. He snapped his pencil as he spoke. 'No,' he repeated, more calmly, 'I don't believe there's any question of that.'

'The inspector is right,' said Oscar, soothingly. 'Daubeney did not murder McMuirtree. He had reason to, perhaps. McMuirtree may have known something of

Daubeney's secret life. McMuirtree made it his business to know all about the secret lives of others. And Daubeney was certainly with McMuirtree at the last. As Edward says, we saw him there, in the dressing room, with McMuirtree's blood on his hands. Daubeney may have pressed the blades deeper into the dying man's wrists, but he did not place them there. Daubeney was not McMuirtree's murderer.'

Willie Hornung puffed at his cigarette. 'Did he at least murder Bradford Pearse?' he asked.

'No,' said the waiter seated on Oscar's right. 'No, George Daubeney did not murder Bradford Pearse.' The man's voice was deep and low; mellow, friendly, and oddly familiar. 'Nobody murdered me, I'm happy to say.'

'Good God!' cried Bram Stoker.

'By all that's wonderful,' called out Wat Sickert, throwing down his cigar and getting to his feet. He moved around the table with his arms outstretched. 'My friend!' he cried. 'My Lazarus!'

Bradford Pearse got to his feet and acknowledged the applause that swept around the table. He embraced Wat Sickert like a long-lost brother.

'And you've been here all evening,' roared Bram Stoker, 'you've ladled out our soup, you've carved our roast, you've poured our wine . . .'

Bradford Pearse broke from Sickert's embrace and looked down the table. 'It's true what they say, Bram – nobody notices the bloody waiter!'

'Well, well,' muttered Conan Doyle, pocketing his watch once more. 'South Norwood will have to wait. Tell us your story, Brad. What happened? Unfold your tale.'

'It's a tale told by an idiot,' said Pearse, his arm still around Wat Sickert's shoulder. 'I've been a fool, Arthur – a bloody fool.' He broke from the artist and looked around the table and bowed apologetically towards us all. 'I own it, gentlemen. I've been a fool to myself – and to my friends.'

Wat Sickert drew a chair from the side of the room and perched himself on it, between Oscar and Bradford Pearse. 'Don't apologise, Brad,' said Sickert warmly. 'We're glad to see you – even without your beard.'

'I do apologise,' said Pearse, seating himself once more. 'I have caused my friends unnecessary anxiety.'

'What happened, man?' repeated Conan Doyle, leaning forward and looking the actor directly in the eye.

'My story's easily told,' answered Pearse. He sat upright in his chair, his broad shoulders held well back. 'That night, when we played Oscar's game, I chose myself as my own victim. I did it partly for amusement's sake – and partly because, that night, at least, I did indeed want to be shot of Bradford Pearse. I was engulfed by money worries, gentlemen – *engulfed*. Indebtedness is the actor's lot, I know. I'm accustomed to it and, as a rule, I take it in my stride – I have good friends; and Mr Ashman is a most sympathetic pawnbroker – but that night I felt quite overwhelmed.' He looked in turn towards Oscar and Wat Sickert and clutched each of them by the hand. 'Those who've had money worries will understand *completely*.' He looked, not unkindly, towards the Douglas brothers and smiled. 'Those who have not, will not understand *at all*.' He took a deep breath and rubbed his face with his thick-fingered hands. Without his beard he seemed much younger than he had done before.

'The morning after our dinner here I travelled to Eastbourne to appear in a play – *Murder Most Foul*, an absurd farrago known in the business as *Play Most Atrocious*. We opened in Eastbourne on Monday night to a limited and profoundly ungrateful audience. On Tuesday afternoon, I sat in my dressing room at the Devonshire Park Theatre, despairing of my desultory and debt-ridden life while reading a borrowed copy of the evening newspaper. In that newspaper, the Eastbourne *Gazette*, I read, on successive pages, of the deaths of the heiress, Miss Elizabeth Scott-Rivers, and of the government minister, Lord Abergordon. Suddenly my plan was hatched! I would follow them to the grave. I, too, could be one of the Socrates Club "victims". If Bradford Pearse died, would not his debts die with him? It all seemed so obvious. It all seemed so easy. I would disappear overnight – over Beachy Head!' He pointed dramatically to Conan Doyle. 'Beachy Head was your idea, Arthur – I owe Beachy Head to you!'

Conan Doyle laughed and stroked his moustache. 'So, it's all my fault, is it?'

'No,' rumbled Bradford Pearse, pressing his palms against the table. 'The folly was all mine. I thought with one bound I could be free. I thought I could do away with Bradford Pearse – and start again, in America! My plan was to begin a new life – with a new name – in a New World.' He looked around the table once again. His eyes were shining. 'It's something we've all dreamt of, haven't we?'

Oscar was gently tapping a Player's Navy Cut against the lid of his cigarette case. 'Only the truly desperate cross the Atlantic Ocean,' he sniffed. 'If one had enough money to go to America, of course, one would not go.'

Bradford Pearse looked at Oscar and burst out laughing. 'Inevitably, my plan failed. I was foiled – as I might have guessed I would be – by the gentleman on my left here.'

Oscar smiled and lit his cigarette. 'Perhaps, Brad, you had forgotten that I'm a man of the theatre myself. I write plays. I'm at home with melodrama. I'm familiar with farce. Your scheme had elements of both. It was, I fear, too wildly theatrical to be in the least bit convincing. Because you're an actor you require an audience. You wanted to be seen to disappear so you lured Sickert and me to Eastbourne by means of a deliberately ambiguous letter. Then, on stage, during the curtain-call, you contrived to vanish before our very eyes. You left a message for us in your dressing room – the single word "Farewel" scrawled in make-up on a looking glass! To heighten the drama, to suggest you fled in haste, you left the word uncompleted . . . But clearly you had not left in haste. You had packed your bags and taken all your most prized possessions with you.'

'I left my Gladstone bag at the cliff's edge,' protested Pearse.

'Yes,' said Oscar, shaking his finger at Pearse by way of mock reproof. 'You left your bag for us to find and in it you left sufficient material for us to know that it was indeed your bag. There was your script, a host of unwanted bills, some inconsequential correspondence, but as I examined the bag I sensed at once that it was nothing more than a stage effect, a mere theatrical "property". The bag contained nothing that you truly valued – no personal correspondence, no diary, no precious pawnbrokers' receipts, no make-up tin. To a travelling actor, his make-up tin is his most cherished possession. You'd not abandoned yours. I knew you were not dead, Brad. I knew you'd simply gone to ground.'

'You're brilliant, Oscar! Fabulous!' cried Bradford Pearse, his eyes ablaze.

'Brilliant,' said Oscar, 'but not brave. Fabulous? Perhaps – but also flawed. I have a weakness for beauty, as you know – and a dread of ugliness that's beyond irrational. And because of them, Brad, I did not discover you in your hiding place when first I should have done.'

'You're losing them, Oscar!' called Lord Alfred Douglas, leaning back in his chair and moving his cigarette from one side of his mouth to the other with his tongue.

'We're not all of us familiar with the peculiarities of the Wilde aesthetic code,' added Charles Brookfield tartly.

Oscar sat forward, extinguishing his cigarette. 'Bradford took refuge in the Belle Tout Lighthouse at Seven Sisters point, a mile or so from Beachy Head. It's an ugly edifice and its guardian – a man of good heart, I'm sure – is a lighthouse keeper of peculiarly disgusting aspect. On the day of Bradford's disappearance, I visited the lighthouse – with Wat Sickert and Robert Sherard here. I realise now that the figure that we glimpsed in an upstairs window was Bradford Pearse – newly shaved. At the time, I chose not to linger at the lighthouse. The keeper was so ugly – he was a grotesque: diminutive, monocular, misshapen – that I turned away from him as quickly as I could. I was wrong to do so. On that occasion, I was the fool. Today, I returned to the Belle Tout Lighthouse. As I expected, I found Brad there and I brought him back here with me.'

'It's good to be back,' said Bradford Pearse warmly, stretching out his left arm and resting a large hand on Oscar's shoulder.

'And what about your money worries?' enquired Bram Stoker, with a furrowed brow.

'Let the world slide, let the world go!' cried Wat Sickert, reaching for his wine glass. 'If I can't pay, why I can owe – and death makes one the high and low!'

Bradford Pearse looked across the table at Bram Stoker. 'They've been sorted,' he said. 'By a generous benefactor.'

'They were not that great,' said Oscar. 'They just seemed so.'

'Oscar has cleared my debts,' said Bradford Pearse. 'He's given me a cheque – for thirteen guineas.'

'I'm expecting a modest windfall,' said Oscar, smiling.

Sickert was on his feet. 'Be merry, friends,' he cried. 'Let's drink to the prodigal's return, gentlemen. Be upstanding. Are your glasses charged? I give you: Bradford Pearse!'

We got to our feet and raised our glasses to the barrel-chested actor who stood before us with shining eyes.

'Your health, Bradford,' said Oscar, draining his glass. 'And yours, Oscar, my dear good friend.'

29

Thirteen Guineas

'Now I'm on my feet, Oscar,' said Conan Doyle firmly, 'I must be on my way. We can't all let the world slide. I've business to attend to in the morning.' He held his Hunter out towards the guttering candles. 'It's nearly midnight, way past my bedtime.'

'Stay till twelve, Arthur,' said Oscar, coming round the table to his friend and placing his hands on either side of the good doctor's shoulders. 'That's all I ask. Stay till the clock strikes. At least see if I manage to live out the day.'

'You'll live out the day, Oscar,' Conan Doyle laughed. 'You'll live for ever.'

'Oh, no,' cried Oscar, confronting his friend with an open palm. 'The life-line stops abruptly. Mrs Robinson has seen untold horrors in my unhappy hand.'

Conan Doyle pushed Oscar's hand away. 'You should not put your faith in fortune tellers, Oscar,' he said earnestly. He breathed deeply and raised his shoulders and looked about the table, nodding his farewell to the rest of the company. 'Goodnight, gentlemen,' he murmured.

All but the police officers and Alphonse Byrd had resumed their seats. Bradford Pearse and Wat Sickert had taken charge of the drinks and were circulating decanters of port, madeira and brandy around the table. Bosie

Douglas was lighting another of Wat's cigars. Charles Brookfield was scribbling a note to himself in a pocket-book. At the sideboard, Byrd was preparing dishes of fresh fruit and a tray of English cheeses.

'We must be on our way, too, Mr Wilde,' announced Inspector Gilmour. 'Duty calls. We must see Daubeney to his cell.'

'You promised to stay until midnight, Inspector,' said Oscar. 'You promised.'

'I think you're quite safe now, Mr Wilde,' answered the policeman, with a chuckle. 'I don't think you're about to be murdered in our midst.'

'Don't you?' asked Oscar, raising an eyebrow. 'I'm not so sure.'

'Goodnight, sir,' said Inspector Ferris crisply, offering Oscar an outstretched hand.

Oscar ignored the policeman's proferred hand and made his way back to his place at the head of the dining table. 'You promised to remain until midnight, gentlemen,' repeated Oscar. 'I'd be obliged to you both if you would keep your word.'

'And you can't go, Dr Doyle,' cried Lord Alfred Douglas, 'or we'll be thirteen at table again!'

The two police inspectors returned to their seats in silence. Shaking his head wearily, Arthur Conan Doyle pocketed his watch, straightened his waistcoat and sat down in his place once more.

Alphonse Byrd laid the fruit dishes and cheese on the table and returned to his seat between Charles Brookfield and Archy Gilmour. Simultaneously, four of the table's candles flared for a moment and abruptly died. The smoke-filled room darkened and fell silent.

'Thank you for your indulgence, gentlemen,' said Oscar quietly. 'I'll be brief. I'll cease upon the midnight hour, I promise you.'

'I'm pleased to hear it, Oscar,' said Conan Doyle, drumming his fingers lightly on the table in front him. 'What more have you to tell us?'

'The truth about David McMuirtree,' said Oscar simply.

'We know all about McMuirtree, Mr Wilde,' said Archy Gilmour. 'Remember – he was one of ours.'

'You know much about McMuirtree, Inspector, but I suspect not all.' Oscar called down the table to Alphonse Byrd, who sat facing him. 'Do you have your watch with you, Byrd? What time do you make it – precisely?'

The club secretary replied: 'I don't have a timepiece on me, Mr Wilde, but I can see the clock on the wall behind you well enough. It's ten to midnight, exactly.'

'Keep me in order, would you, Byrd? Let me know when my allotted time is drawing to a close.'

'As you please, Mr Wilde,' said Byrd, bringing the tips of his fingers together and resting them against his lips. His beady eyes narrowed. Steadfastly he gazed at Oscar. I let my own eyes roam around the table. Every man there was looking directly and intently towards our host. Once again, Oscar Wilde held us in his thrall.

'I sometimes think,' he began, examining the plume of smoke that slowly rose from his cigarette as he spoke, 'that God, in creating man, somewhat overestimated His ability. David McMuirtree was blessed with many of the Almighty's greatest gifts. He was born in Dublin, for a start. He had a keen mind and an easy charm. He had physical strength, physical courage and – after a fashion – physical beauty, too. As a personality, he had individuality – originality even. As a boxer, he possessed power and prowess. But as a man, he had a singular failing. *He lacked all feeling.* He cared for no one but himself.

'David McMuirtree was, in turn, as we know, a magician's assistant, a magician, a fairground entertainer, a policeman, a champion boxer and a police informer. He was also – by instinct and by calling – a pitiless and indiscriminate blackmailer.'

Archy Gilmour shifted in his chair. 'Are you sure of that, Mr Wilde?'

'Oh, yes,' said Oscar lightly, drawing on his cigarette. 'He could not help himself. He showed his true colours to my friend Robert Sherard on the first occasion that they met – repeating to him a sad and sordid story concerning my wife's father . . . He sought to frighten my friend Lord Drumlanrig here by inviting him onto Westminster Bridge to pour poison into his ear . . .'

'Primrose-scented poison, was it?' murmured Charles Brookfield.

'Indeed,' said Oscar, 'it was. The more outrageous the rumour, the readier McMuirtree was to peddle it. He knew everything about everybody. He knew more about me than I knew myself! And he used what he knew, at first to charm and then to terrify.

'McMuirtree was a man who *used* other men, who exploited their weaknesses for his own profit – and his own pleasure. And in his life he used no one man more cruelly than the unhappy creature who sits facing me now – the night manager of this hotel, our club secretary, my time-keeper, Mr Alphonse Byrd.'

The eyes of the room turned and fell on the cadaverous figure of Alphonse Byrd, hunched forward at the foot of the table, his fingers, joined as if in prayer, pressed tightly to his lips. He remained as he was, staring fixedly at Oscar, motionless.

'It was Byrd, of course, who murdered David McMuirtree. Byrd, who'd been born a gentleman, but never lived as one. Byrd, the skilled magician who lacked what the great John Maskelyne termed "the immortal spark". Byrd, who'd been McMuirtree's friend and partner, until McMuirtree abandoned him to pursue his own career. Byrd, the "gentleman", who, from first to last, was humiliated by "half-a-gentleman".

'When they were young, David McMuirtree used Alphonse Byrd – casually, carelessly, without consideration. Twenty years later, Byrd – night manager at a fashionable hotel and privy to the secrets that come the way of all night managers – was being used by McMuirtree still, when it pleased him, as a means of useful introductions, as a source of helpful hearsay.

'In time, the worm turned – as it is wont to do.

'When, in this room on that fateful Sunday night, we played my foolish game of "Murder", Alphonse Byrd named David McMuirtree as his victim of choice – of course he did.

'And when, as club secretary, collecting the slips of paper from around the table, Byrd discovered that two others had also chosen McMuirtree as their murder victim, an idea began to form in his mind . . . If others despised McMuirtree . . . If others wished to see him dead . . .

'Byrd collected the slips from around the table. He placed them in his little magic bag. And as he did so, he saw that two of the slips were blank. On the spur of the moment – as no more than a whim – he decided to take a risk. As, to the assembled company, he read out the names on the slips of paper – not necessarily in the order in which he drew them from the bag: sleight-of-hand is part of Byrd's stock in-trade – he decided to announce that the second blank slip of paper was, in fact, another – a fourth! – that named McMuirtree. Byrd sought to suggest that McMuirtree – his friend – was a man surrounded by enemies . . .

'That evening as we played our game, in his mind Alphonse Byrd played with the idea of murdering David McMuirtree. On Sunday night, I imagine, it was little more than an idle fancy – a dangerous and delicious dream. But on Monday morning, when Byrd learnt of the death of Elizabeth Scott-Rivers, and on Tuesday when he read of the death of Lord Abergordon, Byrd saw that his dream might become a reality. He sensed that, suddenly, his destiny was calling. And he seized the moment. He claimed the hour. He killed his own parrot.'

'Hardly a crime,' muttered Bosie Douglas. 'It was a revolting creature – fractious, repellent.'

'But Byrd loved that parrot,' I said, addressing Oscar. 'Everyone told us that.'

Oscar smiled at me. 'And because Byrd loved his parrot, and because the parrot loved and trusted him, he was able to take it in his hands and wring its neck without the parrot making a single sound – without the least flapping of wings, without the merest fuss.' Oscar looked about the room complacently. 'I knew that it must have been Byrd who killed the parrot because only Byrd could have killed it silently.'

Charles Brookfield leant forward and rested his note-book on the dining table. 'You are telling me that it was Mr Byrd who killed the parrot, are you?'

'I am, Charles,' said Oscar, sucking the last out of his cigarette. 'That's why I seated him on your right tonight. I felt it was the least I could do.' Oscar widened his eyes and extinguished his cigarette. 'After all, you're paying thirteen guineas for the privilege.'

Brookfield turned in his seat and sat back and gazed fixedly on Alphonse Byrd, tilting his head slowly to one side and then the other – as a man might apprise an auction lot or study an unfamiliar piece of sculpture. Byrd did not flinch. His immobile features betrayed nothing. Inspector Gilmour began to ease himself away from the table.

'My time-keeper is silent.' Oscar glanced over his shoulder at the clock that hung above the dining-room door. 'Three minutes more, and then I'm done.' He raised his voice a little and quickened his pace as he resumed his story. 'Alphonse Byrd murdered Captain Flint in his office on Tuesday morning, the third of May. He killed the parrot with his bare hands, tore the feathers from its back and then squeezed some of the poor creature's blood into a silver hip flask – just such a flask as I have here.' With one hand he held open his jacket; with the other, from an inside pocket, he produced an elegant silver drinking flask. 'Never forget, gentlemen, that Alphonse Byrd is a magician – trained by the great John Maskelyne. Byrd may lack the immortal spark, but he was tutored by a master. He secreted the bird's body, blood and feathers in a drawer in his desk until he needed them. At a little before three o'clock that afternoon, when the coast was clear, he slipped from his office into the hotel lobby and – in a matter of moments, in the twinkling of an eye – he created the macabre scene of carnage that, minutes later, my wife and Edward Heron-Allen discovered there.

'Byrd is, as McMuirtree was, a showman. But, unlike McMuirtree, Byrd, by his own admission, lacks courage. He set himself on the path to murder when he killed Captain Flint, but he did not truly commit himself until later in the week – when he heard the news of the disappearance and presumed death of Bradford Pearse. It was then, and only then, that Byrd decided that the gods were indeed on his side. But, of course, it is when the gods wish to punish us that they answer our prayers . . .'

Oscar picked up the silver hip flask from the table and slowly turned it over in his hands. 'Alphonse Byrd may lack courage, and *panache*, but he does not lack ingenuity. He murdered David McMuirtree in a manner most ingenious. He might have killed him in Tite Street at our magic show – but that would have been too obvious, too dangerous: Byrd himself would have been on the scene and the first to be suspected. No, Byrd contrived to kill McMuirtree at one remove – surrounded by admirers, in the Ring of Death at Astley's Circus, while Byrd himself was here, at the Cadogan Hotel, surrounded by witnesses, a mile and more away. Like all the best magic effects, the murder of David McMuirtree was achieved with beautiful simplicity. The concept was all. The execution, next-to-nothing. All Byrd had to do was tamper with McMuirtree's boxing gloves and send his victim on his way . . .'

'Did he line the gloves with cockspurs as I suspected?' asked Edward Heron-Allen.

'No,' said Oscar. 'Cut-up bits of razor from a magician's home-made guillotine.'

The clock above the door began to strike the hour. Archy Gilmour and Roger Ferris got to their feet and positioned themselves at either side of Alphonse Byrd. Oscar looked along the table and smiled.

'It's midnight,' said Inpector Gilmour.

'Yes,' answered Oscar, quietly, 'midnight . . . And it seems I'm still alive.'

Arthur Conan Doyle pushed his chair back from the table. 'Are you surprised?'

Oscar laughed. 'Not entirely, Arthur – but Mr Byrd may be.' Gilmour and Ferris took the impassive Byrd by the arms and pulled him to his feet. He offered no resistance. His face betrayed no feeling.

'I believe,' said Oscar, 'that Mr Byrd hoped that by now I, too, would be dead or dying. He did not choose me as his murder victim, but once McMuirtree had been successfully despatched, I think he saw no reason why I should not be next.'

The policemen pulled Byrd's arms roughly behind his back. From his coat pocket, Ferris produced a pair of handcuffs and slipped them over the prisoner's wrists.

'As he sees it,' Oscar went on, 'life has not been kind to Alphonse Byrd. *I* have not been kind to him. I have a beauty in my life that makes his ugly. I've snubbed him, taken him for granted – treated him as a servant when, in fact, he's a scholar and gentleman . . .

'But Alphonse Byrd is not a gentleman. Nat, the page-boy at this hotel, he's a gentleman. Antipholus, the black boy from the circus – *he's* a gentleman. Brian Fletcher, a young actor we encountered on our way to

Beachy Head – now he's a gentleman! But Alphonse Byrd . . . what's he? He is as most murderers and bullies are: a funny little man, a whey-faced nondescript nobody – riddled with resentments, the victim of a million imagined slights. He's neither a gentleman nor, indeed, a scholar.'

'We'll take him with us now, Mr Wilde,' said Archy Gilmour, pulling Byrd away from the table and pushing him towards the door.

Oscar continued speaking. He would not be stopped. 'Byrd told me that he had spent a term at Oxford, but I knew at once that it was a lie. I asked him which was his college – and he answered, simply, "New." No man who has been to New College *ever* calls it "New".'

Gilmour and Ferris stood with Alphonse Byrd by the dining-room door. 'Goodnight, gentlemen,' grunted Gilmour. 'We'll be in touch with those of you from whom we'll need statements.'

'I think you'll need this,' said Oscar, waving the silver hip flask in the detective inspector's direction.

'What's that?'

'Evidence, I imagine,' said Oscar lightly. 'It contains the wine that Mr Byrd poured into my glass tonight. It contains the second glass of that wine, to be precise. I allowed Daubeney to drink the first before I realised that it had been adulterated.'

'What are you saying, Mr Wilde?' asked Inspector Gilmour impatiently.

'I'm saying that while Byrd may not be a scholar, he nonetheless appreciates a classical allusion. As I am the founder of the Socrates Club, and he is the secretary, he thought it appropriate that I should die as Socrates did.

Mr Byrd sought to murder me tonight with the juice of a plant from his allotment – *conium maculatum*: poison hemlock. I'll not be pressing charges, however. I only drank a drop.'

'What about Daubeney?' asked Conan Doyle, getting to his feet and moving towards the door. 'I'd better see him.'

'Yes, Doctor,' said Oscar. 'Perhaps you had – though I doubt that he's in mortal danger. I tasted the wine – there was not enough poison in it to kill a man. Our club secretary is one of those sad creatures who never get anything completely right. It's even possible that McMuirtree would have survived his ordeal in the Ring of Death if Daubeney hadn't been on hand to push the blades deeper into the boxer's severed wrists. Poor, pathetic Alphonse Byrd. Take him away. He lacks the immortal spark.'

Gilmour and Ferris bundled Byrd out of the room. Conan Doyle followed them, calling on Willie Hornung to accompany him. 'Better do as I'm told,' said the young man, pushing his spectacles up his nose and waving to the room as he went. 'What a night, Oscar! I'll not forget it. Thank you!'

Oscar stood alone at the head of the table, his arms hanging loosely at his side. He was only thirty-seven, but, suddenly, he seemed quite old – washed-out, washed-up. His face, that, moments before, had been so alive and full of colour as he told his tale, was ashen. As he looked about the room he appeared confused: his eyes flickered, his eyelids drooped. As he reached into his cigarette case I noticed that his fingers shook.

'What a night, indeed,' chortled Edward Heron-Allen, stepping forward and shaking Oscar warmly by the hand. 'You're extraordinary, my friend – a phenomenon . . .'

'He writes plays too, you know,' said Bosie Douglas, adjusting Oscar's tie proprietorially. 'For a pre-Raphaelite, he's quite the Renaissance man!'

'Congratulations, Oscar,' said Lord Drumlanrig. 'A *tour de force*. You should have gone to the Bar. Why didn't you? Have you considered politics? I mean it. Rosebery wants men like you.'

Oscar smiled wanly. 'A politician . . .' he began – and then he stopped. 'And I am wary of lawyers,' he said. For a moment, I saw fear in his eyes. I sensed him searching for an aphorism that did not come.

'We are staying with our mother tonight, Oscar,' said Bosie, leaning forward and kissing Oscar lightly on the cheek. 'I'll see you tomorrow. Lunch at the Café Royal as we agreed?'

'Of course,' said Oscar. 'One o'clock.'

'Good night, Oscar,' said Lord Drumlanrig.

'And if you see Papa,' added Bosie as he pulled his brother with him towards the door, 'shoot him for me, won't you? I don't think I dare murder him myself with you on the case.'

Oscar smiled and watched the two young men link arms and go on their way.

'Quite brilliant, Oscar,' boomed Bram Stoker, putting a comfortable hand on his friend's shoulder. 'Drumlanrig was spot-on. It was indeed a *tour de force*. You out-Irvinged Irving.' He looked into Oscar's face and smiled. 'No wonder you're drained. Go home now and have a hot tub and a hot toddy. That's what the Guv'nor does. Works every time.'

Charles Brookfield stood at Bram Stoker's side. He was holding a cheque for thirteen guineas. 'Here you are, Oscar,' he said. 'I believe this is what I owe you.'

'Thank you,' said Oscar, inclining his head towards Brookfield. He took the cheque, examined it, folded it and slipped it into his jacket pocket. He looked directly into Brookfield's eyes. 'And what did you think, Charles?'

'What do you mean?' asked Brookfield.

'What did you think?' repeated Oscar.

'Of you? Just now?'

'Yes,' said Oscar. 'Of me – just now.'

'Since you ask, Oscar,' answered Brookfield, slowly, weighing his words as he spoke, 'Since you ask . . . I thought it was rather like your speech at the opening of *Lady Windermere* – brilliant in its way, but wrong – ill-judged . . . just a touch self-regarding, just a touch too much. Your arrogance, Oscar, will be your undoing.'

'Don't listen to Brookie, Oscar,' cried Bram Stoker. 'He isn't Irish. He doesn't always understand. You were brilliant, my friend – quite brilliant. There's no other word. And you restored Pearse to us! How about that?'

Bradford Pearse and Wat Sickert were standing together by the doorway. Sickert was holding a cigar, resting an elegant right elbow on Pearse's broad left shoulder. 'We're going to the Arts Club,' he announced, 'now – to celebrate the prodigal's return.'

Bradford Pearse nudged Sickert playfully. 'Will there be entertainment, Wat? Will some of your models be joining us, eh?' The barrel-chested actor roared with delight at the prospect and punched the air. 'Thank you, Oscar,' he cried exuberantly. 'Thank you, dear friend. It's so good to be back. The lighthouse was delightful, but the amenities were limited.'

'Are you going to grow another beard, Brad?' asked Bram Stoker, moving to the door, taking Charles Brookfield with him. 'These pink cheeks of yours are quite disconcerting.'

'I thought a moustache this time – like Sickert's here. What do think? I've played the old sea-salt long enough. I thought I'd try my luck as a young buck about town.'

'You don't want to play any more waiters,' said Charles Brookfield drily. 'You won't get the notices.'

'I'm an ac-taw,' said Pearse happily, 'I play whatever comes my way.'

'Are you coming our way, Oscar?' called Sickert as the group gathered at the dining-room door. 'Are you up for a nightcap?'

'No, I'm taking Bram's advice. It's late. I'm for my bed. Robert will walk me home.'

'Good man,' said Bram Stoker, acknowledging Oscar with a small salute.

'Goodnight, gentlemen,' said Oscar, raising his hand to his friends.

'Goodnight, Oscar.' 'Goodnight, Oscar.' 'Goodnight, Robert.' 'Goodnight, Oscar – well done!'

As the foursome left the room, waving and hallooing as they departed, Wat Sickert lingered. He turned briefly and looked towards Oscar with pleading eyes.

'Have no fear, Wat,' said Oscar gently. 'It's fine. Go now. I know you didn't touch the girl.'

Oscar and I walked back to Tite Street together, arm in arm. The air was still. The night sky was clear. In the black roof of the world the stars shone bright. As we walked, Oscar regained much of his energy. As we crossed Sloane Square into the King's Road and a dog-cart came hurtling out of the darkness and missed us by an inch or two, Oscar began to laugh in a way that I had not heard him laugh for a month or more. It was an easy laugh, happy and unforced. 'I have survived,' he chuckled. 'I have lived through Friday the thirteenth, Robert, and not been murdered after all!'

On the far side of the square, when we had reached the safety of the pavement, I asked him: 'Who was it who chose you as their murder victim, Oscar? Do you know?'

'It was Edward Heron-Allen,' he said, still chuckling. 'He confessed it when he brought me his prized cock-spur. He said that if I was dead, he could marry Constance. I told him if I was dead, *you* would marry Constance!'

I laughed. 'Did you really, Oscar?' The notion was absurd, but, even so, to hear it spoken out loud pleased me very much.

'I did – but I'm not dead and you shan't. And Mrs Heron-Allen is alive and well and no doubt offering young Edward wifely consolation as we speak.'

We had stopped beneath a street lamp. In the pale and yellow gaslight I could see that Oscar was smiling. He seemed happy once again. He lit a cigarette – the last of his Player's Navy Cut.

'You know,' I remarked, 'for a time, I thought that Heron-Allen might be the murderer?'

Oscar threw his match into the gutter. 'I thought you were convinced that it was young Drumlanrig?'

'I was – later. I was absolutely certain of it.'

Contentedly, we resumed our walk, arm in arm once more. 'The things one feels absolutely certain about,' he said, 'are never true.'

As we turned left, into the first of the little alleys leading towards Tite Street, I paused for a moment and asked: 'If it was Heron-Allen who named you as his victim, who was it who named Constance as theirs?'

'Can you not guess?' he asked, walking on. 'It was Charles Brookfield, I am afraid.'

'Brookfield?'

'Indeed.'

'Did he tell you?'

'No – my grid told me. By a process of elimination. It can only have been Brookfield.'

'Brookfield wanted to murder Constance?' I said, appalled.

'It was only a game, Robert,' said Oscar. 'No doubt Brookfield wished to put my wife out of the misery of being married to me.' He spoke without rancour. He sounded almost amused by the idea. 'He is a curious character, our Mr Brookfield . . .'

'Indeed,' I said, tartly.

'Do you think that he was right about my performance tonight?' he asked, glancing up at the sky as he spoke. He did not wait for my reply. 'I think that perhaps he was,' he said.

Suddenly, as we reached the corner of Tite Street, he burst out laughing again. 'You know that, at first, I believed that Brookfield was our murderer. It was Mrs Robinson who pointed me in his direction. When she examined the map of my hand, she said: "Where this brook abuts this field, Mr Wilde, I see a whirlpool – and

384

it worries me" . . . I assumed that my hand was telling her that "Brookfield" would prove my nemesis!'

'And was it not?'

'I think not,' said Oscar, laughing quietly. 'Mrs Robinson is paid a guinea a reading. She must say something. At our party, she met Mr and Mrs Brooke, the Rajah and Ranee of Sarawak, and Miss Bradley and Miss Cooper, the eccentric poetesses jointly known as "Michael Field". Mrs Robinson slipped their names into her reading of my palm – and I heard what I wanted to hear, not what she was telling me.'

'Are you sure?' I asked. 'I thought that you put your trust in Mrs Robinson.'

'I do. I have done. And, no doubt, I will again. But I must remember that fortune-telling is allied to the world of entertainment. It's sometimes difficult to tell the truth from the trickery . . . Leastways, Brookfield was not our murderer.'

'But he despises you, Oscar.'

'Does he not have cause? I snub him. I reprove him for wearing gloves indoors. At dinner, I have him seated below the salt.'

'Brookfield despises you and yet he can't keep away from you. He's like a moth about a flame. He despises you not because you snub him, but because he envies you.'

'Ah,' said Oscar, smiling. 'Is that it?'

'It is,' I said, emphatically.

We had reached 16 Tite Street. Oscar had his key in the door. 'Beware of envy, Robert,' he said, looking at me earnestly. 'Look what envy did to Byrd . . . Look what envy's done to Brookfield . . . Envy is the ulcer of the soul.'

'"Envy is the ulcer of the soul",' I repeated. 'That's brilliant, Oscar – one of your best. I've noted it in my journal, have no fear.'

'But have you given credit where it's due? It was Socrates who said it first. *Socrates* – known just by the one name, you note. Socrates, I think we can agree, has joined the ranks of the immortals.' He turned the key in the lock. 'What will become of us, I wonder, Robert? Will we join the ranks of the immortals? What will be our destiny?'

He sighed and pushed open his front door. The house was silent, but not unwelcoming. There, set on the small side table in the hallway, beneath a flickering gas lamp, was a Chinese malacca tray. And on the tray were two champagne glasses, an ice bucket, a chilled bottle of Perrier Jouët and a note in Constance's round, firm hand:

Bravo, Oscar – best of husbands, best of men.

Oscar's eyes were full of tears. He looked at me and smiled. 'I'm not inclined towards a hot toddy – whatever that may be. But a glass of champagne before bed, Robert . . . isn't that the way to end the day?'

Postscript

'What will become of us, I wonder, Robert? What will be our destiny?'

The world knows what became of Oscar Wilde. After the triumphs of 1893 came the trials of 1895 and disgrace, imprisonment and exile. Constance died in Genoa in 1898. Oscar died in Paris in 1900. He was forty-six. As he said, 'My cradle was rocked by the Fates.'

The world knows, too, what became of Arthur Conan Doyle. Thanks to Sherlock Holmes, he found fame and fortune around the world. Thanks to his manifold qualities – his integrity, his courage, and his service to his country during the Boer War – he found honour, too. He was knighted by King Edward VII in 1902.

Thanks to Conan Doyle, young Willie Hornung found fortune, also. At Arthur's suggestion, Willie created a bestselling character to rival Sherlock Holmes – a professional confidence trickster and jewel thief named Raffles, 'the amateur cracksman'. And, thanks again to Arthur, Willie Hornung found love as well. In 1893, Willie married Conan Doyle's younger sister, Connie, and he named his first-born 'Arthur Oscar' in honour of the two men he most admired: his brother-in-law and Oscar Wilde. '*Nomen est omen*,' he said at the child's christening.

Bram Stoker, having created Dracula, died in 1912. Willie Hornung died in 1921. Arthur Conan Doyle died in 1930. Walter Sickert and Edward Heron-Allen are living still. Wat is now one of the grand old men of English art and Edward is best known, I suppose, for his scurrilous novel, *The Cheetah Girl*. Bosie is alive still, too. We meet now and again, when I'm in England, and talk of old times and drink vintage champagne in Oscar's honour.

Bosie married. I never much cared for his wife. (I don't believe that he did, either!) His brother, Francis Drumlanrig, died in 1894, aged twenty-seven – shot dead while out hunting in Somerset. Was it an accident? Or suicide? Or murder? No one knows for sure. To the last, his father, the Marquess of Queensberry, remained convinced that Drumlanrig and Lord Rosebery were lovers. It was Queenberry's great obsession. And to Queensberry's great disgust, in the same year that his son died, Lord Rosebery succeeded as prime minister.

Rosebery kept faith with his promise to Arthur Conan Doyle. His administration outlawed cock-fighting in Scotland. And, in his turn, in the same year, 1894, Bram Stoker kept faith with Conan Doyle. He persuaded Henry Irving to produce and star in a play by Conan Doyle. The piece was called *A Story of Waterloo*. It was the last of the great actor's great successes.

Henry Irving, however, could not be persuaded to play the part of Sherlock Holmes on the stage. The first actor to portray Holmes in the theatre was Charles Brookfield. Yes, it's true.

Brookfield maintained his obsessive interest in Oscar as the years went by. In the early months of 1895 it was

Charles Brookfield who supplied the police with the names and addresses of several of the disreputable young men who, at his trial, gave evidence against Oscar Wilde. And on the evening of 25 May 1895 – the day on which, at the Old Bailey, Oscar was found guilty of gross indecency and sentenced to two years' imprisonment with hard labour – Charles Brookfield and the Marquess of Queensberry organised a gala party to celebrate the verdict. They shared the cost of it. Brookfield contributed thirteen guineas.

Acknowledgements

Writing a book is a lonely business. This is the second in my series of Oscar Wilde Murder Mysteries. In writing it I have been encouraged by the great generosity shown towards the first. I am especially grateful to a number of distinguished writers – David Robinson, Alexander McCall Smith, Anne Perry, Stephanie Barron, Stephen Fry, Roger Lewis, Lee Langley and Theo Richmond among them – for their kind words and generous encouragement. During the bleaker hours imprisoned at the word processor, such kindness makes a difference.

I am grateful, too, for the sustaining support of a variety of friends – ranging from my best friend, Michèle Brown, to my good friend, Merlin Holland, Oscar Wilde's grandson and biographer, who put me right when I went wrong with Volume One (and did so with great grace) and I trust will do the same again should he have cause. I hope that my portrait of Oscar Wilde is accurate: if you spot any errors do please write to tell me.

As ever, I am indebted to my literary agent, Ed Victor – and to more than the tune of fifteen per cent. I have been involved in publishing for forty years: he is simply the best. He also employs the best and I am especially indebted to his foreign rights manager, Morag O'Brien, who, with charm and skill, has introduced this series of books to publishers throughout the world. I am grateful to her, not only for her professionalism, but also for the fact that, because of her, I have made, and am making, new friends in countries as various as Spain and South Korea, Lithuania and Brazil.

In the United Kingdom and Australia, the series is published by John Murray – the publishers of Arthur Conan Doyle. I am profoundly indebted to Roland Phillips and Kate Parkin and their colleagues at John Murray in London, to Trish Grader and her colleagues at Simon & Schuster in New York, to Emmanuelle Heurtebize and her colleagues at Editions 10/18 in Paris, among many others, for their considerable creative and commercial contribution to the series. From the first, Kate Parkin has also been a matchless editor, guide and friend. I am very grateful to her and to Jitesh Patel, the inspirational designer of the covers for the UK and US editions.

'Nothing that actually occurs is of the smallest importance,' said Oscar in his *Phrases and Philosophies for the Use of the Young*. I don't believe he meant it. Saying thank you is important. I am very grateful to all those who have made a contribution to the making of this book – the named ones and the unnamed, too – and I am especially grateful, of course, to you for reading it. There would not have been much point otherwise. Thank you.

GB
London, 2008

Read on for an excerpt from the third volume in the
Oscar Wilde series:

Oscar Wilde and the Dead Man's Smile

Coming soon from John Murray

'I want to eat of all the fruit of all the trees
in the garden of the world.'

Oscar Wilde (1854–1900)

London, Christmas 1890

'Do you recognise him?'

'He has the look of a murderer, has he not?'

'Do you think so?'

'Yes, I do. It's his smile, Robert. Never trust a man who shows you his lower teeth when he smiles.'

'But the poor wretch is dead, Oscar.'

'The rule applies, nevertheless.'

'And this is just a waxwork.'

'But it was sculpted from life, Robert, or at least directly from the cadaver. It's a point of honour with the Tussaud family, you know. They will have had access to the body within hours of the execution.'

It was mid morning on Christmas Eve, Wednesday, 24 December 1890, and with my friend, Oscar Wilde, I was visiting the celebrated 'Chamber of Horrors' at what was then London's – England's – the Empire's – most popular public attraction: Madame Tussaud's Baker Street Bazaar. Oscar was at his most ebullient. As we toured the exhibits, peering through the flickering gaslight at the waxwork effigies of the more notorious murderers of recent years, my friend's moon-like face shone with delight. His eyes sparkled. His large frame – he was more than six feet tall and, now thirty-six years of age, tending to corpulence – heaved with pleasure. Nothing amused Oscar Wilde so much as the wholly improbable. 'Tis the season to be jolly,' he chuckled softly, 'and we are bent on horror, Robert.' He glanced at the multitude around us and beamed at me. 'It is the anniversary of Our Lord's nativity and all London, it seems, is making a pilgrimage to a shrine to child murder.'

Certainly, in its sixty-year history, the Baker Street Bazaar had never been busier than it was on that day. Thirty thousand people had stood in line to see Tussaud's latest sensation: an exact reproduction of the sitting room in which, only ten weeks before, Eleanor Pearcey had battered her lover's wife and baby to death. Mrs Pearcey had piled her hapless victims' corpses onto the baby's perambulator and dumped them on waste ground near her home in Kentish Town. John Tussaud spent £200 – the price of a small house – on acquiring the perambulator and other souvenirs of the murder, including the murderess's blood stained cardigan and the boiled sweet that the innocent baby was sucking on as he was killed. John Tussaud's investment reaped a rich reward. In those days, entrance to the Baker Street Bazaar cost a shilling a head.

Oscar and I had not paid the price of admission, however. Nor had we queued to get in. We had gained access to Tussaud's via the staff entrance in Marylebone Road as special guests of the management. We were due to meet up with our friend, Arthur Conan Doyle, and Doyle was a friend of Madame Tussaud's great-grandson and heir, John Tussaud. Arthur had arranged the visit as a Christmas treat for Oscar and Oscar had arrived bearing a Christmas present for Arthur. The two men had only known each other for fifteen months, but they were firm friends. Their intimacy – their ease with one another – surprised me because, as personalities, they were so different. Oscar was Irish, an aesthete and a romantic. Oscar was flamboyant: he revelled in the outrageous. Arthur was Scottish, a provincial doctor and a pragmatist. Arthur was stolid: he respected the conventional. But both were writers of high ambition, with keen intellects and lively sensibilities, and both were fascinated by the vagaries of the human heart and the workings of the criminal mind.

Oscar was five years older than Arthur and, in 1890, undoubtedly the better-known. The pair had been introduced to one another by an American publisher, J. M. Stoddart, who, on the same evening, in August 1889, had commissioned a 'mystery adventure' from each of them. For Stoddart, Doyle was persuaded to write his second Sherlock Holmes story and Oscar conjured up his novel of beauty and decay, *The Picture of Dorian Gray*. Doyle's Holmes adventure, *The Sign of Four*, was well received and helped consolidate the young author's growing reputation as a skilful spinner of satisfying yarns. In its way, *Dorian Gray* helped consolidate Oscar's reputation, too. The book was denounced as immoral. The *Athenaeum* called it 'unmanly, sickening, vicious'. The *Daily Chronicle* derided it as 'a tale spawned from the leprous literature of the French Decadents – a gloating study of mental and physical corruption'. It was banned by the booksellers W H Smith.

Oscar envied Arthur his creation of Sherlock Holmes. Arthur envied Oscar his way with words. Arthur had no reservations about *Dorian Gray*. He considered the work subtle, honest and artistically good. He respected Oscar both as a writer and as a gentleman. And, amusingly, he also reckoned that Oscar had the qualities essential in a private detective: 'a retentive mind, an observant eye, and the ability to mix with all manner and conditions of men'. Arthur told Oscar that if ever he should write another Sherlock Holmes story he would invent an older brother for the great detective and base him on Oscar. 'Do so, Arthur, please,' said Oscar. 'Your stories will stand the test of time and I have immortal longings.'

Madame Tussaud's, that Christmas Eve morning, was packed to overflowing, but even among the crowds and in the half-light of the Chamber of Horrors, Messrs Doyle and Tussaud had no difficulty in finding us as we hovered between the reproduction of Mrs Pearcey's sitting room and the ghastly waxwork of the grinning murderer with the exposed teeth. Oscar was both the tallest man in the room and the most conspicuous. He was dressed for the season: his elaborate bow tie was holly red; his dandified frock coat was ivy green; and in his button hole he sported a substantial sprig of mistletoe.

'Merry Christmas, Oscar!' called out Conan Doyle, pushing his way through the throng towards us. 'Season's greetings, Robert.'

Doyle held out his right hand towards Oscar. Oscar ignored it and, passing the brown parcel containing Doyle's intended Christmas present to me to carry, embraced the good doctor in a mighty bear hug. Oscar knew that this hug embarrassed Conan Doyle, but it was the way in which he always greeted his friend: Arthur's handshake was almost unendurable. Doyle was not tall, but he was well-built, sturdy, fit and strong, and the vice-like grip of his hand was as forbidding as his fierce moustache. Conan Doyle's dark walrus-like whiskers would have done credit to a Cossack general.

'I'm sorry I'm late,' said the young doctor, prising himself from Oscar's warm embrace. 'The train from Southsea was delayed. A body on the line. Most unfortunate.'

'It is the time of year,' murmured Oscar. 'Some people will do anything to avoid a family Christmas.'

Arthur sniffed and furrowed his brow disapprovingly. 'May I present our host, Mr John Tussaud?' he said, taking a step back to introduce us to his companion.

Mr Tussaud rose briefly onto his toes, nodding his head briskly towards each of us as he did so. He was a slight, chestnut-haired fellow in his early thirties, with a drooping moustache and mournful brown eyes that blinked amiably behind wire-framed spectacles. He looked more like a mild-mannered schoolmaster than a purveyor of horror to the masses.

'Thank you for your hospitality, sir,' said Oscar, with a gentle bow. 'And congratulations on the show.' He looked about us at the crowds, two or three deep – men and women, gentlefolk and workers, children and babes in arms – trooping steadily past the exhibits, mostly in silence. 'It is a triumph.' John Tussaud flushed with pleasure and pushed his spectacles further up his nose. Oscar went on: 'I was particularly taken with the half-sucked sweet retrieved from the dead baby's mouth.'

'Yes,' said Tussaud eagerly, 'the sweet does seem to have caught everybody's imagination. It's raspberry-flavoured, you know.'

'Good God, man,' exclaimed Conan Doyle. 'Did you taste it?'

'Only briefly,' said Tussaud with a nervous laugh. 'I felt I should. The visitors like as much detail as possible.'

'I understand completely,' said Oscar soothingly. 'Your visitors need to know that what they're witnessing is the genuine article. The more corroborative detail you can give them the better.'

Tussaud looked up at Oscar gratefully. 'You understand, Mr Wilde.'

Oscar smiled at John Tussaud and touched him on the shoulder. 'I was telling my friend Sherard here that all your waxwork models are drawn from life – or death, as the case may be.'

'Absolutely,' replied Tussaud, seriously. 'We insist on it – wherever possible. With the murderers, of course, we're very much in the hands of the authorities. Some prison governors let us in prior to the execution, so that we can make a model of the murderer while he's still alive. Others won't let us in at all – or only give us access to the murderer's body after the execution has taken place. That's not very satisfactory, to be candid.'

'Hanging distorts the features?' suggested Oscar.

'It can do, I'm afraid,' replied Tussaud, lowering his voice as a group of young ladies pressed past us. 'From a waxwork modeller's point of view,' he continued, *sotto voce*, 'the ideal method of execution has to be the guillotine. My great-grandmother was so fortunate in that respect, starting out in this line of business in France at the time of the Revolution. The Revolutionary Tribunal in Paris sentenced 16,594 people to death, you know. The guillotine was invented to cope with the numbers.'

'You are a "details man", I can tell, sir,' said Oscar, smiling.

'I have the complete list,' murmured Tussaud. 'All the names.'

'Your great-grandmother must have been spoilt for choice,' said Conan Doyle grimly.

'And run off her feet,' added the great-grandson. 'Families wanted death masks of their loved ones. Those who were about to die wanted to be immortalised in wax. The demand was incredible – one head after another. I believe her health suffered as a consequence. She was a remarkable woman. Have you seen her death mask of Marie-Antoinette? It's one of her best.' Tussaud's spectacles glinted in the gaslight as he raised both hands and beckoned us to follow him.

He led us away from the throng and through an unmarked door, across a darkened corridor and through a second door into a smaller exhibition room, entirely lit by candlelight. There were no crowds here, just half a dozen visitors standing behind a rope cordon gazing at an assortment of individual human heads lolling on scarlet cushions.

'This is my favourite room,' said Tussaud, lowering his voice once more and gesturing proudly towards the exhibits. 'Look. To the left, we have the revolutionaries. Robespierre is the third one along. And to the right – slightly elevated, you notice – we have Louis XVI and his Queen.'

'Their faces seem bigger,' said Conan Doyle, gazing at the waxed visages of the royal couple. 'Their faces appear to be larger than those of the revolutionaries . . .'

'They are larger, Arthur,' said Oscar quietly. 'They were better fed.'

'And behind you,' announced Tussaud in an excited stage whisper, 'we have Citoyen Marat, murdered in his bathtub by Charlotte Corday.'

'Oh my,' murmured Oscar, turning round, 'that is most life like.'

'Marie Tussaud was among the first on the scene.'

'In at the kill,' whispered Oscar, impressed.

'She made it her business,' said Tussaud earnestly. 'It *was* her business. She told the story of her time. She was an artist – a portraitist who worked in wax instead of oils. Monsieur David's famous painting of this very scene is based on her waxwork. Monsieur David was a family friend. So was Marat. And Rousseau. And Benjamin Franklin. Marie made models of them all. She knew all the great men of the age. And the women, too.'

'I envy her,' said Oscar quietly, turning his back on the bath and surveying once more the row of severed heads. 'I should have liked to have met Queen Marie-Antoinette.'

'You have met Queen Victoria, haven't you?' asked Arthur, playfully.

'It's not quite the same thing,' murmured Oscar.

'Marie Tussaud met everybody,' repeated her great-grand-son, proudly.

'Oscar's met everybody,' I said, defensively.

Oscar smiled. 'Not Robespierre, alas.'

'But you met the man who tried to assassinate Queen Victoria, didn't you?' I persisted.

'I did, Robert. Once. And very briefly.' Oscar turned to John Tussaud, adding by way of explanation: 'The man was an unhinged versifier named Roderick Maclean. A poor poet and a worse shot.'

Mr Tussaud laughed and looked at his watch. 'It's lunchtime, gentlemen. I want to hear all about Queen Victoria's would-be assassin over our lobster salad and roast pheasant.'

'Lobster salad?' repeated Oscar, happily. 'Roast pheasant?' He looked at Conan Doyle with shining eyes. 'You are the best of friends, Arthur, and you have the best of friends.'

'I'm taking you to our new restaurant,' explained John Tussaud. 'We shall dine by electric light to music provided by Miss Graves's Ladies Orchestra. They have promised to give us a selection of tunes from the Savoy operas.'

'Gilbert and Sullivan,' said Oscar, genially. 'I have met both of them.'

'Oscar's met everybody,' I repeated. 'Poets, princes, artists, assassins . . .'

John Tussaud was leading us towards the stairway at the end of the exhibition room. We passed a familiar profile.

'Yes,' said Tussaud, nodding at the bust: 'Voltaire. Marie Tussaud knew Voltaire.'

Oscar paused. 'How I envy her!' He sighed. 'I met Louisa May Alcott once,' he said, 'the author of *Little Women*. She was a little woman.' He gazed fixedly at Madame Tussaud's head of Voltaire. 'And I met P. T. Barnum,' he added. 'And, through him, of course, I met Jumbo the Elephant. It's not quite Voltaire, but it's something.'

Conan Doyle burst out laughing. 'You're impossible, Oscar!' he cried. 'Jumbo the Elephant? I don't believe you.'

'It's true,' protested Oscar.

'It can't be.'

'Give him the manuscript, Robert.'

I handed Conan Doyle the parcel that I was carrying.

'This is my Christmas present for Arthur,' Oscar explained to John Tussaud. 'It's some holiday reading – something for him to puzzle over at his Southsea fireside.'

The manuscript was wrapped in brown paper and tied up with string. Conan Doyle turned it over slowly in his hands.

'They're all there, Arthur,' said Oscar teasingly. 'Louisa May Alcott, Jumbo the Elephant, the man who tried to shoot Queen Victoria . . .'

Conan Doyle looked up at Oscar and furrowed his brow. 'What is this?'

'As I say: your Christmas present, Arthur. Last year you gave me *The Sign of Four*. This year I'm giving you this. It's a manuscript – and a challenge. It's a story from my salad days. It's an account of a year and a half of my life – a while ago now. Before I was married. Before I was a family man. Before my responsibilities had made me fat. It's a story that begins in 1882, when I was in my mid twenties, footloose and fancy free. A time when I travelled the world and came to know some remarkable men and women. Not Robespierre and Marie-Antoinette, not Voltaire, to be sure, but remarkable nonetheless . . . Longfellow, Walt Whitman, Sarah Bernhardt, Edmond La Grange . . . Names to reckon with – and people you've never heard of.' Oscar glanced towards John Tussaud. 'I met an executioner once. He was the world authority on executions. His knowledge was encyclopaedic and extraordinary. He was a huge admirer of your great-grandmother, as I recall.'

Conan Doyle balanced the package on the palms of his hands as though assessing its weight. He brought it up to his face as if by sniffing at it he might better estimate its value. 'Is it autobiographical?' he asked.

Oscar turned to Conan Doyle and smiled. 'It's my story, Arthur, but it's Robert's handiwork. Robert is my biographer – and not nearly as uncritical as I would like. Robert wrote what you're about to read: he is my recording angel – my Dr Watson. He witnessed much of what occurred himself, as you'll discover, but I saw it all as it unfolded – from the beginning. It's a true story, Arthur, every word of it. I suppose you'd call it a murder mystery. Of course, it can't be published – at least, not in my lifetime. Much of it is libellous. Some of it's salacious. And, as yet, the story is incomplete. The manuscript's unfinished. It lacks the final chapter. I want you to read it, Arthur. I want you to read every word – even though some of it will make you blush. If you want you can show it to your friend, Sherlock Holmes – he's made of sterner stuff. And then, when you've read it, and pondered long and hard, I want you to tell me – I need you to tell me – who you think the murderer is.'

He turned back to our host and widened his eyes. 'Now, Mr Tussaud, kindly lead us to your lobster salad. The sight of all these wax cadavers has given me the most tremendous appetite.'

1

America

On 24 December 1881, Oscar Wilde set sail for the United States of America. He went in search of adventure and gold. Within weeks, he had found a portion of both.

Oscar had recently turned twenty-seven and, in England, his claim to fame was that he was famous for being famous. He was a celebrity, in the tradition of Lord Byron and Beau Brummell, but more Brummell than Byron, more style than substance. 'Evidently I am "somebody",' he noted at the time, 'but what have I done? I've been "noticed". That is something, I suppose. And I have published one book of poems. That doesn't amount to much.'

As a young man, first at Trinity College, Dublin, and then at Magdalen College, Oxford, Oscar had achieved every academic honour within his reach. He rounded off his under-graduate years by securing an Oxford 'Double First' and winning the coveted Newdigate Prize, the university's chief prize for poetry. But what was his real ambition in life?

'God knows,' he said, when asked. 'I won't be an Oxford don anyhow. I'll be a poet, a writer, a dramatist. Somehow or other I'll be famous, and if not famous, I'll be notorious. Or perhaps I'll lead the life of pleasure for a time and then – who knows? – rest and do nothing. What does Plato say is the highest end that man can attain here below? "To sit down and contemplate the good". Perhaps that will be the end of me too.'

Though in public Oscar denied it, privately he considered the possibility of an academic career. He would have liked to have been offered a fellowship at his old college. It did not happen. Oscar was highly intelligent, very witty, wonderfully charming, and he had the most perfect manners. He beguiled many people, but not everybody. There was something about him – the motion of his hips, the fullness of his mouth, his flowery turn of phrase, his quixotic turn of mind – that some found disconcerting and others disagreeable. 'Oh, he's brilliant all right,' said one of his tutors, 'and delightful in small doses, but don't get too close. There's danger lurking in the hinterland of Mr Oscar Wilde.'

When Oscar left Oxford, cushioned by a modest legacy from his late father, he floated down to London, the capital of the British Empire, and made his mark on the metropolis with outlandish views and an outrageous appearance. 'Only shallow people do not judge by appearance,' he declared. He had always been partial to dressing up. In his last term at Oxford he appeared at a ball disguised as Prince Rupert of the Rhine. In his first season in London he took to going out in a bottle-green velvet smoking jacket edged with braid, wearing a cream-coloured shirt with a scalloped collar and an over-abundant orange tie, taffeta knee-breeches, black silk stockings and silver-buckled shoes. He became a champion of beauty and a self-styled professor of aestheticism. 'Beauty is the symbol of symbols,' he declared. 'Beauty reveals everything because it expresses nothing. When it shows us itself it shows us the whole fiery-coloured world.'

Thanks to his charm, Oscar was invited everywhere. And everywhere he went, he made himself conspicuous. It was a matter of policy. 'If you wish for reputation and success in the world,' he advised, 'take every opportunity of advertising yourself. Remember the Latin saying, "Fame springs from one's own house." ' He was a master of self-advertisement. When he went to first nights at the theatre, in the minutes before the curtain rose, he would appear, in rapid succession, in all parts of the house – in the stalls, in the dress circle, in the boxes on either side of the proscenium – attired in a flamboyant evening suit of his own design and sporting an unlikely flower in his buttonhole. The young Oscar Wilde was determined to be noticed.

And he was. Soon after his arrival in London, the satirical magazines of the day started to publish spoofs and squibs at his expense. He began to feature in newspaper cartoons and caricatures. He was lampooned in music-hall sketches, in stage farces and then, most famously, in April 1881, in Richard D'Oyly Carte's hugely successful production of W. S. Gilbert and Arthur Sullivan's comic operetta, *Patience*. Oscar was at the first night and much amused. He recognised the piece for what it was: not a personal attack on him, but a good-humoured and pleasingly tuneful skit on the absurdities of the Aesthetic movement.

The success of *Patience* changed Oscar's life. On 30 September 1881, he received a telegram from Colonel F. W. Morse, Richard D'Oyly Carte's business manager in New York, inviting him to undertake an American lecture tour to coincide with the operetta's American production. Oscar did not hesitate. On 1 October 1881, he wired his acceptance to Colonel Morse. The young poet was in want of money and exhilarated by the prospect of crossing an ocean and discovering a continent. 'I already speak English, German, French and Italian,' he explained to his mother. 'Now I shall have the opportunity of learning American. It will be a challenge, I know, but I must try to rise to it.'

He equipped himself with a new wardrobe – including a warm Polish cap and a befrogged and wonderfully befurred green overcoat: he was warned about the New York winters – and found an expert on oratory to give him elocution lessons. 'I want a natural style,' he told his instructor, 'with a touch of affectation.' He prepared carefully for his American adventure. He hoped it might prove the 'making' of him.

Oscar set sail from Liverpool on the afternoon of Christmas Eve 1881 on board the SS *Arizona*. He was apprehensive. The *Arizona* was the fastest steamship then crossing the Atlantic, the holder of the Blue Riband, and Oscar did not much care for speed. The *Arizona* had also recently survived – but only narrowly – a mid-Atlantic collision with an iceberg.

In the event the crossing was calm and hazard-free. It was the arrival that proved more of an adventure. The *Arizona* docked in New York harbour on the evening of 2 January 1882. It was too late to clear quarantine, so Oscar and his fellow passengers were obliged to spend a further night onboard ship. The gentlemen of the New York press, however, were impatient for a first sighting of the much-vaunted Mr Wilde. They would not wait till morning. They chartered a launch, came out to sea and, in Oscar's phrase, 'their pens still wet with brine, demanded that I strut before them, like a prize bantam at a country fair.'

The journalists were a little taken aback by what they found. Oscar was not the delicate exotic they had been expecting. According to the man from the *New York Tribune*: 'The most striking thing about the poet's appearance is his height, which is several inches over six feet, and the next thing to attract attention is his hair, which is of a dark brown colour, and falls down upon his shoulders. When he laughs his lips part widely and show a shining row of upper teeth, which are superlatively white. The complexion, instead of being of the rosy hue so common in Englishmen, is so utterly devoid of colour that it can only be said to resemble putty. His eyes are blue, or a light grey, and instead of being "dreamy", as some of his admirers have imagined them to be, they are bright and quick – not at all like those of one given to perpetual musing on the ineffably beautiful and true. Instead of having a small delicate hand, only fit to caress a lily, his fingers are long and when doubled up would form a fist that would hit a hard knock, should an occasion arise for the owner to descend to that kind of argument.'

Oscar did not engage his interlocutors in fisticuffs, but nor, in the main, did he endear himself to them. 'I tried to be amusing,' he later confessed, 'and engendered snarls where I had hoped for smiles. My efforts at drollery were taken for disdain.' He was asked how he had enjoyed his ocean crossing.

He replied, 'The sea seems tame to me. The roaring ocean does not roar. It is not as majestic as I expected.' His remarks appeared beneath the headline: 'Mr Wilde Disappointed with the Atlantic'. He gave the impression of arrogance.

And he compounded that impression on the morning after his ship-board press conference. Disembarking from the SS *Arizona* and passing through customs, he responded to the customs officer's predictable enquiry, 'Have you anything to declare, Mr Wilde?' with a well-prepared reply: 'I have nothing to declare except my genius.'

Some thought this vastly amusing. Others thought that young Mr Wilde was riding for a fall. And, to an extent, he was. His first few lectures were not a success. He said too much, too quickly, and in too soft a voice. He failed to hold the attention of the crowd. His audiences were disappointed; the critics were unkind.

Oscar was undaunted. 'What possible difference can it make to me what the *New York Herald* says?' he asked. 'You can go and look at the statue of the Venus de Milo and you know that it is an exquisitely beautiful creation. Would it change your opinion in the least if all the newspapers in the land should pronounce it a wretched caricature? Not at all. I know that I am right, that I have a mission to perform. I am indestructible!'

In public, Oscar was defiant. In private, he acknowledged that he had work to do. And he did it. He simplified his lecture; he improved his presentation; he moderated his language; he added some jokes that everybody could understand. He turned a potential disaster into an unquestioned triumph. Ultimately, during the course of 1882, Oscar delivered a total of more than two hundred lectures in one hundred and sixty towns and cities across North America, from New Orleans to Nova Scotia, from northern Massachusetts to southern California. 'Oh yes,' he would say in later years, 'I was adored once, too. In America I was obliged to engage two secretaries to cope with the correspondence – one being responsible for the demand for autographs, the other for the locks of my hair.

Within six months, the first had died of writer's cramp; the other was entirely bald.'

In fact, Oscar did have two companions on his travels, but neither was a secretary. Colonel Morse supplied him with a 'man of business', Aaron Budd, a clerk from D'Oyly Carte's New York office, and a personal valet, a young negro called W. M. Traquair. 'I did not care for Mr Budd,' said Oscar. 'He looked after our railroad tickets and counted the takings. He was efficient, but not interesting. He rarely spoke, he never smiled and the pallor of his skin was disconcerting. I believe he was an abstainer and a vegetarian. By contrast, I cared a great deal for Washington Traquair. His father had been a slave. He was my servant, but he was also my friend. He was not a great talker and he could neither read nor write, but he had a wonderful smile and he laughed at my jokes. You have to love a man who laughs at your jokes.'

In the course of his tour, Oscar made a great deal of money and, as he put it, 'a rich assortment of new acquaintances'. In New York, he met the celebrated novelist, Louisa May Alcott, then in her forties and at the height of her fame. 'She was a small but profoundly passionate woman,' he recalled. 'She told me the plot of a story that she was revising at the time. It was entitled *A Long and Fatal Love Chase*. As she recounted the tale, she held my hand in hers and tears filled her eyes. I asked her why she had never married. "Oh, Mr Wilde," she said, "if I tell you, will you keep my secret? It is because I have fallen in love with so many pretty girls and never once the least bit with any man."'

It was in New York, too, that Oscar met the great showman, Phineas Taylor Barnum. Oscar was lecturing at the Wallack's Theatre on Broadway and Barnum came with a party of friends 'to see what all the fuss was about'. What Barnum made of Oscar's disquisition on 'Art and the English Renaissance' history does not record, but Oscar reckoned the encounter a success. 'When I spoke to Mr Barnum of Giorgione, Mazzini and Fra Angelico, he assumed they were a trio of Italian acrobats. Mr Barnum lacked education, but he had style. He came to my lecture and I visited his circus. I was pleased to do so. After the spectacle, at my insistence, he introduced me to his prize attraction, Jumbo, the African elephant. "I must meet him," I told Mr Barnum. "His name will be remembered long after ours have been forgotten." "I should hope so, Mr Wilde," answered Barnum. "He cost me ten thousand dollars." '

Oscar brought back many good stories from his year on the American lecture circuit. Probably his favourite anecdotal set-piece concerned his time in Leadville, Colorado, high up in the Rocky Mountains. There he addressed audiences comprised of ordinary working men – labourers and mine-workers in the main. Because the miners were mining for silver, Oscar chose to read to them extracts from the autobiography of the great Renaissance sculptor in silver, Benvenuto Cellini. 'I was reproved by my auditors for not having brought Cellini with me. I explained that he had been dead for some little time, which information elicited the enquiry: "Who shot him?" '

When, later, Oscar was asked if he had not found the miners 'somewhat rough and ready', he replied: 'Ready, but not rough. There is no chance for roughness in the Rockies. The revolver is their book of etiquette. This teaches lessons that are not forgotten.'

The mayor of Leadville, one H. A. W. Tabor, known as the Silver King, invited Oscar to visit the Matchless Mine and open a new shaft named 'The Oscar' in his honour. Oscar was delighted to oblige and, dressed in all his aesthete's finery, was ceremoniously lowered into the mine inside a huge bucket. Once he had inaugurated the new shaft, employing a special silver drill for the purpose, the miners invited him to dine with them at the bottom of the mine. 'They laid on quite a spread,' he recalled. 'The first course was whisky; the second course was whisky; the third course was whisky; I have little recollection of the dessert.'

That evening, Mayor Tabor offered Oscar further entertainment at the Leadville casino. According to Oscar, 'Drinking rather than gambling appeared to be the business of the place. It was crowded with miners and the female friends of miners.

The men were all dressed in red shirts, corduroy trousers and high boots. The women wore brightly coloured evening dresses cut so low that their breasts were almost entirely exposed. The floor was covered with sawdust and the walls hung with huge, gilt-framed mirrors. In a corner of the main saloon was a pianist, sitting at an upright piano over which was a notice that read: "Don't shoot the pianist; he is doing his best." '

On his second (and final) night in Leadville, Oscar returned to the casino. This time, he went alone. Mayor Tabor had business to attend to in Denver; Aaron Budd, Oscar's business manager, was not a drinking man; and Traquair, the valet, was barred from entry because of his colour. Oscar began the evening by the piano, surrounded by young men in red shirts and young women with full bosoms. He made them laugh and they made him smile. Four-and-a-half hours later, having eaten nothing and drunk too much, he found himself in a different, darker, corner of the saloon, seated alone with two men in check shirts and a young woman who leant towards him across the table dusting her breasts playfully with a little lace handkerchief. As one of the men plied Oscar with drink and the other removed his wallet from his coat pocket, two pistol shots rang out across the room. One shot blew the whisky glass from Oscar's hand; the other sent his wallet spinning into the air.

Instantly, as the shots were fired, Oscar's trio of drinking companions fled the scene, and Oscar, bewildered, slumped slowly to the floor. The man who had fired the shots crossed the room, helped Oscar to his feet and accompanied him out of the casino, down the deserted street and back to his hotel. The man's name was Eddie Garstrang.

2

Eddie Garstrang and Edmond La Grange

Eddie Garstrang was thirty-seven, ten years older than Oscar. He was several inches shorter than Oscar, and slimmer, more wiry, with a small head, pale yellow hair, milky blue eyes and a disarming, open smile. He was a professional gambler, known throughout the Midwest, so he told Oscar, as 'the man who never loses'. He was also a professional marksman, a sharp-shooter of exceptional skill and daring. At least, that's what he claimed, and Oscar saw no reason to doubt him. Garstrang boasted that the great P. T. Barnum had once seen him in action and offered him a starring role in his circus. Eddie Garstrang had decided against working for Mr Barnum. He was determined, he said, to be his 'own man'. He had declined Mr Barnum's offer politely, to be sure. He was softly spoken and a firm believer in what he termed 'old-world courtesy'. He was not as others were in Colorado. He did not chew tobacco or drink whisky. He did not wear a red shirt and corduroy trousers. He dressed in a tailor-made woollen suit of sober check and sported a white and lavender columbine in his buttonhole. Oscar found him fascinating.

On the morning after the incident in the casino, the pair met for breakfast. It was not a pre-arranged encounter. At around ten o'clock, Oscar, unshaven and still groggy from the night before, made his way into the hotel dining room in search of coffee and found Garstrang already seated at his table.

'Good morning, Mr Wilde,' said Garstrang, getting lightly to his feet and extending a hand to Oscar.

'Good day, sir,' replied Oscar, croakily, accepting Garstrang's hand. 'I must thank you. I recognise you. You are my rescuer from last night, are you not?'

'I have that honour,' said Garstrang. He bowed towards Oscar with a smile.

Oscar seated himself at the table. 'Is there coffee?' he asked, rubbing his eyes fiercely with clenched fists.

'There is,' said Garstrang, pouring Oscar a cup. 'And it's hot.'

'And strong, I hope.' Oscar lifted the cup and sipped at the coffee. He looked up at Garstrang who was still standing and smiled at the stranger. 'I'm in your debt, sir. I know it. What do I owe you?'

'Nothing, Mr Wilde.'

'You must want something. How much?' Oscar slipped his hand into his coat pocket and produced a green snakeskin wallet. It was one of his favourite possessions, a twenty-first birthday present from his mother. He examined the scorch mark at the wallet's edge. Garstrang's bullet had done no more than lightly nick the snakeskin

'The pleasure of your company for breakfast is all I ask,' said Garstrang.

'Whisky was my supper,' said Oscar, returning the wallet to his pocket, 'coffee will be all my breakfast, but you're welcome to share it.' He smiled and nodded to the older man. 'Be seated. Please. And remind me of your name? I'm afraid that my recollection of last night's adventure is somewhat hazy.'

'Garstrang – Edward Garstrang. I don't have a card. I've run out.'

'But you do have a gun,' said Oscar, smiling. 'That I recall.' He took another sip of coffee and looked about the deserted dining room. He leant across the table towards Garstrang and added, conspiratorially: 'Was anyone hurt last night?'

'No, I'm a good shot – and it was very close range. I'm a marksman, not a murderer.'

'Why did you come to my rescue? – Do you mind if I ask?'

'You're a visitor – and a distinguished one at that. We don't get many poets in velvet knickerbockers passing through Leadville. You were being taken advantage of at the casino last night, Mr Wilde, and that's not nice.' Garstrang paused and smiled his disarming smile: he had tiny white teeth pressed tight together. He poured more coffee into Oscar's cup. He added softly: 'Of course, in my way, I was taking advantage of you myself.'

Oscar's brow furrowed. 'Were you, Mr Garstrang? How?'

'With my little gun I came to the rescue of the great Oscar Wilde. It'll make a useful paragraph in the newspaper. I could use the publicity. I need to be noticed. I like to be talked about.'

'For reasons of business or self-esteem?' Oscar asked, leaning back and opening his silver cigarette case. The hot coffee was reviving him.

'Both,' replied Garstrang, striking a match and leaning forward to light Oscar's cigarette. 'Do you understand that? I think if anyone does, it should be you.'

'I understand completely, Mr Garstrang. A man who is much talked about is always attractive, whatever the truth. One feels there must be something in him after all.' Oscar drew slowly on his cigarette and gazed steadily into Garstrang's blue eyes. Oscar was the younger man by a decade, but they sat face to face as equals. 'What brings you to Leadville, Mr Garstrang?' asked Oscar.

Garstrang laughed. 'I was born in Leadville.'

'You do not look like a man who was born in Leadville.'

'I'm pleased to hear it. I have travelled quite widely.'

'To Europe?'

'To New Orleans. I work on the riverboats that travel up and down the Mississippi and Ohio rivers. The bigger boats all have casinos now and that's where I earn my living. I'm a professional gambler, Mr Wilde. I play cards and I never lose.'

'If you never lose,' said Oscar, 'where's the excitement? Isn't the risk part of the reward?'

'I don't play for excitement. I play for money. I am a gambler because, as a child, I realised that I hadn't the physique to be a cowboy or a miner and I did not wish to be a sales clerk as my father had been. My father was as most men are – nothing. He lived, he died. He might as well never have been born: he left no mark upon the world. I was fifteen when my father passed away. He left me with nothing but a firm grounding in mental arithmetic and an old Colt percussion revolver. I don't know why he kept the gun: he never used it. When he died I had nothing but the Colt, a few sticks of furniture, a rented room and a change of clothes. That's when I determined to make my fortune. That's when I decided I was going to be rich.'

'And are you?' asked Oscar.

'Not yet,' replied Garstrang, 'but I shall be. I'm getting there, slowly. I am determined.' He refilled Oscar's coffee cup and sat back folding his arms across his chest. 'Do you understand what I'm saying, Mr Wilde?'

'I understand you perfectly,' said Oscar. 'Every man of ambition has to fight his century with its own weapons. What our century worships is wealth. Money is the deity of our day. To succeed in our time one must have cash. At all costs.'

A silence fell between them. Garstrang broke it, changing the subject and saying how much he had enjoyed Oscar's lecture. He had heard him in Denver at the beginning of the week. They talked of this and that – of Oscar's poetry, of Cellini's autobiography, of Garstrang's prowess at poker and his facility with a gun. Eventually another silence fell. Oscar extinguished his second cigarette and looked carefully at his companion. It was the milkiness in Garstrang's blue eyes that made him appear so weak, he decided. And the fact that his narrow face was smooth and pale and hairless. Oscar reflected that he and Edward Garstrang were probably the only two white men in the entire State of Colorado that day not to be wearing either side-whiskers, a moustache or a beard.

'Is your mother still alive?' Oscar asked.

'No,' said Garstrang. 'I never knew my mother. Rather, I knew her, but I don't remember her. She passed away when I was small.'

'Do you have brothers? Sisters? Uncles? Aunts?'

'I have no family, Mr Wilde. I travel alone. I like it that way. I'm a loner, unbeholden.'

'We have much in common, I think,' said Oscar pleasantly, pushing his chair away from the table and beginning to get up from his seat. 'We are both outsiders, Mr Garstrang, observing our lives even as we live them.' He held out his hand towards his new friend. 'To become a spectator of one's own life is to escape the suffering of life, I find.'

Oscar had got to his feet because, over Garstrang's shoulder, through the open dining-room doorway, he could see the silhouette of Washington Traquair, the valet, hovering anxiously behind the glass door that connected the outer entrance lobby to the hotel itself. As a negro, Traquair was not permitted beyond the outer lobby. 'My man is waiting for me,' explained Oscar. 'Kansas is calling.'

'Thank you for your company,' said Eddie Garstrang, getting to his feet as well and shaking Oscar warmly by the hand.

'Thank you for yours,' said Oscar, 'both this morning and last night. This morning you entertained me. Last night you saved my life.'

'I saved your wallet, that's all,' said Garstrang, laughing, 'and your dignity, perhaps.'

'My wallet and my dignity – that's a great deal. I'm grateful. I won't forget you, Mr Garstrang.'

Oscar continued on his tour. He travelled from Colorado to Kansas to Iowa and Ohio, then up the east coast to Canada, then down to Memphis and New Orleans, across to Texas and up to New England and Canada once again. There were more memorable encounters along the way. In Salt Lake City, Utah, Oscar was presented to the President of the Mormon Church of Jesus Christ of Latter-day Saints and met five of the venerable gentleman's seven wives and one of his thirty-four children. Oscar noted that the opera house in Salt Late City was the size of Covent Garden and 'so holds with ease at least fourteen Mormon families'. In

Atlanta, Georgia, Oscar came close to blows with the Pullman car attendant who told him that although his valet, Traquair, was indeed in possession of a valid sleeping-car ticket, nevertheless, as a black man, he could not take advantage of it. It was against the railroad company's rules. In Lincoln, Nebraska, Oscar got his first taste of prison. He was taken on a tour of the Lincoln penitentiary and introduced to a number of the inmates. 'They were all mean-looking, which consoled me,' he said, 'for I should hate to see a criminal with a noble face.' He was shown into the cell of a convict who was due to be hanged in a few weeks' time. 'Do you read, my man?' asked Oscar. 'Yes, sir,' replied the convict, showing Oscar a copy of Charlotte M. Yonge's sentimental novel, *The Heir of Redclyffe*. As he left the cell, Oscar murmured to the prison governor: 'My heart was turned by the eyes of the doomed man, but if he reads *The Heir of Redclyffe* it's perhaps as well to let the law take its course.'

The tour ended in New York City in mid October 1882. All in all, it had been a success. Oscar had earned himself a substantial sum (in excess of $5,000, after expenses) and considerably raised his profile on both sides of the Atlantic. His mother wrote to him from London: 'You are the talk of the town here. The cabmen ask me if I am somehow connected with you. The milkman has bought your picture! In fact nothing seems celebrated in London but you. I think you will be mobbed when you come back by eager crowds and will be obliged to shelter in cabs.'

Oscar decided not to hurry home. He was enjoying being fêted in New York. 'If my presence is advertised in advance,' he reported to Lady Wilde with satisfaction, 'the road is blocked by admiring crowds and policemen wait for me to clear a way. I now understand why the Prince of Wales is in such good humour always: it is delightful to be a *petit roi*.'

But Oscar stayed on in America for another reason. He was revelling in his present celebrity, certainly, but he was also making serious plans for the future. He had ideas for two plays that he wanted to write – period dramas that he hoped to see presented in New York the following year – and he was the recipient of an unusual literary commission from an unexpected source. As he told his mother, excitedly: 'I have come to America where the greatest living Frenchman has done me the greatest possible honour by inviting me to work with him on the greatest piece of theatre in the English cannon.'

The French actor-manager, Edmond La Grange, was preparing a new production of *Hamlet* and suggested to Oscar that he might like to assist him with the translation. La Grange was one of Oscar's boyhood heroes. Oscar had seen him on stage in London and Dublin in several of his greatest roles. He had seen him in Paris, too, at the Théâtre La Grange on the Boulevard du Temple, in *Le Roi Lear*. He had even met him once, briefly, on the seafront in Dieppe in August 1879. Oscar had felt emboldened to introduce himself because Oscar knew the actress Sarah Bernhardt – Oscar worshipped Sarah Bernhardt! – and Bernhardt and La Grange had recently appeared together in Molière's *Amphytrion*. Now, in New York, in the fall of 1882, Oscar got to know the great man. Oscar Wilde, aged twenty-seven, and Edmond La Grange, aged sixty, became friends.

La Grange was in America doing what Sarah Bernhardt had done before him: taking the continent by storm. There were differences between the two great players, of course: Sarah's storm was more spectacular than La Grange's. La Grange was remarkable, but Sarah was divine. And Sarah was a woman. When Madame Bernhardt toured America in 1880, her personal luggage comprised forty costume crates and seventy trunks for her off-stage dresses, coats, hats, furs and fragrances, and her two hundred and fifty pairs of shoes. Monsieur La Grange travelled with three suitcases and a make-up box. Madame Bernhardt's entourage included two maids, two cooks, a waiter, her *maitre d'hôtel* and a *bonne p'tite dame* to act as companion and secretary. La Grange came with an elderly dresser and 'Maman', his eighty-two-year-old mother.

Edmond La Grange's repertoire was less extensive than Sarah Bernhardt's – he brought five productions to America:

she had brought eight – and his celebrity, his 'star status' as we call it now, could not rival hers, but, as actors, as masters of their craft, they were in the same league, and, according to the critics, his supporting company, though smaller, was superior to hers, and in New York, at Wallack's Theatre, playing in Molière, Racine and Corneille, in French, his takings equalled hers. And like Madame Bernhardt, Monsieur La Grange was paid in cash.

It was perhaps surprising that Oscar's and La Grange's pathways had not crossed before. La Grange's four-week Broadway season was the culmination of a four-month cross-continental tour and the great French actor and the young Irish aesthete were both appearing under the auspices of Richard D'Oyly Carte. Indeed it was Carte's man, Colonel Morse, who eventually effected the introduction. 'Edmond La Grange speaks damned good English, but he damn well refuses to do so,' Morse complained to Oscar, chewing on the small cigar that appeared permanently fixed to the corner of his mouth. 'La Grange maintains that French is the official language of diplomacy and therefore the only language to be used in inter-national relations. Whenever I dine with him after the show, he jabbers away at me nineteen to the dozen and I can't follow a word he's saying. You speak French, Wilde. You can have dinner with him. You can talk to him. He'll understand you. You might even understand him, God knows.'

Edmond La Grange and Oscar Wilde understood one another well. They got on famously from the start. Oscar spoke fluent, flawless French, and was soaked in the culture and heritage of *la belle France*. He was honoured to have dinner with his hero and more than happy to talk with him. He was happier still to sit back, wide-eyed with admiration, listening to whatever the great man had to say. Oscar loved the rich, deep timbre of La Grange's voice. Oscar revelled in the orotund, slightly archaic turns of phrase the actor employed. Oscar adored La Grange's myriad theatrical stories: 'They are full of base lies, of course, but they contain a higher truth.' La Grange, at the time, was rising sixty-one, but he crackled with energy. He was not especially tall, but his posture was impeccable and his 'presence' undeniable. He was not especially slim, but he was loose-limbed and moved with a dancer's grace. (That said, there was nothing effeminate about him. Far from it.) He had thick white hair swept back over a high, lined forehead. His face was weather-beaten, but he had a fine profile: strong cheekbones, a Roman nose and huge, humorous brown eyes. He was an actor (to his fingertips), as dramatic in his manner offstage as on, a gambler, a risk-taker, in love with the theatre, in love with life.

La Grange and his company were set to return to Europe on the SS *Bothnia* on 27 December 1882. La Grange proposed to Oscar that he return to Europe on the same ship: it was steaming to Le Havre, via Liverpool. On the journey they could work together on their translation of *Hamlet*. And Oscar, learning that, while in America, La Grange's old dresser – a faithful retainer who had been with the company for more than thirty-five years – had unfortunately died, proposed to La Grange that the Frenchman take on the young black valet, Tracquair, as his new dresser. 'I can vouch for him in every particular. He has laid out my shirts from Peoria to Pawtucket. He knows his business and you may trust him with your life. He has a face of jet and a heart of gold.'

'Does he speak French?' asked La Grange.

'He speaks the language of devotion,' answered Oscar.

On the day of departure, Wednesday, 27 December 1882, Oscar was among the last passengers to board the ship. 'Saying goodbye to a continent is not something that can be rushed,' he explained. Besides, at the dockside there were admirers – and the press – to contend with. When, at last, as dusk was falling, he arrived onboard, he found La Grange and his entourage already comfortably installed in the *Bothnia*'s grand saloon, drinking champagne. To Oscar's surprise, there was an addition to the party.

Standing immediately behind La Grange, leaning over his shoulder, whispering into his ear, was Oscar's blue-eyed friend from Leadville, Colorado: Eddie Garstrang, the professional gambler, 'the man who never loses'.

Garstrang straightened himself and bowed towards Oscar, quite formally.

'What the devil are you doing here?' asked Oscar, in amazement.

Edmond La Grange looked up at Oscar and smiled. 'Monsieur Garstrang is my new personal secretary, Oscar. I won him at cards.'

Follow in the footsteps of
Oscar Wilde

with Gyles Brandreth's
exclusive walking guide to

Wilde's London

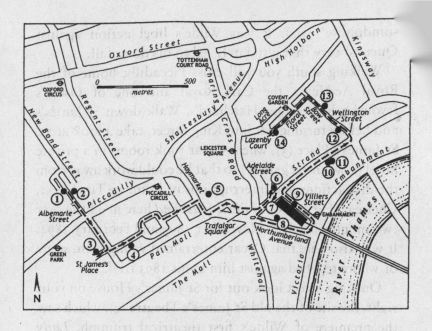

✦✦✦ A Walk in ✦✦✦
Oscar Wilde's West End

When you are next in London, you can take this hour-long walk through Oscar Wilde's West End, visiting several of the locations featured in *Oscar Wilde and the Candlelight Murders* and *Oscar Wilde and the Ring of Death*.

The walk begins in Mayfair, at the north end of Albemarle Street, London W1, home of **Brown's Hotel** (1), from where Oscar Wilde made phone calls, and where Alexander Graham Bell made the first telephone call in England. Opposite, at number 13, is the site of the old **Albemarle Club** (2) where Oscar was a member. It was here that the Marquess of Queensberry, so enraged by Oscar's romantic involvement with his son Bosie, left his visiting card accusing Oscar of 'posing as a omdomite' (*sic*). It was Wilde's libel action against Queensberry that ultimately led to his downfall.

Walking south you will cross Piccadilly, home of the Royal Academy, the Café Royal and one of Oscar's favourite bookshops, Hatchard's. Walk down St James's and before turning left into King Street, take a look at 10 **St James's Place** (3), where Oscar took rooms in a private hotel (now an art gallery) so that he could work away from the distractions and interruptions of home in Tite Street, Chelsea. He wrote *An Ideal Husband* here in a little over two months between November 1893 and February 1894. It was also here that Oscar entertained young men, some of whom testified against him in his 1895 trial.

On King Street look out for St James's House on your right, the site of the old **St James's Theatre** (4), which saw the premiere of Wilde's first theatrical triumph, *Lady Windermere's Fan*, in February 1892. His most celebrated play, *The Importance of Being Earnest*, opened at the theatre in February 1895 to rapturous applause, despite the Marquess of Queensberry's best efforts to sabotage the event with a public denunciation of Oscar. Arriving with a prizefighter, he tried and failed to gain admission by the stage door. It was only a few days later that Queensberry famously left his card at the Albemarle Club. The St James's Theatre was demolished in 1957 to make way for an office block; Laurence Olivier, Vivien Leigh and Winston Churchill led the campaign to save it.

Continue west until you reach Haymarket, where you will see the **Theatre Royal** (5) straight ahead of you. It was here that *A Woman of No Importance* opened in April 1893, followed by *An Ideal Husband* in January 1895. Charles Brookfield played the small part of a

servant, Phipps, despite his rocky history with Osca.
Now head down Haymarket, left onto Pall Mall and.
after crossing Trafalgar Square, pause at the foot of
Adelaide Street to admire **A Conversation with Oscar
Wilde** (6), created by Maggi Hambling in 1999 and the
only statue of Oscar Wilde in England. The inscription
reads, 'We are all in the gutter, but some of us are looking
at the stars', a line from *Lady Windermere's Fan*.

From here cross the Strand, passing **Charing Cross
Station** (7), where Oscar regularly took the Underground
home to Sloane Square. When Oscar arrived in London
in 1879 the city's population was about 4.7 million; when
he left for France in 1897 it had increased by about fifty
per cent. The new Tube network made it possible for the
growing mass of Londoners to escape crowded slums into
new suburbs – including that of Conan Doyle's South
Norwood – thereby relieving the pressure of overcrowd-
ing and ugly tenement development from the city centre.

Now turn left down Northumberland Avenue, stopping for refreshment in the **Sherlock Holmes pub** (8)
where, in the upstairs bar, Holmes's rooms from 221b
Baker Street have been recreated. (Look closely and you
will spot Oscar's photograph and visiting card on
Holmes's mantelpiece.) Continuing up Villiers Street,
look out for the New Players Theatre on the left. This was
once home to **Gatti's-in-the-Arches** (9), the celebrated
music hall built by Carlo Gatti in 1867 in the undercroft
of the new Charing Cross Station. Originally a working-
class form of variety entertainment, music hall was at the
height of its popularity in Oscar's day, attracting audiences from all walks of life. By 1895, Gatti's boasted a
grand café and billiard saloon, and counted Rudyard

ɔling (a Villiers Street resident) among its patrons.

Turn right onto the Strand, a smart promenading street ᴧn Oscar's day, taking in the **Savoy Theatre** (10), the first public building in the world to be lit by electricity, and home of Gilbert and Sullivan. Their 1881 opera *Patience* was a satire of the Aesthetic Movement, and particularly of Oscar Wilde. But rather than damage his reputation the play served merely to propel Oscar even further into the limelight. Adjacent to the theatre, and built on the back of its great financial success, is the **Savoy Hotel** (11), where Oscar frequently stayed on his nights away from home. It was evidence from one of the chambermaids at the Savoy that helped lead to his conviction on charges of gross indecency in the notorious trials of 1895.

Crossing the Strand and heading north on Wellington Street you will pass the **Lyceum Theatre** (12), home of the great Sir Henry Irving, the first actor to be knighted. Irving and his general manager, Bram Stoker, were both friends of Wilde. Heading north, pause at **Bow Street Police Station** (13) where, following the collapse of his libel case against Lord Queensberry, Wilde was arrested and formally charged at the beginning of April 1895.

Turning west down Floral Street, continue for 200 yards before cutting left down Lazenby Court to the small wooden-fronted **Lamb and Flag pub** (14), also known as the 'Bucket of Blood' because of the bare-knuckle boxing held there, largely in secret. The sport was bloody, crude, illegal and notoriously corrupt until 1892 when the Marquess of Queensberry's rules – introducing gloves, rounds and protecting the injured man – were finally accepted, and boxing began to enter the realms of respectability.

An interview with Gyles Brandreth

Would Oscar Wilde really have made a good detective?
Absolutely. He had many qualities that would have made him ideal as a Victorian detective and principal among them is this: he was an Irish gentleman, an outsider, and, unlike the average Scotland Yard detective, could move easily within all ranks of English society. He knew the Prince of Wales and he knew common street prostitutes. He knew actors, aristocrats, tradesmen, poets and politicians. Victorian England was a very class stratified society and an ordinary Scotland Yard detective was unlikely to be a gentleman. Therefore if he had wanted to interview a duke on a murder charge, he would have had to go through the servants' entrance. Oscar would have gone up to the front door. Secondly, while Oscar was a great talker – George Bernard Shaw described him as 'the greatest talker of his time, perhaps of all time' – he could listen as well as talk. Listening intelligently was a skill he had learned at his parents' salons in Dublin – and a great detective needs to be a great listener. He was also a classical scholar and therefore a disciplined thinker with the advantage of a wonderfully retentive memory. And, crucially, Oscar was a poet with a poet's eye. He observed, he listened, he reflected and then – with his extraordinary gifts of imagination and intellect – he saw the truth. He wasn't the original Sherlock Holmes, but I do believe that Mycroft Holmes (the more indolent and more brilliant older brother of Sherlock Holmes) is based on Oscar Wilde.

...ing of Death you give one of the characters your middle
...me, Daubeney. Are the books full of such riddles?
...es. Daubeney is my name, but it's also a name given by
Oscar to one of the characters in his plays. Throughout all
the books there are, I hope, incidental treats for people who,
like Conan Doyle and Walter Sickert, are into anagrams,
acrostics and different kinds of wordplay. I create cross-
words and word games and I used to write puzzle books, so
the puzzle element of a murder mystery is fascinating to me.

Was Robert Sherard really in love with Constance Wilde?
We know a lot about Robert Sherard, but the truth is we
don't know about his feelings for Constance. I put a lot of
myself into Robert, though, and all I can say is that Mrs
Wilde was beautiful, highly intelligent, amusing and generous, a musician, a linguist and a published author; the
thinking man's attractive woman!

So how do we know what's fact and what's fiction?
Aha, you don't! That's all part of the mystery . . . But, gen-
erally speaking, anything that you think is real almost certainly is real, even the truly strange bits. Remember the
French bookshop and the monkey? It's true. The parrot at
the Cadogan Hotel called Captain Flint? True! Everything
about the Rational Dress Society, and Oscar's two half-
sisters who were burnt to death? And about Constance's
father being caught exposing himself in the law courts?
True. In fact, some of the reality I feel I have to tone down
because people would never believe it otherwise.

Read more . . .

Gyles Brandreth

OSCAR WILDE AND THE DEAD MAN'S SMILE

Oscar Wilde investigates a series of gruesome murders in Paris's theatre world

Paris, 1883. Oscar Wilde has come to the city of decadence to collaborate with France's most celebrated actor-manager, Edmond La Grange. But Oscar discovers dark secrets lying at the heart of the La Grange company and is confronted by murders both foul and bizarre. In order to solve the crimes, Oscar risks his life – and his reputation – embarking on a dangerous adventure that takes him from bohemian night clubs to an asylum for the insane, from a duel in the Buttes de Chaumont to the gates of Reading Gaol.

'It's a great book . . . there's enough wit and intelligence here to make it more than a "guilty pleasure" . . . an intelligent read with good characterisation' *Scotsman*

'Thrilling and richly atmospheric' *Sunday Express*

Order your copy now by calling Bookpoint on 01235 827716 or visit your local bookshop quoting ISBN 978-0-7195-6990-6 www.johnmurray.co.uk